DEEP HEX

THE DEEP SERIES - BOOK SIX

NICK SULLIVAN

This is a work of fiction. All events described are imaginary; all characters are entirely fictitious and are not intended to represent actual living persons.

Copyright © 2023 by Nick Sullivan

Cover design by Shayne Rutherford of Wicked Good Book Covers

Cover photo by Zenobillis/Shutterstock.com

Interior Title Page Art by AArrows/Shutterstock.com

Copy editing by Marsha Zinberg of The Write Touch

Proofreading by Gretchen Tannert Douglas and Forest Olivier

Original maps of TCI provided by Daniel J LeVin and VicsitTCI.com

ISBN: 978-0-9978132-8-9

Published by Wild Yonder Press

TURKS AND CAICOS ISLANDS

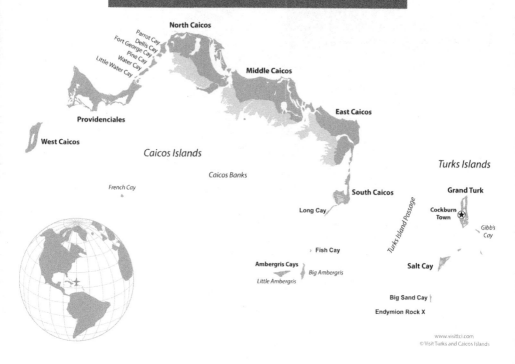

North Caicos

Parrot Cay
Dellis Cay
Fort George Cay
Pine Cay
Water Cay
Little Water Cay

Middle Caicos

East Caicos

Providenciales

West Caicos

Caicos Islands

Caicos Banks

Turks Islands

Grand Turk

French Cay

South Caicos

Cockburn
Town

*Gibb's
Cay*

Long Cay

Turks Island Passage

Fish Cay

Ambergris Cays

Big Ambergris

Salt Cay

Little Ambergris

Big Sand Cay

Endymion Rock X

www.visittci.com
© Visit Turks and Caicos Islands

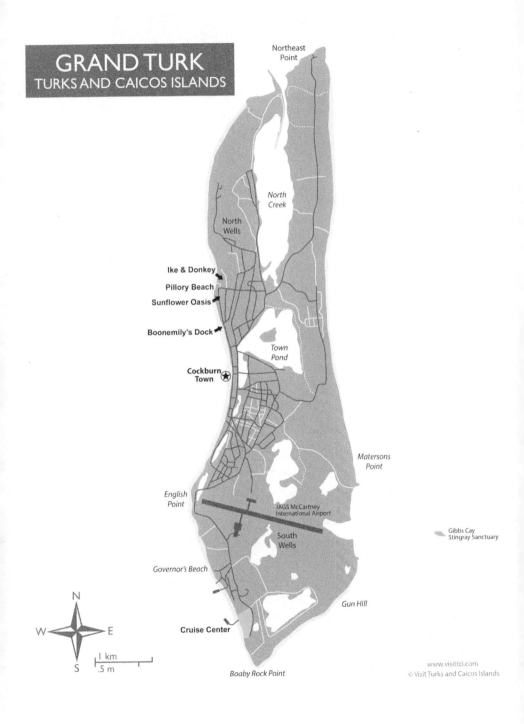

GRAND TURK
TURKS AND CAICOS ISLANDS

Northeast
Point

North
Creek

North
Wells

Ike & Donkey

Pillory Beach

Sunflower Oasis

Boonemily's Dock

Town
Pond

Cockburn
Town

Matersons
Point

English
Point

JAGS McCartney
International Airport

Gibbs Cay
Stingray Sanctuary

South
Wells

Governor's Beach

Gun Hill

N
W — E
S

Cruise Center

1 km
.5 m

Boaby Rock Point

www.visittci.com
© Visit Turks and Caicos Islands

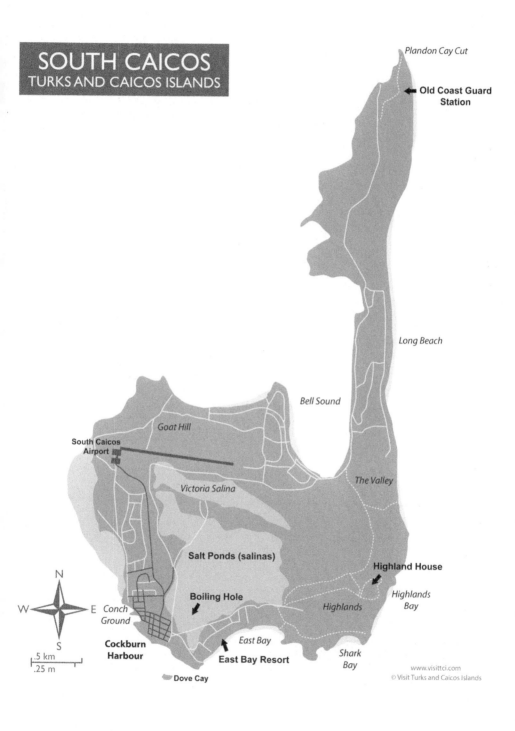

SOUTH CAICOS
TURKS AND CAICOS ISLANDS

Plandon Cay Cut

Old Coast Guard
Station

Long Beach

Bell Sound

Goat Hill

South Caicos
Airport

Victoria Salina

The Valley

Salt Ponds (salinas)

Highland House

Boiling Hole

Highlands
Bay

Conch
Ground

Highlands

Cockburn
Harbour

East Bay

Shark
Bay

East Bay Resort

N
W   E
S

.5 km
.25 m

Dove Cay

www.visittci.com
© Visit Turks and Caicos Islands

To Sean Griffin, Michael Tibbetts, Jorika, Mateo, Melina, Dwaine, Roshane, Neil, Laura, CJ, Lincoln, Darell, Heidi, John, and everyone else at the School for Field Studies, East Bay Resort, Reef Divers, and Clearly Cayman. You all made this book possible.

ONE

"Are you sure you want to do this?"

Mateo Delmar looked up at the young man who'd spoken. "Absolutely," Mateo answered with an easy smile. The East Bay Resort divemaster sat on one of the sloping concrete walls that enclosed a square pool of seawater. The small body of water looked more like a hot tub in an ancient Roman spa than what it really was: part of a series of obsolete sluice-gates and the opening to a subterranean cave system, ominously named the "Boiling Hole."

"Okay, then." The other man checked his smartphone. John was the dive safety officer at the School for Field Studies on the southern end of the island and had been assisting Mateo with his explorations of South Caicos for several years. The wind that whipped across the salt ponds blew sandy-blond locks of hair into his face and he clawed it aside. John's exceptionally long hair had led many of the staff and students to refer to him as "Scuba Jesus."

"See, this is why you should put it up, out of the way,"

1

Mateo chided. Tall and deeply tanned, the Colombian divemaster's head was similarly blessed, but he kept much of his long, black hair cinched into a bun.

John found what he was looking for and tapped the screen on his phone. "Okay, low tide was three hours ago. This is as good a window as any."

Mateo turned to some of the college-age SFS students who were clustered below in the little gazebo beside the concrete enclosure. "The Boiling Hole is three to four hours behind the tides in the bay. And three or four hours after high tide, this water will be so disturbed, it will look like it's boiling. This is one of the reasons I believe there is a complex cave system connected to it. I think it may extend toward the highlands to the east and to the bay to the south, likely with a number of twists and turns before it eventually reaches the sea. If it was a straight shot, the tidal delay would be much less."

"How do you know it reaches the ocean?" a student asked.

Mateo pointed off into the salt flats nearby. "See those needlefish there? They probably came in through the Boiling Hole. And there is another karstic sinkhole not far from here, that we know for sure was connected to the ocean."

"Karst...?"

"Oh, sorry. A 'karst feature' is formed when rock—especially porous rock, like limestone—is dissolved over time. Blue holes... cenotes... these are all examples of this. Anyway, to the south of here is the Turtle Crawl. It's less than 500 feet from the ocean, so the timing of the tides would have been much closer there."

"Why aren't you exploring that one first?" another asked.

Mateo grabbed a fin and pulled it on. "Can't. They sealed it off after a child drowned."

Another student, a lanky girl with doe eyes, poked her head

over the wall and looked down into the depths. Unlike the shallow waters in the surrounding salt ponds—known as salinas—the murky depths of the Boiling Hole resisted efforts to see beyond a few feet in depth. "What happens if it starts 'boiling' while you're in there?" she asked, sounding more fascinated than concerned.

Mateo shrugged. "That might be a question for another day, but today I'm only looking to examine the entrance and any nearby connections. I'll be out long before the tidal shift reaches here. We've tested the currents with a flowmeter over a number of days, and I'm confident I've got an hour or two to play with."

John lifted an assembled set of gear: regulator, wing-style BCD, and a single side-mounted tank. Mateo had selected the more streamlined buoyancy control device for this entry, in the event the entrance was more cramped than expected. Since this was an initial reconnaissance, a single tank would suffice; nevertheless, a backup pony bottle was clipped to the opposite side. John brought it to the top of the wall and set it down behind Mateo.

In moments, the divemaster was suited up. He let out a long, slow breath. "Here we go."

"I'll expect you back in twenty minutes," John cautioned, removing the carabiner end of a safety line from the finger spool that was clipped beside the pony bottle. He drew the line across to an eye bolt they'd attached to the gazebo and hooked it into place as Mateo let out some slack.

"I still think thirty minutes would be safe enough for today, but I'll be back in twenty if it makes you happy." Mateo placed the second stage into his mouth and slipped over the side, gripping a weathered wooden gate that hung over one of the three exits of the Boiling Hole. Then he ducked his head under.

"How's the viz?" John asked, as the SFS students and staff clustered along the gazebo side of the enclosure.

Mateo waggled a hand, then flashed an "OK" sign, probably indicating the visibility wasn't great, but acceptable. With that, he descended in an upright position, the top of his head quickly disappearing from view.

"And now we wait," John said.

"What's that door thing he was holding onto?" the wide-eyed girl asked, pointing at the weathered rectangle of wood, a hinged flap with a chain attached. The one on the western side of the enclosure looked like it had been snapped off at some point.

"Those are sluice gates. The influx of seawater would be controlled here, and at a few other places; if the salinas needed more seawater, they'd open them up. You all know how these salt flats would work?"

One young man raised his hand. "Evaporation?"

"Yes, very good. They would fill the salinas with a shallow layer of saltwater, which would eventually evaporate, leaving the salt behind. You've probably seen a few places where there's a layer of salt glistening on the surface."

"Why aren't they still collecting it?" a blond-headed student asked.

"Well... a number of reasons," John replied. Some of the students were fairly new, and didn't know the history of the salt industry in South Caicos. "Colonists from Bermuda came down to the TCI for salt as early as the 1600s. And there was a lot more organized salt collection going on a bit later, in the 1700s—mostly over on Grand Turk and Salt Cay—but they needed more. South Caicos had a lot of flat wetlands in the interior, so it made for an ideal spot to expand. And word was, the salt produced here was ninety-eight percent pure! Though that might've just been savvy advertising."

John pointed out at the expanse of square ponds that stretched far to the north and east. "You can see all the dividing walls they built to create different sections; they could transfer the contents of one into another as it got saltier and saltier. Those old windmills here and there would help direct the brine to where the salt was eventually collected. And all the donkeys you see around the island? Those were used to transport the salt to the bay, and from there, smaller boats would take it in batches to the waiting ships. And you may have seen some ballast stones on some of your dives? The ships would ditch their ballast and replace it with salt."

He nodded out to a nearby flock of flamingos that were high-stepping their way through one of the salt ponds. "But now, these salt flats are just a lot of briny ponds. The flamingos love shallow, salty water; they eat the tiny crustaceans and pinkish algae that thrive in it, and that's what gives them their pink color."

"Wow! Cool!" a wide-eyed student enthused.

"So, what happened to the salt industry?" the blond kid asked again.

"Oh, right! Sorry, got off track. Here, the waters of the harbor are too shallow for large ships, so it was more cost-effective to move the industry over to Great Inagua in The Bahamas. They have deeper water near the shore and large ships could come right to the pier."

"Hey... I think Mateo's coming up," the girl with the large eyes said.

Below the bubbles from the divemaster's scuba tank, a dark shape could be seen rising toward the surface. John frowned, checking his watch. Suddenly, Mateo breached, spit the regulator out of his mouth, and grabbed hold of the nearest sluice gate.

"You're early," John said with concern. "Is everything all right?"

"No..." Mateo gasped.

"What's wrong?" John asked, stepping up onto the concrete rim of the enclosure and preparing to jump in to assist.

Mateo shook his head and held up a hand. "No... stay there... I'm okay." He swallowed. "And call the police."

"What? Why?"

"Because there's a body down there."

TWO

TWO DAYS LATER. ENDYMION ROCK, 15
MILES SOUTHEAST OF SALT CAY

Boone Fischer led his group of divers over the sand of the sea floor toward the looming mass of Endymion Rock. The undersea feature had earned the moniker when its namesake, the HMS *Endymion*, had plowed into the uncharted reef back in 1790, sinking the warship in relatively shallow water.

Boone spotted an anchor chain almost immediately and signaled the divers who followed in his wake. Draped along the side of the reef, this heavy, stud-link chain was not connected to the *Endymion*; it led to another hapless ship, the *General Pershing*, which had also succumbed to a too-close encounter with Endymion Rock in 1921. Boone would save her for later, and instead directed the group toward the remains of the *Endymion*, just below and to the side.

Two massive bower anchors were the first indication of the ship's presence. Both were partially encrusted in corals and sponges from over two centuries on the seabed. Just beyond lay the remains of the *Endymion* itself. Several cannons were piled together, evidence that the ship had likely rolled during her brief plunge. Covered in marine growth, they almost appeared as a single mass.

A small group of divers clustered around, the family of four from Missouri—the Douglases—excitedly looking about. The father's eyes were locked on the viewscreen at the back of his expensive camera rig, while his wife wrangled their teenage daughter and son to join her beside Boone. Behind them, a sixth diver approached with gentle kicks. Lincoln Forbes flashed Boone a quick "OK" signal. Boone replied with the same, thinking how lucky he and Em had been to hire the man.

Ever since forming Bubble Chasers Diving back in Cozumel, Boone and Emily had resolved to always hire a local or two to help them run their op. Living a nomadic, island-hopping life-style meant they had to learn everything from scratch: dive site locations and layouts; local laws, lingo, and customs; where to live, what to eat. And often, Caribbean countries *required* busi-nesses to employ locals, as had been the case in both Cozumel and Little Cayman. In fact, in Coz, they'd made Ricardo Pérez co-owner with them, to comply with Mexican law.

Before Boone and Emily had relocated to the Turks and Caicos, they'd put out a call for divemasters and captains, and had struck gold with Lincoln Forbes. Like many in the TCI, Lincoln was from one island, but lived and worked on another. Originally from South Caicos, he'd briefly been a taxi driver in bustling Providenciales before becoming a divemaster and boat captain and relocating to Grand Turk. Fortunately, GT was where Boone and Em were hoping to set up shop, so Lincoln acted as a scout for locations and opportunities before they even left the Cayman Islands.

Boone descended beside the cannons and pointed two fingers to his eyes before directing the group's attention to the sea floor. A single cannonball lay in the sand. While Mr. Douglas moved forward with his camera, Boone repositioned himself farther along what he knew to be the remains of the warship's hull. The HMS *Endymion* had been a forty-four-gun "fifth-rate" sailing ship, just shy of what the Royal Navy considered a true frigate. Hailing from the age of sail, she had been of mostly wooden construction, so the majority of her hull had rotted away from two centuries of exposure to seawater and shipworms. Nevertheless, enough clues remained. Having rolled over, the remnants of the hull were covered in a layer of six-inch iron ballast bars, and a line of upthrust bronze ribs revealed the location of the ship's keel.

Moving along the side of the wreck, Boone scanned the sea floor for something else to show off. Endymion Rock was quite far from Grand Turk, and he'd only dived it a few times, but one of the dive instructors at Salt Cay Divers had given Emily and Boone a detailed underwater tour shortly after they'd arrived in Turks and Caicos. Since most of the site was at a fairly shallow depth, they had been able to spend nearly an hour learning every detail.

There they are. Spotting his quarry, Boone descended to the sand and waited to catch the eye of one or more of the divers. The teenage boy, Branson, spotted him first, and Boone motioned the youth over. The other divers soon followed. Reaching down, Boone plucked a small sphere from the sand, where it lay in a cluster of its companions. He held it between his right thumb and forefinger and made a "pistol" with his left hand. Holding the tiny sphere in front of his left forefinger, he dropped the thumb, miming the firing of his finger-gun, then moved the sphere through the water to show them what it was: a musket ball. Boone looked down and carefully placed it in the exact spot he'd taken it from, then swept his hand through the water, indicating all of the other bits of eighteenth-century ammunition.

Wide eyes behind masks greeted him as the divers clustered around. Suddenly, a double clang interrupted them, and Boone looked around, scanning for his fellow divemaster. Lincoln carried a reef stick, a thin metal rod he used for pointing things out, and Boone knew the sound it made when the local man used it as a tank banger, higher in pitch than a bang from the stainless-steel carabiner that Boone preferred.

There! Lincoln was off to the side, his reef stick dangling from a strap on his wrist. His hands were stacked, one clasping the other, and he waggled his thumbs—the underwater signal for "turtle." He pointed at an approaching shape and Boone grinned behind his regulator. A sizable leatherback was skimming across the sand, angling to pass by the wreck. Largest of the sea turtles, they were a rare sight, and Boone had only spotted a few during his countless dives; hawksbills and greens were the most common sea turtle varieties in the area, with loggerheads a close third. Camera leading the way, the father kicked hard to get ahead of the big turtle, with mother and daughter following his fins.

Boone glanced back to see where Branson was and spotted the teen near the musket balls, his hand just leaving the pocket of his BCD. Like many buoyancy control devices, the one the youth wore had small pouches at the side, held closed by Velcro. Branson looked up and met eyes with Boone, then abruptly turned away and started after his family. With a quick flutter kick of his fins, Boone headed him off and simply held out an upturned palm.

Branson looked at the hand, then up at Boone, who waggled his fingers twice. *Gimme.* Caught, the teen appeared to sag in the water. Reaching to his side, he dipped his hand under the Velcro and came out with a closed fist. He placed an object in Boone's hand and swam sheepishly away. The divemaster retraced his kicks and returned the pilfered musket ball to its mates. *Maybe I shouldn't pick one up to show it off,* Boone thought. *It could be considered an invitation.* He turned and swam after his flock, who were following Lincoln and watching the leatherback turtle as it ascended for a breath of air from the surface.

After exploring the rest of the *Endymion* wreck, the group followed Boone over to the remains of the *General Pershing*. Chief among the sights to see were the stockless anchor and early diesel engine, both an evolution in technology from the nearby wreck of the earlier sailing ship. Boone circled the family as they examined the wreck, sneaking a peek at the father's pressure gauge; during their dives this week, he was always the first to run out. At this shallow depth, Mr. Douglas had plenty of air left, so Boone gave the group a healthy amount of time to explore before catching Lincoln's eye and giving a questioning shrug.

Lincoln checked his dive computer for the elapsed time, then flashed Boone a quick "OK" sign and a thumbs up, the hand signals coming one on top of the other. He capped the sequence off with a shrug. The thumbs up clearly wasn't a suggestion to ascend immediately, but indicated they could end the dive. Basically, he was replying, *Sure, we could head back.*

Boone got his bearings and kicked toward the sand flats they'd anchored in. While most dive sites in the Turks and Caicos had fixed moorings, the TCI Reef Fund had opted to avoid one at Endymion Rock, not wanting to make the site easy to find for amateur souvenir seekers. Boone unclipped his carabiner and rapped his tank thrice. Once he had all masks facing him, he flattened his hand and chopped it twice toward the sand.

Boone had just spotted the anchor line when his ears were greeted with a most unusual underwater sound: music. Specifically, the opening strains of "Octopus's Garden" by The Beatles. Boone chuckled into his regulator and looked up at the underside of their dive boat. He quickly spotted the acoustic culprit dangling down from *Lunasea*'s starboard side. Emily was having a little fun with their latest gadget, an Oceanears underwater speaker they'd picked up in Provo last week. The primary purpose of the device was to issue a diver recall in the case of an emergency, but Boone wasn't surprised that Em had found another use for it.

He looked back and found their little group jamming to the beat. Well... as much as one could "jam" to Ringo Starr's bouncy, playful tune. Mom and Dad were dancing together, the daughter—Bethany—was doing a version of the twist, and Branson was looking all around, trying to figure out where the music was coming from. Sound traveled in the water slightly more than four times faster than in the air. Human brains weren't wired for that speed, and determining the direction a sound was coming from underwater was nearly impossible. Boone was impressed with the speaker's quality; the music seemed to be all around them, and was only a little distorted. If need be, someone aboard the dive boat could actually speak to the divers below, explaining the nature of an emergency and what action they were about to take.

Boone caught Lincoln's eye and indicated he would go up first, leaving the local divemaster to watch the divers during their safety stop. Lincoln signaled "OK" and Boone ascended to fifteen feet just as the song ended and a new one began. He shook his head, grinning into the regulator mouthpiece as the strains of "Yellow Submarine" now filled the ocean.

Fins in hand, Boone ascended the ladder to the swim platform with the muted tones of The Beatles' song rising from the water below. He found Emily dancing barefoot on the deck, arms outstretched. With her hair in braids and wearing cutoff shorts beneath a festive Baja hoodie, Emily had a hippie vibe going, an appearance only strengthened by a green-lensed pair of John Lennon sunglasses perched atop her button nose. She had not been wearing *those* at the start of the dive.

Em grinned ear to ear and pointed at him. "Sky of blue…" she intoned expectantly.

"Sea of green," Boone replied, tossing his fins under the port bench and swiftly removing his gear. He nodded toward her attire. "How long've you been planning this?"

"Whatever do you mean?" she replied with an impish smirk, strolling up to him with an air of innocence.

"You're telling me you're *not* trying to channel a hippie chick?" He rose and looked down at her. With his six-foot-four height, it was a long way down to her smiling face.

She tilted her chin up and raised her fingers in a vee. "Peace, love, and music, man."

"I wouldn't mind skipping to number two on that list."

Emily's eyes sparkled and she bit her lip. "Groovy. But we've got divers in the water."

"Still doing their safety stop." Boone lifted her new sunglasses up onto her forehead. "Where'd you get the funky shades?"

"Provo. Right after we got the underwater speaker. Figured

with your love of old-timey music, you'd appreciate my christening it with a little British Invasion."

"Yeah, about that... don't get me wrong, I loved every minute of it, but... the fish might not. Studies have shown human noise pollution can be disruptive to marine life."

"Happiness hoover," Emily pouted.

Boone laughed. "What?"

"You know... a hoover of happiness, sucking up all the fun. Like a joy vacuum. Only more British."

The sounds of a diver breaching came from astern. Boone leaned in to give Em a brief but passionate kiss before heading aft to position himself alongside the ladder. Mrs. Douglas—Lisa—looked up at him, offering her fins. "What an amazing dive! I hope Mark got some good pictures!"

"I'm sure he did," Boone said, helping her up the ladder and directing her to a spot on the port bench. He returned to the platform to take Mark Douglas's underwater camera rig, bringing it forward to the freshwater rinse bin.

Emily was nearby, taking her phone from where she'd laid it beside the Oceanears receiver and tapping the screen to silence the music. Branson reached the starboard bench and she quickly stepped across and guided his tank into a slot.

"Why'd you stop the music?" the teen asked.

"Oh, sorry, mate," Em replied, her South London accent truncating some of her words. "'Fraid that aquatic jam was a one-time bit o' fun."

"Aww!" Bethany whined as Boone helped her to a spot beside her brother. "Why?"

"Well, you see..." Em began, catching Boone's eye before affecting a professorial tone and poshing up her speech, "... studies have shown, human noise pollution can be disruptive to marine life."

"I've heard about that," Mr. Douglas said from the opposite bench. "Sonar from submarines can really mess with whales and dolphins."

"I don't think John, Paul, George, and Ringo would have the same effect," Boone replied, reeling in the speaker. "But just to be safe, no more undersea concerts."

THREE

"I was really hoping to see some humpback whales," Mrs. Douglas said wistfully.

"Afraid you're a few months late for that," Emily said, soaking up the sun as she lay on a towel on the beach, her face tilted skyward. Her Beatles joke now over, she'd ditched the smaller Lennon sunglasses for her enormous lime-green shades. Gone too, was the bulky Baja hoodie and cutoffs. Today she'd worn her bikini with the green fish-scale pattern. Boone liked to call it her "Aquagirl" uniform. Em assumed that meant he liked it.

"Well, we'll just have to come back," Mr. Douglas announced. "When's the best time to see the humpbacks?"

"If you shoot for January 'til early April, you'll see plenty," Boone answered, reclining in the sand in a beat-up pair of board shorts. "February and March are the peak months; the migration is in full swing then. We probably would've seen quite a few on our trip down here."

"They love the deep water in the channel between Grand

Turk and South Caicos," Em explained. "Columbus Channel... or the Turks Island Passage. It runs down past Salt Cay... and here, too." She waved a lazy hand to the west, past the *Lunasea*, which lay at anchor in the shallows.

"What island is this?" Bethany asked, looking around. The islet itself was flat, devoid of any structures and with very little in the way of foliage.

"Big Sand Cay," Boone said. "Uninhabited. And one of the best beaches around. Figured it'd be a good place for our surface interval. It's on the leeward side, so not much sargassum."

"Man, that stuff is stinky," Branson said, his mouth stuffed with watermelon.

"Don't talk with your mouth full, sweetie," Mrs. Douglas admonished.

Branson waved a gnawed-upon rind. "We were in Cancun last year, and there was more seaweed than sand."

"South Caicos, where I'm from... it comes in on de channel side," Lincoln said from where he sat in the surf. "Less on de south coast. East Bay has a tractor to gather it up every morning."

Branson crab-walked over to the cooler that Boone had brought ashore and grabbed two more wedges of watermelon, cramming one into his mouth.

"Branson, don't be greedy," Mrs. Douglas whispered.

"S'all hunky-dory," Emily assured them. "There's plenty. Local grocer had a bunch of 'em and I got a stonking big one! Normally, we just have oranges or apples for after-dive snacks, so this was a treat!" Em reached in to grab a slice herself and was surprised to find there actually wasn't much left. *Blimey, that kid must be half melon.*

17

"So... do all the dive ops go to the Endem... Endemon...?" Bethany trailed off.

"*Endymion*," Emily provided. "From Greek mythology. He was some smokin' hot shepherd that the Moon fell in love with."

Bethany giggled and Boone smiled. "Emily here is an encyclopedia of trivia," he said. "But to answer your question, no... it's a long haul to Endymion Rock, so only a few of the dive ops will do it. Salt Cay Divers aren't too far, so they come here a fair amount. But for those on Grand Turk, it's a lot of fuel and time to get here."

"Unless you've got the *Lunasea*!" Em declared, sweeping her hand toward the Delta Canaveral at anchor. "She's got a bit more pep in 'er step than most dive boats." Emily decided to skip over the reason for that extra speed: the dive boat had been altered to act as a drug runner in Honduras, with a long range and excellent top speed—provided the seas were relatively calm. Looking out beyond the shallows, Emily noticed a few whitecaps that weren't there before. She turned to Boone, who was also gazing out to sea. Emily opened her mouth to say something, but he seemed to know what she was thinking.

"Yeah, I see it. Weather was supposed to cooperate today, but looks like the wind's picked up a bit."

"Second dive... let's pick a northern one, yeah? Get us that much closer to Grand Turk?"

Boone nodded. "Kelly's Folly?"

"Good choice," Em replied. That dive site was near the northwest point of Salt Cay, just seven miles from the southern tip of Grand Turk, and ten miles to their dock. "And if Salt Cay Divers are on it, Northwest Wall is a good backup."

"Works for me," Boone said. He reached over and took

Emily's wrist, turning it so he could check the surface time on the face of her Shearwater Teric dive computer.

"Get your own," Emily said with a laugh.

"Left it on the boat."

"No, I mean you should get your own Teric."

"My old Aeris is still going strong." He shrugged. "If it ain't broke..." Boone lifted her hand, turning her wrist from side to side. "You only got this 'cause your friend AJ had one."

"Maybe. Shut up. Besides, it's gorgeous! Does everything you could want and isn't much bigger than a dive watch." She glanced at it, confirming what she already knew—their surface interval had been more than sufficient. Even though their dive at the *Endymion* had been a long one, they'd rarely dipped below fifty feet; a relatively shallow dive plan.

Boone rose. "We should get a move on," he said. "Before it gets too rough."

"Chop-chop before the chop?" she said with an expectant grin.

Boone chuckled and reached down to offer her a hand, then pulled her to her feet. At four-foot-eleven, she only came up to his bare chest. "I'll get the cooler. You wrangle the herd."

"Wrangle the herd?" Emily drawled, cocking her head. "Sounding a bit like a cowboy, Buckaroo Boone. Didn't know they had those in Tennessee."

Boone smiled and grabbed hold of the Igloo full of drinks and snacks. "Lincoln! We're heading out."

Lincoln nodded and rose from the surf. "I gwan start 'er up," he said, shuffling through the shallow water toward the dive boat. Boone followed with the cooler.

Emily gathered her beach towel and adjusted her sunglasses. "Oy! Saddle up, you lot! We're going to head up to Salt Cay for our second dive. Gather up everything, yeah?"

"Don't eat the seeds, Branson!" Mrs. Douglas scolded, as her son quickly wolfed his last wedge of watermelon.

The teen gathered up his pile of rinds and looked around. Emily pointed to the nearby beach scrub along the low dunes. "Our scaly friends will take care of those!" A trio of iguanas watched the divers, blinking in the hot sun. "Iguana wanna watermelon?" Emily blurted rapidly. "Say that three times fast."

Branson tossed the rinds toward the iguanas. The sudden movement spooked two of them, but seconds later, all three had pounced on the melon rinds. Not far away, others appeared.

Emily made a last check for any garbage, then left the pristine beach, hot on the heels of the Missouri family. In the shallows, the *Lunasea*'s engine burbled to life.

As the *Lunasea* bobbed above the Kelly's Folly dive site, Boone watched with amusement as Emily finished up the briefing with her usual flair.

"And when we're back to the mooring line, I'll see if I can find some little nudibranchs for you, yeah?" She nodded toward the father. "Mark, get your camera's macro settings ready!" She pulled up the top of her green-and-black shortie wetsuit as she looked over the side of the boat. "Getting a little choppy, so I'm gonna pop down now and wait for you. When you stride in, don't muck about too long at the surface; don't want anyone getting seasick. Just descend to join me by the mooring line. Lincoln will follow the group. And Boone... well, Boone will sit up here and miss out on all the great stuff we're gonna see."

"Lincoln and I will help everyone to the stern," Boone said. The boat was rocking as the winds picked up, and he didn't want anyone faceplanting on the deck in their gear. He watched Emily reaching for—and missing—her wetsuit's zipper, so he snagged it and zipped her up. "Pool's open, as soon as Em hits the water."

Emily sat on the port bench and geared up with impressive speed. Boone brought her lime-green fins to the platform and extended a long arm toward her.

"How gallant," she said, rising and taking two sure-footed steps on the rocking deck to take his hand. "Thanks much."

Boone assisted her with her fins, and then she took a giant stride into the water—although "giant" wasn't exactly a word Boone would apply to the petite Brit. He turned to the rest of the group. "Okay... who's first?"

Once Lincoln descended after the Missouri divers, Boone returned to the shade of the cabin, popped open the cooler and looked at what was left. The ice had long since melted, and he reached into the water to grab a Switcha, an uncarbonated lemon-lime drink bottled in The Bahamas. It took its inspiration from local limeade—also called "switcha"—that was popular in the Turks and Caicos. Boone chugged half of it in one go, then capped it and headed up to the flybridge. Putting his feet up, he settled in for a quick nap in the shade of the blue bimini top.

Forty-five minutes later, the sound of a diver breaching the surface brought Boone to the swim platform. Mark Douglas handed up his expensive camera rig and Boone took it, backpedaling to quickly set it in the rinse bin before returning to the ladder to take the diver's fins.

"Fantastic!" he said, out of breath.

"Careful placing your feet on the ladder," Boone cautioned, as the *Lunasea* rose and fell in the waves.

The sea state wasn't really that bad, but divemasters had to deal with varying levels of experience, and it didn't hurt to be cautious. Fortunately, Mr. Douglas had no difficulty extricating himself. Boone guided the man to his bench slot, then went back to assist his wife. Lincoln was close on their heels, and scrambled up behind them as other heads popped to the surface.

"Oh my God!" a feminine voice cried.

Boone scrambled to the stern with Mr. Douglas close behind.

"Bran's coughing up blood!" Bethany screamed.

Branson was holding onto the trailing line with a pool of reddish material floating in front of him, red spittle on his lips. Emily was alongside the teen, looking closely at him. He abruptly spit up another gout of scarlet liquid, spattering Em's mask.

"Gross!" Bethany cried.

Boone dived in and swam over to them.

"Everyone calm down!" Emily called out. "He's fine."

"Is that blood?" Mr. Douglas asked frantically. "Is it an embolism?"

"Not unless he has watermelon seeds growing in his lungs," Emily said, a trace of amusement on her face. She plucked a seed from her mask. "See?"

"He's just seasick," Boone reassured them.

"I ate too much," Bran said, looking a little green around the gills. "Felt kinda sick near the end."

"Yeah, half a watermelon in your tum-tum and a rocking boat'll do that." Em said, before ducking her head under to rinse off her face and mask.

"Let's get you aboard," Boone said, guiding the youth toward the ladder.

———

"I don't need to go to the hospital," Branson whined.

"And I don't want to take any chances," his father insisted.

The *Lunasea* was heading back to Grand Turk with Emily up top at the flybridge wheel. Boone was below, crouched beside the divers who were gathered around Branson. The teen looked a lot better.

"Mark, just to reassure you... motion sickness isn't unusual on these longer open-ocean trips, and I'm pretty sure that's what this was."

"We all took the Dramamine you suggested," Mrs. Douglas insisted. "This morning before breakfast."

Boone caught the flicker in Branson's eyes. The kid squirmed on the bench.

"I... umm... I think I forgot."

"Oh, Bran!" his mother muttered with exasperation. "And I told you to stop stuffing your face with all that melon!"

Boone reached out and tapped the aluminum water bottle Branson held. "Keep drinking. Little sips."

"Look," Mr. Douglas said, "I'd just feel better if we had him looked at."

Boone nodded. It was human nature to have a degree of anxiety about a child's safety, and you couldn't put a price on laying a parent's fears to rest.

"We have DAN insurance," the father said.

"That's good," Boone said. Too many divers didn't have dive accident insurance from the Divers Alert Network, so he was glad to hear this. "Although it would only help you in the case of an actual dive accident. A bout of seasickness wouldn't be covered. But we know a guy at the hospital. Don't worry, we'll take care of everything. Won't cost you a dime."

Lincoln looked over at Boone and raised an eyebrow.

"That's not necessary," Mrs. Douglas said.

Boone shrugged. "Our boat, our watermelon. I insist. The hospital's not far from our dock. I'll run you over there and get you set up. We'll hang onto your gear, but take Branson's computer with you, so the doc can see your dive profile." He rose and headed for the ladder. "Let me talk to Em, and I'll call ahead."

Boone climbed up to join Emily at the wheel.

"How's melon boy?" she asked.

"He's fine. But his dad's pretty anxious. Wants to run him by the hospital." He looked down at the gauges. The *Lunasea* was capable of impressive speed, and yet... "Twenty-three knots. Can we nudge it up a bit?"

"We could, if you want to make everyone relive their lunch," Em said. "Too choppy to floor it. Sorry. Once we get to GT, I can go inside the reef. Throttle up then."

"No, it's not an emergency. And there's probably a cruise ship in today." Driving at top speed inside the reef was frowned upon, with lots of smaller pleasure craft and watersports using the shallows. Bubble Chasers Diving was still a newcomer to the Turks and Caicos, and he didn't want to ruffle any feathers. "Let's stay in the channel."

Lincoln came up to join them. "You really gwan pay for a trip to de hospital?" he asked.

"Oh... we *are*?" Emily asked, then shrugged. "Fair enough. Our watermelon could be considered the catalyst."

Boone laughed. "I said as much." He turned to Lincoln. "First, that hospital is pretty much a clinic. Not too expensive.

And we know one of the docs there." He didn't feel the need to add that they weren't hurting for money. The two divemasters had been blessed with a pair of sizable windfalls during the last few years.

As the low silhouette of Grand Turk appeared on the horizon, the divers joined them on the flybridge, enjoying the wind in their faces. In minutes, a massive cruise ship came into view, nuzzled against the large concrete pier that jutted from shore.

"Whoa!" Bethany stood up and pointed. "It's huge!"

Boone took out his phone and checked the calendar on the cruise ship terminal's website. All residents on Grand Turk used the schedule to know what kind of a day it was going to be. Some businesses wouldn't bother opening if a ship wasn't scheduled. By the same token, some locals wouldn't venture south of the airport if there *was* one in port. Boone found today's date on the schedule. "That's the *Carnival Freedom*. About 3,000 passengers."

"Isn't that the one that caught fire?" Em asked.

"What?" Mrs. Douglas spluttered.

Boone waved a hand dismissively. "Just one side of the double-funnel. Or smokestack, or whatever you call it. Caught fire while it was at the pier over there. Guess they fixed it."

As the *Lunasea* flashed past the cruise ship terminal and approached the airport, a low-flying helicopter roared overhead, heading out to sea.

FOUR

Viktor Gusev looked out the window at the massive cruise ship, his eyes scanning her upper decks as they flew past. He spotted a volleyball court, a swimming pool, and a water slide before the helicopter roared over the sparkling waters of the lee side of Grand Turk. A dive boat was below, bow-on to the passing helicopter, and Viktor had a momentary glimpse of blond hair, tanned skin, and feminine curves just below the blue bimini top that shaded the captain's chair. He pressed his face against the window, looking back as the helicopter rushed past. Sure enough, there was a beautiful woman at the wheel, but then the boat was lost from view.

The Russian debated asking his pilot to circle, but quickly dismissed the impulse. That would call far too much attention this close to the cruise port. Instead, he glanced across to his fellow passenger in the rear of the AW139. Paz Cisneros was engrossed in a folder of schematics, the collection of papers threatening to overwhelm the drop-down table in front of him. An electronic tablet doubled as a paperweight and kept the pages from spilling onto the carpeted floor of the executive helicopter.

"Have you solved our power problem?" Viktor asked.

The Cuban didn't reply, running a finger along a line on one page, then tapping the tablet and scanning the screen.

"Paz!"

"*Que?*" The engineer looked up. "I'm sorry, you said something?" he asked in English.

"I asked if you've found a solution to the power problem," Viktor responded in kind. Since he didn't speak Spanish and Paz didn't speak Russian, they had defaulted to English during their brief working relationship. Both spoke it quite well, so communication wasn't difficult between them.

"I believe I am on the right track," Paz replied. "As you know, the compact solid-state battery we used on the last test was a prototype..."

"I am painfully aware," Viktor said, remembering the acrid, fishy smell of the electrical fire. And... *other* odors. "We'll need to do the next test outside of my property."

"A prudent precaution," Paz replied. "But the data from our test, along with the footage of the combustion that occurred... it provided enough information for my contact to make some adjustments to the solid-state battery."

"How long will it take him to provide us with an updated version?"

"Three days."

Viktor slammed a fist down on the armrest of his seat. "Too long!"

Paz shrugged, unperturbed. "The actual fabrication will require less than a day. But we must take into consideration the flight time from Nagoya, Japan, where the factory is." He adjusted his glasses and tapped the screen of his tablet several times before typing on the digital keyboard. "Nagoya to Los Angeles to Miami to Providenciales... approximately thirty-five hours, in addition to the day of fabrication."

Viktor ground his teeth, wincing as he put pressure on what was likely another cavity. "And from Provo... an additional flight or boat ride," he muttered.

As the most populous of the Turks and Caicos Islands, Providenciales—or "Provo"—was the site of the international airport. But even after cargo landed there, it still had to get to South Caicos. Which meant additional time. Additional screening.

"How soon after it arrives can we test it?"

Paz smiled. "Five minutes or less. The interface will be the same; he has simply adjusted the thickness of the shielding around the anode and cathode collection layers to restrict the expansion of the lithium. We believe the combustion was a result of deformation or 'creep' in the lithium, which reached some of the wiring."

Viktor nodded as if he understood everything the bespectacled engineer had just said. "Additional shielding. How much heavier? Portability is the entire point."

"The materials are lightweight. I anticipate an increase of no more than fifty grams." Paz returned to his tablet and began typing notes.

"I suppose you can work on our other venture while we wait for the new battery," Viktor suggested.

Paz didn't look up from his screen as he replied, "I will devote some thought to it, once I'm finished collating the data on this."

Viktor looked out the window, scanning for humpbacks in the channel. When he'd first arrived, there had been many, but he hadn't seen any in the last month. He spotted a trawler headed north and watched it briefly. Possibly a fisherman, but it was equally likely to be a smuggler, with a cargo of drugs or migrants, bound for The Bahamas. The helicopter banked slightly, and the boat was lost from view, replaced by the cliffs on the eastern coast of South Caicos. Along the ridge stood a line of four long buildings, with more behind: the remains of a resort that never opened. Rumor had it, the resort had been a bit of a "white elephant," a money-laundering project that went off the rails. With over a thousand rooms, these buildings had stood for many years, until a luxury real estate firm had bought them up, along with more than half the island. The firm opened its own high-end resort nearby and used part of the abandoned complex as staff housing.

Much of the low island appeared arid, with very little in the way of trees, but there was a long stretch of verdant green just to the north, where the firm's resort was located. There, along the beach, lay several villas, with additional buildings on the cliffs above. Viktor had dined there often, and found the restaurant to be quite excellent. And while the resort itself was lovely, its presence served a more lucrative purpose: the sale of plots of land and the construction of luxury villas for wealthy foreigners. Foreigners like Viktor Gusev.

Below, a rough, sandy road carved a line along the scrub-filled cliffs. The plots for future homes were laid out in a grid, many with power boxes pre-installed in anticipation of construction. Occasionally, a beautiful home would flash by, but the project was still in its infancy. To date, less than thirty plots had homes on them. Viktor had purchased his own slice of tropical paradise at the far northern border of the real estate company's holdings, just to the south of the old US Coast Guard station, a relic of the Cold War.

The pilot's voice came over a speaker in the back cabin. *"Cinturones de seguridad. Estamos aterrizando."*

"Seat belts. We are landing," Paz translated, securing his papers before he secured himself.

Viktor was already strapped in. They had made this flight numerous times, and while Viktor didn't speak Spanish, Diego —his pilot, and a former Colombian Army aviator—tended to say the same thing every time, and the foreign phrases had become familiar. He'd asked the man to use English a number of times, but that request was battling with old habits and years of routine.

The helicopter slowed to a hover and dropped down on the makeshift pad Viktor had ordered constructed. Although "constructed" was a bit of a misnomer; he'd simply bought the neighboring plot and had laborers strip an area of vegetation and level it. Sand and dust flew as the pilot lowered the AW139 to the ground, its skids touching gently and imparting a slight bounce to the occupants of the cabin. As the engine wound down, Viktor and Paz unbuckled their harnesses but remained in their seats while the cloud of sand dissipated. The clicks of switches being flipped sounded from the cockpit, as Diego went through his shutdown routine.

Outside, a burly member of Viktor's security detail approached to open the passenger hatch and lower the collapsible stairs. "Welcome back, sir," he called out, stepping back as the dust settled.

"Thank you, Sergei," Viktor said, stepping down. He did a double take, looking at the man. Heavily muscled, he was wearing a navy-blue tracksuit, his thick neck sporting a gold chain. "Why do you dress like that, Sergei? You're a walking stereotype."

"It's comfortable," the man said defensively. "I've been working out, and a lotta my clothes don't fit so good no more."

Viktor sighed. "Anything exciting happen while I was away?"

"Baptiste got one of the Jeeps stuck in the sand again. Pierre and I had to go down and winch 'im out."

Like Viktor, Sergei was Russian. But while Viktor hailed from Kaliningrad, Sergei was born and raised in Brighton Beach, and spoke with a pronounced Brooklyn accent. Despite his parentage, his command of Russian was almost as bad as Paz's, so he spoke English with Viktor as well.

"Where did he get stuck?" Viktor asked.

"One of those offshoot roads, south of the marina. Or whatever that mess is gonna be."

"I suspect it will eventually be the marina they hope for. Provided the correct palms are greased." Viktor had heard from a few locals that Reefview—the resort company that now owned much of the island—had dredged a large expanse of the landscape on the bayside of South Caicos, but had stopped work when the TCI Planning Commission got wind of it.

Paz carefully descended the steps and followed Viktor and Sergei as the two Russians approached the villa set into the cliff. The area was tastefully landscaped with local plants and low trees, and the size of the opulent structure wasn't apparent from the road. The roof peaked in six places, the villa being one cohesive building with the appearance of several structures joined together by glass and porches.

The decision to move his base of operations to South Caicos had come a little over a year ago. The location was well suited to Viktor's needs, with its proximity to a number of smuggling routes, and the government largely stayed out of residents' hair, with excellent terms for the purchase of property.

31

Viktor stepped into his tropical palace, smiling as he took in the vaulted, wood-beamed ceiling over the expansive living room. Its sliding glass doors were open at the moment, and he had an unobstructed view across the swimming pool courtyard to the sparkling ocean below. The lightweight curtains billowed in the sea breeze, and he noticed that most of the windows were open as well. He took in a deep breath... and frowned. Sometimes, sargassum accumulated on the wind-ward shore below, but this wasn't that. The scent of a lemony household cleaner permeated the air, but underneath it...

"Kirana!" he called out.

A clattering sound came from the attached kitchen, and his housekeeper came into the room. "Yes, Mr. Goose?"

Sergei snickered, and Viktor caught Paz cracking a smile. He locked eyes with the Indonesian woman. "Gu...*sev*," he enunciated.

Kirana ducked her head in obeisance. "I sorry. Yes, Mr. Gusev."

Viktor waited a count of three, then spoke slowly. "I can still smell it."

"I sorry, Mr. Gusev. I try. I run out of cleaner. No one here to get more."

Viktor sighed. "I'll send someone. Make a list."

As she scampered back into the kitchen, Viktor shot Sergei a look. "Have Baptiste go pick up supplies. That is, if he can keep from getting stuck in a ditch."

In addition to his security detail, drivers, and pilot, Viktor employed a small staff for the villa: a cook, a housekeeper, a maintenance man, and two groundskeepers. There had been a *third* groundskeeper, but he had proved... troublesome. Some of the staff were Indonesian, some Haitian, and none of them had proper papers; a useful bit of leverage. As part of their employment agreement, none were allowed to leave the villa. The only stores on the island were all the way down in Cockburn Harbour, a thirty-minute drive along the rough roads.

"It's not that bad," Paz said, sniffing the air.

"You didn't pay for this place," Viktor muttered.

"True. But once we make delivery, you'll be able to rebuild the entire room, if you want to. Speaking of which..." The Cuban turned and headed into one of the adjoining wings. "I'll be in my office."

Viktor stepped into the courtyard and looked out at the horizon, then down at his swimming pool. Water was at a premium on this arid island, but he had arranged for his pool to be filled with fresh water. It looked very inviting. Stripping off his clothes, he lowered his naked body into the lukewarm water.

———

Paz Cisneros set the folder of documents and the electronic tablet on his desk before picking up a spritzer of lens cleaner and a microfiber cloth. He gave his glasses a careful cleaning, then turned and stepped toward the workbench in the far corner. Midway, he stopped, looking down at the floor. In the center of the room, the faded remains of scorch marks radiated out from a central point, like the rays of a black sun, drawn in charcoal. Yes, the fishy odor of the electrical fire was still there. And it wasn't alone. Paz looked into the corner. Soaked into the wood floor, the faint stain there had a different origin.

FIVE

"C'mon, Boone! Kiss the tiki!"

"Not gonna do it."

Boone and Emily sat on stools at the Ike and Donkey Beach Bar, situated beside Pillory Beach—hands down the prettiest stretch of sand on Grand Turk. Part of the Bohio Dive Resort, the Ike and Donkey was a small, open-air bar with stools all around. Surrounding it were tables, awnings, red umbrellas, and palm trees. The resort itself was taking a pause for renovations, but the bar was too popular to stay closed. That being said, having one of the main dive ops on the island on a temporary hiatus hadn't been bad for Bubble Chasers Diving's business.

"It's good luck to kiss a tiki," Emily insisted, shoving her clear tiki glass at Boone's face, the grimacing head full of frothy piña colada. "Conversely, it's bad luck *not* to kiss a tiki."

"Pretty sure you just made that up," Boone said, smiling.

"Maybe I did..." Emily made her voice husky and menacing and whispered, "...but are you willing to take the risk?"

Boone was saved by a call coming in, as Emily's green-cased phone buzzed on the bar beside her drink. Their local divemaster's number was on the screen; after they'd returned from the dives, he'd said he had some errands to run, and had left them at the dock. Em answered and tapped the speaker button. "Heya, Link! Whassup?"

"Just checkin' in 'bout de Douglases... and whether we'll be divin' tomorrow?"

"We're waiting to hear," Boone said, "but I'd lay odds we'll be diving first thing in the morning."

"Okay den."

"If you have other plans, we can make do with just Em and me."

"No, I'll be dere. I need to get over to South Caicos sometime to see my muddah, but she'll keep."

"Is she okay?" Boone asked.

"Oh, yeah, yeah, yeah. She fine. She jus' wants me to fix her stone wall. Been crumblin' since Irma. I'll get over dere on my day off."

"Okay. We'll text you once we hear from the hospital. We're over at the Ike and Donkey, if you're feeling lonely." As Lincoln hung up, Boone noticed the bartender giggling, and he looked over at Emily, who had started doing something while he'd been talking to Lincoln. He discovered her making out with her tiki glass. Her efforts to keep an intense, passionate look on her face fell apart in short order, and she snorted a laugh into the glass, sending the top layer of piña colada flying. The bartender, still chuckling, grabbed a rag and mopped it up.

"Sorry, Lizette. But Boone rejected my tiki buddy and I had to make it up to 'im."

"S'okay Emily, I could use de laugh." She smiled at Boone. "You want a Tiki Colada too?"

"Nah, I gotta drive. Gimme an I-Soon-Reach."

"Can or bottle?"

"Whatever you grab first."

Lizette went to the cooler and fetched a cold bottle of Turks Head Brewery's "session beer," a low-alcohol lager that went down smooth in the hot, sunny weather of the Turks and Caicos Islands.

"Is that good?" a bar patron asked. She and a young man were sitting around the corner of the bar from Boone and Em and had been watching Emily's antics.

Boone took a sip and sighed with satisfaction. "It is." He held up the label so they could see it.

"I-Soon-Reach... that's a funny name."

Lizette jumped in. "It's from Turks Head Brewery over on Provo. All of deir beers are named for Turks and Caicos sayings. So dat one... let's say you was waitin' on a friend who always late. And you call him and say, 'Where y'at?' And he say, 'I be jus' down da road. I soon reach.'"

The pair chuckled at that.

"And 'Down-Da-Road' is another beer," Boone chimed in. "An IPA. And they've got a couple others... 'I-Ain-Ga-Lie' is tasty."

"I-Ain-Ga-Lie is Belonger talk for 'I ain't gonna lie,'" Lizette explained.

"Belonger?" the man asked.

"Dat's a name for a native-born resident of Turks and Caicos," Lizette said.

Boone noticed they had a pamphlet with them with a Carnival logo on it, and figured they were with the cruise ship. Most cruisies stayed around the terminal with its copious shops and a jumbo-size Margaritaville, but some intrepid souls always made it up to Pillory Beach. He sipped his beer again.

"This beer's refreshing, but my favorite one is the Gon-Ta-Nort Amber."

Lizette was ready for that one. "'Gon ta Nort' means you goin' over to North Caicos. And there's a new beer for *South* Caicos... Gon-Ta-Sout Stout. But you can only get dat at de taphouse at de brewery in Provo."

"And... Provo is?" the woman asked.

"Providenciales," Emily inserted quickly. "It's the island with most of the population, most of the businesses, most of the big hotels, and the International Airport. But this island— Grand Turk—is the capital of the Turks and Caicos. Well, specifically Cockburn Town," she clarified, pronouncing it "COH-burn," the way most locals did.

"Oh, *that's* how you say it?" the man said, and his wife giggled.

"Yeah, the way it's spelled, it looks like some kind of naughty STD, but it actually comes from Sir Francis Cockburn. English bloke. And you know we Brits love to chop off a consonant here or there. Sir Francis was governor of The Bahamas back in the day."

At the look of confusion, Boone stepped in. "The Bahamas had a lot of influence on the history in TCI. I learned a few things from the museum downtown, but Trivia Girl here can explain better than me."

"Right-o." Emily made a show of sucking in a big breath, then launched into her spiel. "The Spanish and French were here, but then the Brits took over. Lots of pirates running around. The Turks and Caicos have been administered by Bermuda, The Bahamas, Jamaica... there was even a proposal to give them to Canada at one point. But eventually they became a separate British Overseas Territory, and got to govern themselves for a change."

Lizette snickered. "Except when de British decide to take back control every so often. Lot of corruption early on. But we've had home rule since 2012."

"And Cockburn Town is the oldest settlement in the TCI, so it's been the capital for ages," Emily added. "Even though Provo has four times as many people."

"Oh, yeah... like in Kentucky," the man said. "Louisville's got way over half a million residents, but the capital is a little town named Frankfort."

"Are you from Kentucky?" Em asked. "Boone here is from Tennessee."

Boone raised his beer. "Howdy, neighbor."

"Right back atcha. We're actually from Delaware, but we moved down there last year. I'm Bill... this lovely lady is Cynthia."

"I'm Emily," Em said, then ratcheted up her South London accent. "Most definitely *not* from Tennessee, guv."

"You from Australia?" Bill asked.

The smile didn't even reach Boone's face before Emily socked him in the arm. Her strong dialect was often mistaken for Aussie, and he liked to tease her about it.

"Right Commonwealth, wrong hemisphere," Em said quickly. "London."

"Boone... that's a nice name," Cynthia mused. "Like... Daniel Boone?"

He nodded. "My mom claimed we were descended from him."

"Are you?" Cynthia prodded.

Boone took another sip. Shrugged. "Dunno. Never seen any evidence, apart from her telling me that's why she named me Boone."

"You should do one of those DNA tests," Bill urged.

"Blimey, that's a brill idea!" Emily gushed. "Hey, I'll do one too! Maybe I'm descended from British royalty."

"Or maybe you *are* from Australia," Boone deadpanned. That earned another punch in the biceps.

Cynthia winced. "Does it hurt when she does that?"

"Used to. I think all the nerve endings there are dead from repeated abuse. This your first time in Turks and Caicos, I take it?"

"First time in the Caribbean, actually! Loving it!"

Boone smiled, nodding. Technically, the TCI weren't in the Caribbean; like The Bahamas, these islands were considered to be in the Atlantic, but they were certainly "Caribbean" in culture and vibe. Boone's phone lit up, but rather than his usual ring, the chorus of "Love Shack" by the B-52's blasted from the speaker.

Boone threw Emily a slow burn look, and the blond Brit bit her lip, stifling laughter. He gripped her shoulder and shook her playfully. "Nice one."

"Boone sleeps like the dead," Em explained to the tourists, who were looking on with amusement, "so I like to unlock his mobile with his thumb and change the ringtone from time to time. Keeps 'im on his toes."

Boone rose from his stool. "Pleased to meet you two," he said. To Emily, he added, "It's the Douglases. I'm gonna take it over there on the beach."

Boone answered the call as he left the vicinity of the bar and headed onto the warm sand. "This is Boone Fischer."

"Hi, Boone, it's Lisa. Thank you so much for being patient with my husband. He's always been a worrywart. It was just what you said. Motion sickness. No signs of any decompression sickness or embolisms or any other scary diving stuff."

"Glad to hear it!" Boone said. "We're less than a quarter mile away. I'll come get you."

"Oh, thank you, that's not necessary. I've already arranged for a cab," Mrs. Douglas replied. "But... I was wondering about tomorrow morning. Can we dive?"

"Of course! We'll just go straight out to The Wall. A nice, gentle, two-minute trip through the shallows. And no watermelons."

Lisa laughed. "And we'll make sure he takes his Dramamine."

"Oh, there'll be no need for that," Boone assured her. "Weather looks good and it really is about the shortest boat ride you can imagine. Heck, people shore dive out to it. And I've got all of your gear safely stored; I'll have it waiting for you on the boat.

After the call, Boone texted Lincoln to let him know they were on for the morning, then pocketed his phone and looked out at the turquoise waters on the inside of the reef. Just a third of a mile out, the color abruptly changed to a dark, midnight blue, where the reef plunged almost vertically to a depth of 7,000 feet. Having come from Little Cayman, with its Bloody Bay Wall, Boone and Em had traded one wall for another. Many "walls" in the Caribbean sloped a bit, but the one here on Grand Turk—and Bloody Bay on Little—plunged straight down in many locations, making for an exhilarating sight when you began your descent.

They'd been here on GT for some time now, and Boone enjoyed the little island. Busier than Little Cayman, no doubt... but not too busy. The cruise ships certainly led to a bit more bustle, but the pier at the terminal could only accommodate two. And Boone and Em had spent a year on Cozumel, where the cruise ship traffic was insane. Good for the local Mexican economy, no doubt, but not at all good for the reefs. Even here, the construction of the cruise ship terminal had resulted in damage to the fringing reef, as a channel was needed. A gap had been torn in the reef and the dredging had caused sedimentation down-current; and just like in Cozumel, areas around the cruise ship terminal showed coral stress and increased algae growth.

Boone heard a braying sound farther down the beach and watched a common Grand Turk commotion. Two dogs chased a pair of donkeys, all four kicking up sand. Boone smiled. On the island of Bonaire, where he'd first met Emily, donkeys were a familiar sight. Here on Grand Turk, salt production was once a major industry, much like on Bonaire. The donkeys were all descendants of the pack animals used in the transportation of salt. And there was another connection to their prior island experiences: the dogs.

In Belize, Emily and Boone had adopted a stray named Brixton—currently being pampered by the owner of the bed and breakfast they were living in. Strays in Belize were called "potlickers." Here in the Turks and Caicos, they were known as "potcakes." Both breeds of canine were essentially mutts descended from various breeds used by colonists for a variety of tasks. And both had acquired their nicknames from the same source: the solidified crust of rice and beans at the bottom of a pot, scraped up and fed to the dogs.

Boone was brought out of his reverie by a wet sensation on his leg. A potcake he'd seen around the resort had come up behind him and was licking his bare calf. He crouched and gave the dog an ear scratch. From the look of her, she was quite pregnant.

"Hey girl... no donkey-chasing for you, huh?"

The dog sat in the sand and panted enthusiastically.

"Hey, let's get you some water." Boone squinted at the afternoon sun. "And how about we go find some shade?"

He headed back toward the bar and beckoned to the dog, but she turned and went off down the beach to the south. "Okay, suit yourself."

Emily was noisily straw-sucking the remnants of her Tiki Colada when Boone came up beside her. The cruise ship couple had left the bar.

"You scare them off?" Boone asked.

"Rude." Em polished off the glass head. "No, I sent them down to Jorika's Moment for dinner! Well... *after* I texted Jorika and made sure she was open. They were going to return to the ship, but I talked them out of cruise ship food."

"Good call." Jorika was their landlord, of sorts. The owner of the Sunflower Oasis, she used to be the chef at the Bohio Resort, and continued to apply her culinary skills at the little kitchen that sat at the front of the Sunflower. Boone had eaten at quite a few places on the island, and her cooking was by far his favorite.

"So, what news of Watermelon Boy?" Emily inquired.

"He's fine. In fact, they want to dive in the morning. Figured we'd just pop out to The Wall."

"Do we need to pick them up?"

"Nope. They're taking a cab back to their hotel."

"Ace! Then, in that case... I may have another drinky-poo."

"I ain't gonna kiss it."

Emily blew a raspberry. "That ship has sailed. Nah, I'll just get an I-Soon-Reach."

As Lizette grabbed one, Boone caught her eye. "Make it two, please. And we'll settle up."

Em arched an eyebrow above her lime-green shades. "Oh, we will, will we?"

"Diving tomorrow... and still need to get dinner."

"Ever sensible, Booney." She took her frosty bottle and looked toward the beach. "I spy with my little eye... something green and invasive."

Boone laughed. "I'll meet you there."

He watched Emily make her way to the beach and turn right, heading for the stand of casuarina trees and the lounge chairs that lay in their shade. Also known as "she-oak" or "Australian pine," the needled trees were not true pines, despite their appearance, but a form of salt-resistant evergreen. And, as with many things in life, there was a bit of a "yin and yang" aspect to them. Casuarinas provided excellent shade, and Boone would be the first to admit that the sound of the sea breeze in their needled branches was one of the most relaxing sounds he'd heard in his brief time on this planet. But on the other hand, the trees didn't belong here in the Western hemisphere, and they tended to out-compete the indigenous flora.

Boone was about to settle the bill with Lizette, but after a moment's thought, he added a bottle of water to the tab. He didn't like to use plastic bottles—there was enough of the non-degradable stuff out there as it was—but he thought he might need it. "And... do you have any bowls?"

"For de potcakes?" Lizette replied without hesitation, fetching a metal bowl from beneath the bar with such speed that Boone figured she had several on hand, ready to go.

"Yeah. There's one I've seen around. She looked a little overheated. She's pregnant."

"Ah, yes... dat's Mama." Lizette laughed. "De name should tell you... dis isn't da first litter she's had."

Boone gathered up the beer, water, and bowl and walked a short distance up the beach. Emily was already stretched out on a lounge chair in the shade of one of the low-hanging branches. The sun was on its way to the horizon, but they had a few hours before sunset.

Emily extended her beer and Boone clinked it as he reclined on the chair beside her. He leaned over to the side and pushed the water bowl into the sand, but didn't yet fill it. This stretch of beach had three or four potcakes that considered it their territory.

"Water bowl?"

"Yep."

"Cool."

They sat in silence for a while, listening to the conversation between the lapping surf and the whispering breeze through the casuarinas. After a time, Mama made an appearance, shambling up the beach. Boone sat up and poured cold water in the bowl. The potcake saw this and went straight to the bowl, lapping noisily.

"Wow. Her belly's stonkin' huge," Emily remarked. "Wonder why she never got spayed?"

"Dunno. But there's gonna be a lotta puppies on the way."

"Y'know... Brixton could use a companion, yeah? Maybe we should adopt one."

Having drunk her fill, Mama went around the foot of the lounge chair and flopped into the sand between Boone and Emily. As one, they reached out to stroke the dog's fur as the ocean and trees continued their soothing discussion.

SIX

The following morning, Emily watched with amusement as Boone carefully closed the hood of the 1988 Ford Ranger, pressing down on it to get the latch to engage. The last time he'd slammed it shut, he'd busted the latch.

"Try it now."

When Emily turned the key and gave the old girl some petrol, the truck burbled to life. Boone came around and hopped into the passenger seat.

"You and your love affair with old bangers," Emily teased. In Cozumel, Boone had driven an ancient Volkswagen Thing that had been in constant need of maintenance.

"*You're* the one who insisted we buy this!" Boone protested.

"Oh, yeah. S'pose I did." Emily had spotted the old pickup in an overgrown yard on the west side of the island and had fallen in love. The ancient Ranger was apple red and had diagonal white stripes painted on the doors, imitating diver down flags. The grille had been replaced, and the interior was more duct tape than upholstery in a few places, but the retired dive shop owner had only wanted five hundred bucks for it.

Besides, they needed a truck. They'd bought a little powder-blue Suzuki Celerio to tool around Grand Turk in, but Bubble Chasers didn't yet have its own dive shop, so they paid to use another shop's compressor to fill their tanks. And the compressor facility was over half a mile from the dock they were using; hence the need for a truck.

The bed of the Ranger was currently loaded with sixteen tanks—two each for Boone, Emily, Lincoln, and their four divers for this morning, as well as two spares. The old truck had decided it didn't want to start, but Boone was a whiz with engines and had mucked about under the bonnet; minutes later they were on their way to the dock.

"Donkey crossing," Boone warned.

Emily slowed as a pair of donkeys crossed Front Street from the beach side to the salina side. The remnants of the salt industry lay in several spots in the interior.

"They're going over to eat the saltwort," Em explained. "Or turtleweed. That ground cover that looks like little jade plants. It grows in high salinity soil. And you can eat it, too. Guess how it tastes?"

"Salty?"

"Blimey, aren't you a bright boy?"

Boone looked over at her as she brought the truck up to speed again. "Another of your Trivia Night knowledge nuggets?"

"A recent acquisition to my brain-vault," Em replied. "The Donkey Whisperer taught me that. After he bought me a drink," she added with a smile.

Boone grunted a laugh. "Where do I start with that?"

"Wherever you like."

"Okay, let's start with, who or what is a donkey whisperer?"

"That's just what I call 'im. His name is Manuel. He's got a goat farm down in the south."

"Shouldn't he be a goat whisperer, then?"

"Don't be so literal. He knows a lot about donkeys, too. Handsome Dominican bloke. Bought me a Tiki Colada, if memory serves."

"Did he kiss it?"

Emily snorted a laugh. "Oh, my... I'm not gonna touch that. But no, he was a complete gentleman."

"Mm-hmm. And where was I?"

"You were busy fixing this bucket of bolts."

"That *you* wanted us to buy."

"Yes. That is correct."

Emily pulled off the road beside the dock, wrenched the manual transmission into reverse, then backed the truck up to the edge of the pier. It was a fairly new dock, located where Front Street met West Road, just two blocks north of the Turks and Caicos National Museum. The dock shared a corner with John's Ocean View Bar & Grill, which, coincidentally, used to be the location of an eatery named Emily's Fish Fry. This sealed the deal as far as Em was concerned. The local fishermen's co-op was a two-minute walk up the road, so the seafood at John's was as fresh as you could ask for.

The *Lunasea* was already tied up at the dock. The Sunflower Oasis—their current lodging—was just a five-minute walk to the north, along West Road. Earlier, while Emily made breakfast, Boone had popped down to the beach, swum out to the dive boat, and brought it to the dock. Lincoln was waiting for them when they pulled up with the tanks.

"You're early," Emily remarked as she got out of the truck.

Lincoln laughed. "You're late."

"Guess why," Boone said, giving the truck a playful thump on the roof as he went to open the rear gate.

Lincoln smirked and shook his head. "You should sell dat t'ing for parts."

"No worries, mate, we got it sorted," Emily assured him. "Boone here's a whiz with engines. He did something-or-other to some thingamabob, and Bob's your uncle, it started right up."

Em helped Boone lug the tanks to the boat while Lincoln stationed himself aboard, taking the tanks as they were handed over and slotting them into various spots on the benches. With only four divers today, he spread them out a little. While the Delta Canaveral could theoretically handle upwards of twenty divers, Boone and Emily preferred smaller groups.

While Boone began assembling the divers' gear at their stations, Emily scrambled up to the flybridge and put her phone in a compartment in the dash. Ashore, a taxi pulled up. Em waved when she saw it was Queen Bee's. The woman that ran it was a fun gal, and gave great island tours. The Douglas family got out and assumed Emily was waving at them, so they waved back. Queen Bee followed suit.

Emily laughed. *And we're waving... and we're waving.* When the taxi drove off, she descended to the deck to assist with their arrivals. Boone started helping them aboard.

"How're you feeling, Bran?" Em asked Branson when he stepped down to the deck.

"I'm fine," the teen said, looking a little embarrassed.

"Good! We've got oranges for today's snack, one apiece. And that's the last you'll hear from me on that," she added with a wink, then grabbed her clipboard and rapidly read through the names of the Douglas family. Finishing that ritual, she returned to the flybridge to start the engine. Boone handled the lines, then stepped aboard as the *Lunasea* backed away from the dock, turned, and headed for the reef.

───────────

As Emily skippered the *Lunasea* over the reef line and the top of the wall, the sea to either side suddenly became a dark blue. Below, Boone rose and grabbed an aluminum boat hook. "Get ready! Almost there."

"Where are we diving?" Mr. Douglas asked.

"Black Forest," Boone replied. He made his way to the bow to secure the boat to the mooring line that was just ahead. In moments, they were over the dive site and Emily descended to run the briefing. She scribbled topography details of the site on a whiteboard as she spoke.

"Right-o! You had some special dives yesterday, but now you'll really get to experience what Grand Turk is famous for: The Wall! We are above one of the largest reef systems in the world, and there are places where this wall drops straight down, like the side of a skyscraper, yeah? Down to 7,000 feet. So don't drop your camera, Mark!"

"It's neutrally buoyant."

"Well, in that case, drop it as much as you like! So, did Boone tell you why this site is called Black Forest? No? 'Course he didn't, lazy wanker. It's named that 'cause there's oodles of black coral down there. Now, normally, black coral prefers deeper water than we can safely dive to. It's sensitive to sunlight, but in this spot the shadow of the overhang of the wall allows it to thrive. It's still deep. We'll be diving to about eighty feet, where there's a lot of it."

"When I was young, I bought a black coral necklace down

in Barbados," Mark said, "but Lisa here told me how endangered it was, so I stopped wearing it."

"Good on you, Lisa! And good on you, Mark, for listening to your wife. Yeah, black coral is like a rhino horn or elephant tusk; not something you should be collecting. The skeleton of the coral is black, and it can be polished to look like onyx. But black coral takes a long, *long* time to grow. Just getting to the thickness of a human hair takes years, and there are some patches of it that are 2,000 years old!"

"What does it look like?" Branson asked.

"That's a good question, Bran... 'cause it won't actually look black! The skeleton of the coral is black, but it's covered in polyps, so the exterior can be all sorts of colors. Here, they're mostly a yellowish-green, but if you shine a dive light on it, it'll look more red. And that's because...?" She looked from Bethany to Bran, and back.

"Red doesn't show up down there?" Bran suggested.

"Bingo! Red goes at less than twenty feet... orange at about twenty-five or thirty. Anyway, Boone or I will point out the black coral. There're different kinds: some are like spindly-armed bushes, some are like long, thin tendrils. And keep an eye out for Graysby groupers—red polka-dotted buggers. This site has a bunch. Also, when we descend along the wall, shine your light in the crevices; there's usually some slipper lobsters. They've got these funky shovel-flippers instead of the long antennae that the spiny lobsters have."

While Emily explained the planned dive profile, Boone slipped into the water off the swim platform and examined the expanse of sand and coral patches that led to the top of the wall, determining the strength and direction of the current. He often looked at gorgonians to see which way the flow was going and how strong it was, but many of the feathery, soft corals had been lost to Hurricanes Irma and Maria. Neverthe-less, there were enough to see there was little to no current, which was typical of many of Grand Turk's dive sites. Boone climbed back aboard and flashed an "OK" sign to Emily as she completed her briefing.

Em plunked her dry erase marker into the basket she'd strapped to the side of the camera table. "All righty, you lot! Pool's open!"

———

The dive was nearing its end, the divers ascending slowly along the top of the wall, when Boone heard the sound of a boat. He looked around but didn't see anything near the surface. Many of the wall dive sites were in a cluster to the north, with more sites spread out to the south, but all were a fair distance away. While the direction of sound was nigh impossible to pinpoint underwater, you could approximate distance from the volume, and this engine—or engines—sounded nearby. The only other named dive site close to Black Forest was The Anchor, which was a shallow dive. This being mid-morning, he wouldn't expect anyone to be diving there just yet; most two-tank morning dives consisted of a deep dive to start, followed by a shallower profile.

Emily was looking back at him. She tugged her ear, pointed two fingers at her mask, then pointed at Boone before laying her palm out and shrugging that shoulder. Boone translated it as: *I hear something. Do you see anything?*

Boone shook his head, shrugged back at her, then flashed an "OK" sign, indicating he didn't see anything, but they were fine. There certainly wasn't any boat between them and the mooring, which was just ahead.

The engine noise continued, but then came an abrupt sound, like a sharp bang. The engine burbled, then died down to a distant thrum before stopping altogether. Boone continued to search for the underside of the boat's hull, but even with the exceptional visibility of Grand Turk's waters, the mystery boat eluded him. The Douglas family continued toward the mooring where Emily awaited them. While the group spent some time searching the nearby coral heads for last-minute sightings of marine life, Boone caught Emily's eye and signaled that he was heading up. After his safety stop, he swam to the ladder, deftly removed his fins, and tossed them up to the deck. He was aboard in seconds.

"Sorry! Be right dere," Lincoln called out from the flybridge. "Was just talkin' with *Caicos Sister*." He started for the ladder, but Boone held up a hand.

"S'alright. You're good. They'll be a few minutes more. You talking about your sister? Or are you talking about a boat?"

"Dive boat. Dey just come over from South Caicos. Captain is an old friend, Doug Cox. Everybody over dere call him Cap."

"They're having engine trouble, I'm guessing."

Lincoln cocked his head. "How you know 'bout dat?"

"Heard them coming in... then a bang. Sounded metallic." Boone climbed the ladder and looked to the south, inside the reef line. There, in the shallows near the mooring for a dive site called The Anchor, lay a forty-two-foot Newton. From the compartment beside the wheel, Boone retrieved the birding binoculars he'd had since Bonaire and trained them on the boat. On the side of the flybridge cockpit, the name *Caicos Sister* was painted. And below that...

"Reef Divers," Boone read. "From the East Bay Resort, right?"

"Yes. *Caicos Sister* is their newest. De boats dey had were on loan from de Caymans but t'ings picked up back dere, so dey went and got dis one. Shame if it broke already."

"Maybe I can take a look during the surface interval," Boone suggested as he restowed his binoculars. "Divers should be coming up now."

"Be right down," Lincoln said. "But first, I'll radio over and ask if dey want some company."

———

Fifteen minutes later, the *Lunasea* lay at anchor in about twelve feet of water. Five minutes before, she'd come alongside the *Caicos Sister*. The Newton had six divers aboard and two crew; they'd come over from South Caicos to dive some Grand Turk sites but had experienced odd vibrations after they'd dived The Tunnels. After dropping Boone and Lincoln off on the Newton, Emily had motored toward shallower water. There were strict rules for anchoring in Grand Turk: all boats had to be south of Pillory Beach and the anchorage had to be completely clear of any coral or structure—sandy bottom only. Coincidentally, the *Caicos Sister* was moored at The Anchor—a shallow dive with an anchor as the main attraction, thought to be at least a hundred years old. Emily had kept well clear of the dive site, dropping their modern anchor into a broad patch of sand a hundred yards away.

At the moment, she and the Douglases were enjoying the sun on the flybridge. Em had brought the cooler of oranges up top, so they could discard their peels into the rapidly melting ice. She popped a slice into her mouth as she watched Boone strip down to his shorts and put on a mask before dropping into the water at the stern. Em rose from the bench to retrieve his discarded T-shirt from the deck, a new one she'd gotten him just last week. Boone loved his ratty old shirts, but quite a few of them were more holes than fabric, and she'd been replacing some of the most threadbare. This one proclaimed: The Turks and Caicos Islands: Beautiful by Nature. She spread the tee out on the bench and sat down beside it.

"Hey, Emily? Why do they call it Turks and Caicos?" Bethany asked, eyeing the shirt.

Em spit an orange seed into the igloo. "Have you seen a little cactus around the island? Dumpy little bugger with a red cap on top?"

"Yeah."

"That's a Turk's head cactus. 'Cause it looks like that red felt cap called a fez. Popular piece of headgear in the Ottoman Empire, back in the day. And the people who ran the Empire were...?"

"Turkish?"

"Gold star to Bethany! You are correct, and that's where the 'Turks' part comes from. Although I did hear an alternate theory from the caretaker at the museum. You visit there, yet? The Turks and Caicos National Museum? Just a couple blocks from the dock."

"We meant to," Mr. Douglas said. "But it was closed when we went by."

"Aww, that's a shame," Em said, thinking. "Did you go by on Monday?"

"Yeah."

"Aha! There wasn't a cruise ship this Monday. Some places will take the day off or have shorter hours. You should go, though. Great exhibits. The staff is super-friendly! And the building is one of the oldest in the Turks and Caicos. Over 180 years old!"

"And... what was the alternate theory? About the Turks part of the name?"

"Oh, blimey, look at me, sailing off on a tangent. The caretaker told me she thought the name came from the fact that a lot of pirates were based in these islands. And, way back then, a lot of piracy was going on in the Mediterranean. Barbary Pirates... ever heard of them?"

"Yeah!" Mr. Douglas said, brightening. "The United States Marines kicked their asses! It's in the 'Marines' Hymn.'" He sucked in a breath. "From the halls of Montezuma, to the shores of Tripoli..." he sang. "The Tripoli part is the Barbary Pirates."

"You a Marine, then?" Emily asked.

"Yes, ma'am," he said with pride. "Logistics, mostly... but if the Marines are gonna fight, they gotta eat and they gotta shoot. Bread and bullets."

"Thank you for your service, Mark!" Emily said. Even though she was British, Em knew Boone would've said it, and she figured she was currently his proxy. "And you are right, those Barbary Pirates were in Tripoli... and a bunch of other places in North Africa... and that area was part of...?" Emily trailed off with an upward inflection. "Bethany, looking at you."

"The... Ottoman Empire? With the Turks."

"Yes! So many people at the time just called pirates 'Turks.' And maybe that's where the first part of the name comes from."

"I like the cactus better," Branson said, daintily eating a single orange slice. No stuffing-of-face with fruit this time around.

Emily nodded. "Me too. And I'd say the Turk's head cactus is the more likely of the two, yeah?"

"And the Caicos part?" Mrs. Douglas asked.

"That comes from the Lucayan language. The Lucayans were the native population that was here—and in The Bahamas—when the Spanish showed up. *Caya hico* meant 'string of islands.' But 'Turk's Head Cacti and Caya Hico Islands' was too long, so they went with Turks and Caicos."

The Douglases laughed. Well... all but Bethany, who was intent on something in the distance. "Your boyfriend's hot," she said distractedly.

"Bethany!" Mrs. Douglas blurted with astonished amusement. Bethany jumped, coming out of her trance.

Em laughed as she turned to face the *Caicos Sister*. "S'alright! I happen to agree with you, Bethy."

Boone had just climbed the swim ladder and stood on the platform, saltwater dripping from his body. He held his mask in one hand and was wiping his face while chatting with one of the dive boat's crew. Even at this distance, Emily could easily make out the details of his sculpted body. With his long limbs and thin frame, Boone had the furthest thing from a weightlifter build, but his physique was wiry, his musculature well-defined.

Most of Boone's exercise regime was limited to swimming, running, and near-daily practice of his martial arts skills. In addition to Brazilian jiu-jitsu, Boone was the equivalent of a black belt in capoeira, another Brazilian martial art. Em figured that the frequent practice of this incredibly flashy, acrobatic combat style was probably at the heart of his phenomenal physique.

"What was he doing down there?" Branson asked.

"Probably checking the props," Emily replied, watching as Boone and the crewman lifted a panel in the deck.

The captain came down to join them, a solid-looking islander with a black stocking cap perched atop his head, its peak flopped over to one side. Boone took a flashlight from the man, then dropped down into the engine compartment. Moments later, he emerged and resumed talking. Emily couldn't hear the specific words, but from the reaction of the crew, she gathered there was a problem. The captain shook his head, and the other crewman appeared to be uttering a curse word or two. Boone spoke some more, then went to the ladder and mounted the Newton's flybridge. In a moment, the *Lunasea*'s radio came to life.

"Lunsea, Lunasea, *this is* Caicos Sister. *Hey Em, you there?*"

Emily grabbed the handset. "I gather all is not well below decks."

"Afraid not. Drive shaft's busted. Pretty hefty crack."

"Oh, shite. And it's a new boat, innit? That's a bloody nuisance."

"Well, it's new to Reef Divers, but it's got a few years on her. I've got a curve ball for you. Let's all head back to the dock. The six divers and their divemaster, Roshane, will join you aboard the Lunasea *and go with you to the second dive. Lincoln too. I'll stay at the dock with the captain, and we'll see what kind of temporary fix we can come up with."*

"Sounds like a plan. See you ashore." Em ended the call and turned to the Douglas family with a bright smile. "So... one of the great things about vacations is you get to meet new people..."

SEVEN

"I think that about does it," Boone called out, rising from the shallows at the stern of the *Caicos Sister*. The Newton's captain, Doug Cox, didn't reply, so Boone waded through the waist-high water to the port side of the hull and pressed his ear against it. Grunts of effort greeted his ear, so he grabbed the gunwale and pulled himself up.

"Need a hand?" Boone addressed the open engine compartment.

Doug's voice rose from below. "Almost done."

Boone went to the yellow-and-red water cooler and grabbed the paper cup he'd jammed into a slot in an overhead beam. In addition to avoiding plastic, most dive ops had switched to disposable, biodegradable cups, and Boone tended to tuck one away after each use. He chugged two cups of cold water before restowing his cup and returning to the aft deck. Doug's head popped up, his black stocking cap drenched with sweat.

"Dat shaft's goin' nowhere!" he said with a pleased grin.

"Go check it out!" He handed Boone his flashlight as they exchanged places.

"You can check my work, too," Boone suggested. "A dip in the water might be nice for a guy who's been in the hold for the last half hour."

"Good plan," Doug said, stepping across to the dock. He made his way to the shore end; from there, it was a simple matter to hop the seawall and wade out to the stern.

Boone ducked into the engine compartment and crouch-walked to where he'd spotted the break in the shaft. The metal had cracked and broken loose; not something that could be fixed on Grand Turk. Instead, they were looking to secure the shaft firmly enough that the boat could safely reach Providenciales running on the one good engine. Boone marveled at the rope-work Doug had done. Using some line and wire that Boone had provided, the skipper had secured the back half of the shaft to the area forward of the break. For good measure, he'd used some additional wire to bind all of that to some interior supports. And then, of course... duct tape. Some was used to secure the knots he'd tied, with more tape wrapping sections of wire tight to the shaft.

Boone came back up and went to the stern just as Doug popped up and stood in the shallows.

"Nicely done!" he called out.

Boone laughed. "Not as good as what *you* did, Cap. And I thought *I* was handy."

"Been workin' on engines all my life," Doug said, as he sloshed his way back to shore. "Where's de prop?"

"It's right there on the edge of the seawall."

Doug grabbed it and came aboard, setting the propeller on top of a milk crate of tools.

"Not sure you even needed the outer lashings," Boone said.

After removing the propeller, he'd secured the exterior part of the shaft to the V-strut it ran through. He'd only used wire, to avoid any drag that lines and knots could have caused.

"Might be overkill," Doug said, sitting on the step amidships on the gunwale. "But don't want de shaft fallin' out in transit. It's a long way to Provo, runnin' on one engine." He grabbed the freshwater hose and pointed the sprayer at his face to rinse off the salt water. The pumps made the same distinctive noise as the freshwater rinse on the *Lunasea*, a series of low, pulsing sounds.

"How long do you think it'll take to get there?"

Doug hung up the hose and removed his stocking cap, wringing it out as he ruminated. "Well, first we got to get our divers back to de resort. From South Caicos... runnin' wit' de one engine, wit' everyt'ing secured like dat, we can probably risk eight knots. Gettin' to de Caicos Marina in Provo will take... 'bout nine hours."

"That's actually not that bad," Boone remarked.

"Long as I got my tunes, I'll enjoy da ride," Doug said, snugging the stocking back on his head. "How long 'til your boat back, you t'ink?"

Boone glanced down at his Aquinus dive watch. "They went up to the McDonald's dive site. Should be back any minute."

"Let's go up top and sit a spell," Doug suggested.

Boone followed him up and sat on a side bench while the skipper relaxed in the captain's chair and turned on the radio. Upbeat music filled the air; it wasn't reggae or calypso, but it definitely had an island feel. There was a rhythmic, jangling guitar, an energetically pounded conga drum, and an odd-sounding instrument Boone couldn't place. He tapped his bare foot on the flybridge deck, enjoying the beat. When it came to a close, a bass voice with a pronounced Caribbean accent came over the speaker.

"Dat was 'Potcake Paradise' by Full Force... a proper ripsaw band outta Grand Turk. And dis is Deejay Ceejay, comin' to you from Radio Bambarra. I 'bout to step out for some lunch, so I leave you with t'irty minutes of reggae, startin' off wit' Peter Tosh! But first... a word from our sponsors."

When Doug flipped the radio off as the commercials started, Boone asked, "What was the unusual sound in that song?"

"A ripsaw. Dat band has a great saw man... name of Zeus. He braces de handsaw against his knee and scrapes a screwdriver along de teeth. By bendin' it, he can change de sound. Ripsaw is de music of Turks and Caicos. A bit like Bahamas rake-and-scrape."

"Radio Bambarra... is that a Grand Turk station?" Boone asked. "I don't listen to the actual radio much. Emily and I usually play music from our phones... or an internet station called Pyrate Radio."

"I love Pyrate Radio!" Doug announced. "But lately I been listenin' to Radio Bambarra. De owner is a Belonger, and he's based over on South Caicos at de ol' Coast Guard station on de nort' side."

"That the guy we just heard with the super-deep Barry White voice?"

Doug laughed. "He sure got a deep voice. Great guy named CJ. He used to be a DJ at one of de popular clubs. Now he go by Deejay Ceejay. Plays reggae, calypso, and ricksaw... dembow and bachata for de Dominican community, and compas and rasin for de Haitians. Dere's a lotta both in Grand and South... CJ likes to give somet'in' to everyone. He even has a story hour."

"Story hour?"

"Yeah... well, it's not an hour. About a half hour a day, he reads from a book. Like an audiobook, but on de radio. Usually Caribbean authors. And he's a poet, so sometimes he reads some poetry."

Boone spotted the *Lunasea* approaching from the north. "They're back." He rose from the bench and made his way to the dock, catching the lines as Lincoln tossed them across and securing the Delta Canaveral to the pier, opposite the Newton. Up on the *Lunasea*'s flybridge, Emily killed the engine.

"You get it sorted?" she called down.

"As sorted as it can be. But that shaft is toast. They'll need to go to Provo."

"And it's a new boat? That is *pants*!"

Boone chuckled. Emily's Londoner slang was a constant source of amusement, and he hadn't heard that one in a while. He started helping the divers onto the dock, listening to the excited buzz. Apparently, it had been a great dive, and he kept hearing one word over and over. When Emily reached the gunwale, he took her hand, pulling her up beside him. He held her against him, looking down into her green-framed sunglasses. "Tell me I didn't miss them again."

Emily laughed. "Right after we went through the arch and hit the wall... bam! In the blue. Five of 'em! I'm telling you, Boone... if I wanna see dolphins, all I gotta do is leave you behind. You're like a dolphin magnet... but the arse end of it."

"Yeah, yeah," he grumbled.

"Like when you flip it around and it pushes stuff away?"

"I got it the first time."

Lincoln stepped across. "Hey, man. You miss de dolphins again."

Boone shook his head. Dolphins were sometimes spotted along the wall, but he always seemed to be on the boat when they chose to make an appearance. At least he'd been lucky enough to witness humpbacks going by.

Roshane, the Reef Divers' divemaster, had gone over to talk to Doug. After a moment, Lincoln joined them and they spoke with him. Finally, Roshane stepped up on the gunwale and addressed the group of divers standing on the dock. "East Bay divers, may I have your attention, please? We got an issue with one of de engines, so we'll need to head back to South Caicos. Why don't you grab some lunch while Doug gets us ready? Lincoln here says John's is great, and it's right dere." He pointed at the building just north of the dock. "Ocean views and seafood! De resort will pick up de tab. I'll walk you over."

The group left the dock, the Douglases following behind, leaving Boone, Emily, and Lincoln with Doug.

"The Douglases will be back in an hour and a half," Em told Boone and Lincoln. "They want to do Tunnels," she added, jokingly pronouncing it "toenails," the way some locals did.

Boone nodded. "They fly out tomorrow evening, right?" Tunnels was a deep dive to ninety-plus feet, and the puddle jumper flight from Grand Turk was unpressurized. You would definitely want a solid buffer of time between a deep dive and an island hopper flight.

"Their flight isn't 'til five, so no worries on the nitrogen," Emily noted. "Oh, and we're taking them to lunch tomorrow."

"We are?"

"We gotta clean and dry their gear and get it to them, yeah? So, I suggested we take 'em for a bite when we drop off their gear. They booked a quickie island tour with Papa J in the morning... and we'll swing by their hotel at noon."

"Sounds like a plan."

"So, whassup with the engine on this beauty?" Emily asked, addressing Doug.

Doug sighed. "I t'ink I know what happened. We got a new guy. Good local kid. When he put de boat to bed a while back, he say he mighta run over de line."

"Oh, bugger," Em said. "Boone did that once, back in Bonaire." She turned and regarded him with innocence. "Didn't you, Boone?"

Boone cleared his throat. "Uh... yeah. Put the boat in neutral as I came up to the mooring line... hopped down to grab the line. There was a huge turtle coming up for air, and I paused to look at it. The boat's momentum took us over the back of the pickup line, and it got caught in the propeller."

"Yeah, dat's what happened here, I t'ink," Doug said. "Line snags in de prop, pulls on de shaft, gives it a little flex... and dat can cause a wobble. When we were comin' across de channel, I felt somet'ing as we got up to speed. Den, comin' up from Tunnels, I opened 'er up, and dat's when we broke de shaft, I bet." He sighed. "Niles isn't gonna be happy. Dis'll bring us down to one boat. And we got a big group comin' on Sunday."

"Who's this Niles bloke?" Emily asked.

"Dive shop manager. From England." He nodded at Emily. "Talks a bit like you."

"You know..." Lincoln mused, "...we don't have anyone scheduled for next week."

"True," Boone replied.

"And I wouldn't mind visiting home."

"You suggesting we sub in for a bit?" Em asked. "I'm game. We've experienced the 'Turk'... might as well try out some Caicos."

Lincoln laughed. "South Caicos has a very different vibe."

"And no cruise ships," Boone noted. "That's a checkmark in the plus column, in my book."

"Reef Divers is pretty strict on who dey employ," Doug noted. "Not much time to check you out."

"We actually subbed for their Little Cayman Beach Resort branch," Boone assured him. "I'm sure you could get sufficient recommendations from them. But we don't know the dive sites over there in South Caicos."

"If you come across, I'll introduce you to Mateo. He can help you with de sites," Doug said. "Man is a modern-day explorer! Knows every site... and discovered half of dem! Roshane is an expert, too. Y'know, he was awarded Outstanding Divemaster by de Dive Industry Association."

"Smashing!" Emily enthused. "I was voted Outstanding Emily, but they took back the award 'cause I was using perfor-mance-enhancing drugs. Mostly coffee and chocolate."

Doug cracked a smile at that. "Okay, we'll run it by de bosses. Give you a call tonight or tomorrow."

"That works," Boone said. "If they want us, we can head across at sunrise on Saturday." He gave Doug his number. "Hey... we gotta run up the road for some fresh tanks, but before we go, can you show Emily that radio station? I think she'd enjoy it."

"Sure t'ing. C'mon up, Miss."

Doug brought them to the flybridge and fired up the radio. Some calypso was just finishing up, and then the deep-voiced deejay came on. Lincoln's eyes went wide.

"Is dat CJ?" he asked Doug incredulously.

"Yeah, mon."

"Dat shows how much I got to get back to South. Last I heard, he was talkin' 'bout starting up a radio station, but I never t'ought he'd do it!"

"Dat Spanish-language Christian station up at de old Coast Guard base closed down after Hurricane Irma," Doug explained. "He got it working again, and Norman Saunders gave him a deal on a lease. Started up last month."

"Omigod, that man's voice is ace!" Emily gushed, as the announcer's rich baritone shifted into the news.

"Okay, it's time for da news around town. De Royal Turks and Caicos Islands Police force announced de seizure of a shipment of cocaine on a short hauler off de coast of West Caicos. And de United States Coast Guard assisted in de rescue of a group of migrants, bound for Provo, when deir boat foundered. Dis week only, Big Mike's Sports Bar, near de South Caicos airport, is offering two-for-one beers if you mention Radio Bambarra.

"And finally, de mystery of de body found in de South Caicos Boiling Hole continues. Cause of death is still unknown. Turks and Caicos does not have its own pathologist, so a coroner from de Bahamas was flown in yesterday. Word on de street is an investigator from de United Kingdom has now been requested."

Lincoln shook his head. "I heard about dat. My sistuh say it was a Haitian man found in dere."

"Found in where?" Boone asked. "He said a 'boiling hole'?"

"It's a seawater hole dat connect to de ocean," Doug said. "Edge of town, just inside de salt ponds. Mateo—dat divemaster and explorer—he's been wantin' to explore de Hole, but he wasn't down more dan a few minutes when he found de body."

Emily shivered. "Blimey. Underwater caves are creepy enough without having *that* happen."

"My sistuh also say dey found somet'ing weird on de body. One of de cops was talkin' 'bout it at Carla and Kenrick's store. Some kinda voodoo t'ing."

The news continued: *"And finally, anuddah boat dat had been carrying Haitian migrants was found on Highlands Beach, north of Gannaway Bay in South Caicos. Immigration found two families sheltering in Highland House, but it is t'ought others may have made it into town."*

―――――――

"Where did you find them?" Viktor asked, as he inspected the two Haitian men who sat exhausted on the ground beside Viktor's South Caicos villa, greedily drinking from bottles of water.

"By de south road," Baptiste said. "Dey were tryin' to reach town, but were too dehydrated to make it."

"Too what?" Viktor asked. Baptiste, too, was Haitian, and his accent was sometimes difficult for Viktor to decipher.

"Dehydrated," Baptiste repeated slowly. "Not enough water."

Viktor grunted, looking down at the migrants.

"What do you want to do wit' dem?" Baptiste asked.

"Well... as it happens... we are short one groundskeeper. Tell them they can work for me for a while. And let them know it's not exactly a request."

Baptiste nodded and began speaking in rapid-fire Creole. The man was formerly of a paramilitary branch of Haiti's police force and could be quite persuasive. He'd probably picked up a thing or two about intimidation from his father, who had been in Duvalier's Tonton Macoute. Viktor watched the men's eyes fill with an uneasy mix of hope and fear. One of the men crossed himself halfway through the presentation.

Pierre, another Haitian bodyguard who'd been in his employ for many months, exited the villa. He saw the two men on the ground and hesitated.

"What is it?" Viktor barked at him.

"Mr. Goose... Gusev..." Pierre caught himself, quickly correcting the name. "Mr. Cisneros wants you."

Viktor went toward the front door. "Pierre... get these men cleaned up and fed, and put them to work." He entered and turned right, bound for Paz Cisneros's office and lab. The Cuban engineer was sitting at a workbench, eyes glued onto an electronic tablet.

"Ah, good," he said, not even looking up. "There is a call for you on the encrypted line."

Viktor went to the corner where the dedicated satellite phone lay. He made an adjustment to the server the call was ported through and lifted the handset. "Gusev."

The caller snickered, and he could swear he heard someone else on the other end laughing in the background. "Ah, Viktor, so good to hear your voice," the man said in Russian. "What is the status of your upcoming shipment?"

"We are expecting a replacement part to arrive tomorrow. After that, we'll need to test it. We can have it ready by..." he looked to Cisneros, who mouthed *Monday*. "Tuesday," Viktor supplied, giving himself some padding.

"You haven't tested it yet?" the man said, amusement in his voice.

"Of course we have! But we're making an adjustment... an *improvement*... so we'll need to test the new configuration."

There was some muffled chatter, then the man returned. "Let's hope it works, *Goose*. If so, perhaps you will redeem yourself, and become a *Viktor* our leaders will find useful. We will be in touch." The call ended.

Viktor seethed at the open disrespect. His name, Gusev, was a derivative of the Russian word for "goose," and his contact had simply called him by the name of the animal. And as for a "useful Viktor," he knew exactly who they were referring to: Viktor Bout.

A Russian arms dealer and former operative for the Soviet intelligence arm, the GRU, Viktor Bout had made quite a name for himself. Currently in American custody, he would likely be exchanged in a prisoner swap at some point. The Americans had even made a movie about him called *Lord of War*, starring Nicholas Cage. Bout's arms dealing had been so extensive, he had been nicknamed The Merchant of Death. Viktor Gusev, on the other hand, did not have the most sterling track record. A number of deals gone wrong—a hijacking of an arms ship-ment, malfunctioning equipment, and two double-crosses—had landed him in the GRU's doghouse.

What's more, rumor had it that Vladimir Putin himself had offhandedly referred to Gusev as "The Goose of Death," saying he did a lot of honking, with no results. The sobriquet had stuck, and from the occasional slips of the tongue among his staff, he was certain the nickname was used here, behind his back.

Viktor ground his teeth... then winced as a lance of pain shot through his jaw. He had always considered paranoia to be a healthy trait in his line of work, and had avoided dentists to keep his dental records from being recorded, but he'd probably need to make an exception very soon.

But if this device works... I will earn their respect. And more. "Paz... we better have this ready for them by Tuesday... for both our sakes."

EIGHT

E mily exited their room at the Sunflower Oasis, pausing to gaze longingly at the inviting swimming pool that dominated the central courtyard. At one end of it, a compact tiki bar lay in wait for thirsty vacationers. The property was adorable—small, but comfortable. Their unit had a full kitchen, but there was also the owner's restaurant, Jorika's Moment, located right on the property. The Sunflower was typical of many residences on Grand Turk, in that most were mom-and-pop operations—no giant, international chains or mega-resorts. For that, you'd have to go to Providenciales.

Em's attention was drawn to a canine collective, positioned in the shade beside the wall that ran along the street. Boone was crouched, stroking the fur of the pregnant potcake dog from up the road at Pillory Beach. Lincoln had arrived to join them for dinner, and he currently had Brixton's leash, the enthusiastic pup straining to greet the newcomer.

"Well, hello there, Mama," Emily cooed, joining Boone. "What are you doing here?"

"She followed me down the beach," Boone said. He'd been up the road, rinsing and hanging up all of the Douglas family's gear to dry. "Brix tried to greet her, but nearly got his snoot nipped."

Em laid her hand on the visiting dog's flank. "Aww... poor girl's gonna be poppin' puppies any day now."

"Jorika fixed her some food," Boone said. "Said she can stay here 'til she gives birth."

"Of course she did," Emily said. "Our landlord is a friend to all pooches." The South African owner of the Sunflower Oasis had three potcakes that lived on the property—Nala, Donkey, and Pepper—all three of whom were taking late afternoon siestas in various patches of shade. Brixton enjoyed their company, and it was good for him to have some playmates.

"I'll set up some bedding in the back corner of the property," Boone said. "There's some good shade under that neem tree."

Emily took Brixton's leash from Lincoln. "Thanks, Link," she said.

"No problem," Lincoln said. He'd dog-sat Brixton on numerous occasions and had a good rapport with the Belizean potlicker. "Are you goin' to bring him to South Caicos?"

"Good question. Boone, what say you?"

"Well... we can make the crossing in an hour, so he could certainly come. On the other hand, we'd probably need someone on South Caicos to look after him on long days. And he's got a lot of friends here."

"That's what I was thinking. Depends on how long we're over there, yeah? You hear back from Reef Divers?"

"Yeah, while I was rinsing the gear. Talked to Niles over at the East Bay Resort. They'd really only need us for the week.

Once that group leaves, it'll quiet down and their remaining Newton and some smaller boats will be more than sufficient."

"Right-o! Brixy, you feel like guarding the Sunflower and playing with your mates?"

The dog looked at her adoringly, wagging his tail.

"Well, that's sorted. So, we eating or what?" Emily asked. "I'm Hank Marvin!"

"You're who?" Lincoln asked, puzzled.

Boone laughed. "She's just being colorful. She means she's very hungry."

"Den why not say dat?"

"It's Cockney rhyming slang," Em explained. "Starvin' becomes Hank Marvin. Don't suppress my Cockney heritage, Link!"

"You're not Cockney," Boone chided.

"I've probably got a touch in there. I'm at least Cockney-adjacent. Okay, then how about I'm *famished*. Does that meet with you boys' approval?"

"Let's grab a table," Boone said, walking toward the little kitchen that stood beside the entrance to the Sunflower's courtyard. "I'll ask Jorika what's good today."

———

Lincoln whistled. "You *were* Hank Marvin!"

Boone grinned, looking at the remnants of Emily's dinner: rib bones on her plate and sauce on her mouth. She took a final bite and set the bone down on the plate with its companions.

"I can't resist her spicy honey pineapple sauce ribs!" Em gushed, sucking the sauce off her fingers.

Boone and Emily ate a lot of seafood in the islands, but

Jorika was particularly good with steaks, ribs, and even lamb. Boone had gone with the rack of lamb with mint jelly, and it had been amazing.

Lincoln was polishing off his chicken marsala curry. Curries were quite popular in the Caribbean and surrounding islands; with the abolition of slavery in the British Empire, indentured laborers from India were brought in, and their cooking had come with them. "Dis is some of de best food on Grand," he declared, setting down his fork.

"Agreed," Boone said. "I'm amazed we haven't put on twenty pounds since we've been here."

"That's 'cause *you* don't gain weight," Emily scoffed. She turned to Lincoln. "Link... Beanpole here claims it's his metabolism, but I'm convinced he's got a black hole in his stomach. And somewhere there's an extradimensional civilization subsisting off his meals."

Lincoln belly-laughed and Boone shrugged. He'd been a tall, gangly kid as soon as he'd hit his growth spurt. After college, he'd begun to exercise with regularity, and while he was still lanky, he'd gained quite a bit of weight, in the form of lean muscle.

"It's fortunate you two didn't have any charters for next week," Lincoln said.

Boone nodded. Summer was low season, and he and Emily hadn't done all that much to drum up business. They weren't hurting for money, but that wouldn't last forever. "Maybe we should kick things up a notch," he suggested. "Spruce up the website, do more advertising. We could go to one of those dive conventions in the States... like the Florida one you did with AJ Bailey."

"If we can keep attempted kidnapping to a minimum, I'd be

up for one. We could have our own booth. Oh! And I've been working on a proper logo for Bubble Chasers Diving."

Boone raised his eyebrows. "Really? I didn't know that. Can I see?"

"Absolutely not. It's a work in progress. But to your point... I must admit I enjoy the amount of freedom we have. All the same, maybe we've been a bit lazy about the biz, yeah?"

Jorika's son came over and removed their plates, and Emily requested a big hunk of the house special rum cake to share. While they waited, Boone thought about the news stories on the radio.

"Hey, Lincoln... that body they found. He was Haitian?"

"Dat's what I heard."

"And the local cops said something about voodoo?"

"Yeah. Somet'ing dey found on de body. But I don't know what."

"That other story... about the boat from Haiti. The migrants? Could that be connected?"

Lincoln sighed. "Not dat group," he said. "Dey just came ashore last night, I t'ink. But smugglers are dropping Haitians off all de time. Dey take deir money, drop 'em on a beach or an uninhabited cay, tell 'em 'Provo is dat way,' den sail away."

"What a bunch of vicious twats," Emily swore. "What kind of minging maggot would do that?"

"One who values money over people," Boone muttered. "So... the two things aren't related, you think?"

"Well, as I say, not dat particular group, but might could be de unfortunate person was a migrant."

"Male or female?"

"Male."

"There a lot of voodoo in South Caicos?" Em asked.

Lincoln waved a hand dismissively. "No, not really. Dere's a large Haitian community, but voodoo isn't somet'ing you hear much about in TCI. I never heard or seen anyt'ing... hmm... except..." He trailed off.

"Yeah?"

"You remember where de radio say dey find de migrants? It's dis creepy old house up on a hill. Called Highland House. Just a ruin. When I was growin' up, folks say dat some people were hung from de rafters in dere."

"Crikey," Em said with a shudder.

"But dat might just be stories. It's sort of... what you call it... a boogeyman house. You go dere at night and tell scary stories."

"Like voodoo stories?"

"No, dat's not why I t'ought of it. Last time I went up dere, I went inside... and on some of de walls were drawin's. Weird stuff."

Lincoln's tale was interrupted by the arrival of Jorika and her famous rum cake. "Here you are! An extra-large piece and three forks."

"Bless you, Goddess of Food!" Emily said, grabbing a fork. "Tuck in, everyone!"

"Looks delicious," Boone said. "Hey...any chance you can look after Brixton for a bit? We're heading over to South Caicos to work for Reef Divers at the East Bay for a week. We can bring him with us, if it's too much trouble."

"No trouble at all. The other dogs like him."

"Thanks a bunch. And thank you for taking care of Mama, too. I'm not sure where her actual territory is..."

"Oh, I've seen her around," Jorika said. "She goes between here and Bohio. My own dog just had puppies. I'll be sure Mama is comfortable, cool, and well fed. And who knows?

Maybe when you get back, there'll be some brand-new puppies! Perhaps you can adopt a friend for Brixton."

Emily winked at Boone and he smiled at Jorika. "The thought may have crossed our minds."

NINE

The next day, Boone and Emily drove both of their vehicles south along the coastal road, toward town. The *Caicos Sister* was gone from the dock, likely almost to South Caicos by now. They pulled up at the boutique hotel the Douglases were staying at and got out. The Turks Head Inne was in a quiet part of downtown Cockburn Town where the streets were narrow, overhung by palms and other tropical trees. Many properties on the street were lined by low stone walls—more for security from donkeys than humans. The Turks Head Inne's white wall had a metal plaque that told some of the building's history. Built in 1830, it was originally a residence for the island's doctor, as well as a dispensary. For a time, it was owned by a Hollywood producer, who used it for housing cast and crew.

Boone and Emily handed over the family's gear, and after the Douglases stowed everything in their rooms, they all assembled on the street. Emily indicated the sign.

"Y'know, a bunch of movies were shot here in Grand Turk. You might be staying in the room of some Hollywood star!"

Bethany smirked. "I looked up some of those movies on IMDB... don't know about 'stars.'"

"I watched one of them on YouTube," Branson said. "*Chupacabra Terror*. So bad it's good. It has that villain from *Breaking Bad* in it."

"Emily here was in a movie," Boone remarked.

The teens lit up. "Really? Cool! Which one?" Bethany asked.

Emily sighed, not wanting to get into the whole story. "*Man O' War*. Sci-fi monster movie with a big, mutated—"

"Portuguese man o' war!" Branson finished for her. "It just came out last month. I saw it!" His excitement faded to puzzlement. "But I don't remember you in it."

"Umm... long story. Do you remember when the heroine jumps into the water to save the pirate bloke?"

"Yeah..."

"That was me, jumping in. Well... the shot from behind was me. I s'pose you could say I was the lead actress's 'stunt bum.' That's probably the only scene left with me in it."

"Oh. So, they fired you?"

"Bran!" Mrs. Douglas scolded.

Emily smiled. "Kinda sorta. I was a replacement for Brooke Bablin, but then she... became available again." She laughed. "Y'know, Boone and I haven't even seen it yet! There's no cinema on Grand Turk, so we're waiting 'til it comes out on streaming." Before any further questions could be asked, she changed the subject. "So, where would you like to eat? There's a great little jerk chicken place called Jack's Shack right on the beach, or we could—"

"Margaritaville!" Branson and Bethany shouted in unison.

"Yeah, the kids have been talking about it all week," Mark said.

Emily caught the expression that flashed across Boone's normally stoic face—a look that said "kill me now." While he loved Jimmy Buffett's music, Boone loathed overcrowded tourist-trap theme restaurants. Em had learned that fact in Cozumel, when she'd made the mistake of dragging him to Señor Frog's. She gave him a look of her own, that said "don't be a stick-in-the-mud," then clapped her hands together. "Margaritaville, here we come!"

"Well, hang on a sec," Boone said, taking out his phone and looking something up. "Margaritaville is in the cruise center, and it's only open if there's a ship..." He trailed off. "Never mind. We're good."

Emily gave him a playful shove. "Boone's driving the truck. One of you gets to rough it."

The Celero wasn't built to carry six, so Boone drove Mr. Douglas in their old Ranger, while Em took the rest, driving south past the airport.

"Wait, slow down!" Bethany pointed out the open window. "I didn't get a good photo of that spaceship when we did the Queen Bee taxi tour."

Emily slowed as they passed by the entrance to the airport, where there was a replica of the Friendship 7 capsule.

"Did Queen Bee tell you about why that's there?" Emily asked.

"Yeah... an astronaut landed in the water near here and they brought him to Grand Turk."

"Not just any astronaut... John Glenn! It was the first orbit of the earth by an American. Actually, there's a newish exhibit about the splashdown in the Cruise Center. Might be able to pop by there, after we eat," Emily suggested. "If it's not too crowded," she added, knowing that it would be. After all, the family needed to finish packing and get to the airport by half past four.

After passing the official cargo port at Grand Turk Harbour, they drove by the entrance to Jack's Shack—easy to miss, because the approach to the seaside joint was flanked by dilapidated warehouses and a boatyard. Emily thought longingly of the jerk chicken as she took them the remaining third of a mile to the cruise ship terminal.

Boone pulled up beside her in the parking lot and everyone got out and went into the Cruise Center, or as Boone called it: "The Compound." Many cruise ship passengers didn't even bother to leave its walls, missing out on the rest of the island. Admittedly, there was a fair amount to do in there, the center being something between an outdoor shopping mall and an amusement park without rides. Passengers filled the duty-free shops and craft stores, ate in the bars and restaurants, or enjoyed a surfside massage. Others simply parked themselves on the beach or in the surf... with a scenic view of the massive cruise ship looming over them. And you might miss the sunset, as it set behind the ship from many vantage points.

It was fairly crowded, so they went straight to Margaritaville to get their names on the seating list. Fortunately, the huge restaurant had a lot of tables, so the wait wouldn't be long, and they were given a pager to let them know when to return. The restaurant and bar was on the corner of a massive pool and a FlowRider surfing machine. The teens didn't have their swimsuits, but there was a Margaritaville Trading Post to amuse everyone while they waited for their table.

"Y'know, there's a Margaritaville in Pigeon Forge, now," Boone said, looking around at the noisy revelry.

"Where's that?" Em asked.

"In Tennessee. You remember me telling you about working as a cleaner at a big aquarium in Gatlinburg? Pigeon Forge is just north of there."

"Odd name, innit? What, they forge pigeons in a blast furnace, or somethin'?"

Boone smiled. "Wouldn't surprise me if there's a store for that. It's a fun place. If you were to pull it up on a map and simultaneously search for 'miniature golf,' 'go-carts,' 'outlet malls,' and 'wedding chapel,' your smartphone would explode."

Emily laughed at that. "Well... I think you should take me there!"

"It's where Dollywood is," he added as an afterthought.

"Blimey, now you abso-frikkin-lutely *have* to take me there!"

"Not many dive industry conventions in that area."

"True, but... maybe we could go visit your mum?"

Boone smiled again, but there was something behind it. "Sure. Maybe."

Em looked up at him. "How far is the place that forges pigeons from the town you grew up in? Kingston, right?"

"Couple hours."

Emily decided to let it lie. Boone talked to his mother on the phone from time to time, but he wasn't particularly forthcoming about his childhood. She'd heard enough to know he didn't think much of his father, a Dutch sailor who'd left his mother high and dry when Boone was very young.

Bethany came running out of the Trading Post wearing a baseball cap with a plush parrot attached to the top. She grinned and held up a flashing pager.

Boone looked toward the bustling restaurant. "Into the belly of the beast."

"I have to admit, that was some tasty grub!" Emily declared, as they exited Margaritaville. She'd been pleasantly surprised to find the menu included a "Chef's Catch" sandwich, and she'd gotten some blackened snapper on a bun with spicy mayo. As a divemaster, she was keenly aware of the seafood she chose to eat, and "snapper" could mean any of a number of species, some of which had healthy populations. Em never ate grouper, though. She knew it was delicious, but the big, lovable critters were often overfished. One old-timer divemaster in Belize had described the size of groupers that he saw when diving getting smaller and smaller every year.

Boone checked his dive watch. "It's still early, if you want to hit the beach or check out any of the shops."

"We don't want to keep you." Mrs. Douglas said.

"We've run the gauntlet of cruisies and we're already in here," Emily reassured her. "Might as well check out a few things, yeah?"

"The craft market is pretty cool," Boone suggested, pointing to the area located between Margaritaville and the exit.

Emily stifled a grin. *He can't wait to get out of here.*

The group spread out amongst the stalls of gaily painted tchotchkes, baskets, and woven items. Emily was admiring a carving of a humpback whale when Bethany cried out.

"Hey! Watch it!"

Em saw the girl go sprawling as a pair of drunken frat-boy types broke into a playful fight, their clumsy scuffle knocking her into a table of knickknacks. Emily went to her immediately. "You all right?"

"Yeah..." she said, though Em could see she'd skinned her knee.

"Oy!" Emily rose and got in the face of the nearest one, who was snickering about the whole ordeal.

"Sorry. No harm, no foul," he slurred.

"Plenty of harm, and you're definitely foul. Why don't you legless plonkers get back on the boat and sleep it off, yeah?"

The young man leered down at her. He looked like he played sports of some kind, his thick neck rising from a numbered jersey. "What did you call us?"

"What, the context wasn't sufficiently illuminating?" Emily spat. "I called you drunken arseholes."

The drunk smirked. "Get outta my face, Tinkerbell," he said. "Unless you wanna wrestle, too..." He grabbed her breast.

The violation was so casual and quick that Emily was caught off guard... but only for an instant. She'd learned a lot of Krav Maga self-defense moves from Sofie Levenstone in Saba, but the one she found the most useful was the wristlock. *And how convenient for this berk to present his hand in so grabbable a fashion.* She whipped her hand up and snagged his hand and wrist, pressing her thumb into the carpals and wrapping her fingers around the side of his palm. In one swift motion, she violently twisted, bringing the big fella to his knees.

His friend moved forward to help, but Boone had been running from the far side of the craft market and stepped in front of the young man. *Now you're in for it,* Emily thought savagely, ready for one of Boone's flashy capoeira moves, or a debilitating jiu-jitsu lock, but the divemaster simply held out a hand and said something in a low, firm voice. His posture and tone made it clear: if the guy didn't stand down... Boone would put him down. The young man's face went pale and he stepped back.

Mr. Douglas arrived from the back of the stalls, ready to unleash Marine justice, but Boone shook his head slightly and indicated a group of men rushing their way. Security had shown up quickly—some from the cruise terminal, and some from the ship. Emily released her assailant.

"She attacked me!" Drunky declared, clutching his wrist.

"This wanker shoved this girl into a table, then grabbed my breast!"

Before the back-and-forth could get any further, Boone held his hand aloft, like a kid offering to answer a math question. With his six-foot-four height and impressive arm-span, it was actually quite effective. The security men looked his way, and before anyone else could speak, Boone took control.

"There's a CCTV camera right there," he said, lowering his arm to point at a camera on the corner of a nearby roof, its lens pointed right at them. "These two are drunk, as any blood alcohol test will show. And they started this fight, as that camera will show." He gestured toward the Douglases. "These US citizens need to catch a late afternoon flight..." He then gestured dismissively to Bro One and Bro Two. "And these two probably want to be on the ship when it leaves in a few hours." He locked eyes with them. "Unless you assholes want to wait for the Turks and Caicos police to arrive and watch the video? In which case, you definitely won't be leaving with your ship."

"Hang on!" Em blurted. "These bastards hurt Bethany! They need to—"

"I'm okay," Bethany said quietly.

Boone looked over at the family. "We can help you get these two charged with something," he said. "But you'll definitely miss your flight home."

Mr. Douglas shifted uncomfortably. "We do need to get back."

"You're with the cruise line, yeah?" Em asked two men in brightly colored polo shirts.

"Yes, Miss," one replied.

"How about you go ahead and review the video. Then you can ban these two from future cruises, when you see what a right pair of tossers they are."

The belligerence had gone out of the two drunks, and one of the cruise ship security men took them aside. The guards spoke with Bethany and her parents, and after a few minutes, Mr. Douglas approached Boone and Emily. "While the idea of having them charged with something is... tempting... the kids have school, I've got work, and our dogs are in a boarding house. Thanks for cooling that off."

Boone nodded. "Sure." He started walking toward the nearby entrance. "But let's get to the parking lot, in case security decides they need a more formal statement."

"What did you say to that guy?" Branson asked, when they exited the compound into the sunblasted parking lot. "He looked like he was about to shit himself."

"Bran!" Mrs. Douglas sputtered... then laughed. "Actually, you're right. He did look like that."

"So? What did you say?" Bran pressed.

Boone looked uncomfortable, then sighed, and spoke reluctantly. "I told him if he went after my girl, parts of him wouldn't work right for the rest of his life."

"Oh, my..." Mrs. Douglas said, taken aback.

"And Emily, what was that you did with his wrist?" Bethany asked, eyes wide.

"It's a wrist-lock I learned from... y'know what, I'll teach you back at the hotel. Boone will be the victim."

After dropping the family off at the Turks Head Inne—and after Emily offered up a quick demonstration of some simple self-defense moves—they bid the Douglases goodbye, went to the car and truck, and drove back to the Sunflower Oasis. They parked in a lot off the main road, planning to give the keys to Jorika, in case the vehicles needed to be moved while they were away. As Boone extricated his long limbs from the old truck, Em headed over to him.

"I like how you handled that scrap back there."

Boone worked his jaw, then said, "Thanks. But you had that guy under control."

"Only 'cause you kept Tweedledumber from joining in." She lifted her sunglasses to her forehead. "To be honest, I half expected you to whip out a fizzy can of dance karate."

Emily expected she'd earn a chuckle from that, but Boone didn't even smile. Instead, he took a breath. "When I saw him grab you like that..." He shook his head.

"Look, you hate losing control, yeah? And you didn't. And honestly... it was the better choice, *not* kicking his arse. You did the right thing."

Boone nodded, then slammed the truck's door. "If I'd done what I *wanted* to do to those guys... *I* would've been the one heading to the police station."

TEN

Boone sat atop the flybridge across from Lincoln, the two men looking astern as the coastline of Grand Turk faded below the horizon, and the sunrise beyond was just cresting the low island. Soon, only the red-and-white cell tower in the middle of Cockburn Town remained visible. A moment later, it vanished as well.

"Water's cooperating today," Emily said from the wheel. "Don't know what the fuel situation is over there, so I'll keep it at a leisurely twenty. Cockburn to Cockburn is about twenty-five miles, yeah?" She laughed. "From one *Cock*burn to another," she shouted, deliberately giving the name a naughty pronunciation and pounding the first syllable.

"I'm amazed you hadn't gone there sooner," Boone said.

"Oh, believe you me, my brain is always shrieking a variety of amusingly filthy things, but I'm working on my maturity."

Boone smiled and thought for a moment. Twenty-five miles was about twenty-two nautical miles. Their boat had an impressive cruising speed, and Em's suggestion was a good balance between fuel conservation and a quick transit. They'd left at sunrise, just after six. "We'll get there just a few minutes before seven. Lincoln, anyone gonna be there to greet us?"

"Dive staff is off on Saturdays," he replied. "So dat's pretty early. Tell you what... let me give you a little bit of a tour of de windward side of South. I can call once we're in range of de cell towers. Drag someone outta bed to meet us at De Bay around eight-t'irty."

"East Bay?" Emily asked, turning her head. "Where the resort is? Pretty skinny water there, yeah? I don't think this Delta Canaveral can manage that. Niles said they keep their Newtons over by the fishing boats."

"You're right, East Bay is too shallow, but de resort is havin' some Aventura catamaran dive boats made dat will be able to go right up to de beach. No, we're goin' 'round de corner to Conch Ground Bay. It's where most of de docks are in Cockburn Harbour. Most people just call it De Bay. Long Cay and Dove Cay shelter it, and cruisers and sailboats will sometimes anchor inside. But first, I'll take you to de north tip." He rose from the bench and peered at the GPS set into the console, shading it with his hand. "May I?"

"You may," Em responded.

Lincoln made some adjustments and when he stepped back, Emily turned the wheel slightly to starboard to align the bow with the new waypoint. South Caicos wasn't yet in view, but to the north, a large cruise ship became visible, on approach to Grand Turk.

"Got out just in time," Boone remarked.

"One of these days, Booney... I'm going to book a Disney cruise for you. Make you wear mouse ears the whole time."

"I think our little cruise on the *Apollo* was enough for me," Boone said, recalling their brief journey on a mega-yacht; a trip cut short by a violent hijacking at the hands of a group of mercenaries.

"Fair enough," Em said. "Hey, Link, what was that radio channel your deep-voiced mate was on?"

"Doug said it's de same as de old Radiovision Cristiana... 530 AM."

Boone chuckled. When Lincoln gave him a curious look, he explained, "In the States, 530 on the AM dial is usually where you get travel advisories, like road closures and detours."

Emily turned on the radio and they were greeted with "Three Little Birds" by Bob Marley and the Wailers. She cranked up the volume and the trio found themselves nodding their heads to the gentle beat, with Lincoln and Boone returning to their benches.

After a few minutes, a shimmer on the horizon resolved itself into their first glimpse of South Caicos. It quickly became apparent that this island had a bit more topography than Grand Turk. Nothing towering like Saba, but a long line of gentle cliffs reminded Boone of certain parts in the north of Bonaire.

"De island is about six miles nort' to sout', and roughly t'ree and a half miles across at de fattest point," Lincoln explained. "Population is about 1,200. Used to be a lot more, back in de day. Provo was de backwater den, and we were known as de Big South! A major salt industry was here... much bigger dan Grand Turk had. Dat all dried up in de sixties when dey moved it over to Inagua. But t'ings were still boomin' when de drug flights were comin' in."

"Wait, what?" Em turned back from the wheel.

"For a while, Pablo Escobar had a hundred planes a day comin' and goin'. De Medellin Cartel t'rew a lot of money around, and de authorities look de udder way. We had a prime minister go to jail in de States for a few years! Nice guy. Owns a lot of businesses here."

"Why here?" Boone asked. "The drug flights, I mean."

"De airport here has a very big runway. America built it in World War II to hunt submarines. And from here, it's not far to de Bahamas or Florida. I was just a boy den, but I remember hearin' de planes all night long. After de flights were stopped, t'ings got quieter... and den Hurricane Ike hit. I was here for dat." Lincoln shook his head and whistled. "You ever been in a hurricane?"

Emily glanced back at Boone, dipping her head to give him a knowing look over the top of her oversized sunglasses.

"Yeah, we've been in one," Boone said. "Irma."

"Oh, dat one hit here, too! And Grand Turk. Most of de roofs on both islands were destroyed. I was livin' in Provo for dat one. Anyway, after de salt left, and de drug flights stopped, and de hurricanes... lot of Belongers moved to udder islands where dere was more work. But we're comin' back now! Fishin' is still de main industry, but de resorts are takin' off. I know East Bay is hopin' to bring in more and more divers every year."

"Speaking of... looks like we're coming up on the reef," Em said.

"Turn north along it... I'll show you Plandon Cay Cut at de north tip."

Boone looked off the port side. Since they were now on the opposite side of the plunging channel from Grand Turk, he had an obvious question. "Do you have a wall on this side, like over in Grand Turk?"

"You'd have to ask de divemasters here. I never dived de east side. But I know Mateo mapped some great sites wit' a lot of swim-t'roughs and tunnels. Dey're across from de fancy Reefview Resort just south of us. I'll show you on de way back."

"Looks like some fishermen are out and about," Em noted, as they passed a pair of fishing vessels. One was small and open —a runabout of some type—with an outboard and two men aboard. The other was larger, with racks of what appeared to be lobster cages.

"Not doing any fishing at the moment," Boone observed.

Lincoln chuckled. "Oh, dey might be. For square grouper."

Emily turned and raised an eyebrow above her shades. "Square... oh. I get it." She'd heard the term before. "Marijuana bales or cocaine bundles, yeah?"

"You said it, not me," Lincoln said with a grin. "Sometimes, de smugglers see a Coast Guard helicopter or plane and dey get spooked. Dump de cargo. De current brings a lot of t'ings over to de east side." He waved the suppositions away. "But dey may just be goin' up to East Caicos. Good fishin' dere. Maybe know a good lobster spot."

Ahead, the deeper blues of the depths gave way to patches of lighter shades as they neared the northern tip of the island. "What's that place?" Boone asked, pointing up at a few battered white buildings up on the clifftop. Windows in the one-story complex were devoid of glass, and a tall, thin pole rose from near the northernmost building.

"Dat's where our tunes been coming from! De old Coast Guard station."

"Looks pretty beat up," Boone noted.

"Yeah... after Irma came through, de Spanish-language radio station left. Last time I looked in dere, de place was a mess. Broken glass and donkey manure. But I guess CJ took over de lease."

"You think he's leasing from the US Coast Guard?" Emily asked.

"Oh, no no... dey left in the eighties, after dey sold de property to a local family." Lincoln smiled. "You remember dat prime minister I mentioned, who went to jail for helping the cartel?"

Boone raised his eyebrows. "You're kidding. And the drug flights... that was in the eighties, too, right? That purchase doesn't seem like a coincidence."

Lincoln shrugged. "Who knows? It's a beautiful area up dere. De family owns most of dat northern tip, includin' de old station. Me, I'm just glad a Belonger held onto dat land. Every-t'in' south of it on de east coast is owned by de Reefview company."

The coastline continued just north of the station, craggy limestone cliffs dropping to the sea. Along the surf line, a thick, reddish-brown mass lined the coast.

"Blimey, that's a fair bit of sargassum!" Emily said.

"Not too bad," Boone remarked. "About the same as on the wild side of Grand Turk." Over the last few years, the seaweed had become a real problem in some areas, as warmer waters and nutrient-high runoffs had contributed to rapid growth. "I heard some Mexican beaches in the Riviera have had it real bad."

"East Bay has a tractor dey use to harvest it every mornin'," Lincoln said. "But not too much down dere, wit' de bay bein' partially protected." He pointed off the port bow. "Dere's de cut... you can go into de shallows for a look, but don't try to go into de bay. Only a foot in most places."

Emily eyed the turquoise waters and found an area that was deep enough for them to turn around in. She idled the engine. "Beautiful spot."

"Plandon Cay Cut is one of my favorite places. Some nice beaches inside de bay, and a lot of young lemon sharks and stingrays." He pointed to the low island on the north side of the cut. "Dat's Norman's Cay. Nuttin' but iguanas and empty conch shells. And farther to de north are a couple more cays and East Caicos."

"Can you get a boat into there from the other direction?" Boone asked.

"Flats boat, you could. And de resorts have kayak tours in dere. But no... bigger boats can't make it in. In fact, from here, you could pretty much walk to Provo. Some guy did it in five days. Only had to swim twice."

"And there's a bigger bay in there, right?" Boone asked. "Inside the 'fishhook'? I was checking out some maps last night... the water seemed pretty skinny up there, too."

"Oh, you're t'inking of Bell Sound," Lincoln explained. "Good bonefishin'. Or used to be. Heard de big resort company tore out a lot of de mangroves to make a nice beach for a bayside bar."

"Fewer mangroves, fewer fish," Boone remarked. Mangroves were a popular place for juvenile fish to find shelter. Predators knew that, and there was usually good fishing nearby.

"Let's start back sout'," Lincoln suggested. "I'll call over to East Bay and wake someone up. Have 'em meet us at de docks."

While Lincoln made his call, Emily maneuvered back outside the reef line and headed south. The reggae music continued, but no announcer came on to interrupt. This early in the morning, it was likely automated. Shortly after they passed the Coast Guard station, Emily let out a gasp.

"Cor, look at that place!"

Boone peered up at the cliff as a villa came into view. Several low roof ridges dotted its length, and there were a number of massive one-pane windows. Two pavilions flanked what appeared to be an infinity pool, the near side of it cascading water, likely to be pumped back into the pool. There was a substantial amount of landscaping around the structure, so he'd missed it as they'd angled in from the channel at the end of the crossing from GT.

"Posh lookin' digs, that," Emily breathed, throttling down. "What do you suppose something like that goes for?"

"No idea," Boone said, taking out his binoculars and training them on the house.

"Dat must be new," Lincoln said, pocketing his phone. "I never seen dat one before. Lot of rich people buying up land, but many of dem don't get 'round to buildin'."

"That seems like a waste," Emily said. "Paying property taxes on an island plot, and not using it. And the taxes on that thing must be astronomical!"

"Actually," Lincoln said with a smile, "de taxes would be zero."

"What? Zed? You can't be serious."

Lincoln shrugged. "Turks and Caicos have no property taxes. Dere's a lot of different fees to pay, but once you do dat, de land is yours."

Boone was still glassing the villa. "Wow... that's..." he said, trailing off.

"What?"

"Oh, nothing," He lowered the binoculars. "Just a really nice place is all. But not that interesting." He opened the glovebox to put them away.

"Give me those!" Em demanded, grabbing the binoculars and training them on the villa. "Gorgeous place. I bet one of those gazebo thingies is for outdoor dining, and the other is for outdoor massages. And that pool is... oh! Oh my. Oops." Emily lowered the binoculars and handed them off to Boone. "Naked bloke by the pool. Completely starkers."

Boone laughed. "Gee, I musta missed that."

"You berk, you *didn't* miss that!" Emily blurted with an incredulous smile plastered on her face. "And you made me look!"

"No, I didn't. You took the binoculars from me of your own free will."

"You cheeky bugger. Lincoln, this sourpuss pretends like he doesn't have a sense of humor, but then he ambushes you."

Lincoln didn't reply, his eyes locked on the ocean to the south. "Can I have dose?"

"What is it?" Em asked, handing them over.

"I have no idea."

Viktor Gusev leaned on the edge of the infinity pool, the relaxing sound of the recirculating waterfall drowning out the surf below. *That boat looks just like... but it couldn't be.* There were plenty of dive boats around, but this one was shaped a bit differently than the ones he'd seen operating to the south, diving the few eastern sites. And the blue bimini cover was the same. But the boat he was thinking of had been in Grand Turk.

The dive boat slowed and the wake vanished. He could make out three people on the bridge in the shade of the bimini, but the rising sun backlit them, making it difficult to see anything distinct. Although one thing became clear: one of the figures—a man, he was certain—was staring up at the house with binoculars.

Instinctively, Viktor sucked in a deep breath and ducked under the water, looking out through the glass wall of the pool —a fruitless exercise when the waterfall was on. What if they were CIA? Or, worse... the GRU? Perhaps his handlers were even more dissatisfied with his performance than he thought. Maybe that phone call two days ago had been to determine if he was in the villa! Viktor felt the burning need to breathe, and he swam back toward the shoreside steps that led down into the pool before rising from the water, naked as the day he was born. He was about to dash into the house, but then froze.

You're being paranoid! he thought, grinding his teeth. A sharp bolt of dental pain from his jaw granted him a searing moment of clarity. The telescope! Up here in the north of the island, far from town, there were no lights anywhere nearby, save the ones on his property. Viktor had mounted a telescope on the retaining wall beside the massage pavilion to view the stars. The Milky Way was absolutely mind-blowing on a clear night.

Viktor fast-walked in his bare feet on the hot paving around the pool and popped off the covers on either end of the instrument. Training it down on the boat, he got a good look at the three figures aboard: two men—one white and one black—and a woman. A petite, blond woman... gorgeous and curvy. *It is the same boat! But what are they doing over here?*

He swung the telescope toward the stern to see the boat's name: *Lunasea.* Viktor's command of English was excellent, so he got the play on words. Suddenly, the stern moved out of frame, his view now filled with foaming water as the boat's engine throttled up. He looked up from the eyepiece, preparing to follow their course, but then something else caught his eye, a half-mile or so ahead of the dive boat.

What on earth is that?

ELEVEN

The boat—if it was a boat—was inside of the reef, and Emily could make out an anchor line pulled taut at the port side amidships; unusual, since most anchor lines ran from a ship's bow, but given the vessel's bizarre shape, it was understandable.

At the bow, a steel mesh drum lay in the water; it looked like it could rotate, but wasn't doing so at the moment. On either side of it, two booms dipped into the water with a thick strip of material stretched between them.

Behind the drum, offset slightly to port, was what looked like a conveyor belt, pitched at about a thirty-degree angle and running sternward. Behind that was a large metal basket or cage. Most astonishing of all was a pair of what appeared to be paddlewheels, housed inside steel cylinders on either side of the stern. The vessel's cockpit was a small, open-air platform on the starboard side, offset from the conveyor. A woman was inside, just looking up from the controls as they approached.

The reef line there was fairly deep, and Emily easily found a place to bring the *Lunasea* into the shallower water. The woman saw them and waved, then gestured for them to come closer. As they neared, Emily could see that the conveyor had glistening clumps of sargassum on its unmoving surface.

"It's some kind of harvester," she surmised, noting the hull was a catamaran of some sort, something she'd not been able to tell from farther out. Em maneuvered the *Lunasea* to the ocean side of the odd boat, taking up station off her starboard, where the offset cockpit was located.

"Ahoy, there!" the skipper of the oddity called out. She was an older woman with graying hair set in a ponytail. Atop that, she wore a fishing cap with a green, transparent visor, and her face was spotted from overexposure to the sun. "Wonder if you could help a gal out?"

"Engine trouble?" Boone called back.

"I hope not! But something's wrong with the starboard paddlewheel. I started turning in circles and the engine was overheating."

"Maybe it's jammed with sargassum?" Emily offered, as she dropped the engine to idle.

"Possible, but they're designed for that not to happen. I was about to hop in and check it out myself, but... I thought I saw a shark."

"Probably just a reefy," Lincoln assured the woman. "And here in de shallows, not likely a big one."

"Yeah, well, maybe... but I confess, I don't even like to see a nurse shark up close." She laughed. "Guess I picked the wrong profession."

Boone was already stripping to his skivvies. "I'll have a looksee," he called across.

Em looked down at his boxers. "Pretty thin material for immersion," she said with a lopsided grin.

"Sorry, no show for you. I'm gonna grab a swimsuit and mask from below."

"Spoilsport."

While Boone went down the ladder, Emily leaned over the side of the flybridge and checked the sea floor beneath. "Lincoln, let's drop an anchor. All sand here, and I don't want to run the engine if I don't have to."

Lincoln went down to carry out her request and Emily looked more closely at the strange boat. She could see collected seaweed in the rear basket, maybe a foot and a half deep. Lincoln called up that the anchor was down and Em nudged the throttle to set it, then killed the engine.

"You hoovering sargassum, I take it?" she asked in the sudden stillness, with only the sound of the wind and nearby surf to compete with.

"Yes!" the woman replied. "This is my first time trying it on the east coast. The water's calmer on the south and west coasts, but there's not nearly as much sargassum over there to test the harvester on. Today had some very flat seas, so I brought it around at sunrise. It was going well, but then..." She waved a hand at her controls.

"No worries, we'll set you right," she assured her. "I'm Emily, by the way. Lincoln is the one who just tossed the anchor... and Boone will be the one feeding the sharks. There's probably a joke to be had with 'chum,' but I'll leave off."

The woman gave a mock shiver. "Oh, don't even joke!" she said with a nervous laugh. "I'm Margaret Earle—Marge—and this is the *Demeter*." She smacked the guardrail beside her.

"Goddess of the harvest! Brill name!" Emily said brightly. "So... that drum-thingie spins and sends the stinky seaweed up the conveyor and it dumps in the back there, yeah?"

"Very good!"

"And those booms you've got sticking out to either side of the collector... with some sort of material between... that's to guide more of the sargassum into the harvester, I'm betting. It can be raised, yeah? Otherwise, that'd be quite a drag on your speed."

"Right again... they raise and lower. But that strip of vinyl will need to be replaced with a fine mesh. Even though it's not that large, when the booms are up, it ends up acting like a little sail, and not in a good way."

Boone stepped off the gunwale and swam over to the stern of the harvester. "I heard your description... very inventive!" he called up from the water. "Kind of reminds me of those collectors that Ocean Cleanup group is using to try and deal with the giant garbage patches in the Pacific."

"Well, that's on a much larger scale," Marge said. "They use extremely long plastic-pipe booms with a skirt below to corral the trash. My device has more humble origins. My brother lives on a lake in New Jersey, and they have a harvester that trundles around, collecting aquatic weeds and algae clumps. I was watching that one day, and flash went the lightbulb!"

"What's that aerial?" Boone asked, pointing. "Next to the controls?"

"Good eye," Marge said, reaching over and telescoping the aerial up several feet. "It's for remote control. The ultimate goal would be for an island to have a small fleet of these, acting autonomously."

"Like one of those robot vacuum cleaners," Boone remarked.

"Yes, exactly. But tides and weather are so variable, you'd need the ability to control these remotely. Ultimately, an operator could monitor three or four of these, taking control if one gets off its programmed route."

"Sargassum harvesting drones... I think you might be onto something." Boone examined the paddlewheel enclosure on the port side. "Stupid question, but I gotta ask... you try reversing it?"

"Yes. Thought maybe that would work, but no dice."

"Back in a jiff," Boone said, securing his mask and ducking under the water.

"You been in South Caicos long?" Em asked while they waited.

"Just a few months. I received a grant to work on perfecting my harvester, and this island seemed like a good option for testing, since the waters aren't as busy as some. The School for Field Studies had a spare room, so I've been staying there. Takes a little getting used to! They don't have air conditioning except in the classroom and computer room, and you only get one freshwater shower per week."

"Is Heidi still running the SFS?" Lincoln asked.

"Yes, she is! She and her husband. I've been picking up quite a few tidbits of marine biology. Did you know sea turtle cheeks are unique?"

"I did not!" Emily said with a smile. "Thanks for the knowledge nugget! I'll file that one away for a rainy day. Hey, what do you do with the sargassum?"

"That's for someone else to figure out," Marge said with a laugh. "It can be toxic when it rots, but I hear Mexico is working on using it for fuel. I'm supposed to have a Zoom call with an environmentalist there next month."

"Yeah, we heard about the biofuel project when we were working in Cozumel."

Marge looked down at the water. "Your friend's been down there a while..."

"Don't you worry!" Lincoln assured her. "De man has gills."

"Boone's fine," Em added. "He's a freediver."

Marge looked toward the stern. "I can feel some vibration..."

Emily laughed. "Y'know, this is the second time this week Boone's been bangin' about beneath a boat. It's actually why we're here. East Bay had one of their boats go down and we're subbing in."

"That explains it. Didn't think I'd seen you three before... or your boat."

"Lincoln is from here originally, but we have an op over on Grand Turk," Em explained. "Came across this morning."

Boone breached beside the harvester. "I found your problem." Emily saw him glance at the harvester's anchor line. "Try it real quick for me? Reverse first... then, when you've got some slack, nudge it forward."

Marge started up the engines, shifting to reverse and gently throttling up. Water churned in front of the paddlewheel. She shifted the transmission and applied a little throttle. The boat slowed to a stop, then moved forward, at which point she killed the engine.

"Wonderful! So... what was the problem?"

"This." Boone had kept one hand under the water, and now he brought it up. In his grip was a rectangular block of white material, wrapped in waterproof plastic.

"Oh ho!" Lincoln clapped his hands. "De square grouper are bitin'!"

"Is that...?" Marge began.

"A brick of cocaine?" Boone finished for her. "Sure looks like it."

"Blimey!" Emily gasped.

"And it feels like a kilo," Boone added, swimming over to

the *Lunasea*. "Lincoln, you mind? Kinda like treading water with a dive weight in my hand."

"Dese waters are known for yellow gold and white gold: treasure and coke!" Lincoln reached down and took the brick. "A fisherman friend once told me... one of dese can sell in de Bahamas for eight or nine t'ousand dollars." He started to turn, but quickly froze. "Oop! De plastic is torn! Got some on de deck!"

"And your arm," Em noted with a laugh. "That's some expensive beauty powder! Put it on the camera table." The table was set into the deck under the flybridge; its surface was covered with a carpet swatch, and it had a low rim around its edge to keep items from sliding off.

Boone swam back to the harvester. "The paddlewheel spokes have a gap between them and the housing," he explained. "The brick had about a third of its length jammed into the gap at the top. The wheel must've snagged it just right and shoved part of it past the spoke. When you tried to reverse, enough of it was on either side so that it couldn't come loose. I had to knead it a little to force it back through."

"Well, I'll be. Hey, you know what? I think it might have a friend." Marge pointed at the harvesting drum. "Something bumped and thumped through there. I figured it was just trash... but now that I think of it, I heard it shortly before the engine trouble."

She stepped down from the cockpit onto the conveyor and crab-walked up to the edge of the basket. Then, lying prone, she reached down into the mass of sargassum. After a moment, she sat up, holding another brick aloft. "Can I give this to you?" she asked Boone.

"Sure. But there might be more buried back there," Boone said, treading water near the stern and looking at the mass of sargassum already collected. He came forward and took the brick before swimming over to the *Lunasea*.

"So... what do we do with it?" Emily asked.

"Turn it in, of course," Boone said.

"Well, yeah, obviously... but where? US Coast Guard? TCI Maritime police? Regular police?" She turned to Lincoln. "What do the fishermen do when they find... 'square grouper'?"

"Uh..." He laughed and shook his head. "Let's just turn it over to the South Caicos police. I'll call dem when we get to de pier."

"Why not now?"

"Remember dose fishermen we saw? Maybe dey need a little time to make sure dey're fishin' for de right kind of fish." He took his phone and went below.

"I'm... conflicted," Em said.

Boone nodded. "Yeah... but they live here, we don't. We'll turn the bricks in when we get to the docks." He went to the edge of the flybridge. "Hey, Marge, do you need an escort?"

"Oh, trust me, you do not want to go at the snail's pace I'll be going. I'm sure it'll be fine, now that you cleared that blockage."

"Well... take my number, just in case. We'll come back for you if you have any trouble." Boone slowly called out the number while Marge entered it into her phone, then Boone went below to raise the *Lunasea*'s anchor while Emily watched Marge doing the same aboard the harvester.

"See you back in civilization!" Em shouted as she turned on the engine.

"Thanks again for the assist. I'll be eating at Triple J's this evening. Saturday night, they do it right! Maybe I'll see you there. Buy you all a drink or three!"

"A generous offer!" Em called back. "Text Boone where to find it, yeah?"

Marge waved goodbye as the *Lunasea* left the harvester in its wake.

"No worries. Everybody on Sout' can point you to Triple J's!" Lincoln said, climbing onto the flybridge. "Best jerk ribs you ever tasted."

"Well, we'll just have to see about that!" Em replied. "Did you, um... call who you needed to call?"

"Turned out de fishermen were fishin' for fish," he said. "Just wanted to be sure. De police might not do anyt'ing at all, and de maritime police hands are full dealing wit' migrant smugglin' and poachers comin' into our fishing grounds from Haiti and de Dominican Republic."

"And the US Coast Guard?" Boone asked from the top steps of the ladder.

"Dey're based over in Inagua. Doubt dey'd come over for a few bricks of powduh." He snapped his fingers. "You know... dey caught a cartel submarine not long ago! Well... it was half in de water, half out... you know about dose t'ings?"

"Narcosubs?" Boone joined Emily at the wheel. "Yeah, we're... familiar with them."

Viktor watched the dive boat and its odd companion as the occupants pulled up anchors. He'd been able to discern that the strange boat was some sort of harvester, its stern basket filled with seaweed. And possibly with something else—the object the pilot had fished from the basket sure looked like a brick of cocaine. The dive boat increased speed and headed for the south as the harvester gently came about and followed suit.

Viktor trained the telescope on the departing dive boat, focusing on the young woman at the wheel.

Someone cleared their throat from behind him, and Viktor turned from the telescope to find Baptiste on the pool deck beside the glass doors to the living room. The man was averting his eyes with a vengeance.

"Yes, what is it?" Viktor grabbed a towel from a stack beside one of the lounge chairs and tied it around his waist.

"De flight has arrived in Provo and de package you've been waiting for is on its way to a boat we've chartered."

"Good. Better than a plane."

"Agreed."

"When can we expect it?"

"About noon, dey say. You want I should get it?"

Viktor nodded. "And I want you to get there before our contact arrives. Pay him and send him on his way. Take Sergei with you. And let *him* drive."

Baptiste rolled his eyes. "Anything else, while we're in town?"

"Ask the cook if she needs anything," Viktor said, making his way back to the villa. He paused at the edge of the pool deck. "Oh... and one more thing. You're meeting our contact at the main pier?"

"Yes."

"See if there's a dive boat there. Blue top. The *Lunasea*. Find out what you can about the owners. Discreetly."

TWELVE

"See dat beach?" Lincoln asked.

They were nearing the southeast corner of the island, and Lincoln was continuing his tour. Shortly after they'd left Marge, they'd passed the Reefview Resort, tucked into well-manicured cliffs. Most of the island seemed quite arid, with little in the way of large trees, but the resort had a tasteful array of landscaping around the buildings that lined the coast.

Now, ten minutes south, Lincoln pointed at a small, curving beach. "De migrants you heard about on de radio? Dat's where dey probably came ashore. And up dere is where dey was found."

On the top of a hill sat a large white building. Even though its roof and walls appeared to be intact, it had clearly seen better days; its gaping windows looked down on them like multiple pairs of eyes.

"Hey Link, is that the haunted house place you were talking about?" Em asked.

"Yes, dat's Highland House. It's off de road between town

and de Reefview. Nuttin' else over dere. Used to belong to a wealthy family, but it's been abandoned long as I can remember."

The coastline curved toward the east, and they soon had a view of a beautiful, shallow bay.

"And dat is East Bay! De resort we'll be workin' for is on de left dere... East Bay Resort."

Emily throttled down when they were across from it. The beach out front was immaculate, and a set of steps rose to the resort itself. The property had two pairs of four-story buildings with an octagonal building in the center.

"Bigger than I expected," Boone remarked.

"De offices and de restaurant and bar are in de middle buildin'," Lincoln said. "You can't see de pool from here, but it's right up from de stairs. Got a swim-up bar!"

"Noted," Em said with a grin. "Where are we staying?"

"Staff housing and de dive shop are 'round de back, beside de tennis courts."

"And me without my racket," Boone said absently.

"Do you play tennis?" Emily asked in surprise.

"I dabble."

"You never dabbled with me." She choked on a laugh. "Blimey, that sounded naughty. I mean, you've never mentioned it."

"Never came up." Boone had actually played in college, and his long reach had given him an edge that had helped him win more often than not. But as soon as the diving bug had bitten him, tennis had become a seldom-indulged hobby.

Ahead, three small rocks rose from the shallows with a larger rock to their left. Farther east, a long, rocky cay stretched into the distance.

"Dose three little rocks? We call dem Huey, Dewey, and

Louie. And dat bigger rock is Dove Cay. Swing out to sea a bit—
we goin' into Conch Ground Bay t'rough de channel between
Dove and Long." He pointed to the appropriately named cay to
the west. "Long Cay runs for 'bout three miles to de sout'west.
Very thin island. Nuttin' but iguanas and seabirds on it. Most
dives we be doin' will be along de sout' side of it."

Emily lined up the bow with the channel and eased the
throttle forward. Boone noticed navigational lights were
perched on the edges of the cays at either end of the channel.
The blues of the channel's waters were significantly darker in
hue than the shallows on either side of it.

"That's not the dock we're going to, I take it?" Emily asked,
nodding her head at an empty wooden pier just inside the
channel. Rows of painted bollards ran along both sides, each
one a different color.

"No, dat's Regatta Pier, and dat area is called Regatta
Village. Queen Elizabeth came to visit Grand Turk and South
Caicos back in 1966. Part of a royal tour. Dey do de Big South
Regatta dere every May!"

"That's what you wanted that week off in May for," Boone
remarked. "You said you wanted to go to a festival."

"It's a lot of fun. Good music, good food. People bring over a
lot of classic boats. A lot of games, a beauty pageant, dominos
tournament, donkey races..."

"People *ride* them?" Emily blurted.

"Well... dey try."

Boone chuckled at that. The donkeys in the TCI weren't
feral or anything, but they weren't exactly tame, either.

"Oh, and sailboat and powerboat races, too. Only one boat
sunk dis year."

"I'm thinking we need to come next year," Boone said, his
eyes scanning the shoreline. There were a number of ruins and

crumbling walls to the left of the Regatta Village; the roofless stone homes were likely victims of either Ike or Irma.

Lincoln pointed to the left of the pier. "Do you see dat church? Red roof, one street back? Dat's St. George's Anglican. Its tower has a big bronze bell dat come from de RMS *Rhone*."

"Wait... isn't that the famous wreck dive in the British Virgin Islands?" Boone asked.

"De same. Pretty sure de BVI would like it back. Jeremiah Murphy, dat pioneer diver in de mid-1800s, salvaged it and brought it here."

"Oh, yeah, he's that Irish bloke who lived on Grand Turk!" Emily exclaimed. "They have a whole exhibit on him at the National Museum. Did all his diving with one of those giant helmets with an air hose."

"First person to dive the sunken pirate city of Port Royal in Jamaica, too," Boone added. "Someone oughta write a book about that."

"Is that another resort?" Em asked, as they passed a second set of buildings up on a cliff above the rocky coast.

"No. See de 'SFS' painted on de wall? Dat's de School for Field Studies Marge said she was stayin' at," Lincoln answered.

Ahead, a small cargo vessel was tied up at a sturdy concrete pier, with five or six men offloading its contents. Beyond that were several smaller piers and jetties, an odd assortment of boats docked along them in places. At the end of one pier, the rusted hulk of a small barge was listing, partially sunk.

"So... where to, Link?" Emily asked.

"You see dat first pier past de cargo ship? Wit' de little shed wit' a red roof? Dat's where dey pick up divers every morning."

"There's a Newton moored out there." Boone pointed into the shallows a hundred yards out. "*Big Sister*. Hey, that one was over in the Cayman Islands when we were there."

"Yeah, I t'ink it's one of de boats on loan from dere." Lincoln said. "Ah, dere's Mateo!"

Walking down the pier that Lincoln had pointed out was a tall, thin man with light brown skin and jet-black hair, some of which was gathered on his head in a bun. He waved at them, then beckoned them to come to the dock, pointing at an empty spot near one side.

"Good-lookin' bloke," Emily observed, as she swung the bow of the *Lunasea* toward the suggested berth.

Boone and Lincoln went below and readied the lines as Emily brought the dive boat alongside the pier. As Mateo stood beside one of the bollards near the bow, Lincoln tossed him a line while Boone took the stern line and lassoed the bollard nearest him.

"Welcome to South Caicos!" Mateo called out. "You have a beautiful boat!"

"Thank you, we like to think so!" Emily replied from the flybridge.

"We mainly use the Newtons," Mateo said, "so it will be nice to try another boat." Mateo spoke with a light accent, but his English was excellent. He looked at it more closely. "I have seen a boat like this before... when I was working in Cozumel."

"Well, that might have been us," Boone said. "We were there a few years ago. Bubble Chasers Diving." He offered a handshake. "I'm Boone Fischer."

"Mateo Delmar."

"Pleased to meet you, Mateo!" Emily said as she hopped across. "I'm Emily! And this is—"

"Lincoln! Good to see you!" Mateo said, smiling warmly. "Back home for a bit, yes?"

"Long as you need us," Lincoln said, stepping across and greeting him.

"We'll find you a mooring spot out in the bay, but for now, you can leave your boat here. This afternoon, we'll bring tanks and put them aboard. We drive a compressor truck right to the pier."

"Sounds good," Boone said.

"I need to run out to the *Big Sister* and get my sunglasses," Mateo said, making his way to a small skiff that was tied up next to a ladder. "Thought I'd lost them kiteboarding in East Bay, but Roshane said he thought he saw them on the boat. Wait here, and I'll be back in a moment to run you over to the resort."

Boone cleared his throat. "Umm... we have one thing we need to take care of before we go anywhere..."

"Oh! Right!" Emily said. "The... square grouper."

Mateo clearly knew what that meant, because he simply said. "How many and where did you find them?"

Boone quickly recapped their encounter with Marge's harvester and Lincoln confirmed he had—eventually—called the police.

"Dey should have been here already," he said. "I'll call dem again."

Mateo nodded. "There are only a few full-time policemen on South Caicos. Probably had another call to attend to. In the meantime, I'll go look for my sunglasses."

"Good hunting!" Em said cheerily.

Mateo smiled and dropped down into the skiff. Once Lincoln released the line and tossed it down to him, the man sped off toward the Newton.

"My sistuh gwan pick me up and take me to my muddah's house," Lincoln said. "I'll be stayin' wit' her. She still got my old bicycle, so text me when you're comin' back here, and I'll join you den."

"Lincoln Forbes, is dat you?"

Boone looked in the direction of the voice and spotted a wiry old man in a small fishing boat tied up behind where Mateo's skiff had been.

"Mister Mack!" Lincoln said, smiling broadly and launching into local speak. "What da wybe is?"

"Een nuttin. I straight. You come to see you muddah?"

"Yessuh! Need to fix up her wall. But we also here to help out East Bay. Dey got to take a boat to Provo for repair."

The old fisherman cackled. "I know! Dat Gardiner boy run over de mooring line. Oh, well... he a good yout'."

Lincoln introduced Boone and Emily to the old man. "And dis is Mister Mackenson Charles... but everyone call 'im Mister Mack. He been fishin' da Big South for longer dan anyone else."

"You fuhst time 'ere?" the old man asked, his dialect thicker than Lincoln's.

"We've been in Grand Turk for a while, but never been over to South," Boone said.

"Well, you pick an interestin' time to visit," Mack said, his voice dropping to a conspiratorial growl. "You hear about de dead man dey found in de Boilin' Hole?"

"Yeah... there was something about it on the radio. But the story said they were waiting for a coroner to come from The Bahamas."

"And an investigator from the UK," Emily added.

"Well, I don't know 'bout dat, but de police bein' hush-hush and de Haitian community is vexed."

"Why's that?" Boone asked.

"De dead man was a Haitian, but no one in town know him. And everybody know everybody."

"Well, he could've been a migrant, yeah?" Em suggested. "Recently arrived?"

"Could be... but usually, migrants don't come 'ere all by deyself."

"The radio said the cause of death wasn't known," Boone said. "But... it was probably drowning, right?"

Mack rose from the deck of his little boat and leaned his arms on the pier, beckoning them closer.

"Maybe he drown, maybe not. But de Boilin' Hole is out in de salt pans, and no one go swimmin' in de Hole." He looked around as if someone might be listening in, then spoke in hushed tones. "And rumor is... it likely murder."

"Murder?" Lincoln said in surprise.

Mack shushed him. "Word is... de man had a voodoo *wanga* stuck in his throat."

"What's a *wanga*?" Emily asked.

Mack laughed. "Never heard of it before, but I ask one of de Haitian fishermen, and he say *wanga* a word for a spell, but it can be de object dat cast de spell. Like a little bag of charms, or a doll."

"And it was crammed down his throat?" Boone asked.

The old man shrugged. "Dat what I heard." He pointed across the bay in the direction of the Reef Divers' Newton. "Divemaster Mateo de one who found de body. Maybe he know more."

———

"Is that them?" Sergei asked.

He and Baptiste had just turned off the main road beside the Seaview Market and were about to drive closer to the pier when they spotted the dive boat with the blue bimini top.

"Boss say dere was a pretty blond woman, a tall white guy, and a local," Baptiste replied, "And dat's what I see."

"Can't make out the name on the boat at this angle," Sergei said, "but that's gotta be them."

"Dey're talking to Mack. Old fisherman. I know him a little."

"Good. We'll see what he can tell us once they're gone." Sergei checked the time on his phone. "We've still got a while before the package arrives. Let's go over to the Sunset Café; get some breakfast. We can eat on the deck and watch for when they leave."

Baptiste nodded and started to back up. Sunset Café had great food and was situated just up the road, catercorner from the Seaview Market. The alley next to the market was the only way in or out from the dive boat's pier, so they'd spot them when they left. Their man was actually coming into that same location, rather than the cargo pier, which had a customs office inconveniently close. With the island's fishermen coming and going from the Seaview pier—as well as occasional cruisers docking to fuel up—one boat doing a quick drop-off would scarcely be noticed.

The two men parked the Jeep and made their way to the deck, choosing a table overlooking the main road that ran from the airport in the north to the East Bay Resort in the southeast. The owner of the Sunset brought them simple laminated menus.

"Coffee?" he asked.

"Yeah," Sergei said, and went ahead and ordered breakfast. As the owner headed back to the kitchen, Sergei felt his phone buzz. He retrieved it and looked at the screen. "It's the boss texting." He frowned.

"What is it?"

"He said to bring back two live chickens." Another text appeared. "No... three."

Baptiste cocked his head. "De store right across de street sells chicken."

"No, he wants live ones."

Baptiste shrugged. "I'm sure someone keep dem. We can ax de old fishermen when we ax 'im about de newcomers. He'll know." He craned his neck, looking across at the alley to the pier. "Although we'll need to wait to talk with 'im."

Sergei followed his gaze and spotted the Royal Turks and Caicos Islands Police Force SUV making its way toward the pier. "What's he doing here?" he wondered aloud.

"Could it be dey know about our shipment?"

"I doubt it." Sergei checked his watch. "And our man's not arriving for a while. He's supposed to text first, once he gets close enough for a signal. I'll have him hold up if the police are still there."

The owner returned with their coffee and a ramekin of sugar packets and creamers. "You hear de news about de murder?" he asked, setting down their cups.

Both men froze. Baptiste picked up a sugar packet and shook it for a moment.

"No... we're over near Reefview," Sergei said. "Haven't been to town in a bit. What murder?"

"A Haitian man dat nobody knows was found drowned in de Boilin' Hole." He leaned in. "Wit' some kind of voodoo t'ing stuffed down his t'roat. Maybe it was some kind of ritual killin'!"

As the owner returned to the kitchen, Sergei slowly turned his gaze on Baptiste, whose own eyes were locked on his coffee cup as he stirred the contents of the sugar packet into his coffee. With his free hand, he adjusted something that hung from his neck inside his shirt.

Sergei spoke in a low voice. "What the hell did you do?"

THIRTEEN

"Normally, you'll go back and forth from the pier in a resort van," Mateo said, as they waded through the sand and seagrass to the beach. The skiff they'd used now lay at anchor in the shallow waters of East Bay. "When it's time to put the boats to bed, you'll use this—or you can use the *Shallow Minded*, that flats boat over there—then, you can just come straight back here. I'll run you back to your boat in a bit. We can pick up your bags then."

Emily was dying to ask about the man's grisly discovery in the Boiling Hole, but Boone had suggested they wait until they were settled in before springing that on him. Likely, it was a harrowing memory. "Glad you found your sunglasses, mate," she said instead.

"Me too. They're my favorite pair," he said, adjusting the polarized wraparounds on his face. "I don't feel whole without them."

"Preachin' to the choir!" Emily said, reaching up to raise her huge, lime-green sunglasses from her nose before letting them drop back into place. "Sunnies and smartphone... don't leave home without 'em."

"True words."

As the trio reached the beach, Mateo said, "The police took the drugs, I assume? I saw them arrive while I was on the Newton, but they weren't there long."

"Yeah, he took the two bricks," Boone acknowledged. "Said he was going over to the SFS pier to wait for Marge and the harvester."

Emily spied three dogs watching them from atop a sand dune off to the side. "I see you've got potcakes here, too. Although... that one's got a leash."

"Yes... the dive shop managers, Niles and Sara, were up late trying to catch them," Mateo said. "Otherwise, they would have been with me to greet you! Since it's the day off, they decided to sleep in." He whistled to the dogs, but they turned and headed inland. "We hope to catch them by next week. Provo sends over vets once a month to offer free neutering and spaying. The potcakes are a bit wilder over here than on Grand Turk or Provo. We want to bring them to the School for Field Studies, where they can socialize with their dogs. They have five."

"That's a lotta pooches," Boone said. "We have our hands full with just one."

"Wait'll we add a puppy," Em said.

"You're getting a puppy?" Mateo asked.

Boone gave Em a sidelong glance. "We're thinking about it. But we haven't really discussed it yet."

They went toward a set of steps that cut through the dunes. "The resort is several feet above the beach, and the buildings are set back," Mateo explained. "We're well-protected from storm surge."

He led them up the stairs to the edge of a large pool with a waterfall coming off the side. A variety of seabirds were hanging out along one edge, and a gazebo bar was set into the right side of it, stone stools visible below the surface of the water.

"Pool bar!" Emily declared, and was about to dash over to it when Mateo stopped her.

"No, let's go this way," he said with hushed urgency, leading them to the left through the manicured foliage. He kept his eyes straight ahead but said, "Do you see the man sitting in the pool at the bar? Bald. Writing in a notebook?"

Emily sneaked a peek backward. "Yeah?"

"He's a writer staying here. Doing research for a book. Every time he sees me, he has a million questions."

"Say no more!" Emily said.

"Besides... the dive shop, equipment storage, and drying room are all in this direction."

As Mateo led them between two of the resort buildings, they passed a housekeeper plucking fuchsia flowers from a row of bougainvillea and placing the blooms in her palm. She smiled as Mateo passed and raised her hand. "Honeymooners coming today!"

"You'll make their room beautiful, I am sure," he replied. They passed a tennis court and reached a parking lot with three small buildings around it. "Here are the dive shop facilities... and over there is the staff housing."

"We're in there, then?"

Mateo looked at her. "They didn't tell you? No, you're not in there... they're putting you up in a suite!"

"I love it I love it I love it!" Emily squealed as they opened the door to the corner suite overlooking the ocean. She swept her eyes across the open-plan room with its full kitchen, dining and living room areas. "Washer and dryer! A little bar nook... coffee maker... and look at the view!"

"I gotta say... I'm impressed," Boone said, taking it all in.

Emily went around the corner. "Two bedrooms!"

"Cool. I'll have somewhere to escape to when you snore," Boone said.

"And I'll have somewhere to banish you to, when you say I snore," Emily fired back. "King beds and full baths in each! I'm thinking this is going to be a great working vacation."

Boone went back into the main area and opened the sliding doors to the balcony. The sea breeze immediately billowed the gossamer, sun-filtering curtains, and the hot, salt-filled air mingled with the air conditioning of the room. Emily made a mental note to dial the A/C back a bit.

"Ace view, yeah?" she said as she joined Boone on the balcony.

"Beautiful." He looked down at her and slipped an arm around her waist, drawing her to his side.

"The writer guy is gone," Emily noted, pointing down at the pool.

"He lost the shade," Boone noted.

"Oh, yeah..." Emily could see that the sun was now past the overhang of the swim-up bar's roof and was beating down on the section of underwater stools that the man had been sitting at. She raised her eyes to the land beyond the resort. "Look!" She pointed. "It's that boogeyman mansion... Highland House."

On higher ground to the east, a mile or two away, the lonely structure stood, its empty windows looking out to sea.

"Sure is," Boone agreed. "Might have to take a stroll up there."

"In broad daylight."

Boone laughed. "I'm with you on that requirement." He thought a moment. "Wouldn't mind seeing the Boiling Hole, too." He looked at his dive watch. "Guess we should get back down there. Grab some lunch, then meet back with Mateo."

"Right-o," Em said, closing the balcony door behind them and pausing to turn up the thermostat. "Back to the pier after, yeah?"

"Yeah. Niles is going to join us. They need to check our safety features and go over proper procedures. Then we'll load the tanks, fuel up, and put the *Lunasea* to bed in the bay."

"Paz!"

Paz Cisneros jumped at Viktor's shout, immersed as he was in a graph of varying ratios of power levels and wavelengths.

Viktor appeared at the doorway to the engineer's workroom. "They just left the main road."

Paz followed his employer out the front entrance to the driveway, where they waited impatiently. A shadow passed overhead, a magnificent frigatebird soaring in the skies above, held aloft by the ocean breeze atop the seaside ridge. Viktor looked up at the bird, and Paz's own eyes were drawn to the top of Viktor's head. Paz knew the man had hair plugs, and with the stiff breeze blowing, the rows of transplants were made starkly apparent, like sad little rows of crops.

Paz tore his attention away from the sight as the Jeep came into view. It pulled up near the entrance and Baptiste and

Sergei got out, the noise of angry clucking sounding from inside the vehicle.

"Took you long enough," Viktor complained.

"The guy was late," Sergei said. "And you wanted us to get you some chickens, so that took a while. Old lady up by the airport had some."

"Let me see the shipment," Paz said.

"Sure thing." Sergei reached back inside the Jeep and retrieved a parcel before setting it on the hood.

"This has been opened," Paz said.

"Well, of course," Sergei said. "I'm not gonna hand over payment to a courier without knowing we got what we paid for."

Paz removed one of the objects from the bubble wrap and turned it over in his hands before putting it back and examining another.

"Well...?" Viktor prompted.

"They appear to be intact and built to the new specifications. I requested six, to account for possible defects in one or two. And this will provide us an additional battery for the backup prototype. I'll need to test these, of course. Charging them will take some time."

"Did you inquire about the dive boat? Was it from Grand Turk?"

"Yes," Baptiste said. "De *Lunasea*. T'ree divemasters came over to fill in for one of de local dive boats dat had an engine problem."

"The young blonde, was she there?"

"Yes. She dere wis' two uddah men, but dey gone when we come back to meet de courier."

One of the groundskeepers appeared around the corner. All four men looked at him.

"*Excusez-moi...* I heard de chickens. You want I bring to kitchen?"

"No, these are not for..." Viktor began, before waving the man away. "We're having a discussion. Leave us!"

The man vanished and Paz was about to go inside to test the new battery modules when he noticed Sergei giving Baptiste an odd, expectant look.

Viktor saw it too. "Is there something else?"

Sergei nudged Baptiste. "Tell him."

Baptiste scuffed a work boot in the sand beside the driveway. "So... you remember when I went to... um... get rid of de test subject? Lucien?"

Viktor looked around to where the groundskeeper had disappeared, then moved closer. "You dumped him in the ocean, did you not?"

Baptiste cleared his throat and looked at his boots. "I... did not." Before Viktor could explode, he continued, "I was on my way to do it, but... de Jeep got stuck. And I was trying to get it *un*stuck... but den the sun was coming up..."

Sergei blew out a disgusted breath and Viktor moved closer, dropping his voice.

"What... did you do... with the body?"

"Dere was a big pool of salt water wi' some mangroves near where I was stuck. I was afraid someone would come along, so I took him from de Jeep and dragged him over dere and dumped him out of de tarp—figured dat make it easier for things to eat de body, yes? I had some rope in de back, so I put a big rock on his stomach and wrapped the rope around it. Rolled him into de water and he sink. I kept trying to get de Jeep out, but it was too stuck."

"And he called me to get him out," Sergei said. "But didn't tell me what he'd done."

"I went back de next night," Baptiste blurted. "To do it proper. But..."

Viktor was trying his best to keep his calm, but Paz could tell the man was about to pitch a fit. "Go on," the Russian directed, clearly seething.

"De body was gone! De only t'ing dere was de rope. I guess de rock pulled loose. I thought I tied it good, but—"

"Where—?"

"The cops have it," Sergei interrupted. He quickly held out a hand, placating. "Hang on boss. This might actually be okay... thanks to the other thing this idiot did. Tell him."

Baptiste lifted his chin, defiant. "I protect myself, is what I did."

"Yeah, so you said. But tell Viktor *how* you protected yourself."

"I feed a *wanga* to de man after we kill him."

"A what?"

"Look, it doesn't matter," Sergei said. "Baptiste is superstitious—he shoved a little voodoo bag in the man's throat to keep its ghost from haunting us or some shit, and the cops found it, and it sounds like they think it was some sort of Haitian ritual killing."

Viktor's anger gave way to contemplation. "Paz... can this be traced to us?"

He thought a moment. "Not likely. The settings had the thermal component too high, so there was some blistering on the test subject's skin—I'll need to adjust that—but the damage might just look like exposure to intense sun. And the salt water he was in will likely confuse things. As for the cause of death, well... that's the whole point of the weapon. Deniability."

The afternoon had gone by swiftly, and Boone was impressed by how tight a ship Reef Divers ran. They met the dive managers Niles and Sara, and Boone couldn't help but notice that the pair collectively shared a lot of traits with Emily. Sara was a young woman from Spain, and like Em, she was both petite and blond. And Niles spoke with a North London dialect —not nearly as thick as Emily's South London accent, but it was fun to hear them banter back and forth.

The staff were pleased with the *Lunasea* and had a lot of questions about the Delta Canaveral. All of Reef Divers' primary dive boats—both in TCI and in the Cayman Islands— were forty-two-foot Newtons. Boone and Em proudly showed off their pride and joy before the Reef Divers staff gave them a rundown of procedures, as well as the nature of the diving here. Mateo promised to go into greater detail over dinner.

It turned out that they had planned to take the newcomers to Triple J's Grill—the same backyard barbecue restaurant that Marge had invited them to.

Now, back at the resort with the sun an hour from the horizon, Boone and Em dropped their bags inside their suite and went down to the parking lot where Mateo and Lincoln were waiting beside one of the resort's vans. Mateo waved as they approached.

"*Hola!* Roshane is going to join us. I think you met him on Grand Turk, yes?"

"We did," Boone said. "But I don't think we actually got to talk with him. He had his hands full keeping the group of divers happy after the issue with the drive shaft."

Roshane came out of the dive shop and trotted over to join them, buttoning up a tropical print shirt.

"Hey, good to see you again..." he began, then squinted his eyes. "Wait a minute... you look familiar."

Boone looked at the man more closely. "Little Cayman? Beach Nuts?"

"Yeah, mon! Dat's it!" He turned to Emily. "You're de one dat won Trivia Night half de time. And you made dis poor man sing karaoke!" He jabbed a thumb at Boone. "He hated every minute of it."

"He's a wet blanket," Emily said. "But I remember you from karaoke, too! You did a brilliant 'One Love' one night."

Roshane waved the compliment off. "I cheated. I'm Jamaican." He shook hands with them both. "I was workin' at de Little Cayman Beach Resort for a while, but now I'm here. Glad to have you two aboard!"

Everyone loaded into the van: Boone, Em, and Lincoln in the back, and Roshane in the front passenger seat. Mateo took them out of the resort, turning west on the road for the short drive toward town. Spotty foliage and scrub lined the road, with very little above a few feet in height. On their right, an expanse of salt flats, divided into salinas by low walls, extended far to the north. Much like in Bonaire, there were groups of flamingos wading in the shallow, salty water.

"There's a lot more salt works here than on Grand Turk," Boone remarked.

"Oh, yes. Much more. It's what South Caicos was known for," Mateo said.

As they reached the edge of town, Boone looked north and spotted a gazebo-like structure in the salt flats, linked to shore by a causeway atop low, stone walls. He glanced down at his phone, checking the Google Maps app he'd opened when they'd hit the road. When in a new place, he'd often use it to quickly orient himself. There was a marker just to the north of their location, and sure enough...

"What are you looking at?" Emily asked.

Boone pointed two fingers at his eyes, then pointed out the window at the structure as they passed it; simple diving hand signals for *Look there.* Emily leaned across him and looked out the window. Before she could say anything, he held up his phone for her, showing her the marker he'd zoomed in on: Boiling Hole. Emily raised her eyebrows.

"We'll ask about it over beers," he said in a low voice, showing the screen to Lincoln.

"Ask about what?" Roshane asked from the front seat.

"Anything and everything!" Emily said. "Love learning about new places. But let's get some beers in front of us first, yeah?"

The van entered the edge of town, which appeared to be laid out in a simple grid. Boone noted that a number of homes appeared damaged, with some nothing more than rubble. Many of the plots were encircled by low, stone walls—likely to keep out roaming donkeys—and many of those walls were crumbling.

Boone remembered Lincoln saying something about his mother needing her wall repaired. "Your mom have a wall like one of these?"

"Yes. She want me to fix it while I'm here."

"We can give you a hand with that."

"Oh... you don't need to."

"Happy to. We won't return to Grand Turk until it's done," Boone assured him. "The great thing about having our own boat... we can go back any time we want."

They passed a number of businesses with hand-lettered

signs, then turned north, traveling a couple more blocks before turning left on Hillgrove Street.

Lincoln jerked a thumb at a yellow-orange building. "Leah's Chicken Bar! Good place for chicken 'n' fries. That place is hoppin' some nights."

Just past the next intersection, Mateo pulled over to the side of the road. "We're here!"

FOURTEEN

On the south side of the street, a low wall with a gate was topped by a hand-painted sign for Triple J's Grill, the red, green, black, and yellow lettering announcing jerk chicken and pork, grilled fish, conch, and lobster. Beyond the gate was a typical Caribbean yard, half sand, half scraggly grass. On the right was a thatch-roofed bar with a row of smokers and grills behind it, and on the left was a squat house with an open sliding door. The back of the yard was fenced, with a couple of larger drum-grills in the back, painted red and black with yellow stripes.

"I don't see Marge anywhere," Emily noted. "Looks like we're the first ones here."

A few folding tables were set out and a young girl was snugging a picnic tablecloth onto one of them. She waved them into the courtyard. "Roshane! Good to see you again. Brought some new folks, I see! I'll let my parents know you're here. Take de big table."

Everyone sat at two tables that were set end to end. Emily

picked up a laminated menu and laughed. "I like their cheeky catchphrase: 'Better meat than down the street.' Ooh, and look at the sides! They've got festivals! I seem to remember you enjoyed those, right, Boone?"

"Fried dough with a little sweet and spice... what's not to like?"

Roshane visited the bar and returned with an armful of plastic bottles topped with colored pour spouts and identified by hand-printed labels. He set them down in the middle of the table. "Dey make deir own hot sauces... wanted to be sure we got one of each over here."

"The pineapple and mango ones are quite good," Mateo said.

"Dose are mild!" Roshane teased. "What, you don't like de heat?"

"Which one's the hottest?" Boone asked.

"Dat'd be dis one," Roshane said, rotating one with a red pour spout so he could read the label.

"Triple J Grill's Blast Your Face Off Sauce," Boone read aloud.

"Challenge accepted!" Emily declared, pulling the bottle over beside her place at the table.

Triple J's carried all of Turks Head Brewery's beers, and everyone ordered one of those. Boone noted most chose the low-alcohol I-Soon-Reach—a good choice for spicy food, and also a good choice for the evening before a busy day of diving. The group ordered their food as the sun went down, and a multi-colored spotlight sparkled to life across the fence and bar as reggae music and the smoky aromas of grilling meats filled the air.

"Mateo... Lincoln said you've done a lot of exploring, looking for new dive sites," Boone said. "I confess, I've always been a bit envious of those early diving pioneers who got to experience underwater locations for the first time. Captain Don, down in Bonaire..."

"Bob Soto, in the Cayman Islands," Emily chimed in. "What was it like, looking for new sites?"

"Exhilarating! It wasn't something I had expected. I came from Cozumel in 2019 to work here at the resort. Then COVID hit."

"Oh, bugger..."

"So... I had a lot of time on my hands," Mateo said. "It was a privilege to be given the opportunity."

"De man is too modest," Roshane said. "Tell dem how many official sites dere were when you started!"

"Nine. And only five moorings."

"And how many now?"

Mateo smiled. "Twenty. Twenty-five if you count the three up by East Caicos, and the two down by Fish Cay. And most have new moorings now. During the time of travel restrictions, we explored from South Caicos all the way up to East Caicos... and all the way down to White Cay and Ambergris Cay."

"Ambergris Cay!" Emily exclaimed. "Boone and I worked there. But I'm guessing you didn't mean the one on Belize."

Mateo laughed. "No, not that far. We have a Big and Little Ambergris Cay. Little is uninhabited. Most people, when they say 'Ambergris Cay' around here, mean Big Ambergris. It is a privately-owned island for very wealthy people. Very small, very exclusive, but it has its own airport and marina."

"Kind of sounds like Caye Chapel, near Caye Caulker," Emily said.

Boone nodded. That exclusive little island off Belize had its own golf course, too. Boone recalled that was where Oliver Price—or whatever his real name was—had been staying. The wealthy Brit had turned out to be a thief and a con man. *And the last time I saw him, he had several pounds of jaguar on top of him. Wonder if they ever found his body?*

"So, Mateo," Emily began, "how did you go about mapping a site?"

"Well... I should say right away that I didn't do it alone. Roshane here captained for me a few times. And Nardo... another divemaster. And Clarence and John from the School for Field Studies did much of the diving with me. We usually used a twenty-four-foot Zodiac with a 200HP engine. Brought along extra tanks on the boat, and we used underwater scooters to maximize the amount of territory we could cover."

"I confess, we don't use scooters much," Emily said. "But they're a lot of fun!"

"So, we would find an area of interest," Mateo continued. "On the first pass, we'd look at the big picture. We would drift dive, and our captain would follow above. If we found a point of interest, we would mark it with a flag buoy on a spool. For instance, if we found an entrance to a tunnel or swim-through, we would mark that with a flag buoy. We also carried a few surface marker buoys—the 'safety sausage' kind—in case we needed more."

"In England, we call sausages bangers," Emily said with a grin, "but 'safety bangers' would get confusing, what with tank bangers, yeah?"

Mateo continued, unfazed. "Also, we can use a safety sausage to send up a dead scooter for a fresh battery."

"Brilliant!"

"What happens to the markers you set?" Boone asked.

"When the captain sees a buoy, he moves in, tags it with GPS and labels it... notes visual shore references. And down below, we are also making notes and sketches. Once the captain has finished tagging it with GPS and making the notes, he deflates it and sends it back to us."

"How long do you do that?" Em asked.

"Depends on the depth of the reef and our air. We usually kept ourselves between sixty and a hundred feet. After sixty to eighty minutes, we ascended."

"An hour at sixty to a hundred feet... that's a lot of time at depth."

"I carried a spare tank," Mateo explained. "And the use of scooters helps a great deal with air consumption. And as far as deco goes, we took our time and staged our ascent."

"And then what?" Em asked. "You go back, yeah?"

"Yes. On the second pass, we return to the sites we marked and do an in-depth exploration. We bring GoPros, dive lights and a spool of guide line for penetration. And for that, we send up the marker buoy and the captain keeps station above the entrance."

"You went into unknown caves?" Boone asked. "Dicey."

"Well, one of them we knew a little about, the Catacombs site. It had no mooring, but some of the men at the Coast Guard station used to dive it. But for any penetration, we were very slow and methodical. Some had no exits, and we deleted those from the list. And anything too deep, too narrow, or just too technical... that was removed from the recreational diving options."

"Mateo, tell dem about de helicopter!" Roshane interrupted.

The Colombian laughed. "That was nerve-wracking. Every once in a while, I would go out on the Zodiac by myself. Just preliminary scouting dives for places we might survey— nothing too deep or technical. One day, I was on the east side, and I hear this roar above the sound of the outboard. I look back and there's a Coast Guard helicopter! And there's a man with a machine gun pointed down at me in the open door on the side."

"Blimey," Emily breathed. "What did you do?"

"Well... I assumed he thought I was a drug runner or something, so I stopped the engine and waved. Then picked up a dive mask and held it on my face. Then lifted one of my Nitrox tanks and pointed at it... then pointed over the side. Then I waited. I could see him yelling back to someone in the helicopter, then he lowered his gun and waved, and the helicopter flew away."

Boone blew out a breath. "Sounds like you handled that well. I'm guessing they're always on the lookout for smugglers."

"Yes. Usually, if a helicopter comes into view, the smugglers will just throw the drugs overboard. And sometimes people find them... as you yourself discovered, yes? Although having them sucked up in a harvester... that's a first."

"Marge said she was going to be here," Em remarked.

"It's still early," Boone said. "So... after you finished your exploration, what came next?"

Mateo took a sip of his beer before continuing. "Once we had the list of potential sites, we went through and determined which ones we thought were worthy of a mooring. We then sent the final list to the TCI Reef Fund with details like depth, coordinates, name... they approved all of them."

Emily leaned forward. "You got to name the sites? Cool!"

"We came up with most of the names together."

"Which one is your favorite?" Boone asked. "Of the sites you explored."

"That's easy. There's a site on the north coast of East Caicos with spectacular spur and groove structures and a healthy reef. I named it Kalo's Garden."

"Kalo... is that a Lucayan word?"

"No... that's my son's name."

"That's a fantastic name!" Emily gushed. "I love it!"

Mateo smiled. "I'm quite fond of it, too. And of him. He's back on Cozumel with his mother."

Boone was about to ask if he knew their previous co-owner and divemaster Ricardo, whose own son would be about four by now, but the arrival of the food interrupted his train of thought. Delicious aromas heralded the arrival of plates filled with ribs and pork.

"I'm not seeing any surf," Emily noted. "Looks like everyone went for turf!"

"De jerk pork is too good to pass up!" Roshane declared, tucking in.

"We get plenty of seafood at the resort," Mateo explained. "With an island whose main industry is fishing, it's in steady supply."

"And lobster is outta season right now," Lincoln added. "Otherwise, I mighta gone for dat."

"I see you found the place!" a voice called out from the gate by the street.

"Marge!" Emily waved from the table. "Pull up a chair and join our yardeque!" When Roshane cocked his head at her, Em added, "A barbeque in a yard, yeah?"

The harvester inventor came through the gate and approached the table; from her interaction with Mateo and Roshane, it was clear they knew her. She took an empty spot beside Boone.

"Do you need a menu?" he asked.

"No, I'm all set. I knew I might be late, so I called in an

order for the grilled fish before they ran out. They get whatever they get, fresh from the docks."

"I heard you might have harvested something more than sargassum," Mateo said.

Marge laughed. "It's certainly been an interesting day!"

"How'd everything go with the police?" Boone asked.

"Fine. Turned out there was only one more... uh... 'grouper' in the sargassum basket. They didn't seem that concerned about it... apparently there was a murder a few days ago, and that has most of their attention."

"Can we ask Mateo about it now?" Emily whispered to Boone, a pork rib slathered in sauce poised before her lips.

Boone smiled as he skewered a plantain on his fork. "Maybe we should eat first before we talk about dead bodies," he said quietly.

"Oh, you're no fun," Emily muttered, before taking a sizable bite from the rib. "Wow, it's so tender!" she said, her mouth half full. "The meat just falls off the bo-aaaaa! Bloody hell!"

Boone laughed as Emily's face reddened and sweat broke out at her hairline. "You poured a bunch of Blast Your Face Off on there and just went to town on it, didn't you?"

Tears in her eyes, Emily nodded vigorously, unable to speak.

"Most folks woulda tried a little bit first."

The young girl who'd taken their orders suddenly appeared with a single-serve carton of milk and set it down in front of Emily, who gratefully tore the end open. "Dat sauce is full of scotch bonnet peppers!" the server said. "I saw her jus' pouring it on dere, and I wonduh: 'is de woman crazy?'"

"That's a phrase we hear a lot around her," Boone deadpanned, eliciting laughs from the table.

Emily paused mid-drink, turned and punched Boone's arm.

She managed to choke out the word "Wanker!" then returned to the milk carton, chugging half of it.

"Yeah, maybe stick to de mango hot sauce," Roshane said, grinning.

"Noted," Emily gasped, then reached over onto Boone's plate and stole one of his festivals. She bit down on the sweet, fried dough and seemed to relax. "Better now."

"So... Roshane... Mateo," Boone began, "what sort of diving are we likely to do this week? I'm guessing most of your day-to-day is to the southern sites?"

"Yes. They are closer than the east coast ones, of course, and the waters are usually calmer there."

"Great divin' all along de south side of Long Cay," Roshane affirmed.

"I'll dive with the *Lunasea* tomorrow," Mateo said. "We have two dive groups coming. The larger one, we'll put on the Newton Custom. It's rated up to thirty-eight divers... well, that's what the little manufacturer's plate in the cockpit says, but we rarely take more than twenty-four. The other group is smaller, and we'll put them on your Delta Canaveral."

"Sounds good," Boone said.

Mateo and Roshane described some of the area's diving while everyone enjoyed their meal. A group of locals waited outside the fence, and Boone guessed they were a couple of families waiting for the double table they currently occupied. The meal finished, Boone caught the server's eye and surreptitiously held out a credit card.

"Oh, I'm sorry... cash only," she whispered.

"Whoops. Hang on." He clawed his wallet out of his pants.

"Oh, no you don't!" Marge said, catching him in the act. "I owe you for the rescue!"

"Wasn't much of a rescue," Boone objected, but Mateo put

an end to the discussion by holding up a wad of twenties. Despite the TCI being a British Overseas Territory, the US dollar was the official currency.

"The resort gave me money to buy you all dinner," he said, taking the bill from the server.

"I suppose it's a good thing," Boone said, "I didn't bring much cash. Is there an ATM on the island?"

"One. T'ree blocks dat way," Roshane said, waving his hand toward the east.

The bill paid, they surrendered their table to the hungry families and went back to the street. Marge said good night and walked toward the School for Field Studies, and Lincoln went with Roshane to go meet some friends at Leah's Chicken Bar. That left Emily and Boone to join Mateo in the van. Emily scrambled into the passenger seat, and once inside, she pounced.

"Mateo... I've been dying to ask—and if it's not something you want to talk about, just tell me to shut my gob, right? But... the body Marge mentioned... you're the one who found it, yeah?"

Mateo looked back at them from the driver's seat. "I did."

"And you were diving in there when you found it? The Boiling Hole?"

Mateo thought for a moment, then turned the key in the ignition. "It's just a few blocks away. I'll take you there."

FIFTEEN

Mateo had just finished explaining the plan for the survey of the Boiling Hole when they pulled up beside the salinas and he drove the van down a narrow, unlit causeway to a small sand parking area. "The Boiling Hole is right over there," he said after Boone and Em had gotten out and joined him in the moonlight. The moon was full, and along with the stars in the clear sky, there was enough illumination to make out the ground, as well as the gazebo-like structure across the water.

"We'll have to walk along this narrow strip between the salt bed walls, so watch your step." Mateo led the way, surprisingly surefooted in his flip-flops.

"Kinda spooky out here, innit?" Em remarked. She looked back toward town; the nearest streetlights were hundreds of yards away.

They walked to the east for a couple of minutes, then turned north, the walkway defining the walls of one of the salt beds.

"I saw flamingos in the waters nearby, on our way over to Triple J's," Boone remarked. "Anything else live in the salt pans?"

"Mostly birds and a few small fish," Mateo said. "I've often seen needlefish. And one of the locals said he's seen juvenile lemon sharks in here one time. I'm convinced the Hole is connected to the ocean. But there may be other connections, also. Juvenile lemons are often found in the mangrove areas to the north."

In minutes they reached the gazebo, which had some seating inside, and was located beside a square of concrete walls. The sound of roiling water was quite apparent. Boone turned on the flashlight function on his phone and shined it over the edge. The surface of the water below was quite disturbed, sloshing up against the walls and rattling a pair of old sluice gates. One gateway was open to the salt pans, and water was pushing through that into the shallows beyond.

"So that's why they call it the Boiling Hole," Emily remarked, looking over the edge.

"Is it always like this?" Boone asked, shutting off the light.

"No, it's placid much of the time. It's tied to the changing of the tides in the bay, but there's a considerable delay."

"How much of a delay?" Boone asked.

"Between three and four hours."

"That's a long time. You probably have a substantial network of passages down there."

"Yes, that is our belief."

"The hour difference in the interval... is that 'inconsistency' consistent?"

"Way to confuse things, Boone," Emily said.

"I mean... is it four hours in the winter, then three hours in the summer? Or is it tied to the moon phase?"

"No, there isn't a clear pattern. It can be different just during the week. I suspect it has to do with weather and currents in the bay."

"Or there could be more than one connection to the sea," Boone surmised. "If the conditions vary, the tide may be entering the cave system in a different way."

"Sorry to interrupt, but can we steer this back to the murder mystery?" Emily requested. "That night you found the body..." she prompted.

Mateo chuckled. "It wasn't night, it was broad daylight."

"Oh, sorry mate! Got swept up in the ambiance."

"We timed the dive to coincide with the morning slack tide in the bay, plus three and a half hours. John, from the SFS, was assisting, and he affixed my guide line to one of the posts there. The visibility wasn't great, so I stayed close to one of the walls and followed it down. There was an entrance to a cave structure about fifteen feet down, and it was on the eastern side, which wasn't what I was expecting."

"Why not?" Boone asked.

Mateo pointed to the southwest. "There's another spot called the Turtle Crawl about half a mile that way. It definitely connects to the ocean—or used to... they sealed it up after a drowning. I assumed that a passage leaving the Boiling Hole would run in that direction."

"Well... caves can go all twisty-turny, yeah? Probably get there eventually," Em suggested.

"Of course. In any event, the passage was wide enough that I wouldn't have to remove my tank, so I decided to do a very short penetration. I hadn't gone more than a few feet in when I found the body."

By now, everyone's eyes had fully adjusted to the starry gloom, and Boone saw Mateo visibly shudder.

"I'm grateful what I came across wasn't a face," he said quietly. "It was a foot. Well... a foot in a work boot."

"Blimey!" Emily gasped. "Bad enough, I say."

"I confess, I felt a moment of panic... but then the training kicked in. I shined a light along the leg and was able to make out that it was a man with dark skin. I thought of this as a drowning victim and tried to retrieve him, but unfortunately, he was wedged in place. I knew I was close to the entrance and had plenty of air, so I removed the guide line spool from its carabiner and played out some line before looping it several times around the ankle of the victim. Then I returned to the surface."

"So, you weren't down there when they retrieved him?"

"No. They sent a two-man team of police divers from Provo."

"And we heard they found something in his throat," Em said quietly. "Something voodoo-ey."

"Yes, I heard that as well."

"So that probably leaves out accidental drowning."

"Wedged..." Boone said quietly.

"What?" Em asked.

"How hard did you pull to try and free the body?"

Mateo thought a moment. "Pretty hard. And from what the police divers told us later, they had to chip at the surrounding limestone to pull him loose."

"When you tried to free him, did you get any more of him through the passage?"

"No. His lower leg was sticking through when I found him, and I couldn't get any more of him over to my side."

"Hmm..." Boone was silent for a while before Emily nudged him.

"Spill it! What's goin' on in your noggin?"

"Well... if someone fell into the Boiling Hole and drowned... or if he was already dead and dumped there... and an outgoing flow pushed him into that opening... then he would've been wedged in place from *this* side, and you shouldn't have had any trouble."

Boone stepped to the side of the Boiling Hole and looked down on the turbulent waters, illuminated from the moon and stars.

"If someone killed that man... they dumped him somewhere else."

———

The next morning at a quarter past six, Boone and Emily met Doug "Cap" Cox by the pool, and they made their way to the beach to wade out to the skiff. From there, Doug took them around to the bay to retrieve their boats.

"I'll drop you at de *Lunasea*, den I'll go over to de *Big Sister* and bring her in."

"There's two of us, if you'd like Boone or me to bring it in for you. Or the skiff."

"I can do it solo," Doug said. "I just tie de skiff alongside and bring dem both in. But if you want to bring de skiff to dock for me, dat'll save some time."

"Boone, that'll be your job," Emily declared.

"Aye, aye, skipper," Boone said, sketching a lazy salute. "Mateo's meeting us at the pier?"

"Yes. And Niles will be along wit' de compressor truck. De resort will bring divers over in several van trips, starting just after eight."

"Lincoln'll be at the pier at seven," Boone said. "His mother's house is just a short walk."

"Good. Roshane will join us about den, too," Doug replied, angling the skiff around an outcrop and skimming along the shallows. They passed the trio of little rocks beside Dove Cay—Huey, Dewey, and Louie—and in minutes they were inside the Conch Ground Bay. He came alongside the *Lunasea*'s swim platform and idled while Boone took a long-legged step across, then turned back to help Emily aboard.

"Too slow!" she sang, having already hopped over. "Get the mooring before you leave me all by my lonesome, yeah? Doug, where do you want me? Left side, or right?"

"I like to put *Big Sister* on de right, and *Caicos Sister* you're replacing is usually on de left, so let's stick wit' dat. Put yourself behind de big lobstuh boat."

"Right-o!"

Boone quickly freed the bow line from the mooring and stepped back aboard the skiff. Doug had them over to the Newton dive boat in seconds.

"You want me to handle the line?"

"No need. You stay wit' de skiff." Doug adjusted his stocking cap and squinted across the bay toward the pier. "Dere's usually a spot on de right between de smaller fishing boats. Find Mister Mack. Old Haitian fisherman, blue boat."

"Met him yesterday," Boone said. "I know right where you mean. See you back there."

Boone settled in at the outboard and headed for the pier at a leisurely pace. The *Lunasea* soon came alongside him, a smiling Emily at the flybridge wheel, the early morning sun shining on her blond hair, which hung down her back in a braid today. She made a shooing motion at him, and he increased speed, intending to get there in enough time to help her tie up at the dock.

Mack was in his boat, arranging some gear. A small cooler

sat on the dock. Boone slotted himself in front of the fisherman's boat and expertly looped a line around the nearest bollard before stepping across and securing the skiff.

"Mornin', Mack," Boone said, glancing across the pier to see Emily on approach.

"Oh! It's you! I was hopin' to see you. After you go yesterday, a man was here, askin' 'bout you and your lady friend."

"Really? Who?"

"Haitian man, name of Baptiste. T'ink he work up near de Reefview Resort, nort' end of de island."

"What did he want?" Boone asked, looking back to see the *Lunasea* nuzzling into the fenders. "Wait, one sec... I'll be back." He crossed the pier and boarded the dive boat, fetching the bow line first. Emily kept the engine idling while he finished securing the boat to the pier.

"Perfect timing," she called out. "Here comes the compressor truck!"

Arriving in the alley, a small truck with a boxy silver back end drove slowly down the pier. As Niles got out of the driver's seat, Mateo exited from the passenger side and the two of them went around the back. Boone looked across to see Mack loading the cooler. He caught the old man's eye and the fisherman waved, then untied from the pier, clearly planning on a morning of fishing. Boone trotted back across.

"Sorry about that."

"S'okay... I would already be out fishin' but my nephew is late. Anyway, dis man Baptiste, I don't know him well, but he bought fish from me a few times. He asked questions about who you were and where you come from. I told him you were divers, and he seem to lose interest. But den he go over and look at your boat."

There was no crime in looking, but Boone sensed there was something more. "Did he go aboard?"

"No... but I t'ink he wanted to. I heard dat camera sound when someone take a picture on a phone... den he seem like he might step over, but he look back and see me watching. Give me a big smile and a wave, den went back toward town."

"Thanks, Mack. Hey, our room has a kitchen—maybe I should hit you up for some fish. What do you usually catch?"

"Snapper and grouper mostly, dis time of year. And lobster and conch when dey're in season. Catchin' lobster... you can make in two weeks what you make in months catchin' fish."

And that's why every Caribbean island has a lobster season, Boone thought. *They'd be near-extinct otherwise.* Boone could see fins, mask, and a pole spear in the boat. "You spearfish, then?"

"Yes. Well, for fish, I do. For lobsters, spears not allowed... have to use a tickler to coax 'em out and grab 'em. I freedive for dem. A diver from France taught a lot of de fishermen how to stay down a long time. He had a house on the island."

"Really! I free dive. Who was the Frenchman?"

"Jacques somet'ing. It was a long time ago. In de eighties, I t'ink." He looked past Boone. "Mateo will know. Dat man has learned more about Sout' Caicos history in a few years dan I have from livin' here mosta my life!"

Boone looked over his shoulder to see Mateo approaching. "Boone, you want to take a look at the compressor?"

"Yes, sure. Thanks, Mack! And we'll grab some snapper from you sometime this week."

The man waved as he started his outboard. Another fisherman jogged up and jumped in, and Mack shouted a barrage of local lingo at the latecomer as he piloted the boat toward the channel.

At the rear of the truck, Boone found Niles already

explaining something to Emily. The back doors were open, revealing the compressor. The unit was divided into two, with a panel on the left for Nitrox, and one on the right for air. Each had three banks of gauges and valves, indicating different levels of fill. In Boone's experience, most dive ops aimed for at least 3,000 psi in a tank, but it could vary. On either side of the unit, two large spools held hoses.

Niles explained how the system worked, then checked a clipboard where he had the numbers of Nitrox divers versus air on each boat. Nitrox had a higher percentage of oxygen than atmospheric air and enabled a diver to stay down longer, the reduced nitrogen content in the mixture allowing for longer no-decompression times. However, its use required a special certification, and many divers simply stuck with air.

They would first run the Nitrox hose across to the *Big Sister* and the air hose over to the *Lunasea*, then switch the hoses and fill the remaining tanks on both boats. Nitrox tanks had yellow and green markings on the top, so occasionally tanks might need to be shifted between boats. Roshane showed up with Lincoln, and everyone got to work. Reef Divers clearly had everything down to a science, and the tank fill didn't take very long.

In short order, the divers began to arrive. Boone and Emily had two groups of four—one from Canada and the other from a diving club out of Charlotte, North Carolina. A larger group boarded the *Big Sister*. They left the dock first, piloted by Doug, with Roshane and Lincoln aboard. Mateo joined Boone and Em.

"I hope you don't mind that we stole Lincoln from you," he said, "but I wanted to accompany you on this dive, and they needed an additional divemaster. They will go to a site on the far end of Long Cay, but I'm going to take us in the other direction, closer to East Bay."

"So... out the channel, hang a left," Emily said. "What's the name of the site?"

"Good Call. It's called that because there's a telecom cable that runs to Grand Turk down there. I'll take us toward the adjacent site, Lost Anchors."

"Where there are anchors," Boone said with a smile.

"Yes! Several. But Good Call has two, as well. They are encrusted with corals, but I'll point them out. Which of you will join me?"

"Boone, why don't you take the deep one, and I'll stay aboard. Switch off on the next."

"Sounds good. Hey, Mateo, you mind if I video the dive briefings? That way we can watch those and be ready to do them ourselves."

"Yes, that's a good idea," he replied, picking up a clipboard. "Let's see if we have all of our divers, and we can get going."

SIXTEEN

The first dive went well, with only some minor buoyancy issues at the beginning. Often, at the start of a trip, a diver might need to adjust their dive weights, and it was something Boone and Em were quite used to. New gear might be the culprit, but often a little unexpected weight gain was the issue. Fortunately, the divers from Canada and North Carolina were all experienced, and once everyone gathered at the base of the mooring line, the dive went swimmingly.

The anchors were quite interesting, and one of them appeared older than the one at the *Endymion* dive site. In addition, they were treated to a pair of reef sharks, several turtles, spotted morays, and a sizable Southern stingray. Boone was impressed with Mateo's abilities. Emily had often spoken of how chill Boone was while diving, with minimal movement and perfect buoyancy, but he thought the Colombian divemaster took the gold medal in the "zen" department.

Back aboard, roll was called, and Mateo instructed Emily to

take them back into the bay and anchor in the shallows north of Long Cay.

"The next dive is very close to the channel," he explained. "Since there's a little chop out here, we can take our surface interval where the water is still."

Once they were anchored, the trio spent some time getting to know the two groups of divers. Oranges were consumed and stories swapped, and soon it was time to head back out.

"We will be diving Airplane next," Mateo announced. "It's the remains of a Convair 440 cargo flight that crashed in the seventies."

"Is it one of Pablo Escobar's planes?" one of the North Carolinians asked hopefully.

"No, sorry. It was just a regular cargo flight. And I'm also sorry to say that Hurricane Irma swept much of the plane over the edge and into the depths. It's mostly debris now. But we get a lot of reef sharks here, and last week one of our divemasters saw a large hammerhead."

That got everyone excited, Boone included. He'd only seen a few, and at a distance. But then he remembered that it was Emily's turn to dive. He looked down at her, and the evil grin on her face told him she'd thought of that, too.

"The site is quite close, so everyone can gear back up," Mateo said. "Emily, go ahead and take us back out, then turn to starboard."

"Actually, it's Boone's turn to take the wheel so I can gear up, yeah?" she said, throwing an innocent smile Boone's way.

While Boone climbed up to the flybridge, Mateo brought in the anchor, and they were soon heading back to the channel. The Airplane site was quite close, and they moored beside the limestone bluffs of Long Cay. Mateo gave a dive briefing, which Boone recorded. Toward the end of it, Emily snuck over to the whiteboard that was affixed to the flybridge ladder with a dry erase marker in hand. While Mateo finished up with his briefing, Emily sketched a hammerhead on the dive profile map. Mateo glanced over to see what she was doing, and she froze.

"Visualize to actualize, yeah?"

He laughed. "Yes! Very good. Please finish. You know, our dive manager, Sara, likes to draw little creatures on the whiteboards."

"Well, of course, it's something all awesome people do," Em said, adding some gills to her creation.

Boone assisted Mateo with the divers, making sure everyone entered the water safely. Emily brought up the rear, decked out in a new shorty wetsuit she'd picked up in Provo— black, with neon green on the sides from sleeves to thigh. Together with her trusty lime-green fins, she was easy to pick out in a group of divers. She gathered her braid atop her head and slid her mask on before letting the braid fall back over the strap.

"Back in a jiff," she said, before dropping in to follow Mateo down to the base of the mooring line, where the divers had been instructed to wait.

And now it was Boone's turn to wait. He climbed back up to the flybridge and turned on the radio, tuning it to Radio Bambarra. He was greeted by "It Wasn't Me" by Shaggy. Boone slid into the captain's chair and put his feet up on the dash.

The song came to an end, and a deep, locally accented voice came on. *"Dat was 'It Wasn't Me' by Shaggy. And let's not forget his good friend, RikRok, singin' de part of de poor man who got caught messin' around. Both of dem hail from Jamaica! And dat was de song dat put Shaggy on de American pop charts.*

"Dis is Deejay Ceejay coming to you from Radio Bambarra. De time is 10:45, and we will be rain-free on dis beautiful day. And

now, how 'bout some old school Trinidadian Calypso with 'Jean and Dinah' by Mighty Sparrow!"

CJ punched the play button, and then cued up the following song, as well as an automated commercial break to follow that. He rose from his chair, stretched, then went to the coffee pot in the corner of the radio station—although "station" was a generous name for it. While the Coast Guard complex spanned several buildings, he was largely confined to an office on the north end, running Radio Bambarra from his laptop. The "radio room" didn't even have a door when he'd first moved in, and he'd only just gotten around to installing a basic aluminum screen door last weekend. For several years after Hurricane Irma, the wild donkeys of South Caicos would occasionally pay a visit to the various rooms of the abandoned Coast Guard station and leave gifts all over the floor. When he'd taken possession of the lease, it'd taken him several days to clean up all of the donkey leavings, as well as a substantial amount of broken glass.

After Irma's destructive visit, the previous tenant—a Spanish-language Christian radio station—had packed up and left. Well, no... they'd actually just left, and didn't pack up at all. In addition to donkey poop and broken glass, CJ had found old mail, invoices, phone books, calendars, and equipment manuals strewn all over the floor. And lining the shelves were ancient monitors and computers, and even an old rotary phone —likely artifacts of the final years of the US Coast Guard's residency.

CJ filled a mug, grabbed a book and several colored highlighters, and stepped out through his freshly installed door to make his way to his hangout spot: a couple pieces of patio furniture and a propane gas grill he'd purchased for a bargain price. He'd had a glass table with an umbrella here, too... for a fleeting amount of time. Being up on a bluff above the ocean had its advantages, as far as the view and the cooling sea breezes. But one blustery day, while he was busy reading the news, a strong gust had grabbed the umbrella and sent the table flying, shattering the glass, and providing him even more shards to clean up. Now, he put his coffee mug on a cinder block, and sat in one of the chairs, cracking the book.

CJ had gotten the idea to read books on the radio from his wife, after she listened to him reading their son a bedtime story. He'd been blessed with a rich, bass voice, and he enjoyed reading, so why not? CJ knew about audiobooks and, after listening to a few, he decided he'd devote thirty minutes of airtime several days a week, reading a selection from a book, usually a chapter or two at a time. He tried to pick Caribbean authors, and today's selection was one he'd had on his night-stand for some time.

Kingston Noir was a collection of short stories, and part of Akashic Books' noir collection. Each *Akashic Noir* anthology was set in a different location, and this one was set in Jamaica. Today he'd be reading a story by Marlon James. He uncapped a yellow highlighter and started marking the dialogue of the main character. His son always liked him to do different voices when he read a story, and that had carried over to his latest venture—although most of CJ's voices tended to sound like some variation of Barry White.

He'd gotten several pages into the preparation when the familiar roar of a helicopter blotted out the sound of the surf below. His neighbor to the south again. Word in town was he was some rich guy from Europe who very few people had actually seen. Although CJ couldn't see the man's villa from here, he'd taken a detour off the road to the Coast Guard station one day to take a look. It turned out to be a very brief look. The large villa was set into the hillside, and much of it was obscured from the road, but he'd seen enough to know not to linger—a man with some kind of assault rifle had started toward CJ's Jeep when he slowed, and he'd quickly brought his tour to an end, driving away as fast as the sandy road would allow. He didn't know what the owner did to earn his money, and he didn't *want* to know.

CJ watched the helicopter lift off before turning to the south. *Wonder where he's off to?* he thought, before returning to his book.

"We will be over Ambergris Cay in ten minutes, Señor Gusev," the pilot announced over the intercom.

Viktor mashed the talk button on the nearby panel. "Good. Thank you. And you understand your instructions?"

"Yes, señor."

Well, that makes one of us, Viktor thought. Fifteen minutes ago, his overlords at the GRU had called with a time-sensitive request. He'd assumed they'd already forgotten what he'd told them about further tests using the new battery and were impatient for an update, but it turned out it was something else entirely. It had been a long time since he'd been asked to do anything that didn't involve arms trafficking, so he was both grateful... and suspicious. Because, while they had told him what they wanted him to do, they hadn't given him a reason for it.

"So... what are we doing, again?" Sergei asked.

Viktor let out an exasperated sigh. "The 'what' is easy. The 'why' is the question. We're to visit Ambergris Cay and have lunch at Calico Jack's."

"Uh... okay." Sergei lifted up the telephoto lens camera he'd been holding in his lap. "Are we going to take pictures of the appetizers?"

Viktor huffed a short laugh. "No, that's for when Diego circles the island before we land. We're to take pictures of every boat in the artificial marina, and the anchorages on the west side."

Sergei nodded, removing the lens cap. "What are we looking for?"

Viktor angled his head to look out the window. "I suspect we'll know it when we see it."

Boone checked his watch. The divers had been down about forty-five minutes, and this was a shallow dive. He flicked off the radio—cutting off Shabba Ranks mid-song—and descended the ladder, then headed to the swim platform and looked down at the water to the stern. Several circles of bubbles heralded the arrival of two of the divers.

"Oh my gosh, that was a big'un!" one of the Canadians spluttered as he reached the ladder.

"Ya, she was a beauty! Did you get some good footage?" his partner asked, holding on to the trailing line several feet back from the ladder.

"You betcha!" He grinned up at Boone and offered his GoPro, mounted on a floating handle-grip.

Boone reached out to take it and quickly set it in the fresh-water rinse bin before going back for the man's fins.

"The hammerhead was there, I take it?" Boone asked, as he helped the man to his spot on a bench, then quickly returned to the stern to accept his partner's fins.

"Still down there when we came up!" the first diver said. "Was swimming around at the bottom during our safety stop. I would've stayed down longer, but first dive and all... you know how it is. I got a little excited and burned through my air."

Mateo came up next, tossing his fins up and stripping out of his BC and tank at the ladder. He was aboard so smoothly that Boone had scarcely finished helping the second diver to her bench before the Colombian divemaster was beside him.

"Beautiful!" he exclaimed. "Hammerhead! A very big one!"

"Yes, so I heard," Boone said, eyes on the next diver approaching the ladder.

Mateo set his gear and mask into a slot before assisting Boone at the swim platform. "You ever see one?"

"Rarely, and always at a distance. Question for ya... and don't hesitate to say no. I'm a freediver. Once everyone's aboard, you mind if I...?"

"If it's still down there, sure. But have Emily stay in and keep her gear on."

When the last of the divers was at the ladder, Emily popped up. "I swear, Boone!" she called out, laughter on the edge of her voice. "We have got to leave you on the boat more often!"

"Yeah, yeah... I heard," Boone said with an aw-shucks smile. "Hey, do me a favor... is it still down there?"

"What, Hammy McHammerface? That's 'is name, by the way. Let me take a butchers."

Boone recognized the odd phrase, since Em had used it before—she was saying she'd go take a look. More of that Cockney rhyming slang: "look" became "hook," then "butcher's hook," then "butchers." When she ducked under, Boone stripped off his shirt and took three strides to his gear, snatching his mask, boots, and fins before returning to the stern. He briefly considered fetching his long freediving fins from below, but decided that wouldn't be worth the time it'd take to get them. Boone was snugging his mask on his face when Em popped up.

"Nope! Hammy has scuttled off to the deep... ohhhhh, you poor bugger, I see what you were up to." Emily's voice went from bubbly to sad as she looked at Boone, his fins in hand and mask on his face. "Sorry, mate. Next time, yeah?"

SEVENTEEN

"Well, that was a waste of time," Viktor muttered as they left the golf cart and headed for their helicopter, parked in a corner of the Harold Charles International Airport. Even though this private island was quite small and had very few people on it at any one time, the runway was nearly as long as the one on Grand Turk.

"At least the lunch was good," Sergei offered.

"Perhaps, but lunch wasn't the point, was it?"

Before they landed, they had made two circuits of the small, private island and taken photos of every vessel they could see in the marina and at anchor. There hadn't been many. Perhaps the photos would contain what his handlers were looking for, but he doubted it. After setting down near another helicopter, they had walked to the terminal and hired a golf cart to take them over to a small bar and restaurant just north of the airstrip: Calico Jack's. One uneventful lunch later, they were back at Viktor's AW139. Their helicopter neighbor from before was now gone, but there was a lovely executive jet parked off to the side. Viktor made a mental note to look into prices for such a plane. If this deal with the new weapon went off as planned, he'd probably be in the market for one.

Once aboard the helicopter, Viktor punched the intercom as the engines spooled up. "Diego... make another circle of the island before we head back. I want to see if there are any new arrivals."

The pilot agreed and looped around the island. Sergei took more pictures, but he and Viktor concluded nothing had changed. Ten minutes later they arrived over South Caicos and Viktor's phone dinged with a text as they came into range of telecom coverage. As expected, it was from Paz.

Viktor read it and shook his head. "It's always something," he muttered.

"What's up?" Sergei asked.

"Apparently, the new components aren't an exact fit, so Paz is having to make some adjustments. We won't be able to test the device until this evening."

"Works for me," Sergei said, then chuckled at some private joke. When Viktor gave him an expectant look, the man added. "Winner, winner, chicken dinner."

Viktor rolled his eyes. "It's not that kind of—"

"Señor," the intercom interrupted.

"Yes, Diego?" Viktor looked out the window. They'd be landing in a minute or less. "Is there a problem?"

"No, señor, but... I had a thought. Back on Ambergris, what were you looking for?"

"That's above your pay grade," Viktor said. Inwardly, he laughed at the irony. Apparently, that information was above *his* pay grade, too... since Moscow hadn't seen fit to tell him.

"Yes, señor. However, if I may... One moment, let me land first."

Three minutes later, Baptiste opened the cabin door. He started to say something, but Viktor waved him away and went to the pilot's door. Diego opened it, but remained seated, his checklist in its metal binder atop his lap.

"Señor, it occurs to me that you were looking for a boat or ship of some kind. And I didn't see much of interest myself."

"And...?"

"Well... I am thinking if you had seen a large ship down there... like a yacht... that might have been different."

"But there wasn't anything like that," Viktor said with annoyance.

"Not yet."

"What are you talking about?"

"Do you remember the helicopter that we were beside when we landed?"

"Yes...?"

"It left before you returned, but while you were at lunch, I spoke with the pilot. He was from Panama, so we talked a little about our homes. Anyway, he had flown there from a superyacht to make some advance arrangements for his boss's upcoming visit."

"Who is his boss?"

"He didn't say. But he mentioned the name of the ship. The *Anya*."

"Change of plans," Mateo announced as he approached Boone and Emily's table in the East Bay Resort's restaurant, the BLU Bar and Grill.

"Pull up a taco," Em said, nudging her plate of fish tacos toward Mateo. "Delish, but I'm stuffed!"

He smiled. "Very generous, but I just had some."

"What's the change of plans?" Boone asked.

"Well... your group has decided to take the kayak trip up near Plandon Bay instead of doing the afternoon dive."

"After a hammerhead encounter?" Boone looked incredulous. "I'd've expected they'd be requesting we go right back out and see if he's back!"

"*You* want to go right back out and see if he's back," Emily teased.

"One of the divers had a little trouble equalizing and wanted to skip," Mateo explained. "But it's such a beautiful day, they decided to do the kayak trip."

"So... rest of the day off, you're saying?" Em asked.

"Well... not exactly. Lincoln is going to work aboard *Big Sister* again, and in the meantime, I have something I would very much like to accomplish, if your boat is available."

Boone reached over and took a slice of plantain from Emily's plate. "Sure. What's up?"

"The TCI Reef Fund is here to replace one of the moorings. Unfortunately, the other Newton being down is a problem. We were going to go over to the harbor and try to hire a fishing vessel, but Doug knows most of the boats, and didn't think any was suitable."

"What happened to the mooring?

"The concrete is badly cracked, and the pin came partway out and is bent. Sometimes a larger vessel will use one of our moorings, but they're not designed for that."

"So, what do you need from us?" Emily asked.

"We'd like to operate the drill from the *Lunasea*. First... do you have the ability to deploy a stern anchor?"

"Yes indeedy. Boone and I added a pushpit bracket to handle one, in case we needed to moor in rough seas. Got the anchor stored below."

"Excellent. And for the drill, there's a powerpack that is fairly large, and ninety feet of hose for the hydraulics."

"She can handle that," Boone said. "We helped with a movie shoot in the Caymans and had a lot of camera equipment bolted securely across the deck near the stern. We actually left some of the fixtures in place, in case we ever wanted to install something temporarily."

"Serendipity-doo!" Em declared. "How deep is the mooring?"

Mateo checked a note on his phone. "Fifty-one feet. The site is Honeycomb, over on the southeast corner. It's all by itself over there, which might be why a passing ship would have used that mooring."

"About how long does the process take?" Boone asked, as he swiped Em's uneaten taco.

"Hard to say. Depends on the material we drill into, but we'll probably be at it all afternoon. Using that drill can be very taxing, so the divers take turns. Five to ten minutes at a time."

"How many divers?"

"Four. Three from TCI Reef Fund and myself."

"I want to drill, too!" Emily proclaimed.

"No offense intended, but... how tall are you?"

"I aspire to five feet."

Boone smiled. "She's four-eleven on a good day."

Em dipped her fingertips into her waterglass and flicked droplets into Boone's face.

"The drill is quite large, I'm afraid," Mateo said. "But I was planning for one of you to be our go-between. You would snorkel near the stern, and relay signals from the divers below to the crew manning the power pack."

"Ooh, that sounds like fun." Em grabbed her napkin from her lap and slapped it on the table. "If Boone is done eating the rest of my lunch, I'm ready to go. I'm guessing you'd like us now-ish?"

"Yes, if that's okay."

"You're the boss-of-the-week, so we're at your service."

An hour later the *Lunasea* was approaching the southeast corner of South Caicos. At the flybridge wheel, Emily looked up at the bluffs above. Highland House stood at the highest point, surrounded by low brush.

"We're almost there," Mateo said from one of the benches. Across from him, Boone was relaxing in the early afternoon sun. Below, the TCI Reef Fund members were assembling gear.

Em looked again at the old manor house on the hill beyond the cliffs. "Blimey, that place gives me the creeps."

Mateo laughed. "It's just an old home, once owned by a wealthy family in the early 1900s. The real estate company that owns Reefview bought the land it's on, but they haven't done anything with it. Rumor is the cartel used it as a place to, uh... punish people."

"Yeah, we heard some of that punishment might involve a rope," Emily said with a shudder.

"I can give you a tour, if you like."

"Hard pass."

"Oh, c'mon Em," Boone cajoled. "Might be fun."

"Seems really arid here," Emily observed, forcing a change in subject. "Kind of like Bonaire, though not quite as deserty."

"Yes, we get strong trade winds, and the rainfall is only about twenty inches a year, but it's double that if you go farther west toward Provo." Mateo swept a hand across the bluffs. "You may have noticed there aren't many trees. About a century ago, they cut down most of the high trees to decrease the humidity and improve the evaporation in the salt ponds."

"I see a buoy." Em pointed ahead.

"Oh! Yes! I love the history on this island, and if you get me going, I can forget what I was doing. That buoy is Honeycomb."

"But I'm guessing we don't want to moor to that, if we're replacing it."

"No, we will anchor above the mooring. Two anchors: your primary, and an additional one at the stern. We've placed most of the mooring pins some distance away from the main reef, but just in case, I will go below and guide the anchors as needed."

"Then you better gear up!" Emily suggested.

In short order, the *Lunasea* was stationary above the drilling area and Emily descended from the flybridge to join the others, arriving just in time to see Mateo climb up the swim ladder.

TCI Reef Fund in Provo had sent a team of four: A man who went by "Tewks" would remain on board to operate the power to the drill and assemble the mooring line system. In addition to Mateo, two women and a man—Zofia, Alizee, and Willis— would comprise the drilling team.

At the moment, the Reef Fund divers were examining the underwater drill, which looked an awful lot like a jackhammer. Alizee spotted Emily. "Ah, perfect timing. I understand you'll be our snorkeler go-between. Let's go over the signals."

Emily quickly learned that there were two signals she'd be seeing most often: an "OK" gesture from the drill operator meant "power on" and crossed forearms meant "cut the power." After receiving the signal, she'd pop her head up and relay it to the boat.

"Boone, you'll be 'surface support' along with Tewks," Alizee said. She gestured at the generator affixed between the dive benches. "That makes a lot of noise, so when the drill's going, you'll remain near Emily and relay a shutdown request to Tewks."

"Got it," Boone said. "Hey, just curious... I'm guessing the driller needs to wear a lot of extra weight to keep from floating around?"

Zofia, a striking woman with elaborate arm tattoos, lifted up a pocketed weight belt and modeled it like a flight attendant showing off a sample seatbelt.

"It's two pocketed weight belts clipped together," Alizee explained. "When it's a diver's turn to drill, they'll ditch their fins, get in position, and then the diver they're taking over for will drape that over the new driller's shoulders. And during the drilling, one of the other divers will use one of the discarded fins to fan away the sediment and debris."

Willis looked at his watch. "We better get a move on."

"Right!" Alizee clapped her hands together. "The drilling takes a long time, and the underwater epoxy we use takes a while to set, so we'd better get wet. Suit up everyone!"

Nearly an hour and a half later, Emily was hanging off the stern ladder watching the drilling, when a deep thrumming reached her ears. The sound of the generator was resonating through the dive boat's hull, so she didn't hear the approaching vessel until it was quite close. She raised her head from the water and was shocked to find a massive yacht passing by on the far side of the *Lunasea*, moving at high speed toward the east. And then the wake arrived.

Emily felt the ladder rise out of the water, hauling her up with it. It wasn't a massive amount of chop, by any means—Em had dived in five-foot seas before, and this was a ripple compared to that. Nevertheless, the sudden wake had an effect on their link to the drill, and Emily watched the hydraulic hose lose its slack and go taut.

Em immediately jammed her mask under the water and was greeted with the sight of two divers frantically giving her the signal to cut the power, the tethered drill floating free of the hole. She did a pull-up on the ladder, hauling herself high out of the water and shouting, "Cut the power! Cut the power!"

Boone was nowhere in sight, but Tewks had anticipated the request and killed the juice to the drill.

"Did you see the size of that thing?" he yelled. "Crazy bastard."

"Where's Boone?"

"On the flybridge. He ran up to radio that idiot to slow down or veer away, but it was already too close."

Emily spared a glance toward the gleaming white hull of the receding superyacht, squinting to make out the name on the stern, then let go of the ladder and dropped back into the water. Alizee was looking up at her, the drill lying on the bottom several feet from where they'd been drilling. The woman gave her a wave. Em figured she'd have flashed her an "OK" under normal circumstances, but since they were using that signal to turn on the drill, a wave from her was sufficient. Em, on the other hand, stuck with standard diver-speak. She pointed deliberately at the drill then pumped an "OK" sign and shrugged.

Alizee gave her an exaggerated nod, then looked over her shoulder as Willis picked up the mooring pin and slid it into the hole. The visibility was excellent, and Em could easily see that the rod was only sticking up a little bit from the sea floor. *Good. Just a few inches to go.*

EIGHTEEN

The drilling done, the divers rested back aboard the *Lunasea*, waiting for Willis to attach the drill and the double weight belt to the line they'd dropped over the side. Once those items were hauled up, they'd call it a day.

"Great work, everyone!" Alizee said. "Except for that little snafu, it went well. What caused the hose to go taut?"

"Huge superyacht, with a bleedin' wazzock at the helm," Emily said.

"Too close, too fast," Tewks muttered. "I've half a mind to report it."

"Sorry we didn't spot it sooner," Boone said, "but I didn't hear it over the sound of the generator."

"Probably on its way to anchor in the bay," Mateo surmised.

Emily scoffed. "No way that stonker can make it through the channel!"

"No, the bigger yachts have to go to the far end of Long Cay and come into the bay from that side." Mateo explained. "Usually, they come in North of Middleton Cay and south of Moxy Bush."

"Wait, what was that second one?" Emily asked with a smile.

"Moxy Bush. It's a clump of mangroves. Lots of frigatebirds make their nests there."

Emily turned to Boone and tipped her big sunglasses down. "Moxy Bush is my new stage name, if I ever find myself starring in a sexy burlesque. Make a note of it."

Boone laughed, then kicked at a coil of line on the deck. "What about installing the actual mooring?"

"Not enough daylight left," Alizee said. "We'll come back tomorrow and finish up."

"You need us again tomorrow?" Emily asked.

"They won't, but Reef Divers will!" Mateo said. "We'll need the *Lunasea* to join the *Big Sister* for the diving again, and the resort's twenty-nine-foot Panga dive boat is sufficient to rig the lines."

Once the drill was brought back aboard, Willis exited the water and the *Lunasea* made its way back to Cockburn Harbour. After passing through the gap between Dove and Long Cays, Emily piloted the Delta Canaveral toward the dock.

"There's the culprit," Boone remarked, pointing toward the setting sun.

Emily turned her head and saw the massive yacht at anchor about a mile away in the shallows of the bay. She throttled down and everyone clambered to the port side to get a look.

"Definitely qualifies as a superyacht," Boone said. "Not as big as the *Apollo*, though."

Emily nodded. Boone was referring to a ship owned by the Othonos family. Boone and Em had been unlucky enough to be aboard when a hijacking had gone down. That vessel had been more of a hybrid between mega-yacht and cruise ship, while this one appeared to be a superyacht of the type that had become popular with the ultra-rich over the last two decades. Em guessed it was three or four hundred feet in length. Gleaming white and possessing elegant lines, the ship's multi-tiered bridge sloped down to an exceptionally long bow.

"Looks like it has a helicopter," Boone said, peering through his birding binoculars. Can't make out the name of the yacht, though."

"It's *Anya*," Emily said. "Managed to read it on the stern right after its wake treated me to a thrill ride."

"Probably named for some rich guy's wife."

"Or mistress..." Emily added, before throttling back up. "Wonder who owns it?"

"Dmitry Evgenevich Rublev," Viktor read aloud. Sergei and Paz were with him in Paz's workshop, gathered in front of a workstation monitor. On the screen was a site for yacht spotters, specifically a page devoted to the 110-meter, 470-ton superyacht *Anya*.

"Sounds Russian," Paz said.

"He is."

"You know him?"

"Not personally, but yes. Yes, I do."

"I thought that, because of the war in Ukraine, oligarchs were having their yachts seized by the West," Paz said. "I read about one captured in Gibraltar... and another in Fiji."

Viktor nodded, a smile growing on his lips. After Russia's invasion of Ukraine, a devastating barrage of sanctions rained down on Russia and her elite. Many of the oligarchs who were in Putin's pocket had been targeted, and a lot of their assets had been seized, the highest profile of which were a number of superyachts. But not the *Anya*. And he knew why.

Viktor leaned back in the office chair. "If a yacht-owning oligarch is an ally of Putin, then yes... his ship might be seized. But if, on the other hand..." He trailed off. "This is what they were looking for in Ambergris," he whispered. "I shall have to give Diego a bonus for his insight."

"What does any of this have to do with our projects?" Paz asked.

"Nothing." *Although... one of them might come in handy,* he thought. "No, this is simply a matter of an asset being in the right place at the right time. The asset being me. The reason the West has not seized this yacht... is because Rublev is a staunch opponent of Putin's war."

"I thought it was a special operation," Sergei said.

"Don't be an idiot. Of course it's a war. A costly one. And Rublev thinks Putin is bringing ruin on the Russian state, setting us back fifty years."

"Well, he's not wrong," Paz said. The Cuban had been against the invasion from the beginning.

"Right or wrong, Rublev was once an ally of Putin," Viktor explained, "but now he's calling for him to step down, and for cooler heads to take over and end the war. And when someone with money or influence speaks out against Putin... their life expectancy is short. This has been happening for years, but since the invasion of Ukraine, oligarchs and businessmen have been dropping like flies. Often several a month."

"Poison," Sergei said, nodding.

"You're thinking of the nerve agent Novichok... or sometimes polonium-210," Viktor said. "Those were mostly used on dissidents or defectors some years back. No, nothing fancy now. Staged suicides, hangings, close-range gunshots... those are popular; a number of businessmen with ties to Gazprom went that way. A chairman and a board member of Lukoil both died mysteriously: one died when he was given a hangover cure with toad poison in it... the other was being treated in the best hospital in Moscow, but somehow managed to fall out of a sixth-story window while smoking a cigarette. Quite a large number have fallen down stairs, fallen off of cliffs or balconies, fallen overboard from yachts. Gravity is certainly cost effective."

"So, you think your... 'employers' are planning something similar for the owner of the *Anya*?" Paz asked.

"Possibly..." Viktor ran his tongue over his aching tooth, thinking. He winced when he pressed his tongue too hard, the jolt of pain granting him a flash of clarity. *If I find the ship and tell them, they'll give me a pat on the back and send someone to do the job. But if I take care of it myself...* He rotated the chair to look at the engineer. "Are we on schedule for the test this evening?"

"Yes. I was about to run the last diagnostic."

"Good. And what about the other venture?"

"Well... it's been on the back burner, obviously."

"I realize that, but humor me. Could it be employed... this week?"

Paz removed his glasses and dabbed at a spot with his shirttail, a habit that was likely more to stall for time than to deal with any actual blemish on the lens. "I believe I've achieved the sixty kilowatts I was aiming for, but the issue is stabilization if they want it ship-mounted. As for using it this week... that would depend on what you want tested."

Viktor looked meaningfully toward the monitor, then back at Paz.

"Oh. Absolutely not," the Cuban said. "The output is sufficient to down a drone or detonate the fuel in an outboard motor... but it would have next to no effect on a ship that size."

Viktor sighed. "I thought as much." He looked again at the monitor. "Sergei... go find Diego. Tell him I want two flights a day to Ambergris Cay." He pointed at the image of the *Anya*. "If he sees that, tell him to take pictures and come straight back and report to me."

"And if we find it?" Sergei asked.

"I will burn that bridge when I get to it," Viktor said, deliberately mangling the English idiom. "Paz, I'm going for a swim. Come get me when it's time to fry some chickens."

———

"You really don't have to do this," Boone protested.

"We insist," Alizee said, leading the way across the street to The Sunset Café. "Treating you to a sunset dinner is the least we can do."

As they reached the base of the restaurant's rustic, wrap-around deck, the old Haitian fisherman from the pier was just descending the steps, counting some US currency.

Boone let the others go ahead to find a table, gesturing Emily to hang back. "Hey, Mack! Good to see you."

"Oh, hello! You comin' for dinner?"

"We are."

"Well, if you were wantin' to eat my fish, now's your chance. Jus' delivered some mutton snapper."

"We'll definitely order that!" Em declared.

"You see de big yacht out dere?"

"We did," Boone said. "Emily had a bit of a close encounter with it when it buzzed the dive boat."

"Yeah, I heard dey was goin' fast. Maybe dey was behind schedule or somet'ing."

"Hey, Mack, just curious if you've seen that guy again," Boone said. "The man who was asking about us... who took a look at our boat?"

"No, he not been by. As I say before, Baptiste work up on de nort' side of de island. Don't see him often."

"Wait, who is this?" Emily asked.

Boone quickly explained what Mack had told him the day before. "Sorry I didn't mention it, but it didn't seem like a big deal." He turned to Mack. "Thanks for the tip on the fresh snapper!"

"Only brought him six," Mack said. "But if dey run out, Sunset make a mean chicken." He cocked his head. "Chicken..."

After a pause, Emily prompted, "Chicken chicken?"

Mack blinked. "You know, Baptiste... before he ask 'bout you two, he ask somet'ing else. He wanna know where he could get live chickens."

"Unless he was looking for 'Chicken of the Sea,' seems like an odd thing to ask a fisherman," Em suggested.

"Not really. He know I be here a long, long time. I send him to a woman I know keeps chickens up in de Flat, sout' of de airport." He shrugged. "Anyway, I better get home to my fam'ly for our own dinner. Guess what we havin'?" As he walked away, Mack clucked like a chicken and waggled his skinny elbows, eliciting a laugh from Emily.

Boone and Em joined the others at a pair of tables they'd pulled together and were greeted by the owner, who took everyone's order and went back to the kitchen.

Just as he disappeared from view, a young man in khaki shorts and a white, short-sleeved, button-down shirt with epaulet patches sewn onto the shoulders jogged across the road from the direction of the pier and came running up the steps to the dining deck. Out of breath, he looked around, presumably for a server. He carried two insulated bags, like one might bring on a trip to the grocery store.

Mateo pointed to the door to the kitchen and indoor bar. "If you're looking for the owner, he's in there."

"Thank you," the man gasped, then ducked inside.

"Whattaya bet he's a crewman from the *Anya*?" Emily said.

"No bet," Boone said. "Probably sent to pick up some ready-made food."

The crewman reappeared in the dining area and sheepishly approached their table. "Um... pardon me. I've got an unusual request..."

"If you're about to ask for a boat safety course for your captain, I'd be happy to oblige," Emily snarked.

The man looked confused for a second, then his eyes went wide. "Oh my gosh, you're from that dive boat we passed! I'm so sorry about that. Our owner was at the wheel at the time. The captain tried to take over, but... well... there's something of a language barrier, and Mr. Rublev can be a bit difficult."

"Rublev is the captain?" Boone asked.

"Oh, no... that's Captain Sorensen. He's from Denmark. The yacht's owner, Mr. Rublev, is Russian." The crewman laughed. "We're quite the melting pot over there."

"Stephen, is it?" Boone read from a slim, gold name badge on the man's chest. "You sound like you're from the States."

"Yeah. Florida. I'm the only American aboard, but we've got a crew of thirty-two from all over Europe, and a few from Indonesia and the Philippines."

"Wait... you're on a superyacht owned by a rich Russian?" Emily asked. "What do they call them... oligarchs? I thought all those fancy oligarch yachts were getting seized, on account of

Russia invading Ukraine. Like that one that got nabbed in Gibraltar."

Stephen smiled. "Unless you're a vocal opponent of Putin and his war. In which case, the West lets you keep your boat. Mr. Rublev is not a fan of Putin." He suddenly looked at his watch. "Look, I'm sorry about that close pass. That wasn't cool. But... my boss is pretty demanding, and he sent me ashore for some fresh grilled snapper for him and his wife and kids, and he read about this restaurant, and..." He waved helplessly toward the kitchen. "The owner said he just got in some snapper, fresh off the boat, but..."

"He only got six, and we ordered four of them," Boone said with a chuckle. "How many do you need?"

"Four... so, I'm short two."

"Em...?"

Emily gave him a lopsided grin. "Chicken chicken?"

Boone rose from the table. "I'll change our orders to chicken."

"Oh, thank you! Look, I can pay you for your trouble."

"Nah, that's not necess—"

"Well, hang on a tick," Em interrupted. "Are *you* paying? Or is the owner of a multi-million-dollar yacht who nearly capsized us paying?"

Stephen grinned. "The second one. Hundred bucks?"

Emily made a great show of thinking, "Hmm, well, gee, I suppose. If we must."

Stephen took out a money clip and peeled off a hundred-dollar bill.

"You got anything smaller?" Em asked with a raised eyebrow.

Stephen laughed and selected two fifties instead.

"Pleasure doing business with you." Emily took the bills

and stuffed them into a shorts pocket. "Drinks are on yacht guy!" she declared.

While Boone went in to change the orders, Em pulled out Boone's chair for the crewman. "Take a load off, Stephen. You want a beer? Your boss is paying."

"Thanks, I would, but I have to grab a few things at the supermarket across the street."

"He's going to do your fish first," Boone said, coming back out.

"Great! Thank you again. I'll be right back."

As Stephen left, the owner returned with drinks on a tray, which he set down on a nearby table. "Mateo, you heard de latest about de body you found?" he asked, as he handed out everyone's order.

Mateo looked uncomfortable and shook his head. "I heard they found something in his throat..."

"Oh, dat! I got some news on dat, too. But de body, dey moved it to de United States after de pathologist from de Bahamas got here and took a look at it. Constable Terrance was by. Now dat it's out of his hands, he share a bit more. For one t'ing... he show me dis."

He took out his phone, pulled up a photo, and turned it to face the table. The image was of a small object in an evidence bag. "Dis what dey found in de man's t'roat."

"Looks like a little bag with a drawstring," Em remarked. "What's in it?"

"Terrance didn't say and I don't t'ink he know, but I show it to Mack just now, and he say it's a *wanga*. Like a little charm. For protection, most like."

"Didn't do a very good job, did it?" Emily said quietly.

"They figure out how he died?" Boone asked.

"No. Dey know de 'when'... 'bout four or five hours before

177

you find him, Mateo. But as to *how* he die... well, dat's why dey move de body to a place wit' better facilities."

"Was it murder?" Boone asked.

"If it was, dey don't know what de murder weapon is. Terrance say de skin on de man's face was blotchy and blistered. Worse... say de man's eyes looked like dey partly melted. But no sign of a wound. Weird death and dat strange bag... maybe he be hexed. Some sort of... voodoo curse."

NINETEEN

Paz made a final series of adjustments and stepped back from the device to join Viktor and Sergei, standing several yards away beside a video camera on a tripod. "Ready for the test subject," the Cuban announced.

"Good. We're almost out of daylight," Viktor said. "Baptiste...?"

The Haitian bodyguard opened a cage that lay in the sandy scrub and extracted one of the chickens they'd managed to procure. The fowl didn't seem particularly pleased with its current situation and flapped its wings in a flurry of feathers. Baptiste brought it over to the tether they'd staked in the ground about fifty yards from the device. Getting the chicken's leg into the loop proved difficult.

Viktor sighed with exasperation. "Sergei, go help him." As the muscular bodyguard went to assist, Viktor looked to the west. Atop this ridge, he could see the sun dipping below the horizon across the shallow waters of the Caicos Bank north of Bell Sound. "We'll need to use the lights."

"What about our neighbor?" Paz asked.

From here, only the flat roofs of the Coast Guard station's buildings were in view, along with the one radio mast and its blinking red light. "He always leaves before the sun goes down," Viktor assured the engineer. "With no lights on that road, who could blame him? We'll be fine. Besides, we're not *that* close." He stooped, took hold of the small spotlight and telescoped its stand, then powered on the light, its forty-volt battery providing plenty of charge.

They had set up their experiment on the border between the nearest unsold plot just north of the two that Viktor owned. There was an old shipping container with kayaks in it on the bay side about a quarter-mile away, but it rarely saw nighttime use. With the exception of the radio disc jockey to the north and the staff of Viktor's own villa to the south, there was no one around for miles.

Sergei and Baptiste rejoined the others, and while Viktor assembled a second light, Paz lifted a small controller with a joystick on one side, various buttons on the other, and a screen in the center. "Targeting camera on."

Viktor looked down at the screen and saw the chicken in closeup, crosshairs settled on the bird. But then it fluttered its wings and moved outside of the reticles. "Shouldn't we reduce the length of the tether?"

"No, that's part of the goal of this test: to see if the device can deal with a moving target. If I can get the recognition software to lock on..." Paz moved the joystick and brought the crosshairs onto the chicken once again, occasionally nudging the controls when the target moved. The crosshairs blinked. "There!"

Several yards away from them, the device atop the tripod moved of its own accord, tracking the chicken. The device was designed to be handheld, but the engineer wanted precision for this test. Paz instructed Sergei to start the video camera to record the test. Baptiste readied a fire extinguisher, in the event this new configuration suffered a battery burn as their last experiment had.

"Are we far enough away?" Baptiste asked nervously. "I saw what dat t'ing did to de groundskeeper."

"The beam is focused and directional. We should be fine," Paz assured him. "Although everyone should put on their eye protection."

The men put on the wraparound safety glasses that Paz had procured from a medical supply company. Used by technicians working around radiation on a day-to-day basis, the leaded lenses of the heavy glasses would offer protection from errant radiation. Given its water content, the human eye was particularly vulnerable to the emissions from the device that now stood so close to them.

Paz flipped up a plastic guard on the controller, revealing a metal toggle switch. "Firing in three... two..."

Microwave weaponry had been around, in one form or another, since the 1970s—at first theoretically, and then more practically. Projected microwave radiation had been extensively tested by the United States military for an "active denial system" to disperse crowds, although its broad, indiscriminate focus and reduced effectiveness versus targets in thick clothing had prevented it from seeing operational use. Anti-drone weaponry utilizing microwaves existed, the energy pulses being used to sever the control link between a drone and its operator, or even to drain their batteries. Both sides in the Russo-Ukrainian conflict were deploying such devices, and many were handheld, operating much like a rifle.

But the weapon that had inspired the device currently

tracking a restless chicken was one that much of the world wasn't even sure existed—which made it an ideal tool for use by clandestine services. Plausible deniability was built in, since it could affect a target invisibly and penetrate many materials.

In Cuba in 2016, members of Canadian and US embassy staff in Havana reported strange symptoms: discomfort, pressure or vibration in their heads and/or ears and auditory hallucinations. These effects lasted for twenty to thirty seconds, and other individuals in adjacent rooms experienced no such sensations.

Over the following years, more incidents occurred among American diplomats and government officials in numerous places across the world, including Moscow, Berlin, Washington D.C., and Guangzhou, China.

Many of the victims displayed persistent symptoms that included vertigo, loss of hearing, nosebleeds, and headaches, and a number of them who received MRIs showed signs of traumatic brain injury. Soon, many were referring to these effects as the Havana Syndrome. Now that the phenomenon had a catchy name, the media and the public took greater interest.

Nevertheless, lengthy studies were inconclusive, and it was even suggested that these incidents were all some form of mass hysteria. The Cuban government came out with its own study, authored by sixteen individuals from the Cuban Academy of Scientists, that declared no known form of directed energy could cause the type of brain injury being reported.

But one Cuban scientist—and engineer—didn't agree. Of the many narratives to explain Havana Syndrome, Paz Cisneros believed the hypothesis that a number of former members of Western intelligence services had suggested: that the symptoms and injuries were the result of a high-tech data-mining method, and the actual targets of the pulsed microwave energy weren't the diplomats, but rather their storage devices: cell phones, laptops, and workstations. And that the effects on the brains and nervous systems of victims were accidental. Collateral damage. As for the likely culprit, Paz put his money on Russia—specifically the GRU.

But if such damage could be done accidentally, Paz reasoned, then certainly this unknown device could be adjusted to do that damage deliberately... and to do it far more catastrophically.

Paz was familiar with a dark-tech project undertaken some years ago by the United States R&D group DARPA, lightheartedly named the Hello, Goodbye, and Goodnight Project. Its goal: to create viable high-power microwave—HPM —weapons.

"Hello" referred to their use to produce auditory hallucinations by microwave-heating of the inner ear—similar to effects that seemed to have occurred in victims of the Havana Syndrome. "Goodbye" referred to area active denial and had led to the riot control system that was being tested by the US military. And then there was "Goodnight." Its goal: lethality. A death ray.

Sources claimed that the Goodnight portion of DARPA's project had proved unfeasible... but of course, that is exactly what one would say if such a weapon actually worked.

Regardless, Paz believed he had enough to go on to begin designing an HPM weapon of his own, and by varying the speed of the pulses on the carrier wave and emitting two variable wavelengths—one piggybacking on top of the other—he had been able to generate a beam that could do massive amounts of damage to soft tissues, skin, and the nervous system at its highest setting. And with further testing at lower settings, he expected he could find the right frequencies to kill a target without overt, outward signs of damage.

His original prototype took up the entire bed of a pickup truck. Unfortunately, attaining portability was a hurdle Paz did not have the resources for. Advances in microcircuits and batteries would allow him to scale down the weapon, if only he could afford these innovations.

Enter Viktor Gusev. After Paz's initial design showed promise, he'd sent out feelers on the dark web, looking for a buyer or investor. An individual had responded, suggesting a meeting at a resort in the Dominican Republic, and wiring fifty thousand dollars as a sweetener.

At first, Paz had assumed the Russian was GRU, but he'd quickly realized that Viktor was, at best, on the periphery of Moscow's intelligence services. The weapons dealer was eager for a success and had plenty of money to acquire the technologies that Paz needed. As an added bonus, he was based in South Caicos, less than two hundred miles from Cuba.

And now, they were on the verge of their final test. If all went well, he would be an extremely wealthy man in just a matter of days.

Finger poised above the switch, Paz confirmed that the crosshairs were still locked on the target. "...one." He flipped the switch.

At first, nothing happened. All four men *might* have heard a sound, might have felt something in the air, but if they did, the sensations were so faint one might believe they were imagining them. But on the other end of the invisible beam, the hapless chicken had no such doubts.

Squawking and shrieking, the bird burst into a frenzy of flapping as the weapon bathed its body in high-intensity microwaves. The tracking software kept the beam focused on the fluttering object, until...

"*Mierda!*" Paz swore, as the chicken suddenly broke loose of the tether and hurtled into the air, leap-gliding twenty feet away before staggering off into the brush, heading north in a wild panic, its squawks fading as it left the glow of the spotlights and vanished into the post-sunset gloom. The weapon continued to track its target, blasting its microwaves after the retreating chicken before the bird was lost to its sensors.

Paz killed the beam and muttered a stream of Spanish obscenities. Viktor patted the man on the shoulder. "This is why I asked for extra chickens. Baptiste, grab another one. And make sure you tether it securely this time!"

Deejay Ceejay hated driving on the rough northern roads in the dark, but he'd gotten caught up in the music and left later than usual. When he'd stepped out, the sunset had been so beautiful, he'd decided to relax and enjoy it.

After the oranges and pinks dimmed, and the sun dipped beneath the horizon, CJ walked along the packed sand and coral of the road beside the Coast Guard station and got into his little blue Honda. He was about to turn on the headlights when a glow caught his eye; a light in the brush atop a rise to the south.

Pretty sure that wasn't there a moment ago, CJ thought. *And there's nothing up there. The nearest house is a quarter mile away— that rich guy with the helicopter.*

Then, a second glow, like a light had been turned on. CJ got out of the car and listened. A breeze off the ocean made it difficult to hear, but he thought he heard voices. Curious, he walked past the unused Coast Guard building south of the one that housed his radio station and headed toward the lights on the hill.

The moon wasn't yet out, but the twilight glow was enough to allow him to pick his way through the scrub. He paused to listen again. *Definitely voices. And... clucking?* CJ pressed forward and was just coming up the rise when the clucks became frenzied squawks. He froze as he heard a voice shout a curse, and the chicken sounds became louder. Then... *something* started to happen to him.

A bizarre buzzing, crackling sound filled his ears and his skin felt hot and prickly. Just as abruptly, the sensation ceased. The fluttering and squawking seemed to be approaching, and CJ was about to take out his phone to use the flashlight when the strange symptoms washed over him again. This time, the sounds in his head were louder and his skin felt like it was burning. Then his head was suddenly assaulted with skull-splitting pain. Thankfully, this second onslaught was shorter than the first.

Deejay Ceejay didn't hesitate; he turned and ran for his car. He started her up and slowly drove down the hill toward the main road, and despite his loathing of driving in the dark, he kept his headlights off until he was well away from the Coast Guard station.

I don't know what the hell just happened... whether those were hallucinations or something else, but just in case...

Reaching the main road, he pulled over to the side, rolled down the window, and tossed a baggie into the brush. It was a recent purchase and he was sad to see it go, but a bad batch of ganja might explain what had occurred. Besides, he was planning on quitting anyway.

Back from the Sunset Café, Boone and Emily joined Mateo on the East Bay beach for an after-dinner stroll—or a "postprandial promenade" as Emily insisted on calling it. The moon was just past full, but still very impressive. Tinted gold, it looked gigantic as it rose above the ocean outside the bay, leaving a pearlescent road in the waters shimmering beneath it.

"It's beautiful," Emily breathed. "Never get tired of it. Luna on the sea."

Mateo laughed. "Luna-sea... I very much like your boat's name."

"I'm quite fond of it," Emily said. "So, what's on tap for tomorrow?"

"Well, several of our repeat divers want to do something a little different, and would like to dive Fish Cay."

"Where's that?" Boone asked.

"About ten miles south of here, on the way to Ambergris Cay."

"The rich folks' private island."

"Ambergris, yes... but Fish Cay is uninhabited. Beautiful beaches. And some excellent diving! I understand your boat is quite fast, yes? Lincoln was bragging about it to Doug."

"Yeah, she's got some pep," Boone said.

"Pep?"

Emily laughed. "Usually, Boone's the one translating for *me*. He means it's fast."

"Pep is good! Given the distance, we thought we'd have you run that dive trip. Two morning dives, then lunch on one of the beaches there, an afternoon dive, and then you'll return."

"Sounds like a plan," Boone said. "You coming with?"

"Yes. I'm one of the few who knows where the best sites are!"

"Is that whole group from the Newton coming over?" Boone asked. "Might be a little cramped."

"No, just eight of them. We'll combine your group with the remainder on *Big Sister*."

"Well, if we've got a long day tomorrow, I s'pose we should... *bring this postprandial promenade to a satisfactory conclusion*," Emily said, letting her rough Londoner accent slide into what she referred to as her "dowager duchess" voice.

Boone laughed and gave her a playful shove so that her feet splashed into the surf line. "If you say 'postprandial' one more time..."

Emily giggled and kicked a glob of wet sand at him. When it came to speaking, Boone was laconic, rarely using three words when one would suffice. A trait that Emily found both sexy and worthy of teasing. "Just 'cause you're deficient in the vocabularic department, doesn't mean the rest of us... *need wallow in your monosyllabic mediocrity.*"

"That's a funny voice," Mateo said, clearly amused.

"*Ooooohhhhh, thank you, my good man,*" Duchess Emily crooned.

"Don't encourage her," Boone said. He pointed into the shallows. "What's that in the water, there? Looks like the remains of an old seawall or dock pilings or something." They were now quite some distance away from the East Bay Resort, and the only light came from the moon and stars.

"Yes, there used to be a resort over here in the casuarinas." Mateo waved an arm inland. "And in waters here, you can see the glowworms. I was curious to see if they would be here, tonight... but it is still too early, I think. Tomorrow, perhaps."

"Oh! I love glowworms!" Emily gushed. "We used to see them in Belize, just after a full moon."

Emily had first noticed this phenomenon when she and Boone were on Caye Caulker. The shallow waters had seemed to glow in patches, with occasional bursts of soft light rising up. Anyone who had been on a few night dives—or even night snorkels—knew that all manner of marine creatures used bioluminescence. But "glowworms" were special, lighting up the waters with their own particular light show.

Ever on the lookout for obscure trivia, Emily had scoured the internet, and had determined the glowing beasties were the polychaete worm *Odontosyllis enopla*, also called the Bermuda fireworm.

"Last night was the full moon, yeah?" Em said. "So maybe tomorrow night."

"Yes, they usually start two days after the full moon... but sometimes it is three or more."

"Well, let's try again tomorrow," Boone suggested.

"Actually, depending on when we get back from Fish Cay," Mateo said, "we could go up to Jerry Camp."

"Where's that?" Boone asked.

"And who's Jerry?" Em added.

"I have no idea who Jerry is, but it's what we call the spot where we have an old shipping container that we store the kayaks in, up near the north tip and the old Coast Guard station. The kayak trips can go right into the beautiful bay beside Plandon Cay Cut. Lots of mangroves, juvenile lemon sharks, stingrays... and glowworms! The best displays I've seen have been there."

"I say we do it!" Emily said.

"I'm also interested in paying *that* a visit," Boone suggested, pointing off to the east. The land was a bit higher in that direction, and only one thing stood on that elevated horizon: Highland House. Its white walls glowed in the moonlight.

"Sure, we can visit it sometime," Mateo said.

"Well, you boys have fun with that," Emily announced. "I'll give it a miss." She stopped and sniffed the air before wrinkling her button nose. "Oh, pee-yew! What is that pong?"

Mateo laughed. "We have a tractor harvester that clears the sargassum from East Bay's beach every morning... and it has to go somewhere."

When he pointed into the gloom near the casuarinas, Emily could make out a huge mound of something in the shadows.

"Cor blimey, that pile of whiffy weed is taller than Boone!"

Boone peered into the gloom down the beach. "Potcake dogs. Looks like the three we saw at the other end of the bay the other day."

Mateo looked "Yes, this is part of their territory, I think."

"Oh, that reminds me!" Emily said, checking the time on her phone. "Let's get back. I'm supposed to call Jorika. We've got a FaceTime date with Brixton!"

"You realize he's just going to hear your voice and go bonkers, wondering where you are," Boone chided.

"I miss the little wubbykins! And hey, maybe Mama's had her pups!"

TWENTY

The following morning, Boone and Emily joined the crews from Reef Divers at the pier. After bringing in the boats and filling the tanks—both the ones for the engines and the ones for the divers—Niles gathered everyone between the boats. "I'm going to be piloting *Big Sister* today... and Doug, you wanted to join the *Lunasea* for the Fish Cay run?"

"Yes, if dat's okay wit' you two," he said, looking toward Boone and Emily. "I want to see what your boat can do!"

"Fine by me," Boone said. "Em and I can dive together, then."

"Absolutely," Niles said. "Mateo will be going along, as he knows the sites there. And I'll steal Lincoln from you again, if that's all right?"

"Sure t'ing," Lincoln said.

"Great. You'll divemaster with Roshane. We'll have a few more divers today, with the combined groups, so we'll add Scott for a third."

"Just don't let him near de wheel!" Doug said.

191

"You have my word on that," Niles responded with a laugh.

"Scott de one who run over de line and bend de shaft on de *Caicos Sister*," Doug explained to Boone and Em.

"All right then, gents and lady, let's get ready for the divers," Niles said. "Mateo will be along with the van shortly."

Boone nodded, looking out across the bay. The *Anya* had weighed anchor and was just starting to move. "Looks like our yacht friend is getting an early start, too."

"Good for her!" Em declared. "Wherever they're off to, maybe they won't feel so rushed this time."

Deejay Ceejay came to a stop outside the Coast Guard station, his wheels crunching in the rough surface of the road beside the main building. Normally, he drove there in the early glow of dawn, arriving in time to greet the sunrise, which was quite stunning when it rose across the channel between South Caicos and Grand Turk. A little coffee, a little meditation... a ritual he enjoyed. But this morning he'd woken with one hell of a hangover... or at least that was what it had felt like. A few extra taps on the snooze button, and his sunrise ritual wasn't in the cards.

Exiting the car, he went around to his hangout spot and sat beside the grill to drink the coffee he'd brought from home. The sun was well above the horizon, but it was still a beautiful sight. Sipping his coffee, CJ felt his gaze straying to the rise in the topography to the south. For the briefest of moments, he thought maybe he should go back up there... see what he could find.

Uh-uh! No sir. Not gonna happen. The strange sensations and sounds were not something he wanted to revisit. *Maybe another day, when the memory isn't so fresh.*

CJ rose from the patio chair and started back to the car to retrieve his laptop and microphone, but froze at the sight of a small shape lying between a stand of stonecrop and the old maintenance bay of the Coast Guard station. A breeze blew across the sand, and the edges of the shape fluttered. Feathers?

Deejay Ceejay slowly approached the object, his mind replaying the clucks he'd heard last night. It was indeed a chicken. And it was dead. And it had no eyes.

"Fish Cay is ten miles from here," Doug said from beside the wheel. Emily was skippering, her pigtails braided and topped by a ballcap, the brim turned backwards to keep it from flying off. Boone and Mateo were below, chatting with the eight divers they had on this trip. They had just left the channel from Conch Ground Bay and were now over the reef and in open water.

"How long's it take you in a Newton?" Emily asked.

"If we're being nice to our fuel, we cruise at about twelve knots. Take 'bout forty-five minutes."

"And your top speed?"

"We never push *Big Sister*... but *Caicos Sister* can hit twenty-five knots."

"Twenty-five? That's adorable," Emily said with a smile.

Doug grinned at her. "You gwan show me whatchu got, or what?"

Em gave him an impish look. "Tell our passengers to have a seat."

Once Doug had informed Boone of Emily's plans, he came alongside her again. "All set."

"Our cruising speed's nearly your top speed," Em said,

making a show of lacing her fingers on the throttle. "And as for *our* top speed... that depends on the sea state, yeah? The *Lunasea*'s hull is built for handling chop, but not cutting through it at high speed. That being said..."

Emily waggled her eyebrows above her big, green sunglasses and eased the throttle forward, slowly bringing the *Lunasea* up to full speed. The dive boat's engine roared and she tore across the water.

Doug whooped and pressed a hand to the black stocking cap on his head. After a minute, Emily throttled down to twenty knots.

"Take the wheel, yeah?" Em said to Doug, then went to the back of the flybridge and caught Boone's eye below.

"You fulfill your need?" he called up.

"The need for speed? Yes, it is officially sated. The seatbelt sign is off, and everyone is free to move about the cabin."

"In that case, I'm coming up."

Doug looked back as Emily returned. "You want de wheel?"

"Nah, you keep on keepin' on."

Doug tapped the single throttle lever. "You only got *one* engine and can hit dat speed?"

"Yeah, a bit of backstory is in order," Em began.

"*Lunasea* used to be *Alhambra*," Boone explained, joining them. "A cartel in Honduras was using a dive op as a front."

"Way to bodge the tale, skipping right to the capper!" Emily protested. "I was gonna give it a slow build."

"Sorry."

"Well, since Boone's ruined everything, I'll skip to the engine. It's a Caterpillar C 12.9. It's a beast! Too big to have two down there, and near as we can tell, the *Alhambra* was a single-engine Canaveral when the cartel got their hands on her and goosed her up."

"So... you renamed her?" Doug asked. "Bad luck, dat."

"We figured keeping the cartel's name wouldn't necessarily be *good* luck," Boone said. "We did a full purging and renaming ceremony."

"Sacrifices to Poseidon, the whole nine yards," Emily added. "She's squared away in the Ledger of the Deep. We even went with a seven-letter name! Good luck, innit?"

"A single engine... bit risky for a dive boat," Doug said.

"Boone here can fix anything that comes up," Em reassured him.

"Well... that's not completely true," Boone hedged. "But I do carry a lot of spare parts and a full set of tools. Breaking down in the middle of nowhere with a full load of paying divers is something I'd prefer to avoid."

Mateo came up top and immediately smiled. "I knew Doug would find a way to get behind the wheel."

"I figured he should get accustomed to 'er, so I can go diving," Em said, sitting on one of the benches.

"Some fishermen out there," Boone noted, as they passed a small boat bobbing in the shallows to the west. "Hey, Mateo, I forgot to ask you... Mack said the fishermen did most of their fishing by freediving with spears, and some Frenchman had taught them back in the day. Jacques something...?"

"Yes. Jacques Mayol."

"Wait... *the* Jacques Mayol?" Boone was stunned.

"The one and only. He had a house on the western side of Bell Sound."

"Who's Jacques Mayol?" Emily asked.

"He was a pioneering freediver," Boone said. "They made a movie about him. He loved dolphins and was fascinated by their ability to hold their breath. Mayol practiced meditation and yoga, and he was the first man to freedive to the 330-foot mark."

"That's insane," Em blurted. "Dare I ask what the record is now?"

"A little over 700 feet, last I heard."

"Yesterday, you said you were a freediver," Mateo said. "How deep have you gone?"

"I don't really do it for records or anything. I'm more interested in how long I can stay down than how deep I get. But the deepest I've gone... well, I freedived to the stalactite overhang in the Blue Hole in Belize. That's about 140 feet."

"You *what?*" Em rose from the bench and gave Boone a double-palmed shove, looking up at him. "I don't remember that! When did you do that?"

"That trip you missed when you were under the weather. That summer head cold."

"Hang on... you mean the one I sat out 'cause I was laid up with a lurgy, and you went ahead without me?"

Boone shrugged. "It was the only day our guests could do it."

Em removed her sunglasses and tucked them in the neck of her T-shirt. "I don't 'ave a problem that you did the charter, it's that you decided to do a dangerous dive without me there! What if something happened?"

"I had Salvador down there with me, with a spare tank. He was manning the boat, so he didn't do the actual dive with the guests. It was a spur of the moment thing."

"Well, next time you feel a momentary spur, check the spot next to yourself and make sure I'm there, yeah?"

Boone looked Em in her green eyes. "Got it. And sorry."

One corner of her lips quirked up in a smile. "Was it cool?"

Boone nodded. "Very."

"You know, there is a blue hole just south of Middle Caicos," Mateo remarked. "Twice the diameter of the one in Belize, and full of hammerheads."

"Hear that Boone? There's your chance for a freedive with a hammy."

Boone laughed. "I think we have enough going on this week, don't you?"

"Ours is 250 feet deep," Mateo said. "Still, 140 feet is impressive."

"I used my freediving fins and extra weights. I'm sure I could go deeper, but that was enough for me."

"You know the story of the first recorded freedive?" Mateo asked.

"If it's the one that happened off the island of Capri, yes... but tell it, so Emily can have another arrow for her trivia quiver."

"Trivia quiver," Em repeated. "I like it."

"Well, in 1949 there were these two men," Mateo began. "An Italian scuba diver and a Hungarian spearfisherman..."

"Sounds like the start of a joke," Em said with a laugh.

"The Hungarian bragged that he could dive to a hundred feet on one breath, and the Italian challenged him to prove it. So, they made a bet—50,000 lire. The Italian dives down to the bottom near Capri and waits in his scuba gear, and he has a cylinder with a piece of paper; the agreement for the bet. Then along comes the Hungarian with nothing but fins and mask, and he takes the cylinder and wins the money."

"Whoa! Fifty thousand smackaroos is a pretty good haul for a hundred-foot dive."

Mateo shrugged. "Fifty thousand lire back then was about eighty dollars."

"We're comin' up on Fish Cay," Doug announced.

Boone looked on the horizon and saw a low island off the starboard bow. They'd been traveling in deeper waters to the east of Fish Cay, and Boone could make out the ocean spray sparkling as the waves washed up against the windward shore.

"Let's go around to the lee side for the dive briefing," Mateo said. "The water is calmer and there are three beaches over there. Very pretty."

Doug turned the wheel to starboard and aimed the *Lunasea* to pass the northernmost point of Fish Cay. Boone was just looking away from the island when he thought he caught movement out of the corner of his eye. He squinted. They were still some distance away, and yet...

"Doug, can you bring us to an idle?" he asked, as he popped open a compartment and retrieved his binoculars.

"What's up, Boone?" Emily asked.

"Maybe nothing. Thought I saw something moving around on the rocks." Boone removed his polarized sunglasses and pressed the binos to his eyes.

"Probably just an iguana," Mateo said.

"It's a man!" Boone exclaimed. "Waving a shirt over his head, looking our way."

"Could be a fisherman, broke down," Doug suggested.

"Budge up!" Emily nudged Doug aside and took the wheel. She began to throttle up. "Have the divers sit tight."

"Take us around to those beaches," Mateo said. "I'll tell the divers to hang on."

Once he was safely down the ladder, Emily pushed the throttle to the stops and the *Lunasea* tore through the water. The jostling their speed imparted to the hull made it impossible for Boone to keep his binoculars on target and he put them away. In moments, they were no longer needed, and he could see the man clearly, still waving frantically. They were moving parallel to the cay, so Boone figured it might appear as if they were heading away without seeing him. Boone stepped to the port rail and waved a long arm over his head. Even from this distance, Boone could see the joy on the man's face. Abruptly, he turned and ran toward the interior, vanishing from sight.

In a minute, the dive boat came around to the leeward side of Fish Cay and the northernmost beach came into view, small and empty and tucked away between two limestone outcrops. Emily continued south and as they passed the middle beach, the third, southernmost beach came into view.

"Blimey..." Emily breathed as she slowed the boat to an idle. "The beach is chockablock with people!"

"I count thirty men and women," Boone began. "No, wait... thirty-one. There's the guy who was signaling us coming down."

"I see some kids, too," Em said. "And that woman in green has a baby."

"Haitian migrants," Mateo said as he mounted the flybridge.

"What are they doing all the way down here?" Em asked.

"Someone dumped dem here," Doug said. "Probably at night, when dey couldn't see where dey was bein' left."

"Back in 2021, we found a group that had been left on Long Cay," Mateo said. "Some of them might pay $2,000 to be taken to Provo or The Bahamas... but the smugglers just find an uninhabited spot with no police around and drop them there. Tell them 'Welcome to The Bahamas' and then leave them stranded. And if some of them don't fall for that, out come the guns."

"Bloody tossers," Emily muttered.

"Some of them are pretty well dressed," Boone noted.

"Dey dress to blend," Doug said. "Might even wear designer clothes, if dey have dem. De smugglers don't always do somet'ing like dis."

"Well, what're we waiting for? Let's pick 'em up," Em said. "Maybe half now, half on a second trip."

"No, not a good idea," Doug said, taking out his cell phone. "Sometimes, de rescued will take de boat from de rescuers. We need police on de scene."

Emily grabbed the mic for the radio. "I'll call for assistance, yeah?"

"Could do, but if I can call de police or immigration office in de harbor directly, dat'd be faster." Doug looked at his phone. "We're ten miles out, but de cell tower is up on de hill above town, so maybe... No. I got no bars."

The others checked their phones, but no one had a strong enough signal.

"We'll try the VHF then, yeah?" Em keyed the mic and broadcast on Channel 16. "Pan-pan, pan-pan, pan-pan," she began, using the distress code for a non-life-threatening emergency. "This is the dive boat *Lunasea*, located on the west side of Fish Cay, ten miles south-southwest of Cockburn Harbour, South Caicos. We have located a group of thirty-plus migrants on Fish Cay, and need police and additional transport, over."

She was just about to repeat the call when a reply came back, the voice tinged with a Scandinavian accent, "*Lunasea, this is the motor yacht* Anya, *at anchor about three nautical miles south of your position. What is the status of the migrants? Is there any imminent danger? Over.*"

"*Anya*, this is *Lunasea*. Migrants are currently on a beach. We don't have any specific evidence of any medical emergency, but there's no telling how long they've been there, over."

"Lunasea... *this is* Anya. *I am seeking permission to assist, over.*"

"Someone was yelling at him in the background," Boone observed. "I'm guessing we're speaking to the Danish captain their crewman told us about."

Emily was about to key a reply when the radio came to life again. "Lunasea, *dis is Officer Troy of de Department of Environment and Coastal Resources in Cockburn Harbour. We have received your information, and will be dispatching a DECR boat to your position once we inform de police and can secure additional officers. We will inform Provo to send a Marine Police unit as well. Over.*"

Doug held out his hand for the mic and Em handed it over. "Troy, it's Doug Cox. You bringin' de *Hammerhead?*"

"*Yes, Doug. Soon as we find a constable, we'll be on our way to you. Over.*"

Doug handed the handset back to Emily. "We won't have to wait too long. De *Hammerhead* is a Whaler with twin 300s. She can hit seventy knots on de flats, but comin' here... she'll probably do about forty. De police boat in Provo is even faster. Trip-350s... one inline, two outboards."

"If they're built for speed, they're not likely built for a lotta passengers," Boone said. "Once we've got a police escort, we can take at least half of the people here."

"I'll let the divers know what's up," Mateo said, and climbed down the ladder just as the radio crackled.

"Lunasea, *this is* Anya. *I've been monitoring your conversation with DECR and will remain at Big Ambergris Cay, out of the way, over.*"

Boone took the mic, "*Anya,* we have over thirty migrants here and might need an additional boat... over."

There was a long pause with no response, before the voice finally returned.

"I'm sorry, Lunasea, *but we won't be able to assist, over."*

"Betcha someone was vetoed by a certain Russian billionaire owner," Em said. "Hope he choked on our snapper."

Boone hung up the mic and went to the railing, looking across at the group on the shore. Many were waving, and he waved back before glancing down at the shallows below. "I'm going to bring the water cooler ashore."

"I'm coming along," Em said. When Boone started to protest, she verbally ran him over. "You need someone to carry the paper cups."

Boone smiled. "In that case, you can carry the first aid kit, too."

"Looked shallower from the boat," Emily spluttered, as she hopped-swam toward the shore, floating the waterproof first aid kit ahead of her.

Boone chuckled as he waded beside her, dragging the yellow-and-red Igloo cooler along, the sleeve of paper cups gripped in his teeth. As soon as Emily had hit the water, it was clear it'd be over her head. For Boone and his six-foot-four height, it wasn't a problem.

Once they reached the surf line and came ashore, the migrants gathered around. Boone realized they had just assumed these people were Haitian, but his ears quickly confirmed that assumption as they picked up the familiar sounds of Haitian Creole, the distinct French vocabulary punctuated with African and West Indian words.

Boone set the Igloo down in the sand and offered cups to the eager hands that surrounded him. Emily knelt beside the water cooler and dug a little divot into the sand beneath the spigot.

A man dressed in a lightweight sport coat and tie stepped up to Boone. "Thank you for finding us. And especially for the water. We have been without." The man spoke English with only a touch of an accent.

"How long have you been here?" Boone asked.

"Since last night. I believe they left us here around midnight but can't be sure. They took all of our phones and watches. Anything of value."

"Sodding bastards," Emily spat.

"Yes. They were. Bastards with guns." He extended a hand. "I am Dr. Ronald Etienne."

"Boone Fischer. And this is Emily Durand."

"*Enchanté.*"

"You a doctor doctor?" Emily asked.

Ronald smiled. "If you mean 'am I a medical doctor,' then yes. And I see you brought a first aid kit; thank you for that as well. We have some minor cuts and bruises among the group, but dehydration was my primary concern."

"Well, hopefully you won't need to wait long. They're sending down a couple boats from South Caicos and Provo."

Far from looking relieved, Ronald appeared sad. "Police and Immigration, no doubt," he said with a sigh. "And everyone will be sent back to Haiti, to do it all over again. Once they save up enough money for another try."

"Where was the ship supposed to take you?" Boone asked.

"Ship? Generous term for that overcrowded trawler. They were supposed to take us to Bonefish Beach on the western side of Providenciales, where a truck would have taken us to the Haitian community of Dock Yard. Once there, some would stay with friends and family in Provo, while others would begin another journey... trying to get to The Bahamas or America or Canada."

"How about you? Where were you headed?"

"Me? I would return to Haiti, once I helped these people reach their destinations. I'm a facilitator of sorts." He appeared to catch himself. "But please don't repeat that."

"Not my circus, not my monkeys," Boone said.

"He means it's none of our business," Emily translated, when Ronald appeared confused by the idiom.

"The boats that are coming are two fast boats," Boone said. "Our dive boat will probably take at least half of you. And we'll probably offer a less bumpy ride."

"Thank you. We'll put the families with you, if that's all right. And I'll come along, as well. We have a pregnant woman, so I should remain close by."

"She's not due, is she?" Em asked with concern.

"No. She's about seven months into the pregnancy."

"Still, I'll keep the speed down with that in mind."

"I'm sure she'd appreciate that."

Boone had noticed that Dr. Etienne hadn't gotten a drink for himself and filled a cup for him.

"*Mèsi*... thank you." He drank the cup down. "I'll speak to everyone. Let them know what to expect."

TWENTY-ONE

Viktor lifted his head from the massage table as the staccato chop of a helicopter reached his ears. Lying under the pergola beside the infinity pool, Viktor had a good view of the ocean below. Soon, the AW139 appeared from the south, slowing to a hover directly across from the pool. Diego caught Viktor's eye and pumped a thumbs up, then jabbed a finger toward the north side of the villa, in the direction of the landing pad. The helicopter nosed down and moved slowly along the cliff.

"I suppose that's it for now, Kirana," he said, climbing down from the table and cinching a towel around his waist.

The Indonesian woman nodded her head and began gathering the sheets and towels. Viktor had been lucky to find her: Kirana doubled as a housekeeper and masseuse, and was skilled at both tasks. And it didn't hurt that she was attractive.

Viktor made his way to his bedroom and threw on some clothes, then hurried out to the landing pad. Diego was just finishing the shutdown process and removed his helmet before stepping down and jogging over to Viktor.

"It's there! The *Anya*!"

"You have pictures?"

"Yes! But I promise you, it is the yacht you are looking for. It is anchored offshore on the lee side of Ambergris Cay, near the small, man-made marina; she is much too large for it."

"Good. Thank you, Diego! Expect a bonus." Viktor left the pad and returned to the villa, debating his options. Information was power; the trick was determining when best to wield it. He reached his office just as his phone dinged. Examining it, he saw a spam robo-text, offering a cure for hair loss along with a link.

"*Svolachs*," Viktor cursed. He recognized the code embedded in the fake URL link, so he knew this wasn't a real advertising robo-text; it was a notification that a call was about to come in on the secure satellite phone. But the hair loss reference was surely a not-so-veiled jab. Viktor had been self-conscious about his steadily receding hairline and bald spot, and last year had undergone hair transplants in Brazil. The results were... disappointing. And yet one more source of amusement to those sons of bitches in Moscow. Viktor resolved to keep the *Anya*'s location to himself, waiting for the maximum advantage.

He retrieved the sat phone from Paz's workshop, waiting for the call. The Cuban didn't even look up, engrossed as he was in his latest calculations. The call came and Viktor turned a dial on the nearby server, making a last-minute adjustment to the encryption before answering.

"This is Viktor," he said.

"Viktor *Gusev*?" the voice on the line said, stressing his last name.

Viktor sighed. "What do you want? I'm very busy."

"We certainly hope so. Have you made those 'adjustments' you needed? Is the device functional or not?"

"It is. We carried out tests on a live subject and the weapon is a success."

"A live *human* subject?"

"No. We used chickens."

A roar of laughter was heard in the background, but the voice on the phone seemed less amused. "We are not paying you to deliver a chicken-killing device, *Gusev*."

"But you already have our data on the weapon's effect on a human subject!" Viktor protested.

"Yes, we do... and the data showed that there was far too much heating of the skin. We need a weapon that can kill without an outward trace. Otherwise, a sniper rifle would be just as useful."

"My engineers solved the thermal effect, boosted the pulse and slowed the wavelengths to better target the brain."

"Wonderful. So... prove it. We will need video as well."

"Goddammit, I already killed one of my staff for you!" Viktor shouted. "I won't kill another!"

"Then I suggest you find someone outside of your staff. We don't care who you use, so long as it isn't a chicken. You have until tomorrow. The ship will arrive at sunrise."

The call ended and Viktor slammed the sat phone down on the table. "Dammit! Paz, what are we going to...?" He stopped, staring at the open doorway. One of the migrants Baptiste had picked up was standing there, eyes wide and mouth open. Viktor couldn't remember the man's name, but he had been helping maintain the grounds the last couple of days. "What did you hear?" Viktor asked.

The man didn't reply, just shook his head in the negative.

Viktor took two steps toward him. "You speak English, don't you?"

The Haitian turned and ran. Right into Sergei.

"Grab him!" Viktor ordered.

His bodyguard easily overpowered the migrant, who was likely still weak from his voyage. Sergei dragged him into the workshop.

"Well... this solves one problem, I suppose," Viktor mused. "But not here. And not where we used the chickens. That was too exposed." After a moment, he smiled. "I know just the spot."

Thirty minutes after Boone and Emily brought the water ashore on Fish Cay, the *Hammerhead* arrived with two DECR officers aboard and a South Caicos constable. No sooner had they motored up to the beach than the marine unit from the Royal Turks and Caicos Islands Police Force came roaring across the waves from the northwest, two armed officers accompanying the captain. After some discussion, the migrants were divvied up onto the three boats. Constable Terrance from South Caicos was assigned to the *Lunasea* as security.

The divers from the East Bay resort helped the Haitian families aboard, after which Mateo and Doug gathered the divers up on the flybridge. Emily climbed up after them to skipper the *Lunasea* back to Cockburn Harbour, while Boone remained below with Ronald and Constable Terrance.

They were halfway back when Boone remembered where he'd heard the man's name. "Constable Terrance... I was talking with the owner of the Sunset Café... is there any more news on that body that was found in the Boiling Hole?"

The man visibly shuddered. "Been tryin' not to t'ink about it." Then he narrowed his eyes. "Didn't know he be tellin' everyone what I tell him. What did he say?"

"Not much. Said the body had no sign of a wound, but the skin was blistered. And the eyes were... damaged."

Terrance shuddered again. "Look like dey partly melted."

"They ever figure out who he was?" Boone asked.

"No. Dey assume he Haitian, but no ID on him."

"If there was no identification, then why assume he's Haitian? Could be from any Caribbean island, right?"

"I s'pose, but he had a tattoo," the constable said, taking out his phone and scrolling through his photos before finding what he was looking for. "A heart wit' '*Chère Roseline*' above and '*Mwen renmen ou anpil amou*' below. Dat last phrase is Haitian Creole. A term of endearment."

"It means 'I love you so very much,'" said Ronald, who was standing nearby.

Terrance nodded to him, then scrolled through more photos and turned to Boone. "You hear what we found in de man's t'roat?"

"Yeah... a little bag. A *wanga*, I think the word was."

"Here... I took a picture of it in de evidence bag." He showed Boone the image, and Ronald leaned in to get a look as well. It was the same photo the restaurant owner had shown them, but Boone didn't mention that.

"I don't know nuttin' 'bout voodoo," Terrance said, "but supposedly dis sort of t'ing is used to cast a spell."

In his peripheral vision, Boone caught Ronald rolling his eyes. Boone glanced at him, and the doctor looked away. "Constable, did you ever find out what was in it?"

"I didn't... but dey open it up in Provo, I hear. It had a lock of hair wit' melted wax on it, and some herbs and ashes. Maybe burnt paper, but my friend don't know for sure."

"Was it the dead man's hair?"

"No. But it come from anuddah Black man, dey say."

Boone looked over at Ronald and could see the man studiously pretending not to be listening in. Boone pointed at the constable's phone. "Do you mind if I take a photo of your photo? I might know someone I can ask about this."

"Well... I suppose. But let me zoom in so you can't see de evidence bag label."

"Good idea." Boone lined up his phone's camera and took a picture of the object on the constable's screen. "Got it. Hey... I understand a pathologist from The Bahamas examined the body, but then they sent it to the States. Any idea why they did that?"

"Because of de CT scan," Terrance said. "A constable friend in Provo told me dey imaged de body, lookin' for de cause of death." He looked at Boone, no doubt enjoying the suspense.

"And...?"

"His brain showed severe trauma and internal bleedin'. Like you'd get from a car crash or somet'ing."

"So, someone killed him with a blow to the head?"

"Dat's just it. No damage to de skull! Not even a bruise. My constable friend hear de pathologist say somet'ing when he call for de body to be moved."

Again, Terrance waited expectantly, until Boone asked, "What did he say?"

"Two words. Havana Syndrome."

As the *Lunasea* came into view of Cockburn Harbour, the *Hammerhead* pulled ahead and one of the DECR officers waved at Emily and beckoned for her to follow them.

"They'll want us to dock at de cargo pier," Doug said. "Immigration is over dere, along wit' a small holdin' area."

Emily followed them to the dock where they'd seen a cargo ship unloading on the day they'd come over from Grand Turk. In minutes, the *Hammerhead*, the *Lunasea*, and the marine police boat were all tied up at the dock. Under the watchful eye of the police, the migrants were gathered in a group near a small building with a sign for Customs and Immigration.

Emily joined Boone, who was speaking with Dr. Etienne. "Ride wasn't too bumpy for your mum-to-be, I hope?"

"Very smooth ride, thank you for that. And thank you both for your assistance and kindness."

"Sorry we couldn't do more," Boone said.

"Yes. I, too, wish I could do more. But for my charges, they will be returned to Haiti, where life grows more uncertain every day. Ever since the assassination of our president in 2021, the country has spiraled into violence. Criminal gangs control more territory than the government now."

Boone put a hand on the man's shoulder. "I hope that all of those you've helped find their way to a better life someday."

Ronald nodded. "I as well." He looked back at the immigration building. "I'd better get back there and help with the interviews, but... that body you and the constable were talking about..."

"I saw you... react when the constable was talking about the magic bag... and about not knowing much about voodoo."

"That is because few do! Hollywood has twisted perceptions of the practice. Vodun is a belief system as much as it is a religion. My mother was a *manbo*—a Vodun healer and priestess—but she was also a Catholic. The two are not mutually exclusive. It was her knowledge of folk remedies that sparked my interest in medicine."

"Did you recognize that little bag?" Boone asked.

"Not that one specifically, and a charm like that is not uncommon in Obeah, either, so it might not even be a Vodun *wanga*. I don't practice any of those religions myself, but I know someone who might be able to tell you more."

Ronald moved closer to Boone, offering his hands to both Boone and Emily, taking their own hands in a grip of thanks... and in the process, moved closer and spoke quietly.

"There is a man I helped come here many years ago. He was an *oungan* in Port-de-Paix. I hear he is working at the East Bay Resort as a groundskeeper. I remember he wore a *wanga* around his neck during the crossing. He went by Anel and would be about my age."

Ronald gave their hands a firm squeeze and released his grip before turning and rejoining the migrants.

Once the police took statements, Boone, Emily, Doug, and Mateo took the *Lunasea* and their group of divers over to the main pier and tied up. It was decided they would go back to the resort for a quick lunch before returning for an afternoon dive or two to compensate for the lost morning. Boone and Em decided to chill in their room, making some sandwiches from a few items they'd picked up at the supermarket near the pier. Sandwiches consumed, the two retired to the main bedroom, planning on a half-hour power nap. While Emily nudged the air conditioning up a couple of notches, Boone set the alarm. Quick naps in the tropics could easily turn into longer snoozes if you weren't careful.

Emily flopped hard onto the bed. "Well, that was a new experience," she said, before sighing and closing her eyes.

"Mm-hm," Boone responded, sitting on the edge of the bed.

Em opened her eyes to find Boone engrossed in something on his phone. "Boone... you gonna join me in a kip, or what? I've got the A/C all ice-boxy."

"Yeah, in a sec."

"What're you lookin' at?"

"Wikipedia."

"Ooooh... doin' some hardcore research? What on?" Emily lay back and closed her eyes again. "Lemme guess. The mating habits of the Lesser Plumed Plover?" Silence greeted Em's ears, so she tossed another. "The life and times of Chunky Jack, the plumpest pirate to ever sail the seven seas?"

That one earned a chuckle, but when Emily cracked an eyelid, she still saw Boone's bare back as he continued to sit on the edge of the bed, reading something on his phone.

"Are you looking at porn? You are, aren't you? Is it Bigfoot porn? I heard that's a thing."

Without turning around, Boone reached a long arm back, snagged a pillow, and tossed it at her face. Emily giggled and grabbed it, swinging it hard against Boone's back. "Put the phone down, you berk. Or tell me what you're looking at."

"Havana Syndrome."

"You mean that thing that's been in the news a few times? Attacks on embassies with microwaves?"

"Yeah... although reading this, seems like some experts think it's just some form of mass hysteria."

"Why on earth are you reading about that?"

Boone turned to look at her, tossing the phone onto the

sheets. "You remember what the owner of the Sunset Café told us about that body Mateo found? The stuff he heard from a police constable?"

"Yeah?"

"The constable who was with us on the ride back said they did some CT scans on the body they found in the Boiling Hole. The victim showed signs of brain trauma... but with no outward sign of injury. They sent the body to the States. Apparently, the pathologist suggested it was Havana Syndrome."

Emily sat up. "I thought it was some kind of ritual voodoo hoodoo."

Boone smirked. "You don't actually believe that."

"Well... no... probably not. But it makes about as much sense as someone zapping a migrant with microwaves."

"True. The guy was probably Haitian, by the way. He had a tattoo in Creole."

"Well, let's try to find that guy Dr. Ron told us to talk to," Em suggested. "Maybe he's got some idea who the victim was."

TWENTY-TWO

After the excitement of the morning, the afternoon dives almost seemed like an afterthought. To make up for the lost morning dives, the *Lunasea* took the Fish Cay group out for a rare two-tank afternoon trip, and Boone and Em went on both, leaving Doug aboard the *Lunasea*. The deep dive at The Maze was fantastic... "aMAZE-ing" as Emily put it. A big green moray was on station, but the real treat occurred near the end of the dive, within sight of the mooring line. Neither Boone nor Emily had ever seen so many drums and high-hats in one place. The beautiful black-and-white fish were usually solitary, but at The Maze they were gathered in groups. Five of the gossamer-finned drums under a coral head to the right, and at least twelve of the stockier high-hats under a deeper coral head off to the left.

For the second dive, Mateo took them to Dove Cay, also known as Safety Stop—aptly named, as the bulk of the dive occurred at about fifteen feet. The dive plan took them to the right of the channel that cut into the bay, and the divers swam along Dove Cay and the smaller "cay-lets," Huey, Dewey, and Louie. Several eagle rays and stingrays skimmed the sand near the crashing surf that pushed through the small cays, and there were stands of rare elkhorn coral to explore. Emily managed to spot a painted elysia—a tiny, brightly-colored nudibranch— which she pointed out to the divers and Mateo, who took particular interest. He signaled her by pointing at himself, pointing two fingers at his eyes, pointing at the little sea slug, shaking his head, then pumping an "OK" sign at her: a series of signals she took to mean "I've never seen that! Thanks!"

Back aboard, Emily took Mateo aside and suggested a night dive, which would catch up the Fish Cay divers on all their missed dives, but the divemaster shook his head. There was no hyperbaric chamber on-island, the nearest one being in Provo. In the event of an accident, a diver would need to be airlifted, and the current airport didn't allow after-dark flights. Upgrades were in the works, but until the new airport was completed, they couldn't do night dives.

The afternoon dives over, they returned to the pier to drop off the guests, then put the *Lunasea* to bed beside the *Big Sister* while Mateo ran the divers back to the resort. Boone and Em were just debating whether they should return the skiff to East Bay themselves when Mateo returned in the van and hopped out.

"You know what tonight is?"

"Monday Night Trivia?" Emily guessed hopefully.

"No... two days after the full moon! Would you like to see the glowworms up at Jerry Camp, on the north side? We can grab burgers to-go from Resha up the street."

"I'm game," Boone said. "What about the skiff?"

"It will be fine at the pier. Let's go."

"Bagsy!" Emily cried, running for the van.

Boone smiled at Mateo's confusion. "It's a British thing. She's calling shotgun."

Mateo laughed. "I don't know what that means, either."

"I'm calling the front seat, slowpokes!" Em said, slamming the passenger door behind her.

They drove two blocks north and Mateo ran inside a small, brown house with waist-high pink walls out front. Several minutes later, he returned with a paper bag containing three foil-wrapped burgers.

"That's a burger restaurant?" Em asked, looking back at the weathered house as they drove away.

"It's Resha's house and these are from her kitchen. She makes great burgers."

"That she does!" Boone said, already chomping down on his partially unwrapped burger.

Mateo drove north through town. "Usually, to go to Jerry Camp and the Reefview Resort, you take the unpaved road from just beside the East Bay Resort. It loops around near the Highland House, then cuts north and runs all the way to the tip. But since we're already in town, we'll go the other way. North to the airport, then the road cuts east along the runway to Bell Sound, where it meets up with the unpaved road."

"Let's fire up some tunes," Emily said through a mouthful of burger. She nodded at the dashboard. "I'd turn the radio on but I don't want to get your knob greasy." The instant the words left her burger-stuffed mouth, she practically choked. "Oh, blimey, I'm sorry, that was positively pornographic."

Mateo blushed and even Boone was laughing hard at that one. "That sounds like something your alter ego would say. Moxy Bush, was it?"

"Aww, you remembered!"

Mateo flipped on the radio and reggae music filled the car, the song coming to a bouncy conclusion.

"Dat dere was 'Dreamland' by Bunny Wailer from his album, Blackheart Man. *De reggae world lost Bunny a little over a year ago, and he will be sorely missed. Little known fact about dat song... it's actually an adaptation of 'My Dream Island' by El Tempos... an old R&B band out of Lackawanna, New York. Y'know... dat's a fun word to say: 'Lackawanna. Llllackawanna.'"* Deejay Ceejay burst into a deep laugh. *"Woo-eee, kiss-me-neck, dis has been a long day and it's almost time for me to sign off, but I t'ink I got one more in me. How 'bout a little touch of de Bahamas, wit' Ronnie Butler..."*

A calypso song with an almost country music feel to it came over the airwaves as they reached the airport and turned right. Boone polished off his burger and Emily looked back and caught him eying hers.

"Don't even think about it," she said, turning away in her seat and taking a hefty bite.

"There's bottled water in the cooler on the seat beside you, Boone."

Boone took one out. "These are like the ones in our hotel room."

"Yes. East Bay has its own reverse-osmosis system. The water coolers you see around the resort are filled from the same source."

Boone chugged half of it as they drove alongside the airport fence and the runway beyond. They passed a group of donkeys, grazing beside the road. "The runway fence has some holes in it," he remarked. "Do the donkeys ever get in?"

Mateo laughed. "It doesn't happen often, but sometimes a plane will have to delay their takeoff or landing while they clear donkeys off the runway." Past the airstrip, the road turned slightly north, where the shallow waters of Bell Sound sparkled ahead. Mateo slowed and pointed at an overgrown road to the left. "We don't have time for a detour, but Jacques Mayol's house lies up that road."

"He still live there?" Emily asked.

"Oh... no, he took his own life in Italy, many years ago. The house still belongs to his family. The real estate company that owns the Reefview bought up most of the land up that road, but Mayol's family refused to sell."

He rolled forward over a small bridge; the waters of Bell Sound ran beneath it and fed an area of mangroves to the south. Minutes later, the paved road gave way to sand and packed limestone as they merged with a rough road from the south.

"That's the road that runs down past Highland House, and then cuts back toward our resort and the town," Mateo said, turning north. "You'll see a few roads to our right that run up to the cliffs. There are many empty lots for luxury homes along those roads, but there are only a few houses and villas built so far."

The calypso song came to an end and Deejay Ceejay's rich bass resonated in the van: *"Dat was 'Crow Calypso' by Ronnie and de Ramblers. Well, de sun is getting ready to kiss de waters of de Caicos Bank, and as you know, ladies and gents, Deejay Ceejay broadcasts out of de old Coast Guard station, and it get very dark up here. Before I go, just a touch of news I suss from de seagrape vine: a group of souls from Haiti was left high and dry on a beach in Fish Cay overnight. A boat from Reef Divers along wit' police and DECR pick dem up and bring dem to Immigration. If anyone have a little extra food or water to bring by, dey might appreciate it. Okay, good people, I be signin' off! Dis has been Radio Bambarra. Until de morrow."*

As the radio went silent, Mateo flicked it off. He slowed and pointed up at some large, rectangular buildings lined with balconies and windows. "That was a resort that never opened... and to the north of it is the Reefview Resort."

"You ever go up to Reefview?" Boone asked, when they passed a sign for it.

"A few times. If they have divers staying there, we provide our services. They have a nice view, and the restaurant is good. And they also have a beach bar on the Bell Sound side, but I don't like to go there."

"Why not?" Emily asked.

"Because of what they did to the mangroves to give that 'beach bar' its beach."

"Ah... right. Lincoln mentioned that. And he told us they were digging a marina somewhere?"

"You mean... that?" Mateo said, as they continued north, and the view to their right was filled with mounds of sand and dirt, standing water, and a notable lack of foliage. "They started dredging after Hurricane Irma but had to stop."

The van continued for another mile before Mateo slowed again. "The turn to Jerry Camp is right here, but we have a little time. I'll show you the old Coast Guard station."

"Ooh!" Emily sat up straight. "That's where Mister Sexy Voice broadcasts from, innit?"

"Yes. We might catch him on the way out." Mateo turned right and started up the hill. Numerous small sheds and oil tanks dotted the landscape on either side of the ascending road, most overgrown with tropical foliage of one kind or another. "The road ends right by the old base. This is the north-ernmost tip of South Caicos."

"What's all that over there?" Emily asked, pointing at a slope on their left. "All that slanty concrete... not flat enough for Coast Guard helicopters."

"That is the largest rain catch system on the island. Used to provide all the water to the base. Probably still doing its job, although I imagine the cistern hasn't been cleaned in years."

The van neared the top of the hill, and the buildings of the Coast Guard station came into view: all one-story, the structures had flat roofs and were painted white. There were many openings for windows, and what few windows there were had broken panes. To the left, at the northern end of the complex, a single spire rose with a winking red light atop it. The building to the right looked like it might have been a dormitory, and the building to the left appeared to be the old station itself, with an open-walled workshop or garage on the near side. Beside it, a man crouched in front of a compact Honda with an open trunk, doing something at ground-level. As the van rolled to a stop, the man looked up, shielding his eyes against the soon-to-be-setting sun.

"That's Deejay Ceejay," Mateo said, turning off the engine.

The man rose and put something into the trunk, closed it, then turned and waved. While he wasn't as tall as Boone, he was close, and a pile of dreadlocks atop his head might actually have given him the edge in a measuring contest. "Mateo, wah gwaan? You givin' a tour? I was just 'bout to head home."

"Good to see you, CJ. We're actually on our way to Jerry Camp to see the glowworms, but they don't start up until after sunset, so I thought I'd show them the old station. Boone and Emily came over from Grand Turk to help out Reef Divers."

"Don't let us keep you," Boone said.

"You need to get home and rest that beeeeeautiful voice!" Emily chimed in.

CJ treated her to a huge grin. "You been listenin' to Radio Bambarra?"

"We have! Ace music!"

"You listen to Story Hour?"

"Not yet, but we've only been here a few days."

"Well, I'd show you around, but I promised Miss Riggs I'd join her for dinner."

"Ooh, a dishy date with a deejay!" Emily teased. "Lucky woman."

CJ laughed. "Naw, it ain't like dat. Miss Riggs old enough to be me granny. She keeps chickens out near de airport, and I t'ink I found one of hers."

"Out here?" Mateo said. "Don't see wild chickens often... the potcakes usually get them."

"I know it. But she's de only one I know keeps live ones, and she said she sold a few de other day. Dis one was running around up dere last night, I t'ink." He gestured toward the rise, south of the other building. "It was... weird."

Emily thought the man was going to say something else, but then he gave his head a shake. "Do you need any help rounding up your friend's chicken?" she offered.

"Oh, no need for dat. It's dead. In de trunk. I t'ink somet'in' wrong with it."

"Well... if it's dead, I suppose that qualifies," Emily said.

"No, I mean... well... it got no eyes."

Boone cocked his head. "Can I see?"

"Ew, Boone. Gross."

CJ shrugged and opened the trunk. "It's in dat cardboard box."

Emily watched as Boone leaned into the trunk, then stood back and thought for a moment.

"The eyes aren't gone, they're..." He trailed off, then took out his phone and took several flash photos.

CJ looked at the setting sun. "Look, I best be gettin' on and you t'ree better hustle, you wanna get to de camp by sunset."

"Sorry we couldn't check out your radio station," Emily said.

CJ smiled. "Most of my radio station is sittin' on de front seat of my car. A laptop and a good microphone. But I tells you what: you two wanna get a proper look-around, come join me for coffee at sunrise sometime." He pointed past the buildings to the ocean below the bluff. "De sunrise here is truly glorious. I never miss one. Well... almost never. Just pop by sometime."

CJ squeezed into the little blue Honda and made a three-point turn, his wheels crunching on the rough road. He tooted his horn twice as he trundled down the hill, and the trio climbed into their van and followed.

Emily noticed a sandy road cutting off to the south along the bluff. "That road... does that go to where the swank homes are? When we were coming into South Caicos from Grand Turk, there was a big villa on the cliff."

"I know the one you mean," Mateo said. "It's near the Dreamgate and Catacombs dive sites. But that's the only place up there. Most of the homes and unsold plots are off of this next one there," he said, as they passed another turnoff halfway down to the main road.

Ahead, CJ's Honda followed the road as it reached sea level and curved south, back toward civilization. Mateo turned right, where the road was narrow and rocky. Occasionally, branches from various shrubs and mangroves scraped the sides of the van. In minutes, the road ended in a sandy area alongside a blue shipping container. The ground sloped down through loose scree to the water of the bay, low mangroves lining the shore. Off to one side, tied up to some of the roots, was a small flats skiff.

"The container is full of kayaks, paddles, and life jackets,"

Mateo said. "Guests from East Bay and Reefview use them to tour the cays and the sandflats up near Plandon Cay Cut."

"Are we going kayaking?" Emily asked.

"No need. If the glowworms make an appearance, we'll see plenty right out there," he said, waving a hand toward the shallows.

Boone went to the edge of the water. "Lemon shark," he commented.

"Aww, a juvenile," Em remarked, joining him. "Little cutie."

"There are many juveniles in here," Mateo explained. "Quite a few nurse sharks and stingrays, too."

Emily looked west at the setting sun. From where she stood, there was an unobstructed view across the shallow waters of the Caicos Bank. "Sunset in three... two... gorgeous."

"How long until the light show?" Boone asked.

Mateo smiled, holding up his phone to his mouth and pressing a button. He spoke a command: "Timer... fifty-five minutes." He lowered his phone. "Glowworms are very consistent. Almost exactly fifty-five minutes after sunset, they'll begin the mating ritual. If they decide to start tonight, that is."

"What... mama glowworm might have a headache?"

"Who knows? It's usually two days after the full moon, but sometimes it's three."

"Well, let's get comfortable," Boone said, sitting in the sand.

Fifty-five minutes later, Mateo's phone trilled as the timer went off. He quickly silenced it and pointed into the dark waters. "There! The mating begins!"

"Bow-chicka-bow-wow," Em chanted with a little hip wiggle.

"Easy there, Moxy Bush," Boone said. "Whoa! This is a lot more than in Caye Caulker."

In the shadowy shallows, flashes of greenish light pulsed. Some points of light seemed to be rising as they strobed, others floated near the surface. The flashes varied slightly in duration, ranging from near-instantaneous to a longer glow.

"The females swim up near the surface," Mateo said, "and release a mucus that glows. The males flash their own signals and aim for the females... then the spawning begins."

"How long does it last?" Boone asked.

"Just ten to fifteen minutes."

They continued to watch the display, and sure enough, after a short span the number of flashes dwindled, until all was dark once more.

"That was amazing," Emily breathed. "Fireworm fireworks."

TWENTY-THREE

Back on the road, Mateo drove slowly, his headlights the only illumination along the rough track. Boone had managed to claim the passenger seat for the return journey, and his eyes swept the sides of the road, looking for donkeys or potcakes. *Or chickens*, he thought.

Some lights glowed up on the cliff as they neared the turnoff for the Reefview Resort, but soon they were plunged into darkness again. This lasted for ten minutes, until oncoming headlights appeared in the distance.

"Someone's out late," Mateo commented.

"They're not moving, whoever they are," Boone observed.

When Mateo's headlights illuminated the other vehicle, they found a white Jeep beside the road, a dark-skinned man at the wheel. The Jeep rocked and sand flew from its wheels as the driver gunned the engine and a second man, mostly obscured by the Jeep, pushed with all of his might.

"This happens a lot," Mateo said, rolling down the window.

"People try to go around a pothole or puddle and they can get stuck in the sand."

The driver took his foot off the gas, and the other man rose from the rear of the Jeep. He was Caucasian, dressed in a black tracksuit and sporting a black ballcap and some expensive-looking sneakers.

"Blimey, that guy's jacked," Emily mumbled to Boone from the seat behind him.

"*Hola*," Mateo called out. "Stuck, yes?"

The driver started to say something, but the man in black held out a hand to him. Boone heard him say, "I got this, Baptiste," before he approached the van. "Yeah. There was a big hole in the road and we tried to dodge it," the man explained, speaking with some sort of New York accent. "Too bad. We had dinner reservations."

"Oh, up at the Reefview?" Mateo asked.

"Yeah. Heard the food there is great."

Odd choice of clothing, for dinner at a swanky restaurant, Boone thought. The driver was dressed in island casual, but it looked like there was something on his shirt. "I'd be happy to help push," Boone offered.

"Oh... no, that's okay. I think I almost got it."

"It's no trouble," Boone said, opening the passenger door.

"I have two boards in the back we use for this sort of thing," Mateo said, opening his door as well. He left the van running and went around to the cargo door at the back.

Boone got out, then turned at the sound of the van's sliding door opening. He helped Emily step down. "Is it just me, or...?" she began.

"Not just you. There's definitely something squirrely about those guys."

As Boone came around the front of the van, he saw the man in the cap talking animatedly in a low voice to the driver. His body bent forward slightly, and Boone spotted a dark shape at the back of the man's waistband. He held out a hand, blocking Emily. "Hold back."

"What? Why?"

"Actually... hop into the driver's seat," Boone mumbled, guiding her gently toward the van. "Just in case."

The man in black straightened up and turned with a smile. "Sure, we'd love a hand."

Mateo arrived with two broad boards. "I'll get these in place," he said, as he went to the front of the Jeep and jammed one under the edge of each tire.

Boone looked at the Jeep. It had tinted windows, but he could make out that the seats were down, the vehicle configured for cargo, but there was nothing in there as far as he could see.

The man stepped in front of his line of vision, placing a friendly hand on Boone's shoulder. "Thanks for doing us a solid," he said, giving Boone a gentle squeeze as he steered him away from the side of the Jeep and toward the back.

"No prob," Boone said. "You sound like you might be a fellow American. Where are you from?"

"Brooklyn. You?"

"Tennessee, originally. I'm Boone." He offered his hand and the man took it in a firm handshake.

"Pleased to meetcha, Boone. And again, thanks so much for helping us out." He called out, "Are the boards in place?"

"Yes," Mateo said, coming around the front. "I'll help out—"

"No, that's okay, we got it, I'm sure. Step over to your van... I bet we'll be throwin' a lot of sand." He grabbed hold of the rear of the Jeep and leaned in. "Okay! Gun it!"

Boone joined in, pushing hard. The tires caught on the boards fairly quickly, and they had the Jeep back on the road in moments. Oddly, the driver drove forward almost ten car-lengths before coming to a stop, brake lights glowing in the dark.

"Your buddy must be hungry, leaving you behind," Boone joked.

"Ah, he's an idiot," the man said, turning and jogging after the Jeep. "Thanks again!" he called back over his shoulder. "Have a good night!"

Boone watched him go, walking over to the two boards, the near ends now embedded in the sand. He picked one up as Mateo joined him and grabbed the other.

"Strange man," he said.

"Yeah," Boone said absently, handing over his board and heading back to the van. Inside, he discovered Emily had scooted from the driver's side to the passenger seat.

"Bagsy," she whispered.

Boone shook his head with a smile and slid open the side door, climbing in as Mateo returned from tossing the boards in the back. Boone leaned forward between the seats.

"I don't think those two blokes were bound for a candle-light dinner," Em remarked.

"No," Boone said.

"They probably live in one of the big houses," Mateo suggested.

"Then why lie about dinner? Also... how common are guns on the island?"

"Guns?" Mateo said in surprise. "I suppose they were quite

common back when the drug flights were coming in, but they are highly restricted now."

"The white guy had a handgun in his waistband."

"That's why you held me back," Em said.

"The driver... he never spoke," Boone mused. "At least not to us. But I heard the other guy call him Baptiste." He looked at Emily. "You remember that man Mack said was checking out the *Lunasea*?"

"That was him?"

"Said he was a Haitian named Baptiste. And that he worked somewhere up in the north, near Reefview."

"Sounds like a likely match. What about the other guy?"

"Well, that's another thing... I introduced myself and stuck out my hand... and he shook it and thanked me for the help, but didn't give me a name. And he didn't seem to want me looking in the back of the Jeep."

"The windows were tinted," Mateo noted, starting up the van and rolling forward.

"Yeah, but I got a little peek. The rear seats were folded down, but I didn't see anything in there."

"I'm taking us the southern way," Mateo explained as he passed the turn for the airport. "More direct to the resort."

About a mile south, Boone leaned farther forward, peering out the windshield.

"Climb into the front with us, why don't you?" Em teased.

"Slow up for a sec?" Boone requested.

The moon was low in the cloudless sky. On a rise ahead and to the left, backlit perfectly by the lunar light, stood Highland House, alone atop its hill.

Boone pointed at the silhouette of the old manor. "Mateo... whattaya say? A little more sightseeing?"

"Oh, no-no-no-no-no," Emily protested. "Uh-uh. With a big heaping bowl of nope and a side order of sod that!"

"It's just an old house," Mateo said. "Although, I've never gone up there at night."

"Yeah, 'cause you possess a modicum of sanity."

"Em, c'mon..." Boone cajoled. "Just a quick look. You can stay in the van."

"Bollocks to that! If you wanna play Scooby Dooby Dumb in a haunted house, you'll need someone sensible with you."

"So... we're going?" Mateo asked.

Em huffed out a sigh. "I don't want to wander around in an old house with nothing but the little lights on our mobiles. You have any proper torches?"

"Flashlights? Yes, I have two big ones."

"Brilliant," Emily muttered. "Just what I wanted to hear."

After a short drive down the road, Mateo turned left and drove up the hill on a narrow track, rolling to a stop about fifty yards from their destination. Above the ocean to the southeast, the moon shined down. The walls of Highland House were pale in the moonlight, and there was a soft glow in the six window-less frames facing them, likely picking up some illumination from openings at the rear of the building.

"Not any less spooky up close, I'm afraid," Emily commented after they'd all piled out.

Mateo dug around in the back and came out with two flash-lights; one fairly standard, and the other a pistol-grip spotlight. Boone took the latter from Mateo and pressed it into Em's hands.

"Here you go. You see any ghosts, hit 'em with that."

"I'll hit *you* with..." she grumbled, taking the flashlight and turning it on. "Blimey-what-is-that!!" she squawked as her beam caught something large moving through the low brush.

Mateo laughed as he shined his own light toward the movement. "Donkey."

Emily turned and punched Boone in the arm.

"What? It startled me, too!"

"Scared the shite out of me," she tittered nervously, shining her light around. "There's a couple more over there, too."

"Yes. Highland House has no doors left, and the donkeys sometimes go inside the ground floor for shelter. Which reminds me: watch your step in there."

The trio approached the manor, steering clear of an open well or cistern that was next to the old driveway. Stepping up onto the cement base that ringed the building, Boone moved inside, Mateo's and Emily's lights throwing his shadow on the interior walls.

"Whoa... I see whatcha mean about watching your step," Boone said, nearly planting his foot in a pile of donkey dung; the interior of the entry room was littered with it. Here and there were signs of human activity: a few candy wrappers, a soda can, a beer bottle... even a discarded windbreaker, covered in dust.

"Be careful," Mateo said. "There are many holes in the old wood floor."

Boone looked down into one such hole, a rectangle of splintered planks. Emily shined her light into the gap, revealing cement supports, limestone, and sand.

"No vampires down there. That's a plus, I s'pose." She shined her light up on the nearest wall and gasped. "But *that*, on the other hand... what the bleeding hell is *that*? Or *those*?"

On the inner wall of the entry room were a trio of large, crude drawings. Boone moved closer, looking at them from off to the side to keep from shrouding them in his shadow. The drawings were incredibly basic, yet surprisingly imaginative. "Looks like they're drawn in chalk. Purple chalk."

"You mean like a kid would use to draw on the pavement for a game of hopscotch?"

"Yeah."

"Not exactly Monets, are they?"

"More like Picassos," Boone said. "No... cave paintings, that's what they look like."

"But what on earth are they?"

"Well... that one over there looks like a naked woman with moth wings... and this middle one, I don't know what the heck that is, but it's got cat's eyes and a crown... and this one next to me... yikes."

"That one definitely wins the creepy contest," Em said.

"It looks like a *centauro*," Mateo said.

"A centaur, yeah," Boone confirmed. "With crazy hair, and holding a scythe or a sickle. And he looks pissed."

"That's 'cause the artist gave 'im angry eyebrows."

Boone laughed. "Almost like a kid drew this."

"Look there," Mateo said, shining a light back the way they had come. Beside the entry door was a smaller drawing: a square with triangles protruding from each side, drawn in orange chalk. And in its center, a blue eye.

"And over by the other exit, just past Moth Girl," Emily said, shining her spot beside another doorway.

A large hexagram took up much of the small wall beside the opening, its interior speckled with little hash marks, like tic-tac-toe symbols. It looked like there might have been three initials in the center, but this drawing appeared to be much older than the others, its yellow chalk faded with age.

"You know anything about these, Mateo?" Boone asked.

"I confess... I've never noticed them. But I've only been up here twice before."

"In broad daylight, I'll wager," Em muttered. "Like a normal person."

"Yes."

Boone headed into the remains of the living room, picking his way carefully past donkey droppings, broken planks, and holes in the floor. A two-landing staircase occupied most of one corner. It appeared largely intact, although one step toward the bottom was caved in, the wood snapped in two in the middle. Boone looked up. Apparently, the floors above hadn't fared much better than down below: beside two beams, a sizable hole in the ceiling yawned overhead. The only light up there came from moonlight glowing through upper windows.

"Mateo, can I borrow your flashlight?" Boone took it and shined the beam through the hole. "Okaaaay..." he drawled, lengthening the word.

Emily added her spotlight to the hole above. "What are you... oh-for-the-love-of... is that a rope hanging from that beam?"

"Looks like it." A rope was wound around a central beam beneath the second-floor ceiling, one frayed end dangling.

Mateo looked up. "You know... they say the cartel used to hang people here."

"Back in the eighties," Boone clarified.

"Yes."

"That rope doesn't look forty years old... and it's coiled pretty loosely. If I had to guess, someone was playing around, trying to be scary."

"Well, it worked. C'mon, let's get out of here," Emily coaxed. "The donkey poop is a little ripe."

Boone sniffed. Yes, the odor of the dung was hard to ignore, but there was something else in the air. "I wanna run upstairs real quick."

"Hell no! I'm putting my foot down!" She shined her light on the floor. "Carefully. I like these shoes."

"Hang on..." Boone said, crouching and shining his own light near her feet. There lay a particularly impressive manure pile with a deep impression in the middle.

"A footprint," Mateo observed.

"From a running shoe, from the looks of it. And recent." And the toe is pointed toward the stairs. He rose from his crouch and shined his light along the steps. "I'm going up. You can stay here—I won't be a minute."

"I'll stick around down here," Emily said. "Try to catch you when you fall through the ceiling."

"Be very careful on those stairs," Mateo warned.

"Yeah, I see the one that's busted. I'll keep to the edges."

Boone carefully made his way up the creaking steps and onto the second floor. The stairs emptied into a large room with numerous window frames. To the left was a doorway leading to a darkened room, and to the right on the south wall were two doorways, open to the air, the moon framed in one of them. *Probably used to be a balcony out there,* Boone thought. Looking up at the rope hanging from the rafters, he was even more sure this wasn't some noose-remnant from the eighties.

"Everything okay up there?" Emily called up.

"Fine. Nothing much in the rope room... gonna check the other part of the house."

Boone kept his flashlight on the floor, eyes on the lookout for broken boards as he stepped into what was likely a master bedroom. The donkeys had likely found the stairs to be an unfriendly obstacle for their hooves, and the surface of the floor was clear of their leavings, although extremely dusty. Or sandy, with all these open windows and tropical breezes. He shined his light across the floor and spotted a print in the sand. Then a pair. *Odd... they're side by side, toes pointed at the wall,* he thought. He shined his light on the wall, half-expecting some more chalk art, but there was nothing there. Boone sniffed the air again. *What is that?* Stepping into the adjoining room and sweeping his light toward the far corner, he got his answer.

He took a moment to compose himself before calling out, "Mateo... call the police."

TWENTY-FOUR

"Hurry up!" Sergei whisper-shouted from beside the darkened Jeep, parked a hundred yards from Viktor's villa.

Baptiste ran up, clutching a balled-up tarp. "Got it," he gasped, shoving the tarp into the back. "Let's go!"

Sergei got into the driver's side and turned them around, heading back down the road. He kept his lights off until they were out of view of the house.

"I don't know where the boss found you," he muttered.

"You were supposed to bring de tarp!" Baptiste protested.

"Bullshit, that was your job. After you got rid of the last one, you were in charge of getting a new one!"

"I *did*, I just didn't put it... never mind," he said sulkily.

"If someone finds that body before we get back..."

"No one will! No one goes up dere at night."

"Looked to me like someone did," Sergei said. "The trash and beer bottles..."

"De yout's sometimes go dere, yes, but not on a Monday

night. Dey got school. And de older kids are at college in Provo until de summer break next month."

Sergei shook his head. "And that's the *last* time I let you drive. We're actually lucky we didn't have anything in the Jeep when those dive people showed up. Otherwise, we'd be disposing of *four* bodies tonight."

"You recognize dem, yes? De ones from Grand Turk de boss was curious 'bout?"

"Yeah. Although, my guess is it was the hot little blonde he was really interested in." Sergei knew his boss had a weakness for the ladies; half the helicopter trips over to Grand Turk or Provo had been to satiate Viktor's needs.

Sergei abruptly slowed as a dark shape moved across the road ahead. *Damn donkeys...* Belatedly, he remembered he'd need to clean the soles of his sneakers.

The decision to do the test just before sunset rather than in the dead of night had made sense to Sergei. The Highland House was very remote, yet it stood on a hill, and while an observer in the distant, populated areas would have no way of seeing anything happening inside during the day, if they'd done the test at night, they would have needed lights. And, with windows lining every wall, that would have been easily spotted by anyone looking toward an otherwise dark and lonely hill.

Paz Cisneros had been pleased with the results of the test, and had gathered up the weapon and his instruments and joined Viktor in the other Jeep, leaving Sergei and Baptiste to clean up. After the last body-disposal debacle, Sergei had insisted he go along with Baptiste, and they'd planned on dumping the body in a spot where the currents would take it away. But they weren't about to drive around the island with a untarped body in the back.

"I still don't know why you did what you did wit' de chalk," Baptiste said.

Sergei rolled his eyes. "And I don't know why you did what you did with that little voodoo bag, so we're even."

"I tol' you... it's for protection. I always keep one wit' me, in case I need to... deal with someone. Sometimes... de ones I kill, dey spirits come back for revenge."

"What, like a zombie?"

Baptiste gave Sergei a look. "Dat a whole diff'rent t'ing. Dis *wanga* I use is to keep de restless spirits from rising from de dead."

"Sure sounds like zombies."

"No, not a *zonbi*. De dead body don't come back... de spirit do. Like a ghost. *Jumbee* is what my mother call dem. She was from Antigua."

"And here I thought you were doing some kinda Haitian voodoo."

"A little a' both."

The Jeep neared the intersection where the main road met the rough, southerly road; the lights of the airport were visible across Bell Sound to the southwest. But those weren't the only lights Sergei could see.

"Shit."

Racing on the road that ran along the airport was a pair of headlights, and above that, the flashing blue-and-red lights of a police car.

"What do we do?" Baptiste asked, as Sergei rolled to a stop.

"We wait."

"Turn off de headlights!"

"Hell no. We're too close. They'd see them go out. But I don't think they're coming our way."

Sure enough, the flashing lights came across the intersection ahead, slowed, then turned and headed south. In the direction of Highland House. They watched in silence for several interminable minutes. Then, the lights began to rise as the police car reached the Highlands.

"Oh, no..." Baptiste whispered.

"You wanted to know why I used that chalk we found?" Sergei said, starting to turn the Jeep around. "Misdirection."

"Here they come," Emily said, looking up at Boone. He'd been unusually quiet ever since he'd carefully descended the steps and suggested they wait outside. While he hadn't gone into any details, he'd told her and Mateo that there was a body upstairs.

The red-and-blue flashing lights vanished behind a rise for a moment before reappearing. The Royal Turks and Caicos Islands Police SUV came to a halt behind the resort van and Constable Terrance got out, along with another policeman.

"You again," he said, seeing Boone.

"Me again. The body's upstairs."

"Any active threat?" Terrance asked.

"Not anymore."

The constables retrieved sturdy flashlights from their vehicle and followed Boone into Highland House. Emily entered as well, but Boone stopped her just inside the doorway.

"Em... you might want to stay down here..."

"Thanks for lookin' out for me, but if you can handle it, so can I."

Boone sighed. "You can't unsee it..."

"I'll remind you that we've both seen quite a bit over the last few years, yeah? Enough chin-waggin'... lead the way."

"I'll stay here, if that's all right," Mateo said.

Boone shined his light on the footprint. "There's a print there in that skat. And watch your step on the stairs," he warned, ascending the stairs with the two officers behind and Emily bringing up the rear.

The four flashlight beams swept the empty room at the top of the stairs. One of the constable's flashlights froze on the rope on the beam.

"What is...?"

"Unrelated, I think," Boone said. "He's in here." Boone led the group into the side suite and entered the back corner room. As one, the four beams of light converged on the corner.

"Oh my God," Constable Terrance whispered.

Emily reached out and found Boone's hand. She gripped his fingers tightly but remained silent.

A dead man sat on the floor, slumped in the corner, his head lolled forward on his chest. One arm was elevated, zip-tied to a pipe; the other was out to the side, secured to an ancient radiator, the two arms together almost like the hands of a clock at three. Both hands hung limply from their restraints, and there was blood on the wrists where the ligatures had bitten into the flesh. The man was dressed in a weathered T-shirt, jeans, and work boots. The sight of the dead body was jarring enough, but there was more to the macabre scene.

"Witchcraft!" the other constable rasped, shining his light on the wall just above the man. A hexagram with a circle around it was scrawled on the surface. Three little X's were drawn inside the center, and the whole thing appeared to have been done in blue chalk.

"There's another downstairs," Boone said. "Although..." He trailed off, then turned and ran his light around the room. It came to rest on a thick nub of blue sidewalk chalk. "Bingo. The wall art downstairs looks like it's been there a while, but this is fresh."

"So is de blood on de wrists," Terrance said, crouching closer to the man and pulling on a pair of latex gloves.

"And look at his ears," Emily said quietly.

Terrance leaned to one side, shining his light on the side of the man's head. "A trickle of blood... both ears." He sighed. "I want to lift de man's head," he announced, as if seeking permission. When no one said anything, he gently shifted the man's head back, leaning it in the corner. He rose and stepped back. "Do any of you know dis man?"

Everyone replied in the negative, and Terrance concurred the man was a stranger to him as well. "He's not a local. My guess... anuddah Haitian migrant."

"What do we do?" the other constable asked.

"We'll need de forensics team for dis. Go down and radio dispatch. He should be dere by now. Have dem contact Provo." The constable started to go, but Terrance stopped him. "Take a photo of his face first. Text it to dispatch and have dem pass it along."

The constable picked his way down the stairs and Boone shined his light on the dead man's boots. After a moment, he crouched beside the man's legs.

"What are you looking for?" Em asked.

"I was wondering if he was the one who stepped in that donkey dung downstairs."

Em looked at the soles of the boots. "They look a bit dirty, but I don't think so. And besides, that didn't look like a boot print; more like a trainer."

"No, you're right, don't think it was him. But look at these." He shined his flashlight at the bottom of the man's jeans, near the hem. "And on the bootlaces too."

"Are those little spikey things seeds?" Emily asked.

"Burrs. Used to end up with a whole pantleg of these things when I went out in the woods in Tennessee. But also ended up with something like this on my shoelaces when I went hiking in Washington-Slaagbai in Bonaire. Some of the desert plants on South Caicos remind me of the ones in that park."

Emily shifted her light to the man's arm hanging from the pipe. She shuddered at the wounds on the man's wrist. "Looks like he tried to get loose. Tried hard."

"Scratches..." Boone said.

"More like gouges," Em corrected.

"No... on his arms. Look." He pointed at multiple faint lines on the man's forearm. "They look scabbed over. Maybe from thorns?"

"Or maybe he's got a cat."

Emily watched as Boone moved closer to the body, looking carefully at the dead man's face. His eyes were lidded, and in the whites that were visible, they appeared heavily bloodshot. Boone sat back on his haunches, then pointed at the corpse's forehead.

"There are some faint circles, a bit larger than a quarter. Kinda like something was stuck on there. And next to them... the skin looks raw. And look... next to his mouth, too."

"Maybe he was gagged with duct tape?" Terrance suggested.

"That's a good guess, actually." Boone looked up at Terrance. "Constable... I don't want to disturb the crime scene or anything, but..."

"I've already moved his head," Terrance replied. "What are you thinking?"

"Can we check..." Boone started, then looked back at Emily and hesitated. "Y'know... never mind."

"You want to check in his mouth for one of those voodoo thingies," she declared.

Boone looked uncomfortable. "Yeah..."

"Do it," Em said firmly. "With the constable's permission," she added.

"I'll open his mouth," Terrance said. "You shouldn't touch de body." He maneuvered to the man's side and gently opened his mouth.

Boone leaned close and shined his light in. "Can you tilt his head back a bit?" he asked. When the constable complied, Boone angled the flashlight, then froze.

"Well?" Emily asked.

"Something's in there, all right." He set down his flashlight and fished out his smartphone. "Em, can you bring that spotlight over?"

Good... Boone the Overprotective has taken a backseat to Boone the Curious. Emily moved closer to illuminate the open mouth. She could definitely see something in there, and it appeared to be fabric.

Boone snapped several photos, then opened one and zoomed in. He held it up to Constable Terrance.

"It look like de one from de Boiling Hole body. Here, take some wit' mine," he said, unlocking his own phone and handing it over.

Boone took several, doing his best to get the camera to focus in on the object that appeared to be tucked into the dead man's throat.

The other constable came up the stairs. "Provo gonna send a team," he said, then stopped when he saw what they were looking at. "Anuddah one of dose bags? I'm tellin' you... dis look like some kind of ritual killin' or sacrifice."

"It does, doesn't it?" Boone said, shining his light on the chalk drawing on the wall.

"I didn't realize hexagrams had anything to do with voodoo," Emily said.

"I'm not sure they do," Boone replied, skepticism in his voice. He swept his light along the man's body, then back to his face. "I don't see any wounds."

"Just like de last one..." Constable Terrance said. "Dey'll probably take de body back tonight. Run tests again."

"Your constable friend over in Provo, will he be there?"

"Probably. Why?"

"I'd be curious to know if they find massive trauma in the brain."

"The test was a success," Paz announced after he plugged in the last of the data. "The heating element has been eliminated. This time, no blistering. Outward signs of trauma were minimal."

"There was some blood coming out of his ears," Viktor noted.

"Only because we ramped the weapon up to maximum at the end. The first three applications were perfect."

"Including the one where Sergei fired it through the wall?"

"Yes. The sensors I taped to the subject's forehead indicated the beam strength was eighty-five percent of the intensity without the barrier. Obviously, different materials will provide a range of results, but it should penetrate most unreinforced walls. And if I cross-reference our data from the test on the chickens, I can extrapolate the effects at varying ranges."

"So... can we deliver this tomorrow morning, as scheduled?"

"Yes. Prototype, spare batteries, schematics, test data, and the test videos... all of it will fit in a suitcase. And a second suitcase for the tripod, imagers, and tracking equipment for remote use."

Viktor nodded. "And... if the need should arise... your earlier prototype could be brought up to specifications, yes?"

"Absolutely. It's already quite functional. Although not quite as subtle in its effects. But that is something I can adjust, now that I have the data."

"Excellent! Good work. By tomorrow morning, we should be very wealthy men."

Footsteps in the hallway heralded the arrival of Sergei and Baptiste. Sergei stood in the doorway but didn't enter the workshop.

"You're back early," Viktor said, suspicion growing.

"Yeah..." Sergei said, reaching up to scratch at his scalp. "So... um... I think it's gonna be fine, but... we had a bit of a snag." Before Viktor could explode, Sergei continued. "But I improvised." He then explained, briefly, what he had done.

"You idiots..." Viktor snarled, then cried out in pain.

"Boss?"

"It's my fucking tooth, you moron. You had me grinding my teeth again." He rose. "What's done is done. And as you say, they may focus on the Haitian community, thanks to Baptiste's superstition. That buys us some time."

Baptiste glowered at that, but stayed silent.

"The transfer goes ahead as scheduled," Viktor announced. *It'll have to*, he thought. *As much as I love this villa, I'll probably need to move on once the deposit hits my Swiss bank account.*

TWENTY-FIVE

Deejay Ceejay completed the last of his morning sequence of sun salutations, exhaling slowly and evenly as he came to rest in the standing mountain pose. He'd been practicing yoga for several months now, after a whirlwind romance with a visiting tourist from Costa Rica. She taught yoga at a retreat there, and she had been eager to teach him. *Taught each other quite a few things,* CJ thought with a laugh, remembering fondly the very beautiful—and very flexible—young woman.

He exhaled again, watching the changing palette of colors as the sun rose. He was about to roll up the mat and fetch his coffee when his eyes settled on a ship, backlit against the brightening horizon. It looked like a small cargo vessel, not unusual for the area, but CJ knew all the ships that brought supplies over from Provo and he didn't recognize this one.

Shrugging, he returned to his Honda to ditch the yoga mat and grab his laptop and microphone. After making his way back to the broadcasting office, he went inside and was greeted by the aroma emanating from his coffeemaker, its timer set for sunrise. He had to tweak the start time occasion-ally during the year, but it was usually waiting for him—provided a storm didn't take down the solitary powerline that ran out to the Coast Guard station, or the island didn't have an outage.

CJ downed a couple of Advil before reaching for his coffee mug. The strange sensations he'd experienced Sunday night had left him with a chronic headache and a bit of vertigo, but thankfully it tended to wane as the day progressed. Armed with caffeine, CJ returned to his hangout spot. His music ran on an automated loop when he left in the evening; the next day, once he was ready, he'd break in with live programming.

Exiting the Coast Guard station, he was greeted with the sound of a helicopter. Probably his neighbor, heading over to Grand Turk. CJ reached his patio chairs and settled into one, sipping his coffee. The helicopter came into view to the south, roaring out into the Turks Island Passage. The cargo ship was closer now, and CJ could make out some crewmen on deck. Then something highly unusual happened.

CJ stared as a cargo container—or what he'd assumed was a cargo container—slowly started to split open from the top. The sides folded down as if on a hydraulic hinge, and the divided roof flattened out as well. In less than a minute, a cargo container had become a helicopter landing pad.

"*Bumba!*" CJ whispered in surprise, reverting to some of his father's Jamaican patois. He rose from his chair to get a better look. The rich guy's helicopter approached the ship, then slowed to a hover before lowering to the deck. After a moment, two men exited the helicopter, carrying... *luggage?*

CJ squinted against the rising sun, watching the activity on the deck. After a few minutes, the occupants reboarded and the helo rose from the ship. The temporary landing pad reassembled itself into a cargo container as the helicopter pivoted and started back for the neighbor's villa.

"Well... so *dat* happened," CJ rumbled, his deep voice awakening with the infusion of hot coffee. After finishing the remnants in his mug, he turned and headed back to his office to start the broadcast. Plugging his laptop directly into the system, he fired up the software and settled himself in front of the mic.

"Dis is Deejay Ceejay with Radio Bambarra, coming to you on a glorious Tuesday morning..."

———

"Blimey, it's a shite morning," Emily mumbled into her coffee.

"Three hours of sleep might be to blame," Boone said, nudging the eggs and bacon in the skillet. The East Bay Resort had great breakfasts, but in order to get a little more sleep, they'd opted to stock their suite's kitchen with the basics.

Emily grunted and rose, padding across the kitchen to lean against Boone. "I like my bacon crispy," she warned.

"You tell me that every time, and I always crisp it up for you."

"That's 'cause I tell you every time," she said into his shirtless back, before pressing a kiss beneath his shoulder blade and refilling her mug. "I'll be on the balcony, sucking down a second cuppa."

Boone finished at the stove and plated their breakfasts. Balancing both dishes, napkins and forks, a bowl of fruit, and his own coffee in his hands, he joined Emily on the balcony.

"All in one go," she said, impressed. "You work as a waiter in your youth?"

"I've got big hands."

Em snorted a laugh. "And big feet. And I'll stop there."

Boone set the food down on a small table between their patio chairs. "Tuck in."

"Ooh... using my lingo. I'll civilize you yet, Tennessee Boy."

Boone nodded at the wall over her head, where an anole was perched. The tiny lizards were common in the islands. "You've got a friend."

Emily looked up at the small, green-brown reptile that clung to the surface. "Oh, that's Nolan."

Boone grinned. "Nolan the Anole?"

"Although that might be Anna..." she said, squinting at it. "I'll know for sure once I'm fully caffeinated."

When they finished their meal, Boone asked, "How you doing?"

Emily sipped her coffee, measuring a response. "Well... no nightmares, so that's a plus. Okay, I guess. You?"

Boone shrugged. "I'm all right. Long as I don't think too much about it."

"Which, of course, you're doing."

"Kinda hard not to... I want to know what happened."

From their upper floor, the beach below was visible, and a small tractor was running along the shoreline, gathering up the sargassum. The man driving it was one of the gardeners Boone had seen around.

"We need to find that groundskeeper Dr. Etienne told us about. He said his name was Anel."

"The voodoo priest?"

"Yeah. Those things on the wall, and those little bags... something's off about it."

"No argument there. Well, let's go down and talk to Tractor Guy. See if he knows him."

Boone didn't have his dive watch on yet, but he didn't need

it; the sun's placement was a sufficient clock. "We don't have time now; we need to bring the *Lunasea* in and fill the tanks. After the morning dives, we'll go find the man."

Paz heard the helicopter's return and went outside to find an angry Viktor storming toward the villa, Sergei walking behind at a respectful distance, carrying two large duffel bags.

"*Ublyudki!*" Viktor swore.

"What happened?" the Cuban asked. "Did you get the money?"

"Yes... and no. Our good friends in Moscow saw fit to transfer the payment to a bank account in Cyprus..."

"Well... that's good, yes? Did they pay the full amount?"

"They paid *double* the agreed-upon amount!"

Paz's eyebrows shot up, but suspicion immediately set in. "Then why are you angry?"

"Because I don't *have* a bank account in Cyprus. Access to it is blocked; bastards called it a 'trust fund.' They will transfer it to me once I complete a second task." He grabbed hold of his jaw and massaged it, breaking away from Paz and going into the villa.

Paz looked at Sergei. "Did they give us a down payment?" He nodded toward the pair of duffel bags.

"No." Sergei set down the bags and unzipped one.

Paz looked inside. "Are those... plastic explosives?"

"Yeah. PVV-5A, they said. Along with detonators, timers... and some blueprints for a ship."

Paz swallowed. "What exactly is this other 'task' they've given Viktor?"

"We have to blow up the *Anya*."

251

After the morning dives, Em and Boone took a stroll around the resort, looking for one of the groundskeepers. The place was well-maintained, so it didn't take them long. A young man was trimming a vast expanse of glossy, light-green leaves that ran along the drop-off above the beach.

"Excuse me!" Emily called out. "We're looking for Anel?"

"Sorry. Not me," the man said with a Haitian accent. He continued tending to the shrubs.

"What kind of plant is this?" Emily asked, running her thumb along one of the leaves. "Almost like a succulent, but not really."

"Kind of looks like magnolia tree leaves," Boone remarked. "I've seen them on a bunch of islands, but never knew what they were."

"I call it beach cabbage but some of de others say sea lettuce," the man said, opening up. "Grows very fast. It likes salt."

"I'm rather fond of salt myself," Em said. "Well, if you see Anel, let him know we were by? We rescued some migrants from Fish Cay the other day, and one of them said we should meet him."

"You were de ones who help dem?" the man said, setting aside his clippers. "T'ank you for dat." He pointed east along the beach. "Anel is workin' on de edge of de property. De Devil's Gut is gettin' very bad."

"Devil's what?" Em asked.

"Anel show you. He de expert on dat."

Emily and Boone took the steps down to the beach, ditched their shoes, and headed east along the surf. Highland House was visible on a rise just past the patch of casuarinas where

Mateo had taken them on a night walk. When was that...? Sunday? Seemed like a lifetime ago.

They spotted a middle-aged man atop a line of dunes, holding a plastic tank by a handle and spraying something onto a large clump of orange vines, thinner than angel hair pasta.

"Are you Anel?" Emily called out. When the man looked up, she quickly added, "Hi! I'm Emily, this is Boone. Dr. Ronald Etienne told us to look for you."

"Oh, yes. He told me you might be around." Anel's accent was very slight, sounding more like a Belonger than a Haitian. "I saw Ronald on Sunday. Brought some food to de people. Glad you found dem. No fresh water on Fish Cay."

"It was lucky our group wanted to dive there," Boone said.

"You battling the Devil's Gut?" Emily asked with a smile.

"Oh, you know it?"

"Never heard the name 'til one of your mates told us, but we've got it over on Grand Turk."

"Well, you might have heard it by anuddah name, it's got quite a few: Strangle Weed, Witch's Hair, de Love Vine."

"Ew. Creepy."

"Nasty stuff. It's a parasitic vine. Latches on to anuddah plant and sucks it dry. See here...?" He lifted a clump of the orange stuff and beneath it were the remains of a bush of some kind, completely gray.

"Blimey, it looks like it's been burned to ash."

"Well, dat's de sun dat do dat. Once de Devil's Gut take all de moisture, de victim goes gray." Anel set down his tank and removed the cap from his salt-and-pepper head, wiping his brow with the arm of his long-sleeved T-shirt.

"What are you spraying it with?" Boone asked. "Weed killer of some kind?"

"I don't like to mess with dat stuff. Dis is a simple recipe I make... a gallon of vinegar, a cup of salt, and some dish soap. It stick to de vine and dry it out. Sun do de rest." He nodded at the patch he was working on. "Dis stuff spread like crazy, so I keep it away from de resort. Dere's a lot more of it up dat way." He pointed along the beach past the casuarinas.

"Highland House is up that way," Boone ventured.

"It look closer dan it is," Anel replied. He sighed, running his hand through his hair for a moment. "Word gets around. I hear what happen up dere. You de ones who found him?"

"Yes." Boone said. "We were wondering..." Then he abruptly trailed off, looking down.

Emily knew the look on his face. "What is it?"

Boone pointed at the groundskeeper's boots. "You've got a bunch of burrs on your laces."

"Oh... yes, dere's all sorts of prickly t'ings on South Caicos. When you maintain de grounds for a place like dis, you run into all kinds of plants."

"That why you wear the long sleeves in hot weather like this?"

"Yes... didn't take me long to learn dat," he said, rolling up a sleeve. Numerous tiny scars lined his forearm. "Most of de groundskeepers have some souvenirs like dis."

"The body had scratches like that... and burrs on the laces of his work boots."

"He weren't one of ours. Everyone is here. And I already seen a photo of his face de police took... dey been asking around de Haitian community. No one knows him." He shrugged. "Dere's probably a few Haitian groundskeepers who work up in de villas and de Reefview in de north. Dey might live on de grounds and not be known to dose of us in town."

"Hey, do you know a Haitian named Baptiste?" Emily asked.

"Common name. I know several."

Boone took out his cell phone. With Constable Terrance's permission, he'd taken a number of photos while they waited for the team from Provo to arrive. "Ronald said you were a priest of some kind?" he prompted.

"I was an *oungan* of Vodun in Port-de-Paix."

"You say 'was'... does that mean you no longer practice?"

Anel shrugged. "It was a calling, so it is not somet'ing dat I turn off, like a light. But officially... I no longer have a temple."

"So... what does an *oungan* do?" Emily asked.

"Nothin' like you see in movies," Anel said with a laugh. "I was a sort of community leader. People come to me with problems and I try to help. I perform some religious services, like consecrations of a home or business or a newborn. Death rites are important, helping a departed loved one find peace. And I know some home remedies to help when someone is sick... but more often dan not, I would just take dem to de doctor. Dat how I meet Ronald."

"Is this something from voodoo? Or, excuse me... Vodun?" Boone held out his phone with the angry-looking centaur wall art pulled up.

"You can say voodoo, I take no offense." He took the phone and shielded it from the noonday sun. "Oh! Dis downstairs at Highland House. I went up dere a few times." He laughed. "No, all dose drawings, some of the yout's do dem. You know, dat place have a reputation, and dey just having fun scaring demselves."

"Like... putting a hangman's noose on the ceiling beam?" Emily asked.

"Dere weren't no noose on dat... just a rope. A local father

255

told me his son took a rope from him and do dat." He chuckled, shaking his head. "Say de boy didn't know how to tie a noose."

"What about this?" Boone said, leaning in and scrolling to the downstairs hexagram.

"Dey do dat one, too," Anel said.

"And... this?" Boone swept it one more time, pulling up the hexagon that was found over the body.

Anel frowned, peering at the smartphone screen. "I never seen dat one. Where dat?"

"It was on the wall over the dead body," Boone said. "Looked to me like it was freshly drawn and I found a chunk of blue chalk that matched it on the floor. There was some suggestion that it might be a part of some voodoo ritual killing..."

Anel's calm demeanor wavered. "Dat nonsense got nuttin' to do wit' Vodun. Hexagrams... pentagrams... dat all European witchcraft. No more a part of Vodun dan brain-eatin' zombies!"

"Boone here had a feeling something was a bit iffy," Emily chimed in. "But we wanted to be sure."

"What about the little bag in his throat?" Boone asked. "A *wanga*, I think it's called?"

"Dis one had one, too, I hear," Anel said, sobering. "A *wanga* is a kinda charm. Usually a packet or bag wit' a selection of specific herbs, and often a form of protection. But you don't put one down someone's throat. Unless..." His eyes went distant.

"Unless what?" Emily asked.

"What was in it?"

"The one from the Highland House... no idea," Boone said. "But the one found in the body from the Boiling Hole, I heard it had a lock of hair, herbs, and ashes."

"A lock of hair... huh. You know, when an *oungan* helps with a death rite, we might use a bit of hair or a fingernail clipping in de creation of a *govi*, to help guide de immortal part of the spirit of de deceased. But it is unusual to use one in a *wanga*."

"Unusual, but not unheard of," Boone said.

"I heard of somet'ing like dis back in de days of Papa Doc Duvalier, but I assume it were just a tale to intimidate. As I say... de *wanga* is often worn for protection. But in dis case, it might be a different kind of protection. It might be dat whoever put it in dere... it's to keep de spirit of de dead man from coming back and seeking vengeance."

Boone thought for a moment, but it was Emily who spoke first.

"Chicken!"

Boone and Anel looked at her quizzically.

"Sorry... brain blurted it out before I had a sentence to go with it. Are chickens used in voodoo? Or is that more Hollywood nonsense?"

"Sometimes a sacrifice is required for certain rites, and a chicken is often used. But dat isn't very common. Besides, dere aren't many live chickens on the island. Only Miss Riggs keeps dem, far as I know. Why? Was dere a chicken at de crime scene?"

"No... Deejay Ceejay found one by the Coast Guard station," Emily answered. "Dead. But not sacrificed or anything."

"Maybe we should head back up there tomorrow morning," Boone suggested. "Take him up on his offer of a sunrise coffee."

TWENTY-SIX

Boone and Em drove north in the pre-dawn darkness, with Emily at the wheel of an orange Jeep. The previous afternoon, they'd rented the vehicle from Harbour Adventures, at the far side of Cockburn Harbour. The owner, Carla, a former schoolteacher from Trinidad, had treated them to some conch fritters that she made on a little hot fryer beside a cooler of beers and sodas.

"You think we'll get more fritters when we return this?" Em wondered aloud.

Boone chuckled. "I think she said barracuda was next on the menu. Can't say I've ever heard of a rental car agency doubling as a liquor store with hot food."

Em slowed as the edge of her headlights illuminated a pair of donkeys crossing the road. "Donkeys and iguanas... the speed-limiters of the Caribbean," she said, accelerating once the way was clear.

Boone smiled. "You miss Bonaire?" he asked.

"Yeah, I do. You?"

"Same. Although most of my fondest memories are tied to the gal in the driver's seat."

Em spared a glance at Boone. "Let's keep racking up memories, shall we?"

Twenty minutes later they reached the bend that led up the hill to the Coast Guard station.

"I see CJ's car," Emily said, rolling to a stop near one of the old buildings.

While Em killed the engine and the headlights, Boone grabbed the thermos and three paper coffee cups he'd gotten from the resort's breakfast area.

As they exited, a deep voice called out, "Up here!" Between the two main buildings, a shadowy form waved at them.

"CJ, it's Emily and Boone," Em responded. "That offer of sunrise and coffee still on? We brought the coffee."

The man gave a rich and resonant laugh. "Well, Muddah Nature will provide de sunrise. I'm just doin' my morning meditations, but please join me."

They walked up to where CJ stood. A couple pieces of patio furniture, a few cinderblocks standing in for tables, a grill, and a yoga mat defined a small area near the drop-off to the ocean.

"Welcome to my little oasis," CJ said, waving a hand at the chairs. "Please, take a seat. Your timin' was good; sunrise comin' in about ten minutes."

Boone poured some coffee for each of them. "Sorry to show up unannounced."

"No worries, mon. I am glad you chose to visit."

"We woulda come here yesterday," Em said, "but we got caught up in an incident."

CJ nodded. "Highland House. I heard 'bout dat. Talked

'bout it on my news segments yesterday. Rumor reaches me, and I report what I can. Constable Terrance confirmed much of what I heard."

"So, you're a reporter as well as a disc jockey," Emily said.

"And a storyteller... sometimes a poet. Used to be a musician... and a taxi driver. A person should be more dan one t'ing."

"And now you have a radio station!" Emily said. "Hey, Radio Bambarra... that name have something to do with the rum?"

"De rum and de radio station name both come from de Bambarra people from West Africa. A Spanish slave ship sunk near Middle Caicos and many Belongers are descendants of dose people."

"So, you run your radio programs from here?" Boone asked.

"Sure do. De old equipment here can broadcast a decent signal. You know what dis place was?"

"Station for the United States Coast Guard," Em said.

"Yes, but de *kind* of station is important. Dis was a LORAN station."

"What's that?" Boone asked.

"Long-range navigation. Before GPS, ships could use de signals from multiple LORAN stations to determine location."

"And now, you pump out Bob Marley to those ships!" Emily said with a smile.

CJ raised his coffee cup to her, then looked thoughtful. "You know... saw a strange t'ing wit' a ship yesterday..." He pointed straight out to sea. "Right out dere."

"What was strange about it?" Boone asked.

"It look like a reg'lar short-haul cargo ship—not de big container ships, a small one like come into Cockburn Harbour from Provo. It had a single cargo container in front of de bridge, and de container... she open up like a flower."

"What?" Emily cocked her head. "This the poet part of you makin' an appearance, CJ?"

CJ laughed. "I s'pose. What I mean is, de cargo container open up, like it was hinged and hydraulic... and de whole t'ing flatten out. And den de helicopter came."

"Said Storyteller CJ," Em teased.

"Where you find dis one?" CJ said to Boone.

"Luck of the draw, I guess," he replied.

"Anyway, de helicopter land on de pad dat de cargo container make. And two men get out of it, carryin' luggage."

"People smuggling?" Em asked.

"I t'ought so at first, but dey hand over de luggage and men on de ship look in de bags. Den one man starts talkin' to de helicopter guys, and dey get angry and start shoutin'. And dat's when I notice... some of de men on de ship have guns. But serious guns, you know?"

"Assault rifles?" Boone asked.

"Yes. So, after a while, a man on de ship comes over and sets down two more pieces of luggage, but de soft kind. He take somet'in' out of one and show it to de helicopter men."

"What was it?" Emily asked.

"Too far away for me to be sure, but might coulda been a brick of cocaine. Anyway, after a while, de two men get back in de helicopter with de new bags, and dey take off and go back where dey come from."

"Which direction?"

"Oh! I should have said. Right over dere." In the dawn glow, he waved toward the south. "My neighbor over dere, he have a big house and a helicopter. It was his. I recognize it."

"Who's your neighbor?"

"Never met the man."

"Hey, CJ... that chicken you found. Did it belong to that woman you know?"

"Mrs. Riggs? Yes. She recognize de feathers. Said she sold it to a Haitian man on Saturday along wit' two others." CJ sat up in his chair. "Here comes de sun!"

Brilliant oranges lit the distant clouds across the channel, and the fiery orb peeked above the horizon. Since Boone and Emily usually lived on the leeward side of islands, they didn't often get to experience a true ocean-horizon sunrise.

"Beautiful," Boone breathed.

The trio sat in silence for several long minutes, enjoying the view.

CJ yawned and stretched. "You want a quick tour before I start my broadcast?"

"Sure thing!" Em said. "Although it'll have to be a quickie. We need to get back to help Lincoln and Mateo get ready for the morning dives."

"Ok, den..." CJ rose, but suddenly wobbled and gripped the arm of his chair.

"You all right, mate?" Emily asked.

"Yeah... just a dizzy spell. T'ink I might have come down wit' somet'ing. Headache not so bad today, so dat's good."

Boone looked up abruptly. "Headache? When did that start?"

"Few nights ago."

"The night before you found that dead chicken?" Boone asked.

"Yeah? Why?"

"Did anything strange happen that night?"

CJ looked at him, then sighed and sat back down. "As a

matter of fact, yes, somet'ing did. I t'ought it was a, uh... hallu-cination from... well, never mind."

"Tell me what happened," Boone pressed.

The deejay laid out everything that he could remember: the lights, the chicken sounds, and the weird—and painful—sensations he'd experienced.

Boone looked to the south. "It happened up there? Can you show me?"

CJ set down his coffee cup and stood, thankfully without an attack of vertigo. He led the way through the scraggly plants and bushes. "It was dark... but I t'ink I was about here when I felt de first... whatever it was. De lights were off dat way."

"Understood. Stay right there, if that's okay." Boone searched the area, but it was Emily who spotted something first, some distance away from where CJ stood.

"Feathers!" she said, waving a chicken feather in the air. "There's a bunch caught in the plants around here. Looks like a lot of chicken prints in this sandy area."

"The lights... were they here?" Boone called back to CJ.

"No... farther dat way!" he replied, pointing past Emily.

Boone continued in that direction, then came to a stop, looking at the ground. He crouched and took several pictures, then returned to the others.

"Some indentations and a lot of partial footprints. But I'm guessing several days of sea breezes has wiped most of them out. Although this heel looks familiar, doesn't it?" He held out the phone to Emily.

"The donkey poop shoe print!" Emily exclaimed.

"Might not be the same one, but..." Boone trailed off, looking back the way he'd come. "Where is your neighbor with the helicopter?"

"About half a mile sout', off a private drive." CJ abruptly winced.

"Headache back?" Emily asked.

"Yes. I got some ibuprofen back in de office."

"Well, let's go get it."

"Listen, CJ," Boone began as they headed back north. "I think you need to get checked out."

"I know. Plan to go to de clinic on de edge of town."

"I think you may need to go to Provo," Boone suggested. "Get a CT scan."

CJ stopped walking. "Why?"

"It's just a theory, but... let's get back to your office and I'll explain."

They started walking again, Emily twirling a chicken feather in her fingers. "Hey... CJ? Did Mrs. Riggs happen to tell you the name of the Haitian she sold the chickens to?

"She did. Man named Baptiste."

———

Baptiste LaGuerre snipped off a tiny lock of hair from behind his ear and added it to the little bowl, which already contained the ashes of a small piece of paper and the remains of three kinds of herbs. Taking the flickering votive candle, he tipped a trickle of melted wax onto the hair. Once it had hardened, he placed the waxy lock into a small pouch before adding several pinches of ash and herbs. Cinching the pouch tight, he looped a cord through the drawstring and hung it around his neck.

A fist pounded against the door of Baptiste's room, and Sergei called out. "Baptiste! Viktor wants to see you!"

Baptiste quickly tucked the *wanga* into his shirt and began disassembling his makeshift altar. "I be right dere. Where he want me?"

"By the pool."

"I hope de man put on some clothes dis time."

"You 'n' me both," Sergei said, his laughter fading as he moved away from the door.

Baptiste opened a drawer and carefully placed a variety of items inside, all components for his shrine to Guede Nibo, a member of Baron Samedi's group of *lwa*—or spirits—with domain over the dead. Guede Nibo was the first to ever die by violence, and he was the patron and guardian of all who died prematurely. Given his line of work, Baptiste had certainly been responsible for swelling Nibo's ranks.

The top of his chest of drawers now spotless, he exited his room and made his way down to the pool. Thankfully, Viktor was clothed, sitting at a small table eating breakfast outside. He did not invite Baptiste to sit.

"There you are. You know the boats at the harbor. Which one has the best speed and range?"

"De DECR boat, *Hammerhead*. No question. Very fast. And decent range, I expect, given what dey do."

"Good. Can we steal it?"

Baptiste shot a look at Sergei, who was seated off to the side. "What? No, I don't t'ink so. Dey keep it at de pier right by Immigration. Cameras, lights... and I'm sure dey've got some way to track it."

Viktor nodded, as if he'd expected that answer. "Who's next?"

Baptiste thought for a moment, slowly shaking his head. "Most of the boats are fishing boats, and not very fast... or skiffs and dinghies without much range."

"What about the dive boats?"

"De Newton dat went to Provo for maintenance was fast... twenty-five knots I heard. But de other one is older. Much slower. Although..."

"Yes?"

"You remember de dive boat from Grand Turk you had me ask about?"

Viktor smiled. "The one with the blue top and the beautiful young woman aboard?"

"Dat's de one. Dey went down to Fish Cay de other day. Rescued some migrants. I was talkin' to Mack, who was talkin' to Doug; dat boat has a crazy engine some cartel put in her. Don't know de top speed, but Mack say Doug say it was flying."

"Hmm... it was called the *Lunasea*, if I remember correctly."

"Dat's right."

"Very well," Viktor said, working his jaw, deep in thought. "We need that boat. Moscow wants us to hit the *Anya* before sunrise tomorrow. According to her itinerary, she'll be leaving tomorrow for the Mediterranean."

Viktor thought a moment. He'd planned on scoring some points by revealing the yacht's location, but apparently Moscow had other ways of tracking her.

"The *Lunasea* is probably out running morning dives," Viktor mused. "Sergei... go down and wait for them to return. Ask to charter them for an afternoon or night dive. Triple their normal rate. Whatever it takes."

"Uh..." This time it was Sergei's turn to sneak a look toward Baptiste. "I'm not sure that's a good idea. For *me* to go down there. Or Baptiste."

"And why is that?"

"Well... they've seen us before."

"So? It's a small island."

"They saw us right after the, uh... 'experiment' at Highland

House. I forgot to mention it. When we were coming back for the tarp, Baptiste ran off the road and got stuck. They came along and helped us out."

Baptiste expected Viktor to rage at him, but instead he just shook his head with a sigh, then tossed his linen napkin onto his plate. "Fine. I'll do it myself."

TWENTY-SEVEN

At a quarter past noon after the morning dives, Emily navigated back along Long Cay, slowing as they came near *Big Sister*, moored at the Troy's Dream dive site. Em waved across to Doug, who had his feet up on the dash; she noticed one foot was waggling to the same beat coming out of the *Lunasea*'s radio, tuned to Radio Bambarra. Doug returned the wave. Lincoln would be down below with one of the other Reef Divers divemasters; their Bubble Chasers Diving coworker seemed to enjoy being with others from his birth island, so they'd kept the boat assignments the same.

Emily slowed as she approached the gap between Long and Dove, then entered the bay and aimed the bow toward their pier. The bouncing rake-and-scrape song on the radio came to an end and CJ came on.

"Hey dere, Belongers... dat was Bo Dog and De Rooters, from our Bahamian neighbors to de north. Just lettin' you good folks know Deejay Ceejay'll be cuttin' out early today. Got to take a trip over to Provo to make sure all my parts work. But before I go, I gwonna

finish up my readin' from Kingston Noir. *Dis is de last short story in de book: 'Monkey Man,' by Colin Channer."*

Emily was only able to enjoy a few sentences of his reading before they came alongside the pier and Boone secured the boat with Mateo's help. Em switched off the radio to better concentrate, and they were soon snugged up against the fenders.

Mateo met the van and joined the guest divers for the return to the resort, leaving Boone and Emily to clean up the *Lunasea* and prepare the boat for the afternoon dive. The pair planned on grabbing a quick bite across the street at Sunset Café.

"CJ's going over to Provo to get checked out," Em told Boone, knowing the flybridge radio couldn't be heard below when the boat was at speed.

"Good. I might be way off base, but couldn't hurt to get himself checked. Headaches and vertigo popping up out of the blue is nothing to ignore."

"Agreed. Hey, you spray down the deck, and I'll grab the compressor hose so we can do the refills before *Big Sister* hogs them."

"Good plan."

Emily stepped across to the pier and went around the back of the compressor truck to power it up.

"Excuse me, sorry to disturb you..."

Emily turned to find a man in his forties, well-tanned and dressed in a pink linen shirt and white slacks. A pair of iridescent wraparound sunglasses were firmly in place on his face, and Em would have found him handsome if it weren't for what she assumed was a bad hair transplant, his hairline reminiscent of a doll's head.

"Is that your boat there?" he asked with a touch of an

accent, flashing a big smile of teeth that looked to be in need of a trip to the dentist.

Emily smiled back. "Yes! I'm one of the owners of Bubble Chasers Diving." She tugged at the tank top she wore. "I've been meaning to get some proper T-shirts made, but haven't finished the new logo."

"You will hear no complaint from me. I think what you are wearing is quite fetching."

Oh, goodie... one of those. "Well... thanks for that," she said with a tolerant smile.

"I apologize if that was forward, or inappropriate," he quickly said. "Where I am from, we can be a bit bold."

"S'all right. I thought I detected a bit of an accent... where you from?"

The man smiled again, and there was a micro-hesitation. "Poland. And you?"

"England. I'm Emily."

"Viktor. Very pleased to meet you, Emily."

"And this here's Boone," she added as he approached. No doubt Boone was wondering what was taking her so long. "My... co-owner."

"Ah, excellent," Viktor said, his sunglasses pivoting to Boone. "My houseguests and I are looking for a dive charter this afternoon. Can your boat reach Ambergris Cay? I hear there are some unspoiled reefs there."

"Yeah, she can reach there easily," Boone said, "but I'm afraid we've got a full boat this afternoon."

"You misunderstand... we would be looking for a private charter. And I promise you, I'd make it worth your while."

"Gee... I don't think we can do that," Emily said. "We're contracted out to Reef Divers this week, three dives a day."

"Oh. That is a shame. But I have a solution! We would be just as happy to do a night dive. Even more so!"

"I'm sorry, but they don't do night dives on South Caicos." Boone said.

Viktor looked annoyed. "This is a Reef Divers rule, yes? But you are your own operation, are you not? Surely you can make an exception for... let us say... four times your normal rate?"

"It's a safety issue. No hyperbaric chamber here, and no night flights."

Viktor waved a hand dismissively. "Then it is no problem! I have a helicopter."

Behind her huge lime-green sunglasses, Emily stole a glance at Boone before speaking. "You... have a helicopter? Wow! Haven't met many guys with one of those."

"Yes. And we have night-flying instrumentation. So, you see? No safety issue."

"I don't want to violate Reef Divers' policy when we're working for them," Boone said. "Besides, we've got a full day of dives tomorrow. But we'll be free Saturday, if you're still looking for a private charter then."

Viktor shook his head and clenched his jaw. He winced, then massaged his cheek. "Then, I suppose that will have to do... but perhaps... perhaps you will do me the honor of joining me for dinner? I confess, being on a small island like this, I don't often meet interesting people."

"What about your guests?" Boone asked. "Your diver friends?"

"Oh, yes, but they are old friends. Always the same boring stories. Please, you must join me. My chef is excellent, and my home is beautiful. Please. Do me this courtesy."

"Where's your place?" Emily asked, still keeping one eye on

Boone. She had a feeling he was about to ask that same question.

"It's on the coast with a beautiful view of the ocean."

"Way up north?" she asked. "Near the old Coast Guard station?"

"Yes."

"Think we saw it when we came over from Grand Turk. Gorgeous place."

"Then you'll come?"

Em now turned her face fully toward Boone. "We've still got the Jeep..."

Boone shrugged. "I'm always up for a good meal."

"Wonderful!" Viktor was all smiles again. "Do you have a map on your phone? I'll show you where to go."

"Sure." Boone opened it up, moved the map to the upper part of South Caicos and zoomed in on a big house on the satellite view. "This you?"

Viktor looked. "Yes. How did you find it so fast?"

"I'm good with maps. And as Em said, we saw it when we came over."

"Then I'll see you at six-thirty, an hour before sunset."

"Is there a dress code?" Emily asked. "We came over with limited options."

"None whatsoever. Wear whatever you wish. Your kind of beauty doesn't require a fancy dress."

With that, he turned and walked back toward the main road.

"You realize he's going to seat you next to him at the table," Boone said with a grin.

"Distinct possibility," Em said, then asked, "Is this a good idea?"

"Probably not, but admit it... you're as curious as I am."

272

"There's a famous saying about curiosity, and it never turns out well for the kitty cat."

"Good thing we're dog people."

———

After the third dive of the day, Boone and Emily returned to the pier to drop off the guests. *Big Sister* was back, and Boone went across to find Lincoln. The young man spotted him first.

"Boone! You miss me yet?"

"Hey man! How's your week going?"

"Been very chill," Lincoln replied. "I t'ought, wit' so large a group, it would be crazy... but our divers, most of dem are veterans. And it's been great catchin' up on what's been goin' on in South Caicos with Doug."

"Listen, we got an invite to have dinner at this rich guy's house up north," Boone said. "Sounds like he wants to do a dive charter sometime. Wanna come?"

"Oh, t'ank you for askin', but Troy and I are goin' out. Gwanna take some ladies dancing at Leah's tonight! Troy's de DECR officer who help wit' de migrants."

"Yeah, I remember him. The fast-boat skipper. Well, you two have a great time! See ya tomorrow."

Returning to the *Lunasea*, Boone and Emily prepared her for the next day, put her to bed in the bay, then returned to the resort to change clothes. Boone hit the shower first, then joined Emily in the master bedroom.

"Why do you think he invited us?" Emily pulled off her tank top and flung it into their makeshift hamper, an empty suitcase lying in the corner.

"He didn't really invite *us*. He invited *you*. I was just in the line of fire. He mighta been wearing sunglasses, but there was no doubt where his eyes were."

"Fair point," Emily admitted, examining the sparse options in the closet. "So, here's a question... if this guy's helicopter is indeed the one that Ceejay saw landing on that ship..." She let the words hang in the air.

"Which it probably is," Boone said, grabbing his least objectionable pair of cargo shorts from a drawer and pulling them on. "Whatever it was doing out there, it's probably why he has a seaside mansion."

"My money's on drugs," Emily said. "That is to say... my money is on *his* money coming from drugs." She laughed and looked over her shoulder at him. "That sounded much more clever when it was still in my head."

Boone smiled, nudging her aside to grab the one and only shirt he had hanging in the closet. "Suitcases full of square grouper? Maybe. Look, we're just going for a nice dinner in a fancy house. If we happen to ask a few questions along the way... so be it."

"Get in, get the lobster, get out."

"How do you know he's gonna serve—"

"He's gonna serve lobster," Em said with certainty, as she narrowed her choices to two sundresses and held them up. "Which?"

Boone tapped the green one with spaghetti straps before slipping into his lightweight, button-down shirt.

"You don't have actual shoes, do you?"

Boone looked at the sandals on his feet. "I have my ratty old sneakers, but I think these are the better bet."

"Agreed. Begrudgingly." Emily laid the dress on the bed and stripped off the rest of her clothes. She tossed them into the hamper-suitcase, then headed into the bathroom. "Shower time." She threw him a crooked smile. "*Not* an invitation. Alas, we don't have the time." Em closed the door with a waggle of her eyebrows.

Boone blew out a breath, then left the bedroom and went out on the balcony. Eyes on the waters of the bay, he sifted through his thoughts.

TWENTY-EIGHT

Emily drove the orange rental Jeep up the long road—or maybe it was Viktor's driveway, as there didn't appear to be anything else along it. Once they crested the hill, the roofs of the villa came into view. The landscaping was impeccable, with a number of plants that probably weren't native interspersed with flowering bushes and palms. The villa itself was inset into the landscape, several steps down from the road.

"I don't see any other cars," Emily noted.

"Maybe there's some kind of motor pool off to the side. But let's just pull over in front."

"In case we need to make a quick getaway?"

"I was gonna say 'so we don't have to go looking for the Jeep in the dark,' but yeah, fast getaway works too."

As they pulled up to a stone-lined entry sidewalk, a dark-skinned man dressed in a white shirt and black slacks rose from a small bench near the walkway. He waved and approached them as they exited the Jeep. "Good evening. Mr. Gusev is expecting you. If you will follow me?" He spoke slowly, and from his accent, Boone guessed he was Haitian.

The man turned and approached the house, descending three short steps to reach a small entry-patio, flanked by a pair of urn fountains, chest-high and constructed of stacked slate. With fresh water so scarce on the island, this struck Boone as an extravagance.

The man opened a glass door and stepped aside to let them in, then closed it after them. "Follow me, please." He walked through an impressive living room with high ceilings and opened a sliding glass door at the far end, leading them to an equally impressive outdoor area, much of it covered in two-toned paving stones. A large infinity pool dominated the space, with seating areas and large pergolas on either side. One of the tables was set for dinner, a linen tablecloth rustling in the breeze. On a raised area to the left, a small bistro table and chairs sat with a commanding view of the ocean. In one of those chairs sat Viktor.

"Mr. Gusev," the man called out, pronouncing the name with care. "Your guests have arrived."

"Ah, good! Welcome!" His eyes roamed over Emily's body before popping back up to her face. "What a beautiful sundress. What are you drinking? Pierre, take their drink orders."

"Just a Coke, if you have one," Emily said. "In the can is fine."

"Water for me," Boone added.

"Water and soda... not very adventurous," Viktor said as Pierre left to get their drinks.

"We've got a full slate of dives tomorrow," Emily said. "Drinking and diving don't mix."

Boone nodded his agreement. Although neither of them

would hesitate to have a beer or two with dinner during a dive week, he agreed with Em's instinct to keep a clear head.

"Well, I hope you will make an exception for dinner. I have an excellent Marcassin Estate Chardonnay chilling. It pairs perfectly with lobster."

Boone caught Emily looking up at him with an arched eyebrow. "Lobster! What a pleasant surprise," she said.

"Yes, I had my people pick up some fresh today."

"Really?" Boone said. "I thought lobster was out of season."

Viktor shrugged. "Anything is available, for the right price. Except your boat!" He laughed. "I'm not used to people turning down such a generous offer for a simple charter."

"Sorry about that," Emily said. "But like we said, we could probably accommodate you and your guests on Saturday."

"Where are your guests?" Boone asked, looking at the dinner table. "I only see four place settings."

"Ah, yes... my friend Paz will join us, but the rest were disappointed there would be no charter, so my pilot took them over to Grand Turk for a night dive. He'll go back for them in the morning."

"How long's it take to pop across?" Emily asked.

"Less than ten minutes."

Pierre returned with their beverages in two iced glasses and Viktor beckoned them up to the small overlook. A martini glass with a single olive sat on the bistro table. "Come! Sit up here. The view is wonderful."

Boone followed, taking a sip of his water. He grimaced. However they were getting their water, they probably needed to change a filter. Emily also made a face after a sip of soda. "Probably the ice cubes," Boone said quietly as they went up the short flight of stone steps. *She asked for it in a can, didn't she?*

"Every once in a while," Viktor said, pointing down at the reef line, "I see a dive boat out there. But not often."

"The winds have to behave," Boone said. "Heard there are some great swim-throughs there... but we haven't dived there this week."

"And yet, I think I saw your boat down there... on Saturday, was it?"

"Yeah, that's when we came across," Emily said. "Might have seen you, too... quite a *lot* of you, if that was you," she added with a wink.

Viktor laughed. "Oh, yes, I was swimming, and with the privacy I have here, I usually don't bother with a swimsuit." Far from blushing, Viktor seemed to puff out his chest a little. "And you were down there with another boat, as I remember. Odd-looking thing."

"A sargassum harvester," Emily explained. "The inventor was having engine problems."

"It had something jammed in a paddlewheel on the side," Boone said. "Guess what it was."

"Sargassum, I imagine." Viktor said.

"Cocaine," Boone said, watching the man carefully. "A brick of cocaine. And there was more in the basket in back."

"Really? Interesting." Viktor picked up his martini glass and tilted it to and fro, catching the light of the setting sun in its icy liquid.

Boone checked in with Emily; she was watching Viktor as well, but the man didn't show any overt reaction.

"Actually, I'm not surprised. On two separate occasions, when I was flying over from Grand Turk, I've seen crew on small boats tossing things overboard... until they realize it's not a Coast Guard helicopter flying toward them." He chuckled. "I wonder if they go back and try to fish the coke back into the boat."

Boone took another sip of water, again noting the off taste. Emily set her soda down on the table, and Viktor's eyes went to the glass.

"Is the cola not to your liking?"

"Oh, it's fine. Just pacing myself. So... Viktor... what's Poland like?"

Viktor's brow knit for a brief moment, but then he smiled and spoke in a rush. "Oh, it is beautiful! I am from Gdansk, on the Baltic Sea. I have not been back in a while, but I hope to return to visit family."

"I must confess, I have a weak spot for pierogies," Emily said. "Some grilled onions and sour cream on those bad boys... scrummy!"

"Delicious," Boone translated when Viktor cocked his head.

"Ah, yes... they are quite good." He slipped an olive from the skewer in his martini and popped it into his mouth. He chewed and abruptly stiffened, sucking in a breath and making a guttural noise.

"You all right, mate?" Emily asked.

Viktor nodded, wincing. "A toothache," he said, massaging the side of his jaw.

"Looks like a bad one, yeah?" Em observed. "Probably should get that looked at."

Boone sensed someone down by the pool and turned to find a small, bespectacled man in a guayabera shirt looking up at them.

"Paz!" Viktor called out, his tooth pain clearly dissipating. "Quit lurking about and join us."

The man below glanced back toward the main house and raised a hand at his side, then came up toward the overlook.

Boone spotted movement beyond the glass doors to the living room. It was probably Pierre or another member of the staff, but something about that little hand motion seemed off. Furtive.

"*Buenas noches*," Paz said as he reached them. "I hope you are enjoying the view."

"It's gorgeous," Boone said.

"Paz is a dear friend," Viktor explained. "We go way back."

"Yes. We do. We are," Paz said, nodding. "*Amigos.*"

Paz struck Boone as a bookish type; a bit socially awkward. His accent was quite familiar. From their time in the Cayman Islands, Boone and Em had encountered many people from nearby Cuba.

"Well, pleased to meet you, Paz," Emily said. "This is Boone, I'm Emily."

"Pleased to meet you, as well." Paz's eyes were on Boone and Emily's drink glasses.

"Thirsty, Paz?" Viktor said. "Go have Pierre set you up with something, then join us at the dinner table."

Paz nodded and descended the steps, glancing back once before vanishing into the villa.

"Forgive him—Paz is a little shy. Please, enjoy the sunset. I'll check with the kitchen and be right back." Viktor rose and went down past the pool, entering the glass doors Paz had just exited through.

"You heard the man, let's enjoy the sunset," Boone said, reaching down and grabbing both their drinks from the little table. "Join me at the rail." He handed her the soda.

"Blech, I'm done with this."

"How much of it did you drink?"

"Couple sips," Emily said, looking at him suspiciously. "Tastes like shite."

"Same. Do as I do... keep the ice." Boone put an arm around her and drew her close, keeping their backs to the villa. Holding the glass in front of him, he extended his forefinger and middle-finger over the ice in his glass, then poured the liquid over the side into the foliage below.

"You think it's drugged, don't you?" Emily said, ditching her cola.

"I don't know," Boone said. "It's got a chemical taste, and that could be from their water-maker, but both Viktor and his friend were eyeing our glasses. Better safe than sorry."

Emily looked over the edge. "No quick exit that way."

"I don't think we're at that stage," Boone said. "But I'll text Lincoln to call us in five minutes. We'll tell our hosts there's a problem with the boat and have to go, then head out before the dinner."

"Much as I'd enjoy a fancy meal, I endorse your plan."

Boone typed the request and tapped Send. He was about to put away his phone but realized he hadn't heard the familiar sound effect that occurred when he sent a text. Looking at the screen, he saw why; the words *Not Delivered* appeared in red next to the unsent text.

"Problem?" Emily asked. When Boone showed her his screen, Em waggled her fingers at him. "Gimme mine."

Boone dug her phone out of a cargo pocket; as often happened on a night out with Emily—particularly when she wore a lightweight dress—he became the pack mule for any items she wished to bring.

Emily took it and tried texting Lincoln; she was met with the same result. "That's weird, innit?"

Boone nodded, glancing around. "We're not that far from town, as far as cell signals go, and we're on high ground." As Boone looked down at the table set for dinner, a woman in a maid's uniform appeared from a side door from the north wing. She appeared to be South Asian or Polynesian, and she carried a basket of bread. As she set it down, she spotted them watching her. Sparing a glance toward the sliding glass door where Viktor had gone, the woman turned and locked eyes with Boone. Ever so slightly, she shook her head, then turned and hurried back inside the side door.

"You saw that, right?" Emily said quietly.

"Yeah. And she looked afraid."

"Sod the lobster, we're out of here."

Boone looked toward the glass doors to the living room, remembering Paz's surreptitious hand gesture. Blackout curtains were gathered to one side of the glass. "I think there's at least one other person in there."

"Maybe that Pierre bloke," Em suggested. "Follow my lead. I'm gonna ask for a little pre-dinner tour of the place. Soon as we get near the front door, we bugger off to the Jeep."

Emily descended the steps and Boone followed her around the pool. Viktor and Paz came outside from the living room as they approached.

"Dinner is ready, if you'd care to be seated," Viktor said. "Ah... you finished your drinks. Can I refresh them for you?"

"Nah, we're good," Em said quickly. "Tiny bladder and all, yeah? Say, I've never seen such a posh place... any chance of a quick tour before we tuck in?"

During this exchange, Boone watched Paz; the Cuban's eyes were locked on their now-empty glasses. Boone's eyes flicked to the curtains. *They moved.*

"They didn't drink it," Paz said abruptly.

Viktor's gracious-host façade cracked. "Dammit, nothing is ever easy. Baptiste!"

Boone's suspicions were confirmed as a man came through

the glass doors, a handgun rising from his side. Boone instantly recognized him as the driver from the stuck vehicle they'd assisted. "You two, hands on your h—"

Boone stepped into him with blinding speed, forcefully throwing a shoulder into Paz as he passed, sending the small man sprawling to the ground. Cut off mid-sentence, Baptiste tried to swing his pistol the rest of the way up, but Boone was already outside of his arm's arc. Boone's preferred combat style of capoeira involved evasion and keeping one's distance, but that wasn't what was called for here, facing a gun. Instead, he employed a Krav Maga move that Emily had taught him. Releasing his empty glass to shatter on the tiles, Boone latched onto both gun and wrist and violently twisted, applying sudden and painful pressure as the wrist was bent to the breaking point, the barrel of the gun inverted to face Baptiste.

The Haitian howled as Boone tore the weapon from his grasp, nearly breaking his trigger finger. Out of the corner of his eye, Boone saw Viktor grab for Emily. Still gripping Baptiste's wrist, Boone followed up with a quick headbutt to the bridge of his nose, spun him toward the pool, then snapped a *chapa* side-kick into the man's breastbone, sending him flying into the shallow end of the pool.

The primary threat dealt with, Boone spun to assist Emily, only to discover she didn't need it. Viktor was on one knee, clutching his groin.

"C'mon!" Em shouted, dashing for the door.

Boone raised the handgun and aimed it toward Viktor, then Baptiste, who was gripping the edge of the pool, dripping wet and wincing. Keeping the gun trained behind, he backpedaled after Emily into the living room.

"Boone!" Em shouted, as Pierre appeared from the north wing and rushed them.

The butler—or whatever he was—didn't appear to be armed, but Boone recognized a fighter's stance when he saw one; he swung the gun to face this new threat, leveling the barrel on the man's chest; Pierre halted in his tracks, raising his hands. At the same instant, Boone saw the man's eyes flick to his right, toward the alcove that housed the front door. Without thinking, Boone pivoted and aimed the gun at the main entryway. "Em, get behind me!"

A muscular man came around the corner, a handgun held in a two-handed shooter's grip. Encountering the barrel of Boone's weapon, his eyes went wide with surprise, and he quickly threw himself backward into the entry alcove. Boone recognized him as the beefy guy who'd been with Baptiste when they'd gotten their Jeep stuck.

"Drop your weapon!" the man shouted from cover, his Brooklyn accent ratcheted up with the sudden burst of adrenaline.

"How about you drop yours?" Boone said. "Toss it out here and we'll be on our way."

"Fat chance. You even know how to use that thing?"

"Definitely," Boone replied with more confidence than he felt. *But I might be a bit rusty.* Growing up in Tennessee, he'd done his share of shooting. And during his time in Bonaire, an old shopkeeper and occasional father figure, Martin Petersen, had taken him out for some surreptitious target practice in the desert north of Rincon. Martin had a pair of Glocks for protection, and the old man had declared Boone's abilities with a handgun to be "decent." But Boone hadn't fired a gun in ages. *In fact, the last time I fired a handgun was when I shot that terrorist on the deck of that narco sub. But it's just like riding a bike, right?*

"You're not gettin' out this way, pretty boy," the goon called around the corner.

Em tugged on Boone's shirt and nodded her head toward the south wing.

"No idea if there's an exit through there," he whispered, then swung his gun to face Pierre, who'd crept several steps closer. "Back up!" Boone shouted.

"Sergei! Where are you?" Viktor's voice called out from the pool area.

"Front door, boss," the unseen man shouted back. "Guy's got a gun."

"Back outside," Emily said, grabbing Boone's hand and pulling him toward the sliding door.

Boone followed, sweeping the gun between Pierre and the entry alcove as he reached out and found Emily's hand. The pair retreated to the pool area. Baptiste was unsteadily rising to his feet and Viktor was just to the side of the doorway, leaning against the glass. Boone swept the gun between them, stepping backward away from them, and toward Paz, who still lay crumpled on the paving stones.

"Whatever you have going on here, we want no part of it," Boone said.

"Well, that's too bad," Viktor said. "We need your boat."

"What for?" Emily asked.

Viktor didn't answer her. "Sergei! Pierre!"

Pierre appeared at the door. Boone flicked his eyes over his shoulder, spotting a pergola over a massage table, a telescope, and yes... a garden path leading to the south. "We're leaving." He pushed Emily that way and took another step back. "Any of you come after us, I'll—"

Boone's ability to speak was interrupted by a searing pain as the muscles in his right leg seized up. He was aware of Emily shouting and a rush of movement as several assailants charged him all at once.

Emily had been a few feet away from Boone when Paz suddenly shifted on the ground, his hand holding something about the size of a remote control for a television. *Bastard was playing possum!* Before she could shout a warning, the Cuban rammed a stun gun into Boone's bare calf, its tips sparking just before it was pressed into flesh. Boone stiffened, his face a mask of pain.

"Boone!" Emily cried. She grabbed the man's hand and pulled the weapon away from Boone's leg. Still prone on the ground, Paz couldn't prevent her tearing it from his grip and kicking him in the face.

Unsteady, Boone tried to raise his gun as Baptiste and Pierre rushed him from opposite sides, the trio grappling for possession of the weapon. Emily stepped in and triggered the stun gun, sticking it against the side of Baptiste's head. The device gave off a staticky clicking sound and the Haitian's teeth clenched, his face a rictus of pain. Boone managed to throw him off and was shifting his focus to Pierre when Sergei suddenly appeared on the pool patio and pistol-whipped Boone, slamming the barrel against his temple.

Tears burst from Emily's eyes as Boone crumpled to the paving stones like a puppet with its strings cut, his gun clattering across the ground. "Bastard!" she cried, hurling herself toward the burly man. Pierre stepped between them and got 50,000 volts for his efforts.

"That's enough out of you!" Sergei yelled, stooping and pointing his handgun at Boone's now-motionless head. "Unless you want your boyfriend's brains all over the ground."

Emily froze, but she maintained her grip on the stun gun.

"Personally, I would prefer Sergei not redecorate my patio," Viktor said. "I just resurfaced it." He looked over at Paz, who was nursing a bloody nose. "Paz, you sneaky son of a bitch... I did not know you had that little zapper on you."

"I retrieved it when they seemed hesitant to drink their drinks."

"You said the drug was tasteless."

"I never said that—I said it was hard to detect. But when I saw the empty glasses, I knew they had poured them out. If they had drained those drinks, they would've been semiconscious at best."

Now that she thought about it, Emily did feel just a little bit woozy—although that could've been the adrenaline. She took a step toward Boone.

"Now, now, none of that," Viktor said, stooping to pick up the gun Boone had dropped. He leveled it at Emily. "Playtime is over. Please drop Paz's toy."

"I drop this, you're just going to kill us," Emily hissed.

"Who said anything about killing you? A beautiful girl such as you, I'd very much like to keep alive. As I said, I need your boat. And... my preference would be for *you* to drive it. You'll come with us... and Baptiste will stay here and babysit your friend. As an insurance policy." He looked out to sea as the thumping beat of rotors heralded the approach of a helicopter. "Diego's back. Perfect timing."

Em looked down at Boone, who was beginning to stir. Glaring at the men surrounding her, most of whom had now recovered from her jolts, she didn't see any way out. Her bare shoulders drooped, and she let her arms fall to her sides. Emily dropped the stun gun with a plastic clatter. "You win, you bloody rotter."

TWENTY-NINE

Viktor checked his watch as Sergei guided Emily toward the Jeep. *A few minutes after eight.*

"In you go," Sergei ordered the petite blonde, as he held open the back door to the white Jeep and ushered her inside.

Viktor leaned in after her. "Remember that charter I asked for? That's all this is. You'll be taking some of us to Ambergris Cay for a little excursion. Actually, it worked out for the best that you didn't drink the drug. Now, instead of waiting for your head to clear, we can get going much sooner. But if you try anything... I'll have Baptiste shoot Boone. On the other hand, if you behave... do as you're told... you and your boyfriend will get out of this alive."

"How do I know you won't just snuff us the minute you get to Ambergris?"

"Assuming you don't make a fuss, I don't see any reason to harm you. Once we've done what we're going there to do, I'll need you to bring us back. And I'll have Boone waiting for you on the pier."

"I'll need to talk to him on the phone. Check in with him during the trip; make sure he's all right."

"Proof of life? Fair enough. But you'll be using one of our phones, obviously. We've taken the pair of phones your boyfriend had. As well as these..." Viktor jingled a set of keys with a floaty on the keychain. "I assume these are for the boat?"

"Yeah."

"And this one?" he asked, holding up a single key on a basic keychain. "For the rental?"

Emily simply nodded.

"I'll leave that in the ignition for you. For when you get back."

"You're a right gentleman, you are," she muttered.

Viktor watched the expression on her perfect face as it fluctuated between anger and despair. *Such a beautiful young woman,* he thought. "Wait here." He started to shut the door on her but had a thought. "Your boat... does it have any dive gear on it at the moment?"

The blonde looked up at him defiantly. "Why?"

"I think you are misunderstanding the power dynamic here. Answer my question... or I'll ask your lover the same question... in a much more *unpleasant* manner."

Emily sagged and dropped her eyes. "Yeah. We've got spare kit. Couple sets."

"And tanks?"

"Thirty-two of them. Full. Some air, some Nitrox."

"See? That wasn't so hard." He closed the car door and took several paces away. "Pierre?"

"Yessir," the man answered, stepping up to him.

"You'll drive us down to the harbor, then come back here and assist Baptiste." He gestured toward Emily. "Keep her company a moment."

Viktor gestured to Sergei, Paz, and Diego to follow him back to the villa. Once inside the living room area, he had them wait while he went to Paz's workshop to fetch Baptiste. Inside, the Haitian bodyguard was sitting in an office chair, swiveling from side to side, eyes on his prisoner. Boone was secured to a sturdy chair in the corner—the very chair that had held their first unfortunate test subject. Each wrist and forearm was zip-tied to an arm of the chair, and each ankle was zipped to a chair leg. The divemaster still seemed groggy, but he managed to raise his head and glare at Viktor.

"Where's Emily?" he demanded.

"Safe and sound. And assuming you sit here quietly, you'll be reunited before daybreak." He motioned Baptiste outside of the room, just out of earshot of their prisoner. "How secure is he?"

"If ol' Lucien couldn't break free while we was frying his brain, I don't 'spect dis man can."

"In that case, shut the door and join us in the living room."

Once everyone was assembled, Viktor laid out their assignments. "Diego, you'll take the helicopter over to Ambergris Cay and wait. We may need you. Paz... I'm counting on you to assist me with the explosives."

The Cuban looked surprised. "Demolitions is not my area of expertise."

"The electronic component for the timers and detonators is most certainly something you'll be better at than I."

"You hired me to design weapons for you and I have done so. Assisting with an assassination is not part of my job description."

"It is now. The money for the microwave weapon is locked away from us until we carry out this task."

Paz sighed. "I looked at what they provided you. Four

magnetic limpets to secure netting containing the linked explosives. They're arranged in a square, approximately one meter per side. The entire block will need to detonate simultaneously in close proximity to the *Anya*'s fuel tanks if you want to do catastrophic damage."

"And I'm certain you had a look at the blueprints for the ship as well?"

"Yes. *Anya* has a steel hull, so the limpets will work anywhere. The best place to secure the block of explosives would be below the waterline, just aft of amidships."

Viktor laughed. "And you say it's not your area of expertise? Excellent work. Sergei, pack some weaponry for us; we may need something more than a few handguns if we hit a snag. And you have dive gear, yes?"

"Yeah. But I haven't dived in a while."

"The yacht is anchored in fairly shallow water. You'll be fine."

"What about tanks?" Sergei asked.

"Already on the dive boat. And there is additional gear aboard, according to the girl. She will be driving the boat."

Baptiste sucked his teeth in disapproval. "You sure dat's a good idea? I can drive de boat for you."

"If you drive a boat like you drive a Jeep, I think I'd rather take my chances with the girl. Besides, the Turks and Caicos are full of shallows and sand banks, and she knows her own boat. I want to get down there as quickly as possible without hitting a reef."

"What you want me to do, den?"

"You are going to stay here and keep our other hostage company. I'll be guaranteeing Emily's cooperation with a promise of his safety. Keep the sat phone handy; she'll probably want to call in and check on him."

"Okay," Baptiste said. "And what do we do with them when you're done with the yacht?"

"Well... I'm thinking I might keep the blonde around for a while," Viktor said, a lustful gleam in his eye.

"And the man? Mister... Fischer?"

"Do you have one of those little magic bags ready?" Viktor asked.

Baptiste reached down into his shirt and brought a *wanga* out, letting it dangle from a cord atop his chest.

"Good. You'll be needing that. And this." He handed over the key to the orange rental Jeep. "Dispose of the body properly this time. Pierre will be back, so take him with you. Leave the Jeep in some secluded area on the north end."

"How do you want me to do it?" Baptiste asked. "Bullet? Garotte?"

"Paz... how easy would it be to set up the backup prototype and give Baptiste a lesson?"

The Cuban smiled. "Five minutes or less. Ease of use is one of its selling points. But I remind you, it hasn't been calibrated like the one we sold. There will be some blistering of the skin."

Viktor shrugged. "Sunburn is common in the tropics."

"A corpse doesn't get sunburnt," Paz said.

"Good! It'll confuse the time of death, then. Now, go teach Baptiste how to use your toy and join me outside."

Viktor went with Sergei to examine his available weaponry, not noticing the door to the kitchen wing silently swinging shut.

Boone tested his bonds, wincing as the plastic bit into his skin. He'd had a run-in with zip-ties before, although these weren't the flex-cuff type he'd been bound with aboard the hijacked mega-yacht *Apollo*. His own arms and legs were strapped to the arms and legs of the chair—ligatures on his ankles and a double helping on his arms at wrists and forearms. *Maybe I can tip it over... break it apart.* He wasn't sure that would do him much good, since the chair was made of metal; his flesh would likely give way first.

Muffled male voices were just audible through the door, but he couldn't make out what they were saying. His head still pounding from the pistol-whipping, Boone swept his eyes across the items on the desk and two workbenches that took up most of one wall and part of another: multiple monitors and computer workstations, a laptop, an array of tools including a soldering gun... and in the far corner atop one of the work-benches, an odd device. Black and vaguely rifle-shaped, it reminded Boone of those pulse rifles in the movie *Aliens*. Although this one was less elegant, with coils and soldered connections exposed along its length, and there wasn't any conventional barrel that he could see.

Boone looked at all the equipment in the room. *There's no way they'd let me see all this and then let me go.*

The door abruptly opened, and Baptiste entered the room, his eyes on Boone. He tossed a key on a ring onto one of the workbenches, then stood over Boone and leaned over, examining his wrists. "Looks like you been pullin' at de ties. Trust me, I been usin' dese for years; you'll only hurt yo'self."

Boone didn't reply, as his own eyes were locked on the small bag dangling by a cord from the man's neck. Behind Baptiste, the small Cuban man, Paz, entered the room.

"Where you turn off dat cell phone jammer?" Baptiste asked. "I got de sat phone, but Pierre don't have one. I may need to talk to him while you're gone."

Paz stepped over to a workstation and clicked on an icon on the screen. "Done." He turned to the corner workbench and lifted the strange device. Gathering a small object that reminded Boone of a battery you'd plug into a cordless drill, he clicked it into place on the underside of the device. "Take this," Paz said, handing it to Baptiste before picking up a tripod stand that lay under the workbench. Without a word, the two men left and shut the door.

Boone looked down at his feet. Scorch marks surrounded the chair he inhabited. Images of the dead man in Highland House rushed into his mind.

Emily had tried her best to chat up Pierre, but the man sitting beside her was no longer the friendly, gracious butler who had welcomed them to the villa several hours ago. Stone-faced and silent, he occasionally glanced at her, but otherwise stared straight ahead, waiting.

Strange they didn't tie me up or anything, she thought. *Probably 'cause they know there's nowhere to go.* Now that the sun was well and truly down, she could see that there wasn't even a trace of man-made illumination in sight, aside from Viktor's villa. Em had debated popping open the door and making a run for it, but quickly realized she could never do that. First, because they would likely catch her. And second... because they had Boone. Tears stung her eyes as the moving image of Boone's limp body crashing to the ground suddenly played out in the theater of her mind. Was he even alive?

He was breathing after that man hit him, she knew. And if they wanted her help, they'd need to let her talk to him; be sure he was okay. *Otherwise... once we're on the* Lunasea, *I'll push the throttle to the stops and ram us into Dove Cay at top speed.*

Her daydream—or "daymare"—was interrupted as the doors to the Jeep opened. The brute who had struck Boone opened the tailgate and started loading a number of duffel bags. Up front, Paz got into the passenger seat, and Viktor opened the door beside her and dropped a small satchel at her feet.

"I apologize for the wait. Could you move to the middle, please?"

Emily glared at him and scooted to the middle of the backseat, arranging her sundress to cover her knees. Viktor reached down and Emily felt his hand against her thigh. When she jerked away, he raised the offending hand; it was holding the near half of the middle seat belt. "Buckle up. Safety first."

She grabbed it from him and buckled in. "Wanker," she muttered.

"Pierre, take the wheel," Viktor ordered.

Pierre exited the back seat of the Jeep and was replaced by Sergei, who gave Emily a leer. Em returned the look, her green eyes shooting lethal daggers. Then her eyes dropped to the man's expensive-looking trainers. *Oh, shite... the shoe prints.*

The Jeep started up and rumbled down the driveway toward the road below.

———

Pierre took them along the rough, southerly route toward town. As the Jeep transitioned from the unpaved road to the paved one, Emily looked to her left at the lights of the East Bay Resort.

"So... your boat is moored in the shallows, not tied to the

pier. And you have to take a boat... to get your boat?" Viktor clarified, as they neared the lights of town.

"Sometimes we swim out to get it," Emily said. "But I'm not exactly dressed for it."

"Oh, I dunno," Sergei said with a lecherous smile.

"Shut up, Sergei," Viktor said. "The skiff you use...?"

"Moored in East Bay, at the resort."

"Well, that won't do. Let's just get to the pier."

Passing by the Boiling Hole, then the Regatta village, Pierre took them into Cockburn Harbour. Aside from a solo bicyclist and a pair of donkeys, the streets were largely quiet. There appeared to be a few locals dining on the patio of the Sunset Café, but the supermarket near the pier was closed for the night. Pierre drove them down the alley to the deserted pier. A variety of fishing boats sat quietly in the illumination of a couple of working lights.

"There are several small boats at the pier," Viktor noted. "Paz... do your engineering skills extend to hotwiring an engine?"

"I'm afraid not."

Sergei laughed. "Good thing you got this boy from Brighton Beach. I've boosted a few cars in my time, I can probably do a boat." He looked out the window to the bay. "And if not, I'll swim out. Her boat's not that far."

"Pull over to the side and kill the lights," Viktor ordered Pierre. "And go with Sergei; I'd prefer he have someone who looks like a local with him, if he's going to go poking around the boats."

As the two men exited, Emily looked at the adjacent pier where the immigration office stood. It appeared closed, with only an outdoor security light currently on. "Pretty risky what you blokes are doing..." she said.

"I can't say I disagree," Viktor replied. "This whole thing was sprung on me at the last minute. Which is why we need your *Lunasea*. I hope it's as fast as I've heard."

"You'll never know if you hurt Boone," Emily said. "How about you let me talk to him while your goons muck about with the fishing boats."

Viktor retrieved the satchel bag from the floor and took out a bulky satellite phone. "Don't really need this yet, but might as well make sure it works." He swung the hinged antenna up and punched in a number. After a moment, he spoke. "Baptiste? How is your guest?" He listened a moment. "Well, he has every right to be angry. Put the phone on speaker and let him know Emily would like to speak with him."

Viktor enabled the speaker on his phone and they heard "... *girlfriend wanna speak wit' you.*"

"*Emily? Are you all right?*" Even the speakerphone's canned quality couldn't disguise the urgency in Boone's voice.

"Boone! Yes, I'm fine! Are you hurt? When you fell, it was..." Emily fought a lump in her throat, willing her mind to stop the replay. "Please tell me you're okay," she said, unable to keep the tremor from her voice.

"*I'm okay. Strapped to a chair in a room that looks like a nerd's paradise.*"

Viktor laughed at that. "Hear that, Paz?"

The Cuban didn't reply as Boone's voice continued. "*Where are they taking you, Emily?*"

Viktor punched the button to silence the speaker and held the phone to his ear. "That's enough chitchat. We're going on a boat ride with your delightful friend as our guide, destination unknown. But if you both behave yourselves, this will turn out just fine. Baptiste, turn off the speaker."

Emily thought back to when Viktor had approached them

at the pier, asking for a charter. *Did he forget he'd specifically mentioned Ambergris Cay to us?*

"Sergei is trying to hotwire a boat, God help us," Viktor said into the phone. After a moment, he added, "They moored their dive boat in the bay, and..." He listened again. "Really?" Turning to Emily, he asked, "Which one is Mack's boat? Baptiste says you were talking to him last week."

Emily pointed out the left window at a small boat at the midpoint of the pier. "That one."

"Thank you. Baptiste, keep the phone handy, I may call again soon." He hung up. "Paz, go bring Sergei and Pierre back. Baptiste knows where one of the fishermen hides a spare key for his boat. We'll redock it in the same place once we bring the dive boat in and load up."

Three minutes later, Emily and Sergei were puttering across the shallows toward the *Lunasea*.

THIRTY

"She loves you, I t'ink," Baptiste said, setting down the sat phone. He sat in the office chair and resumed his aimless swiveling.

Boone didn't respond to the man's assertion, instead saying, "That bag around your neck. That's a *wanga*."

Baptiste ceased his swiveling. "How you know 'bout dat?"

"We talked to a real *oungan* about the little bags found in the bodies. I doubt he'd approve of how you're using it, though. They're supposed to be worn for protection."

"It *does* protect me!"

"Really? How does shoving a magic bag down a corpse's throat protect you?"

"I don't know what you talkin' 'bout," Baptiste said, resuming his chair swiveling.

"Yeah, you do. The body in the Boiling Hole... the one in the Highland House. That was you, wasn't it?"

"I didn't kill dose men."

Boone smirked. "Maybe not directly. I'm guessing your boss

or his egghead buddy did the actual killing. Probably with that thing there, right?" Boone nodded his head at the odd device Baptiste had brought back with him when he'd returned. "The Cuban guy show you how to use it?"

Baptiste didn't reply, but his chair-swiveling slowed, his eyes on Boone.

"Let me guess... microwaves." When that got a twitch of response, Boone continued. "Pretty unpredictable, I'd bet. You know... when you and your buddies were out frying chickens with that thing, you messed up the disc jockey at the Coast Guard station. Can you imagine what you'd do to your own brain, if you fire that off in a small space? Like this room? Microwaves bouncing around... might boil your eyes, too."

Baptiste looked back at the device, unease evident on his face.

"I thought maybe your boss was just a drug smuggler or something, but this is some next-level evil. No wonder you're wearing that *wanga*."

"Dis ain't for me," he said.

"I figured," Boone replied. "So, what's the deal with sticking it in the people you murder?"

Baptiste huffed a scornful snort. "Not somet'ing you would understand."

"I dunno, I'm pretty open-minded. And at the moment, I'm a captive audience."

Baptiste chuckled at that. "I s'pose so." He lifted the bag and kneaded it in his fingers. "Dis *wanga* is tied to me, wit' offerings to de *lwa* spirit Guede Nibo. Him be de guardian of all who die by violence. I put dis wit' de body, it keep de victim's *jumbie* from seeking me out."

"For revenge."

"*Oui, pour revanj,*" Baptiste replied in Creole.

Boone leaned forward in the chair, locking eyes with the man. "If you or your friends hurt Emily... there aren't enough *wangas* in the world to keep me from coming back and sending you to hell."

Baptiste blinked, taken aback. He opened his mouth to speak, but was interrupted by a tremendous boom from outside, its shockwave shaking the room. The glass panes of the one window in the workshop rattled and glowed with a flickering orange light. Baptiste jerked, sending his office chair into a half-spin. He lurched to his feet, grabbed his handgun, and ran out of the room.

An explosion, followed by fire, Boone thought. *No idea what caused that, but it's now or never.* He strained at the plastic ties, ignoring the pain. They barely budged. He was just about to try and tip himself over when a pair of women appeared at the door, their eyes wide with adrenaline. Boone recognized the older of the two as the woman who'd shaken her head in warning to Boone and Emily when she'd come out to bring bread to the dinner table. She had a steak knife in her hand and she knelt on the floor before going to work on the ties on Boone's ankles.

The younger of the two carried kitchen shears, and she quickly began snipping at the four ties on Boone's arms. "I am Kirana. This is Mia. We must hurry."

Mia said something in a language Boone couldn't identify, anger in her voice.

"What did she say?"

"We are Indonesian, and Mia's English is not so good. She says she couldn't let them kill another."

"They kill Lucien!" Mia spat, her serrated steak knife sawing through one of his ankle bonds. "I know they did! He gentle soul!"

"Some migrants came here last week," Kirana said, "and we think they killed another one of them. And then we overheard they are going to blow up some big yacht."

"Near Ambergris Cay?" Boone asked, remembering the location Viktor had originally asked for a dive charter to.

"I'm sorry, I didn't hear where." Kirana was done with one of his arms and Boone took the shears from her and went after the tie on his left wrist. The blades wouldn't snip through the tough plastic in one go, and he had to work the shears several times to cut it. "What was that explosion?"

"The maintenance man punctured the tank they use to fuel their helicopter and started a fire," Kirana said. "I hope he is all right!"

"Well, that ought to get the police here," Boone said, removing the last of the arm restraints just as Mia sawed through the one on his other leg. "Is there a way out from this wing?"

"No. The nearest door is the front."

"You two get to safety and call the police," Boone urged.

"We have no phones. Only Viktor and his men have them."

"Well, the police will get here soon, if that fireball was big enough. Hide until then."

Mia said something, angry tears in her eyes.

"She says we will be deported."

"You may have stopped some very bad men. Tell the authorities everything you've seen, and I bet they'll work something out with you."

Kirana and Mia dashed from the room and Boone turned to the workbenches. He'd already figured out what he'd grab if he ever got free: the sat phone and the key to the rental Jeep went into his pockets. He was about to flee, but then turned back to snatch the strange contraption. Holding it like a rifle, he ran from the room.

Leaving the south wing, he hurried toward the front door, only to encounter Baptiste turning the corner from the entrance alcove. Surprised, the man reached behind himself for his pistol, only to find himself staring down what passed for a barrel on the microwave gun.

"Y'know, this is actually pretty easy to use. Very ergonomic. Hands on your head... nice and slow. Otherwise, I'm gonna nuke your brain like a breakfast burrito."

Of course, Boone had zero idea how to use the weapon, but Baptiste didn't know that; and he'd seen the Haitian's unease when he'd talked about possible effects. Baptiste slowly raised his hands and placed them on his head.

"Turn around." When Baptiste did as he was told, Boone fished the handgun out of the man's waistband; it was the same one he'd taken from him before. He checked the safety. "Good way to blow a hole in your butt cheeks, with the safety off. Now... where are our cell phones?"

"Don't have dem. Viktor took dem."

"To Ambergris Cay?"

Baptiste didn't offer any confirmation, and suddenly an engine and the rattle of crunching sand and gravel sounded from outside.

Police? No... much too soon for them to get here all the way from town. Without hesitation, Boone raised the gun and administered some pistol-whip payback, slamming the butt of the weapon into the man's head. Unlike in the movies, a single hit wasn't enough, so he bashed Baptiste again to send the goon to the floor. Woulda preferred if it had been the other guy, Boone thought.

Dashing out the front door, he practically collided with Pierre, who was staring at the flames just to the north.

"What is happenin'...?" He froze. "You!"

The barrel of Boone's gun was hovering an inch in front of the man's forehead before he could act. "We've got to stop meeting like this, Pierre. Where's Emily? Tell me if you want to live."

"Hey man, I just work here. Dey left in her boat. I watched it go, den came back here like I was told."

"Gimme your gun."

"I don't have one, I swear!" He lifted his shirt and turned in a circle.

Boone remembered the man's fighting stance when he'd faced him earlier and wasn't about to let down his guard. "Lie on the ground, face down. Toss your phone and your keys to the side."

"Don't shoot! I'll do it!" Pierre hit the sand and tossed the requested items.

Setting the microwave gun down, Boone scooped up the items and pocketed them. He knelt beside the man and pressed the gun to his temple. "Where are the others going with Emily?"

"I don't know!" the man shrieked. "Some other island!"

"Why? What are they doing?"

"I don't know, dey don't tell me much."

"You know *something*," Boone insisted, increasing the pressure on the man's temple."

"Dey gonna blow up some big boat!"

"What boat?" Boone roared. "And how are they going to do it?"

"I don' know, I swear!"

Just north of the compound, flames had engulfed much of the low scrub, and black, oily smoke rose from beyond the north wing's roof. Boone flicked his eyes toward the villa, imagining Baptiste regaining consciousness... retrieving another weapon. *I need to get to the harbor!* "What's the code to unlock your phone?"

"Zero five zero one!"

Boone rose, grabbed the strange weapon, and was about to bolt for the orange Jeep, but then turned to face the one Pierre had arrived in. *I've got his keys, but just in case...* He raised the gun and pumped two rounds into the nearest front tire. Pierre whimpered at the gunshots as Boone ran to the rental and jumped in. Executing the quickest three-point turn of his life, Boone aimed the Jeep down the driveway and took off in a spray of coral and sand.

"Slow down!" Viktor demanded.

"I thought you wanted to get there fast," Em shouted over the roar of engine and wind, her teeth chattering. While she loved the thin, breezy sundress she was wearing, it was not designed for the flybridge on a nighttime ocean voyage. They were roughly ten miles from Ambergris Cay, according to the chart plotter. She and Viktor were on the flybridge, while the others were below.

"It's too rough!" Viktor complained. "We're bouncing too much. Sergei and Paz have delicate work to do."

"There's more chop tonight," Emily said, throttling back to a more manageable ride. "What sort of work they doing?" she asked. When Viktor didn't reply, she tried another question. "What's in those bags?"

"That is not your concern."

Em had watched Paz and Sergei bring aboard four bags, and she knew what was in two of them: one was a standard scuba gear bag, and another was a long case for disassembled fishing rods—but, of course, there weren't any rods in there. Sergei had briefly unzipped it to retrieve a stubby assault rifle and loaded a magazine into a slot behind the grip. But the other two duffle bags were bulky, stuffed full of something.

"Look, I'm doing what you asked. Just want to know what I'm in for. I'm guessing you're not going fishing or diving."

"Actually, Sergei will be diving," Viktor offered.

Emily gave him a sideways glance. "What on earth are we doing, going out to a private, rich-people's island in the middle of the night?"

"We are making a delivery," Viktor said, with an odd smile on his face. He retrieved his satellite phone from the dash and placed a call. "Diego... is the yacht there?" He listened a moment. "Is it lit up? Any people on deck?"

A yacht? At Ambergris Cay...? Emily remembered the superyacht *Anya* had gone there—and that its owner was Russian. As Viktor finished the call, she listened carefully to his accent. Although his English was impeccable and his accent slight, it reminded her of someone she'd helped arrest on Grand Cayman: a mercenary named Tolstoy.

"Is the anchorage visible from the airstrip?" Viktor nodded to himself and ordered, "Go ahead and land. I don't want to arouse their suspicions." He hung up.

"You're not Polish, are you?" Emily stated. It wasn't a question.

Viktor ignored her. "How soon until we get there, at this speed?" he asked, peering at the illuminated dials on her dash.

"I dropped us down to twenty knots when you were havin' a whinge about the bumpy ride, so about thirty minutes."

Viktor shook his head, thinking. "It's not late enough yet. Bring us down to five knots."

Emily frowned and throttled down as he requested. She shivered violently, her dress wet from the spray. Taking her hands from the wheel, she vigorously rubbed her bare arms.

"Listen... this dress isn't gonna cut it. I'm freezing."

Viktor looked her over, a barely disguised gleam of lust in his eyes. "Yes, I can see that."

Emily crossed her arms over her chest. "Look, if I go hypothermic, you'll have to pilot yourself. I've got a hoodie down below. Can you handle the wheel while I grab it?"

Viktor gave her a suspicious look.

Emily threw her arms out at the expanse of ocean on all sides. "Where am I gonna go?"

Viktor waved toward the ladder. "Don't take longer than a minute, or I'll call Baptiste and deliver some punishment to your friend."

"Yeah, about that... I'll be wanting to check on Boone again when I get back."

"We'll see."

Emily scrambled down the ladder. Sergei and Paz had something laid out on the deck just aft of the ladder, working in the illumination of a flashlight that Sergei held, his back to her. She paused, trying to see what it was. She was about to move closer, but decided to grab her Baja hoodie first.

Quietly, she stepped down into the small hold beside the marine head and grabbed it off a hook. After a moment's thought, she slipped off her sandals before returning to the deck. She paused, looking around for the bag Sergei had weapons in, but it was nowhere in sight. She continued toward the two men who were kneeling on the deck, hunched over their work. Emily took three silent, barefooted steps closer.

"Why have we slowed down?" Paz asked, leaning over an object in Sergei's beam. "Not that I am complaining... it's making our work much easier."

"My guess, the boss probably wants to hit them when they're all asleep," Sergei replied. "We were gonna get there too early."

Paz must have spotted movement over Sergei's shoulder, for he straightened up from whatever he was working on. "What are you doing down here?" Sergei's flashlight beam slashed across her face, blinding her.

By way of explanation, Emily held up the Baja hoodie. "I was freezing my arse off. Viktor said I could grab this."

"Well, you have it," Sergei said. "Get back up there."

Em slipped on the hoodie and turned to the ladder to begin her ascent. The flashlight beam might have spoiled her night vision, but not before she'd seen what the two men were working on. Paz had been tinkering with something that looked very much like a timer. And, although the small, whitish blocks laid out on netting in a grid looked a lot like the bricks of cocaine they'd found in the harvester, the wiring linking them together convinced Emily they were something else entirely.

His headlights piercing the darkness, Boone tore down the rough road to the south, knowing it would likely get him to the harbor a minute or two faster than the airport road. *Provided I don't swerve into a ditch,* he thought. *Or hit a donkey!* He braked as he nearly did precisely that. Boone honked the horn but the pair of donkeys just turned to look at him. He thought about using Pierre's phone to call Lincoln, but like many of his generation, memorized phone numbers were a thing of the past. The police were likely on their way to the fire; indeed, he'd seen flashing lights off to the west during his drive. Still...

Boone turned on the phone and was greeted with the lock screen. He punched in the code Pierre had given him and then dialed 911—while some Caribbean islands still used the UK code 999, the TCI had followed The Bahamas' lead and gone with the American digits. The phone began to ring. And ring.

Boone put the phone on speaker and set it on the passenger seat, then leaned on the horn again. This time one of the donkeys moved off, but the other remained stubborn. Boone swore and aimed the Jeep for the edge of the road. Maneuvering around the animal, he winced as branches from the roadside scrub shrieked against the orange Jeep's paint job. Once he was rolling again, he increased speed, hands locked on the steering wheel in a vise grip. Suddenly, the ringing on the phone stopped, and a voice with a light Turks and Caicos accent came on the line.

"Nine-one-one, what is your emergency?"

Where do I begin? Boone thought. "My name is Boone Fischer. I'm calling from South Caicos. I'm guessing I'm speaking to someone in Provo?"

"Yes, you are correct. What is the emergency?"

"I need to talk to someone in the South Caicos police station."

"They have a direct number—"

"There's been an explosion at a villa just south of the Coast Guard station."

"Yes... our phones have been busy with that. Are you there?"

"No, I just left there... but you need to tell the police there may be one or more armed individuals on the premises." Boone had Baptiste's pistol and Pierre had been unarmed, but he had little doubt there were other weapons in the house. And for all he knew, there were other goons there amongst the staff. "There are two women from Indonesia. Mia and Kirana. They helped me escape. Separate them from the others and they can tell you more."

"How do you spell those names?"

"No idea. Listen... write this down... there are three men and a kidnap victim on a boat, traveling between South Caicos and Ambergris Cay. At least, I *think* that's where they're headed. The boat is a Delta Canaveral named *Lunasea*. Luna like the moon, sea like the ocean. Did you get that?"

Silence greeted him. Boone looked down at the phone and stared at the black screen. He thumbed the power button and an "empty battery" symbol taunted him. *You have got to be kidding me!* He tossed the phone aside, thinking. He could drive directly to the police station... but every moment he stayed on the island put Emily farther and farther away. Besides, he didn't have any idea where the police station was. He actually knew very little about places in town, other than the resort, and some restaurants...

"Leah's Chicken Bar!" he said aloud. Lincoln had said he and Troy were going there to take some ladies dancing. *And Troy's with the DECR!* He remembered what Doug Cox had said about their boat: it could hit seventy knots on the flats. Likely far less on the open ocean, but it would be much faster than the *Lunasea*.

Boone looked at the clock on the dash: just before eleven o'clock. Many places closed early in the islands, but if this was a dance club, it probably catered to a later crowd; hopefully they'd still be there. Boone remembered it was just up the street from Triple J's Grill—Lincoln had pointed Leah's out as they passed it—and he was pretty sure he recalled the route Mateo had taken.

Fifteen minutes later, Boone pulled up across from Leah's, the pounding bass of the dance music audible through the Jeep's windows. He jumped out and found Lincoln outside, talking to a beautiful young woman.

"Heyyyyyy, Boone! You and Emily done wit' your fancy dinner?" His grin faltered as Boone drew closer. "What de hell happened to you?"

"No time to explain! Is Troy here?"

"Yeah, he's inside," Lincoln said, his face grim.

"Get him! Please hurry!"

Lincoln dashed in and Boone spared a moment to apologize to the woman Lincoln had been chatting up. "Sorry to ruin your date."

She didn't acknowledge the apology but stared at him instead. "You got blood on de side of your face," she said.

When Boone raised his hand to his temple, his fingertips were greeted with dried blood, no doubt from the love tap from Sergei.

"Dere's blood on your wrist, too. You should go to the clinic," she said earnestly.

"Eventually," he said, as Lincoln appeared with Troy in tow. Boone turned and ran across to the Jeep.

"What's goin' on?" Lincoln asked, as he and Troy piled into the vehicle.

"They stole the *Lunasea* and they've got Emily!"

"What? Who's got her? What are you talkin' about?"

"I'll explain on the way to the pier." He turned and looked back at Troy. "The DECR pier. Please tell me you've got the keys to the *Hammerhead* on you."

THIRTY-ONE

"How much longer?" Emily asked, bundled into her Baja hoodie.

Viktor looked at the clock on the dash. "Fifteen minutes more, and I'll check in with Diego. I don't want anyone on deck when we make our delivery."

"Of drugs."

Viktor looked at her with a smile. "How did you guess?"

Emily didn't see any percentage in revealing what she strongly suspected. No, it wasn't "suspicion." Sod that. *Certainty*. These bastards were going to blow up a yacht. Kill a whole crew of wage-earners just to assassinate one man.

"Viktor..." Paz's head was at the top of the ladder. "We are nearly ready. Sergei is getting suited up."

"Excellent. I will check in with Diego shortly. We'll proceed once the *Anya* has bedded down for the night."

The head disappeared and Emily could hear quiet conversation below.

"If we've got fifteen minutes, how about letting me talk to Boone."

"After I make the call to Diego."

Emily eyed the marine VHF radio. Paz had disabled it when they'd come aboard, and she doubted it was something she could fix in the scant seconds she'd have available if Viktor was momentarily distracted. *But maybe there's something else I can do to bollocks things up.*

Boone had explained everything as best he could, and had used Lincoln's phone to call Provo's 911 center again, this time providing as much detail as he could. He'd learned that TCI's police boats and helicopter were dealing with a late-night migrant-smuggling intercept, but the seriousness of Boone's suggestion earned a promise to reach out to the US Coast Guard, which likely had assets at its Bahamas base on Great Inagua, 140 miles away.

Boone's instinct to procure the *Hammerhead* had been good; assuming the *Lunasea* was indeed heading to Ambergris Cay, they'd be able to reach it far sooner than anyone else. Troy guided the center-console fast boat through the gap between Dove and Long Cays and opened her up.

"A bit choppy!" he shouted, "but I t'ink I can maintain forty-five or fifty wit'out bangin' us up too badly!"

"Uh... Boone? What are we going to do if we catch them?" Lincoln asked.

Boone had to admit that he hadn't figured that part out just yet. With only Baptiste's gun, Boone didn't exactly have the firepower to take on Sergei, Viktor, and Paz—he had little doubt they'd brought along something more substantial than a few handguns. Boone took the gun from his waistband and checked the magazine; pressing a thumb down on the rounds inside, the bullets only gave slightly, so at least he had nearly a full mag. He jacked the chamber back a half an inch and confirmed there was a round in there, as well. *Not enough.*

"Troy, you don't happen to have a gun or two aboard, do you?"

"Are you kidding? Dis is a Department of Environment boat."

"What about dat t'ing?" Lincoln asked, pointing at the vaguely rifle-shaped device that now lay on the deck.

"I don't think that'll help," Boone said. "That's more like a piece of evidence than a long-range weapon."

Over the roar of the dual outboards and the hiss of the ocean spray, Boone almost didn't hear the unfamiliar trilling coming from a cargo pocket of his shorts. Digging into the pocket, he pulled out the sat phone he'd liberated from the villa. He stared at the unfamiliar number on the phone, instinctively knowing who it was.

Shit... "Troy! Throttle down!"

"What? Why?"

"Please, just do it! I don't want them to hear the engines. Lincoln, umm... how's your Haitian?"

The Belonger shot him a confused look. "What you mean?"

"This call is going to be for the Haitian goon who was standing guard over me. Name of Baptiste. Can you sound Haitian?"

Troy had brought them down to a low idle and overheard the exchange. "I know Baptiste. Hangs around de harbor, asks a lot of questions." He waggled his fingers, beckoning for the phone. "Give here. I deal wit' Haitians all year long. Some are good friends."

"The guy who's likely calling is named Viktor. If he asks, I'm still strapped to a chair with zip ties."

"Say what?" Troy said, incredulous. The phone continued to ring.

"They're checking on me," Boone said in a rush. "Emily may have demanded they call—she called once before. Tell the man I'm sleeping. Say as little as possible."

Troy nodded and answered, his natural Belonger dialect switching just a bit toward a passable Haitian, "*Bonswa*, Viktor." He listened a moment. "*Padon*, but I was takin' a piss. He sleepin'." Troy suddenly cleared his throat and coughed. "Dunno. T'ink maybe I comin' down wit' somet'in'." He listened some more, raised a finger to Boone, then shouted "Hey! Wake up!"

Boone wasn't particularly good at lying. And, as Emily was only too happy to remind him from time to time, he would've made a terrible actor. He did his best to imagine himself back in the chair, then took the phone. "Emily?"

"She's here," Viktor's voice replied. "Don't worry, this will all be over soon."

———

Emily listened as Viktor spoke to Baptiste. "Why did you take so long to answer?" He frowned. "You sound... strange. What's wrong with your voice?" Viktor listened, then sighed. "Well, drink some orange juice or tea or something. Wake up our guest."

Emily could hear a shout over the phone. She swallowed, waiting in the near silence, with only the sound of the waves lapping against the hull. Then, after a pause, Viktor spoke to someone else.

"She's here," he said. "Don't worry, this will all be over soon." He thumbed the speaker button and held the phone toward her. "All right, you lovebirds, say hello to each other."

"Emily, are you there?"

Em's heart rose into her throat at the sound of Boone's voice. "I'm here and I'm okay. For the moment, at least."

"What does that mean?" Boone asked. "Viktor, what are you planning?"

Viktor gave Emily a warning look and waggled a finger at her. "As I've been telling your lovely friend, we are just making a delivery. She's quite the boat driver! Once we're finished, she will bring us back, and you two can be reunited."

Sergei climbed the ladder and was about to speak, but Viktor raised a finger to his lips. The muscular goon was stuffed into a wetsuit like an overcooked hotdog about to burst, and had a dive knife strapped to his left leg above the dive bootie. While Emily and Boone on occasion would carry a knife or sea snips to free marine life from fishing line, she had no doubt Sergei had it on because he thought it looked badass.

Emily leaned toward the outstretched sat phone. "Boone... are you all right? How's your head? That guy hit you hard."

Sergei snickered at that and Viktor shushed him.

"I'm fine. Can't wait to see you again. In fact, once we're back together... I'd love to take you out for some karaoke."

Emily frowned. *What the f—?* Sergei must've hit him harder than she thought; Boone hated karaoke with a white-hot passion. *Unless he's trying to tell me something.* "Oh, really? What song?"

"Lynyrd Skynyrd's big hit, of course. I'll even play air-guitar on the solo."

For the first time in a long while, Emily felt a twinge of hope. "It's a date. And maybe we could take a vacation in

Belize, after. To that lovely island north of Caye Caulker, yeah? Assuming we don't get kidnapped by a barmy Russian again."

"And that's enough of that," Viktor said, withdrawing the phone. "You Americans... so frivolous." He thumbed off the speaker function. "Baptiste...?"

Emily glanced over her shoulder at the dashboard, taking in the navigation screen, the clock, and the non-functioning marine radio, trying to come up with a plan. The ghost of a smile came to her lips. *Viktor said Baptiste's voice sounded strange... what if it wasn't Baptiste?* Emily knew in her heart that Boone had gotten away. The song Boone was referencing was "Free Bird."

Boone covered the phone and locked eyes with Troy. "You're up, 'Baptiste.' Say as little as you can."

Troy took it and answered, "Yeah?" and listened for a bit, then said, "Okay." He hung up and handed the phone back. "I t'ink he bought it."

"I hope so. Floor it! We can still catch them. They had the call on speaker and there was no engine noise, so I think they're sitting somewhere." He looked up at the small mast. "What's your radar's range?"

"Your dive boat has a flybridge, right?" Troy asked, as he brought the *Hammerhead* up to fifty knots.

"Yeah."

"Den we may get a return on her out to about eight miles. But dat's in calm seas. And if she's close to Ambergris Cay, we might not pick her out from de clutter."

"Okay. Keep on a straight line heading for Ambergris. Emily confirmed that's where they're heading."

"How'd she do dat?" Lincoln asked.

"She mentioned wanting to take a vacation to the island north of Caye Caulker in Belize. That island is also called Ambergris Caye, although they spell the 'cay' with an 'e' at the end. We used to work as divemasters on both islands."

While Troy wrestled the fast boat through the chop, Boone thought about the call. Viktor had said they were just making a "delivery," but both Kirana and Pierre had said he was going to blow up a big boat. He'd taken a chance with that Lynyrd Skynyrd remark, figuring a foreigner like Viktor wouldn't know their music catalog. *Wait a minute... Viktor said he was Polish... but Emily just made a crack about being kidnapped by a Russian.* Boone stiffened as he realized what "big boat" they were likely targeting.

"Is the VHF open on sixteen?"

"Of course."

"I know who they're going after. There was a superyacht named the *Anya* down in Ambergris. Owned by a Russian. We have to warn them."

Troy looked down at the plotter. "At this speed, we'll be in VHF range of Ambergris in just a few minutes."

———

The *Lunasea* was back up to thirty knots, Diego having confirmed that the yacht was now largely quiet. Emily watched Sergei struggling with the back zipper on his wetsuit. He caught her eyes.

"It's been a while since I wore this," he said defensively, then came beside her and turned his back. "Zip me up."

"Sod off, I'm driving."

"I'll do it!" Viktor snapped, rising and pinching the zipper

319

together. Gritting his teeth with effort, he dragged it closed, then yelped and clutched his jaw. *"Khuy!"* he swore, moaning in pain.

"Your tooth, boss?"

Viktor nodded angrily.

"Bet you need a root canal," Emily said with some pleasure.

Viktor ignored her, snapping at Sergei, "You know what to do?"

"Yeah."

"Then gear up. Once we're close, we'll anchor and you can... make the delivery."

Emily watched as Sergei moved stiffly toward the ladder and carefully descended. *That suit is a size too small, at least. Too much time in the gym, I gather.* If the need arose for swift action on his part, Sergei wouldn't have a lot of agility. She filed that observation away. Looking ahead, she could now make out a glow on the horizon. She was running out of time!

"Kill the running lights," Viktor ordered. The sat phone rang on the dash and he grabbed it. "Yes, Diego?" His eyes grew wide. "What?" He dashed over to the aft railing. "Paz! Get up here and enable the radio!" He came back to Emily and shouted in her ear, "Increase speed!"

"Any faster, and we'll be smacking the waves hard," she cautioned.

"Do it!" he roared.

The Cuban scrambled up top and reached behind the radio, wincing as he tried to restore the connection. Em figured he must've just unplugged it from the battery to keep her from jumping on and radioing for help.

"What is going on?" Paz asked as he fished around behind the unit.

"Diego says the *Anya* is lit up and weighing anchor. Crewmen running on deck."

"Got it!" Paz declared. The digital screen on the marine radio lit up.

"What channel is the emergency channel?" Viktor shouted the question at Emily.

Not a boater, I take it. No wonder they needed me. While she was tempted to stall for time, she was as curious as they were. "Channel 16. Here, I'll—"

Viktor gripped her wrist. "Keep your hands on the wheel! Paz, you do it."

Paz tapped it in and the radio sprang to life mid-broadcast.

"*...advise you get underway immediately. Repeat. Mayday, mayday, mayday... to the motor yacht* Anya, *we have reason to believe an attack on your vessel is imminent. Strongly urge you to get underway immediately!*"

"I know that voice..." Viktor hissed, disbelief on his face. He grabbed the sat phone and put in a call. After a few moments, he hung up. "Baptiste is not answering. Boone Fischer escaped. That's him on the radio!"

"He has certainly alerted the authorities. We have to abort," Paz said matter-of-factly.

"*Nyet!* This is my last chance! If I fail at this, it will be *me* falling from a balcony!" Again, he went to the aft rail. "Sergei, take off the scuba tank and get up here! Bring the weapons!" The man shouted something that Emily couldn't hear over the wind, and Viktor responded. "The yacht is underway! Change of plans! Hurry!"

Ahead, Emily could now see the superyacht, fully lit up on the horizon. From the small bow wave, she must have just gotten underway. To the left, a few lights were visible on the private island of Ambergris Cay, including a line of runway lights that extended out over the water, the end of the airstrip perched on some kind of jetty.

As Sergei hauled himself up the ladder, the long bag over his shoulder, Viktor spoke quickly. "They've been alerted, so no need for stealth. We're going to come up alongside them. Sergei, you'll set the charges above the waterline as close as you can to the spot Paz showed you. I'll arm myself and shoot any crew member that tries to interfere. Paz, you'll pilot the boat and put us where we need to be."

Emily looked at the yacht. The crewman they'd met said there was a crew of thirty-two aboard, plus who-knew-how-many guests. *Boone's safe,* she thought. *I've got to end this now.*

"Sergei, take the girl below and put her in the head." Viktor continued. "I'll radio Diego to spool up the helicopter. We'll beach the boat and get to the runwa—"

Bracing her bare feet on the deck, Emily spun the wheel to port as hard as she could, aiming the *Lunasea* at Ambergris Cay's airstrip jetty, sending the three men flying to starboard. With the Delta Canaveral now traveling at nearly top speed in the choppy waters, it was only an instant before she took a wave squarely on the bow. The boat bounced violently and Paz flew over the rail, his cry drowned out by the roar of the engine. Still packed into his wetsuit, Sergei went down hard, and Emily was pleased to hear a metallic thud as his head hit the bench.

Viktor managed to hold on, but just barely. He reached for her, fury in his eyes. Em took aim and slugged him squarely in the jaw where he'd been nursing his toothache. He howled in pain and dropped to his knees, clutching his face.

"Better grab the wheel, Vic!" Emily cried, before straddling the port rail and dropping down to the gunwale beside the cockpit. She immediately grabbed hold of the nearest railing and practically crawled her way aft, eyes locked on the grid of explosives that were now balled up under the starboard bench. Without hesitation, she grabbed hold of the netting and pulled it toward her, eyes searching for the timer. *There! Please, let it be basic...* Fortunately, the device seemed idiot-proof. *So easy, even a Sergei can use it!* her mind gibbered at her.

Emily felt the boat start to turn; Viktor had it back under control. Looking up from the timer, she saw the *Anya* moving along the starboard side as the *Lunasea*'s bow slewed toward the superyacht. Looking up at the flybridge, she could see Sergei rising unsteadily to his feet, blood flowing from his forehead. He squinted down at her, trying to focus. *There's no time... and no other way.* Em powered the timer on, punched the "minutes" button once; the digits now read 00:01:00. She stabbed her thumb down on a green button in the center. The "one" in the minutes place instantly vanished as the seconds started to race downward. *59... 58... 57...*

Emily pressed her palm to the deck of the *Lunasea* for the last time. *Sorry, old girl.*

"Hey! What's she doing?" Sergei slurred, gripping the flybridge rail beside the ladder.

What I have to. Silently continuing the count, Emily dragged the mass of explosives out from under the bench, rushed several feet toward the forward hold, and hurled it down the steps. Out of the corner of her eye, she spotted Sergei's legs, halfway down the ladder. Up top, Viktor was shouting something.

50... 49... 48... Sergei might get to it in time. Thinking again of the forty-plus people aboard the *Anya*, Emily reached through the rungs of the ladder, released the safety catch on Sergei's dive knife, and with two swift motions, yanked it free of the sheath and rammed the blade straight down into Sergei's instep. The big man yowled in pain and surprise, instinctively grabbing for the knife. Woozy from the head-strike on the flybridge bench and clumsy from the undersized wetsuit, Sergei lost his balance. Plunging backward with a surprised yelp, he crashed to the deck on his back, his head bouncing off it with a sickening thud. Moaning, he tried to sit up.

42... 41... 40... I think? Lost count. Emily was about to run for the swim platform and dive off, letting the *Lunasea*'s momentum increase the distance between herself and the impending explosion, but she paused for a second, ripping free one of the orange life jackets on the side of the cabin. After a moment's hesitation, she grabbed a second one. *Hope I don't regret this.*

Emily tossed the vest to Sergei as she ran past him and he managed to catch it, with a look of confusion on his face.

"Jump overboard!" she shouted. "If you're anywhere near this boat when she blows, the shockwave in the water will kill you!" With that, she scrambled onto the swim platform and hurled herself sternward, the life jacket gripped in one hand. Landing in the *Lunasea*'s wake, she spluttered as roiling salt-water enveloped her face.

Glancing back in the darkness, she spotted the dark shape of Sergei clumsily lurching over the side, clutching his life vest. Gripping her own by a strap, Emily swam vigorously away from the receding dive boat.

THIRTY-TWO

"There! I see the *Lunasea*!" Boone cried.

They had picked up a radar return off the western coast of Ambergris Cay several minutes ago, and then two smaller blips resolved as they drew closer. The *Anya* had been visible first, lit up like a Christmas tree. As they ate up the range, the dive boat came into view; she was running dark, her lights off.

"She's headin' right for de yacht!" Troy shouted.

"Floor it, Troy! Get us closer!" Boone retrieved their solitary firearm and disengaged the safety.

They were still over a half mile away, tearing across the waves.

Emily had lost track of her mental stopwatch, but she was sure it was nearly time. Still aimed at the *Anya*, the *Lunasea* was far away now, the unlit boat vanishing into the darkness. Then, night became day.

Viktor throttled down as he approached the massive ship. "Sergei! We're almost there! We can still do this! Are you ready?" He heard nothing from below, so he slowed even further and stepped to the aft rail. "Sergei! Where's the bomb?"

His question was answered by a white-hot flash of light and an ear-shattering boom.

Viktor Gusev—The Goose of Death—took flight.

"NOOOOOO!" Boone's scream tore itself from his throat as the *Lunasea* vanished in a massive explosion, the shockwave almost visible as fire rushed out in all directions. Debris hurtled outward, bits and pieces splashing into the surrounding waves. And one of those pieces of debris looked human.

Boone stared in disbelief at the expanding ball of fire and oily smoke curling up into the air above the shattered remains of the dive boat. The gun slipped from his nerveless fingers and clattered to the deck. He followed, slumping to his knees. Tears flowed down his face.

"Emily..." he croaked.

Even at this distance, Emily felt the hot wind as it buffeted her face. Debris landed nearby, and she nearly laughed out loud when the speaker of her recently purchased Oceanear smacked into the water beside her. That brief moment of hysteria was snuffed out by the sobering sight of the burning wreckage of the Delta Canaveral, its hull almost unrecognizable in the flickering light of the burning oil slick that surrounded it.

The *Lunasea*, her pride and joy, was no more.

Emily swallowed, fighting back tears. She shook her head violently, then set her mind to the task at hand—getting out of this alive. The sea state was rough, and waves buffeted her face. She looked at the yacht, which was now barreling away at top speed—no doubt fleeing from what the crew rightfully believed was an attack. To her left, the runway lights of Ambergris Cay glowed in the distance. That was her best bet.

The woven cotton of her Baja hoodie was soaking up water like a sponge, weighing her down, so she stripped it off and consigned it to the deep. Her sundress didn't offer much in the way of insulation—the water temperatures in June were warm, but she usually wore a three-mil wetsuit for night dives. Shrugging into the life vest, she prepared to make the long swim to shore. She had only taken two strokes when the roar of a boat's engines rose above the sound of the waves.

"Lincoln! Get on de spotlight!" Troy yelled. "Look for survivors!"

Boone blinked back tears, pushing down the despair and grief. Emily could still be alive! *She might be hurt... dying... drowning...*

He stood, eyes scanning the waves as the *Hammerhead* slowed and approached the debris field. Lincoln swept the powerful spotlight across the burning waters.

"There's a body!" Lincoln called out.

Boone felt terror rising in him, but Lincoln added information.

"The body's male!"

"Keep looking!" Boone shouted.

"We have to bring him aboard," Troy said, motoring over to the figure that floated facedown.

Boone grabbed hold of the gunwale and slipped over the side, biceps straining as he held on with one hand. He grabbed hold of the clothing of the man and dragged him to the side of the boat. Troy idled the engine, and he and Lincoln pulled the man aboard. Boone hauled himself out of the water and rolled onto the deck, coming face-to-face with Viktor. The man's features were savaged by cuts and burns, and his eyes stared up at the sky, seeing nothing.

"He's dead," Troy remarked.

"Good," Boone spat.

"I think there's someone else out there!" Lincoln pointed to port.

Boone lurched to his feet and stared into the darkness. A male voice was calling for help. "It's not her," he said softly.

Troy took the wheel again and brought them over to where a man was waving his arms, his burly torso packed into an orange life vest from the *Lunasea*.

"Where's Emily, Sergei!" Boone shouted as the man flailed about.

"Help me!"

Boone reached his long arms down and grabbed hold of the man, pulling him partway up. Once Lincoln and Troy had him, he let go and went back toward the bow. Searching the deck, he spotted the handgun he'd dropped. Boone picked it up and stalked back to Sergei, who was now sitting on the deck, slumped against the center console.

Without a pause, Boone aimed the gun at Sergei's face. "Where is she!" he hissed though gritted teeth.

"She saved me!" he cried, raising his hands. "Well, she stabbed me first, see?" He pointed at a bloody bootie. "Right before the explosion, she tossed me this life vest and told me to get off the boat. Then she dived in."

Boone felt woozy as hope flooded through him. "Where did she jump from?"

"The uh... whattaya call the back of a boat?"

"Stern."

"Yeah, that. We were going really fast at the time."

"How soon after she went in did you jump?" Boone asked, urgency in his voice.

"I dunno... ten... twenty seconds?"

Boone looked at the remains of the *Lunasea*, then back toward Ambergris Cay. He pointed along the path he believed the dive boat had taken. "Troy, take us back that way, nice and slow. Lincoln, you're on the spot."

"Hey, we gotta look for Viktor!" Sergei protested.

"You wanna find Viktor? Peek around the console there," Boone said.

Sergei craned his neck around; he spotted Viktor and stiffened.

"Congratulations, you found him," Boone said, then slammed the pistol into the back of Sergei's head. One sledge-hammer blow was enough this time, and the goon crumpled.

"What you do dat for?" Troy cried out.

"He's a killer, and we can't afford to be watching our backs while we search for Emily," Boone said without emotion. "Besides, I owed him one."

Emily had watched the spotlight approach the burning wreckage. Without hesitation, she'd begun swimming hard toward the flames. Although it was closer than Ambergris Cay, the boat was still a considerable distance away. *Maybe next time... buy some life vests with a strobe light on 'em,* she thought. Her muscles were starting to burn when the boat suddenly turned, heading right toward her. The powerful light pierced the darkness, scanning the waters ahead of the boat.

Emily stopped her swimming and waved her arms. "Oy! Over here!"

Boone tried to slow his breathing, the adrenaline still coursing through him. The minutes ticked by, with no sign of Emily. There was quite a bit of debris, though. One black disc coasted by their bow wave. *Was that the Oceanear?*

Suddenly, a high-pitched voice sounded across the waters ahead. Boone turned. "Troy! Kill the engine!" When the rumble stopped, Boone strained his ears. This time, he was able to make out words.

"Oy! You wankers! Why'd you stop? A bit to your starboard!"

Emily! "Lincoln! Put the light off the starboard bow!" In moments, a familiar blond head was spotlighted, the reflective panels on the life vest below flashing in the illumination.

"Oh, thank God!" Boone cried, his voice quavering.

Troy brought them alongside, and Boone dived in, knifing through the water toward Emily. Breaching beside her, he engulfed her in his arms, scissor-kicking to keep them from sinking.

Emily felt Boone's body shudder as he held her tightly. He pulled back, and in the light from the spot, she could see the sheen of moisture in his eyes that had nothing to do with the waves that buffeted them.

"Emily! I thought... I thought you..."

"Shhh... I'm all right. Nearly snuffed it, but..." She was about to make a wisecrack about staying alive for that karaoke date he'd promised, but she trailed off and clutched him fiercely, giving in to her own tears.

THIRTY-THREE

GRAND TURK. THREE DAYS LATER.

"She'd be at anchor right there," Emily said softly.

"I know."

The couple sat on the low seawall beside the pier they'd been using, the very same pier where Boone had helped Doug with the *Caicos Sister* a little over a week ago. Out across the Columbus Channel, the sun was about to set.

Boone reached over and scratched Brixton's haunches, but the dog kept his chin on Emily's thighs, looking up at her. Ever since they'd gotten back to Grand Turk, the potlicker pup had stuck to her like glue, sensing her sadness. Of course, Boone was also upset by the loss of their boat, but for Em, the *Lunasea* had been her baby.

Emily sighed again, reaching up to remove the green John Lennon sunglasses from her face and hook them into her tank top in preparation for the sunset. Her favorite shades had been aboard the dive boat, hanging from the dash.

The colors on the horizon deepened as another beautiful day in the tropics came to a close. And beyond that horizon, out of sight, lay South Caicos. It had been a whirlwind three days since the destruction of the *Lunasea*, and Boone reached to his side and picked up the Gon-Ta-Nort beer from the wall, taking a deep swallow while he thought about everything that had happened.

Shortly after Emily's rescue, a United States Coast Guard helicopter had arrived. Spotting the flames, the chopper came to a hover above the wreckage of the dive boat, and Troy had contacted them via the radio. Emily quickly informed them that there was a third man in the water somewhere, as well as a co-conspirator in a helicopter over on Ambergris Cay. But apparently that helicopter had already fled, and despite a lengthy search in the waters near the island, Paz Cisneros was not found.

The USCG flew Boone and Emily to the Cheshire Hall Medical Centre in Provo for a medical evaluation. Boone was discovered to have a mild concussion, while Emily was determined to be in reasonably good shape, despite flirting with hypothermia. Police arrived to take their statements, and Boone and Em ended up staying at a hotel near the airport before taking a morning plane back to South Caicos. They were surprised to find Deejay Ceejay was booked on the same puddle jumper. CJ had gotten the CT scan that Boone had suggested and was expecting results in a few days.

Lincoln picked Boone and Em up at the airport and filled them in on the goings-on since the fire at Viktor's villa. After the blaze had been extinguished by the single, airport-based fire engine, the South Caicos police discovered a number of undocumented workers who had been kept in a modern-day version of indentured servitude. They were more than helpful in providing a wealth of information about various activities of the owner and his cronies, including two likely murders. Two of his underlings escaped before the police arrived, but the Haitian bodyguards were later captured when the Jeep they were traveling in ran off the road and into a salt pond.

The body recovered from the explosion of the *Lunasea* was positively identified by INTERPOL as a low-level arms dealer and former GRU operative, Viktor Gusev. His remains were offered to Russia, but Moscow denied any knowledge of the man. His bodyguard, Sergei Mikhailov, was cooperating. The strange weapon Boone had brought with him to the *Hammerhead* was taken aboard the USCG helicopter during the rescue and would soon be in the hands of American researchers.

Back at the East Bay Resort, Emily ordered Boone to bed before speaking with Mateo and Niles. With no boat, and a concussed Boone not able to dive, it was decided that Lincoln would team up with Mateo and take a smaller group of divers on one of East Bay's smaller, shallow draft boats to finish out the week. Boone and Em would then be flown home on Saturday, one week after they'd come over to South Caicos. Lincoln would remain behind to fix his mother's wall. Boone had offered to stay and help, but their coworker insisted he go back home and "rest up your busted head."

Now, back on GT, Boone and Em watched the sun drip below the horizon.

"Pretty," Emily said. Her own beer, an I-Soon-Reach, sat unopened on the wall beside her.

Boone draped his arm around her, and she let her head fall on his shoulder.

"What're we going to do?" she asked.

"Dunno."

They sat in silence for a few minutes, then Boone spoke again.

"Y'know... Bonaire... Saba... Belize... we didn't have our own boat." When Em didn't reply, he added. "Long as I have you, I'll be happy."

Emily nuzzled his cheek and gave him a peck. "And long as I have you, *I'll* be happy. But I'd be even happier if we had the *Lunasea*, too."

"Well... we've still got a hefty chunk of change in the bank. And maybe that oligarch will send us a reward, for you saving his life."

"Fat chance," Em muttered. Probably halfway across the Atlantic by now. Not even a ta-muchly, ungrateful wanker."

"All I'm sayin' is, if we need a new boat, we'll get one."

Emily sighed. "Too soon to think about it."

"Agreed." Boone finished his beer and shook out the can.

Without taking her head off of his shoulder, Emily retrieved her untouched beer and handed it to him. "Here. Not feeling boozy."

Boone set it down next to his empty, unopened.

"But I am feeling peckish. Shall we walk back to Sunflower? See if Jorika's cooking?"

"Sure." Boone picked up the cans in one hand and offered Emily his other. She took it in hers, and the two of them walked north in the gathering twilight, Brixton trotting by their side.

———

Back at the Sunflower Oasis, Jorika wasn't in the kitchen, so they retreated to their room for a few minutes. Emily fumbled at the pockets of her shorts, then swore.

"Sodding hell! I keep reaching for my mobile!"

"I know... I've done it too. Crazy how much we rely on those things."

"Well, we're gonna need to get new ones, right quick."

"Sounds like we've got a plan for tomorrow," Boone said, as he tucked the unopened beer into the room fridge.

"Tomorrow's Sunday. The Digicell store won't be open."

"Bugger."

Emily laughed at his use of her Britishism, and he smiled.

"I was hoping that would get a giggle out of you."

Em sat down at the little desk in the room and wistfully opened a spiral-ring notebook that lay beside a cup of colored pencils. Inside were drawings of potential Bubble Chasers Diving logos. Emily had always been a doodler, and probably could have made a go of it professionally, if the diving bug hadn't sunk its buggy teeth into her. She flipped to the fourth page where her favorite was and smiled. *Yes... that's the one. Just need a little more detail on the dolphin.*

"That the logo you've been working on?" Boone said from behind her shoulder.

Emily quickly shut the notebook. "No peeking! Still not done. Besides... not much call for it, at the moment."

"There will be. We've still got most of our gear that was in our East Bay suite, and in the drying room. Reef Divers will bring that by, next time they take a trip to the GT Wall. We can talk to the local dive shops... see if any of them need a sub or two."

"And we've still got that fantastic red, dive-flag truck," Em said with a laugh.

"Not sure that's in the plus column," Boone said.

Emily looked up at him, her eyes straying to the stitches in his hairline above his right ear. "How's your head? You on the mend?"

"I think so. Just a little tired. But I'm guessing you are, too."

"Exhausted. But still starving."

"Then let's go see if Jorika's opened up yet."

They went outside into the courtyard beside the pool and made their way to the door into the kitchen of the little restaurant.

"Still not there," Em said. "Might need to gnaw on your arm for sustenance to tide me over. Lemme pop in there for some barbecue sauce."

"I hear something..." Boone said, ear cocked. "Around the back. Sounds like... squeaks and whimpers."

Emily's face lit up. "The puppies!" She dashed around the side of the rooms, toward where the neem tree stood, shading the far corner of the property.

There, they found Jorika and her son, as well as another woman who Em knew to be a vet with Provo's Potcake Place K-9 Rescue organization. Mama lay on her side on a blanket, with seven puppies mewling and wiggling around her, their eyes still shut.

"Omigod, they're so cute!" Em squealed, dropping to the ground beside the group. Brixton flopped down beside them, wagging his tail.

"Mama had them earlier today," Jorika said.

"All healthy," the vet added.

"How's Mama?" Boone asked.

"She seems to be doing well. Although she'll need to be spayed. She's getting a little old to be popping out puppies."

Boone crouched beside Emily and laid a hand on the mother's flank. "Good job, girl."

Emily added her hand beside his and stroked the potcake's fur. Mama exhaled a sigh, then looked up at them with big, adoring eyes.

"Jorika tells me you're thinking of adopting one of these little rascals," the vet said.

"We'd thought about it, but..." Boone trailed off. "How hard is it to adopt out all the puppies?"

"Oh, we have an easier time with the puppies. And as you know, we have a program where tourists visiting Provo can take one home with them."

"Well... in that case..." Boone looked at Emily.

Em watched as Brixton belly-crawled closer to Mama and gave her several supportive licks. She looked at Boone and nodded. Smiling, she turned to the vet.

"We'd like to adopt Mama."

— END —

Keep reading for The Afterword, for an inside peek at what was based on fact, and what was made up... but first:

If you enjoyed this book, please take a moment to visit
Amazon and provide a short review; every reader's voice
is extremely important for the life of a book or series.

Boone and Emily will return in another installment of
THE DEEP SERIES

If you'd like advance notice of their next adventures, head on
over to
WWW.NICKSULLIVAN.NET
where you can sign up for my mailing list. If you're like me, you

hate spam, so rest assured I'll email rarely. Be the first to know when my next book is available!

Follow me on **BOOKBUB** to get an alert whenever I have a new release, preorder, or discount! And it will bring me joy. The more followers I have, the more powerful I become!

And check out other authors who set their tales on the water, near the water, or under the tropical sun at **WWW.TROPICALAUTHORS.COM**

Looking for a little more Boonemily? Watch them team up with characters from Wayne Stinnett, John H. Cunningham, and Nick Harvey! Check out *Graceless* and *Timeless*, the first two books in the Tropical Authors "Less is More Series." And since the release of *Deep Hex*, Boone and Em have returned in another in that series, *Faceless*.

AFTERWORD

I had been planning to set a book in Turks and Caicos for some time, having fond memories of a dive trip to Grand Turk many years ago. And when I tucked a hint into *Deep Focus* that I might set my next book in TCI, one of my readers reached out with an idea. (Thanks, Sean!) It turned out he knew two of the owners of Clearly Cayman, who manage dive resorts in Little Cayman and Cayman Brac, and Sean had taken a trip to their new East Bay Resort (EBR) in South Caicos.

In short order, I was in talks with Michael Tibbetts of Clearly Cayman to come check out East Bay. If the name "Tibbetts" is familiar to you, it's because it's one of the most common names in the Cayman Islands, and Michael is likely related to some of the earliest settlers. He suggested I come to South Caicos, and immediately intrigued me with all sorts of information about the island's history.

My reader Sean and Michael Tibbetts both recommended I talk to Mateo Arias, a Colombian divemaster who had been working at EBR since before COVID. I sent him a few initial emails and received a flood of detailed information. It turned out that, in addition to being a skilled underwater explorer, he was quite the historian!

I admit, I knew absolutely nothing about The Big South, and my original plan had been to base Boonemily on Grand Turk, and put the baddy in Provo (Providenciales). I like Boone and Em to be in sleepy places, so GT would fit that bill. But once I learned more about South Caicos, I thought I might set a good portion of the book there.

It was my first trip outside the US since COVID, so I set up a two-week stay instead of my usual one week, planning to dive and research for one week, and write for the second. It was already too late for the humpback migration, so I went in mid-June—which worked out for me as things were a bit quieter. The flights were uneventful—apart from being seated next to a man who was wearing the exact same shirt—white, with little blue sharks—that I was wearing. I took that as a good omen. Although, in retrospect, it could have meant I would soon be eaten by sharks.

Let me say that my experience at the East Bay Resort was fantastic. The staff was helpful and answered my non-stop barrage of questions with patience and grace. And if one person didn't know the answer, they usually put me in touch with someone who did. The food was great, the room was beautiful, and I loved that pool! Yes, I did a lot of writing on one of the stools at the swim-up bar, until the sun crested the roof and drove me away.

I was thrilled to learn that EBR's dive op was Reef Divers, the very same op I'd dived with at the Little Cayman Beach Resort, and at Cobalt Coast in Grand Cayman. The dives in South Caicos were great—I was aboard *Big Sister*, on loan from the Caymans—and I had as many encounters with reef sharks as in Saba, as well as plentiful eagle rays and turtles. And yes, that unusual mass-gathering of spotted drums and high-hats that I tucked into the book actually happened at—let me check my Teric dive computer app—The Maze!

As usual with my Afterwords, I'll be chatting a little about what was based on fact, and what I may have fudged a bit. But first, let me extend some Big South thank yous to several Belongers and EBR staff who went out of their way to help make *Deep Hex* a better book:

First and foremost, thank you Mateo Arias, for your phenomenal knowledge of South Caicos history, and your incredibly detailed descriptions of your own adventurous activities. While the *real* Mateo had not yet dived the Boiling Hole at the time of this book's release (he was planning to), he deserves much of the credit for tripling the number of dive sites available to EBR's Reef Divers, using his downtime during the COVID lockdowns to explore much of the surrounding area. That being said, he always made sure to share the credit with a number of Belongers and School for Field Studies staff who assisted him during the exploration and mapping. Mateo went through their exploration methods, and also gave me pages of detail about the TCI Reef Fund's mooring ball drilling procedures, in addition to plentiful information about the dive sites I was unable to visit, as well as describing the outlying cays to the south, and the humpback migrations that I'd missed.

Mateo's knowledge of local history was extensive, and he took me on a half-day excursion all over the island. I filled pages of my notebook with details about Highland House, the salt industry, the Coast Guard station, French freediver Jacques Mayol, real estate development and habitat destruction, the bell of the *RMS Rhone*, Queen Elizabeth's visit, glowworm displays, details about all the type of boats EBR had, as well as some fascinating tidbits about the darker history in South Caicos with the drug trade in the eighties.

Thank you to Neil and Laura, dive managers for Reef Divers during my stay. Neil is a Londoner, and he really does talk a bit like my imagined Emily, and Laura really does doodle fishes on whiteboards—again, like Emily. Neil explained in detail what may have happened to the drive shaft of one of the Newtons shortly before I arrived. And that leads me to a big thank you to Dwaine "Cap" Cox.

Dwaine, with visual aids from some photos Mateo had taken, told me about the crack in the drive shaft, as well as the masterful rigging they came up with to get it safely to Provo. Apparently, the wire and ropework earned high praise from the boatyard folks when they saw it. Dwaine taught me a tremendous amount about engines, and confirmed for me the fastest boat in the harbor was the *Hammerhead*.

Thanks to Roshane—who also goes by Kevin—who was indeed voted Outstanding Divemaster by the Dive Industry Association, and received a cool reef pointer from them. Roshane gave me all sorts of useful "knowledge nuggets" and gave a lot of good divemaster advice. Also, he was working at the Little Cayman Beach Resort at the same time I was there! Small world.

Thank you to the various members of the groundskeeping staff who showed me the local flora, as well as telling me about their experiences with Hurricane Irma and some smaller, more recent storms. Thank you to the resort drivers, Lincoln and CJ, who took me to places in town and told me a bit about life for Belongers. CJ wasn't a deejay, but he did have an amazing, bass voice that immediately made me want to put him in front of a microphone.

Thanks to Heidi at the School for Field Studies, for giving me a tour of the facilities, answering a slew of questions, and introducing me to the school's five potcakes. Thank you to Darell, owner of the Sunset Café in Cockburn Harbour. He was a gold mine of recent history and some fairly juicy gossip, much of which I didn't dare put in the book.

And of course, my sincere thanks to Michael Tibbetts, and the whole Clearly Cayman family for setting me up in such a lovely room, and facilitating my research. Thank you to Daniel J LeVin and VisitTCI.com for the use of their island maps... and for having such a wonderful website! There is a phenomenal amount of detail on there for all of the TCI, from history, to attractions, to flora and fauna—I used it extensively in my research.

Over on Grand Turk, my thanks to Jorika, owner of the Sunflower Oasis. During my first trip to Grand Turk, she had been the chef at the Bohio, and it was some of the best food I've ever had in the islands. Now she has her own place and her own restaurant (now called The Fisherman's Wife). And yes, they have potcake dogs at the Oasis. I flew over to Grand Turk to revisit some of the old haunts, and Jorika gave me a tour of some of the businesses the locals use, and we had a good time at the Ike and Donkey Beach Bar, one of my favorite watering holes. Best of all, I got to meet the litter of puppies her own dog had just had. And thank you to Lisa at the National Museum in Grand Turk, for answering a number of questions and telling me about their Early Diving exhibit.

And now, let me dive into the "fact or fiction" portion of the afterword. Where did some of the material come from?

COVID-19: "Hey, Nick, didn't you say in the foreword to *Deep Devil* that The Deep Series wouldn't deal with COVID? But you mentioned it in this book." Yep, you got me. I made that original decision primarily because I was sick of it, and because —to be completely accurate—Boone and Emily would basically just be sitting on a couch somewhere, waiting for the islands to open back up. That would've been a great book: *Deep Cushions*. But I had to bring it up in *Deep Hex*, because it was that very shutdown that enabled Mateo to do his extensive exploration. And because the lockdown in the Cayman Islands lasted much longer than in the TCI, it led to many of the Reef Divers boats from Brac and Little being brought over to South Caicos, in a multi-day, multi-boat journey. The *Caicos Sister* was an invention of my own—I didn't want one of EBR's actual boats to break down in my fictional story. The resort plans to get some Aventura catamarans, which will be able to operate directly from East Bay's shallow waters.

The watermelon incident: One of the divers on the *Big Sister* told this story; apparently some kid threw up some watermelon and the parents freaked out. I had no choice but to steal this bit.

The Ike and Donkey Beach Bar: Is it real? Why yes, and I love it. On the grounds of the Bohio Dive Resort, the bar is right off the prettiest beach on the island, Pillory Beach. Yes, they have clear tiki glasses, yes, the potcakes roam nearby, and yes, they've got you covered if you want a cold beer from Turks Head Brewery. The day I arrived, the staff had *just* been told that the Bohio Dive Resort was about to close for renovation, but I'm hoping by the time you read this, they'll be back, better than ever. Quick side note: When I dived there, ages ago, the head divemaster was "Scuba Steve," and he had a thick, working-class British accent. One dive guest in my group asked him if he was Australian.

The migrants on Fish Cay: This was based on a real situation that happened in November, 2021. Several of the dive staff and a few locals recounted a group of twenty-three Haitians being discovered on Long Cay. But in this case, a visiting dive boat didn't spot them—they were in view of Cockburn Harbour when the sun rose.

The sargassum harvester: I made this up. I've been tracking the increase of sargassum over the last decade, and the East Bay Resort has a tractor that harvests along the bay shore every morning. I live on a lake, and while writing the first chapters of this book, I was watching our lakeweed harvester puttering around. Ding! Inspiration. I confess, I had intended for the bad guys to make use of this device (remember that antenna for drone operation?) but the story went another way.

The Coast Guard station and a radio station there: I was fortunate enough to go inside the station, dodging donkey droppings as I explored the buildings. The far room on the north end had clearly been the office for a Spanish-language radio station, as was evidenced by all of the invoices, correspondence, and instructional manuals I found. I figured if an actual AM radio station operated there before Hurricane Irma... why not after?

Deejay Ceejay's "Story Hour": As many of you may know, in addition to writing, I've been narrating audiobooks since the 1990s. My earliest experience with recorded-audio format was "The Radio Reader" on NPR, with half-hour segments of a book read aloud by producer Dick Estell, doing a chunk of a book every day until the book was completed. I figured I should resurrect that idea. And the "Kingston Noir" I had CJ reading from? I've narrated a bunch of these Akashic Noir collections of mysteries.

Highland House: Yes, this place is creepy. All of those drawings on the walls? I didn't make those up, those things were on the walls. That angry centaur was the weirdest. And there was a hexagram, which worked out well with my planned title. And yes, there was a rope hanging from the beam up on the second floor. I had heard from multiple sources that people had been hanged there during the height of the drug trade, but putting on my Boone cap and examining it, it was clearly a newish rope. My description of everything being done by kids having fun and doing things to spook each other was a guess, but I suspect my hypothesis is correct.

Pablo Escobar and South Caicos: Yep. Hundreds of planes a day in the eighties. It was a refueling stop from flights from Colombia, on their way to The Bahamas or the United States. They made a Tom Cruise movie about one of the pilots-turned-informant: *American Made*. And the TCI Chief Minister—equivalent of a Prime Minister—who was busted for taking money to look the other way for the flights? He still lives in South Caicos, and I had lunch with him. Norman Saunders is quite charming and told me a lot about life in The Big South, all the way back to the fifties. And yes, his family owns the old Coast Guard station and the land it is on.

Square Grouper: The Columbus Channel, or Turks Island Passage, is a popular smuggler's route, and if the Coast Guard shows up, cargo ends up in the drink. Twice during my stay, I was told fishermen had found square grouper, but no one would ever say *which* fishermen.

Dive computers: Boone has an old Aeris and Emily has a cutting-edge Teric. That's because I just got a beautiful Teric from Shearwater... but I also have my old Aeris, still going strong. I took my Teric out for a spin for the first time in South Caicos, but I thought it'd be fun to have the Aeris on my other wrist. So, I basically had Boone on my left and Em on my right. That Teric is fantastic, by the way. I referred to its profiles—

saved on an app on my phone—many times while writing this book.

Viktor Gusev, The Goose of Death: At the time I began writing *Hex*, Viktor Bout, "The Merchant of Death," was still in US custody. And I had a bet with myself that I would get my book out before Bout was released; I lost that bet. A notorious arms dealer and likely GRU operative, Bout has quite a reputation. Rather than create a similar supervillain, I thought it would be more fun to create someone who both idolized and resented Bout, a scoundrel whose deep insecurities motivated him as much as any other trait. Gusev was made up completely.

The microwave weapon: Paz's device was based on some very real projects and much of the exposition in the book is based on researched sources. The Havana Syndrome is a real phenomenon, although there is a great deal of speculation about the causes. About halfway into the writing of my book, I watched a CNN special, "Immaculate Concussion: The Truth About Havana Syndrome," and made some tweaks based on a few tidbits of newer information. As to the effects of the hypothetical weapon, I pumped that up into the realm of borderline sci-fi, in the interests of making it a greater threat.

The oligarch-owned superyacht, *Anya*: There is no such yacht. The oligarch-owned superyacht *Anna*, on the other hand... was in South Caicos the week before I arrived. I fictionalized the oligarch aboard my yacht, because I don't want to mysteriously fall off of any balconies.

Russian businessmen and officials dropping like flies: Absolutely true. Heck, I couldn't keep track. Three more died in India—two in a hotel room, one on a boat—while I was writing the last chapters. I even narrated a book about assassinations of expat Russians throughout history called *The Compatriots*.

It's not a new phenomenon, but the tempo certainly seemed to increase in 2022.

Boone missing out on dolphins: This is a running gag for my old dive buddies. We went to Grand Turk over a decade ago and loved it. Then I got a Broadway gig, acting in the musical *Newsies*, and my friends decided to go back to Grand Turk without me. I have never seen wild dolphins while at depth. Naturally, my buddies saw free-swimming dolphins off The Wall, and attributed that to my not being there. I intend to kill each and every one of them in my future books. There was a great hammerhead near The Airplane site the week before I arrived in South Caicos, but of course I didn't see it.

Triple J's Blast Your Face Off sauce: Is it that hot? No, it is not. But where's the fun in that? The food there is absolutely delicious, though!

The glowworms (or Bermudan fireworms): I was fortunate enough to be in South Caicos during the full moon, and Mateo took several of us down the beach (where I had my version of Mateo take Boone and Emily) and we got to witness the glow-fest. Here's a fun bit of trivia: Columbus wrote in his diary that he saw lights in the waters, and some have speculated that it was Bermudan fireworms. But I'm a research nerd, and I looked up the moon phases for October, 1492. The full moon was October 5th. However, his entry said the lights occurred on October 12th at 10:00 p.m., so it wasn't glowworms. Too long after the moon, too late at night.

And finally, before I move on to some additional acknowledgements, a word about this book's title. This being the sixth book in The Deep Series, I would have loved to name it *Deep Six*! But there are already so many books with that title, including ones by the tropical adventure titans Clive Cussler and Randy Wayne White. So, I went with the Ancient Greek for six: hex. And *Deep Hex* worked well for my plans for Baptiste.

My thanks to all of my friends at Tropical Authors. As I write this, we've just added our fiftieth author! And in the wake of the novella *Graceless*, I teamed up once again with authors Nicholas Harvey, John H Cunningham, and Wayne Stinnett to write a Tropical Authors novel, *Timeless*! The book hit the USA Today Bestseller list, and the TA "Less is More" series is continuing with all new authors, with *Shameless* which was just released, and with *Priceless*, *Faceless*, and *Ruthless* in the pipeline. If you're interested in beach reads set by the ocean, under the sea, on boats, islands, and coastlines, be sure to sign up for the Tropical Authors newsletter for lots of deals from your favorite tropical authors.

Thank you to all of my beta readers: John Brady, Joan Zale, Mike Ramsey, Drew Mutch, Jason Hebert, Deg Priest, Bob Hickerson, Tom Tewksbury, and Malcolm Sullivan. Many of you have extraordinary backgrounds in diving, boating, and writing and you all kept me on my accuracy-toes and made some wonderful suggestions.

A big thank you to Shayne Rutherford of Wicked Good Book Covers for helping this picky ol' author with the cover design he was looking for! This cover is one of my favorites, and the adjustments Shayne made to my original mock-up were fantastic! And thanks again to John Brady for helping me create that first pass cover to work from.

Thanks to my editor, Marsha Zinberg of The Write Touch, for taking my crazy story and giving it a better shape, and improving my grammar, punctuation, and plotting. Gretchen Tannert Douglas and Forest Olivier for their eagle-eyed proofreading skills. My thanks to Karl Cleveland for his work on my

DeepNovels.com website; don't go spotting any more dolphins without me, or I will punish you in a future book!

And finally, as always, thank you to my readers—and my listeners, you audiobook fans. This time, I'm not sure where "Boonemily" will be next—and having read this book, I bet you got the feeling that they're not sure, either. But I have little doubt they'll land on their feet. Until then, stay safe, stay sane... and keep seeking the sun.

ABOUT THE AUTHOR

Born in East Tennessee, Nick Sullivan has spent most of his adult life as an actor in New York City working in television, film, theater, and audiobooks. After narrating hundreds of titles over the last couple of decades, he decided to write his own. Nick is an avid scuba diver, and his travels to numerous islands throughout the Caribbean have inspired this series.

For a completely different kind of book, you can find Nick Sullivan's first novel at:
www.zombiebigfoot.com

Made in United States
Orlando, FL
23 September 2024

51868566R00221